## Praise for The A

"The magic is believable, the ⌐⌐⌐⌐⌐⌐⌐, and the twists, turns and myster⌐⌐ ⌐⌐ ⌐⌐ solved glue your eyes to the page. You will never forget these characters or their world."
—*Jacqueline Lichtenberg, Hugo-nominated author of the* Sime~Gen *series and* Star Trek Lives!

"Alastair Stone is like Harry Potter meets Harry Dresden with a bit of Indiana Jones!"
—*Randler, Amazon reviewer*

"Somewhat reminiscent of the Dresden Files but with its own distinct style."
—*John W. Ranken, Amazon reviewer*

"I am reminded of Jim Butcher here...Darker than most Urban Fantasy, not quite horror, but with a touch of Lovecraftian."
—*Wulfstan, Amazon Top 500 reviewer*

"If you like Harry Dresden and The Dresden files, or Nate Garrett in the Hellequin series than this series is for you."
—*Amazon reviewer*

"Once you enter the world of Alastair Stone, you won't want to leave."
—*Awesome Indies*

"I've been hooked since book 1."
—*Penny B. McKay, Amazon reviewer*

"It's getting hard to come up with something better than great to describe how good this book was."
—*Ted Camer, Amazon reviewer*

"You cannot go wrong with this series!"
—*Jim, Amazon reviewer*

"Warning—don't start reading this book if you have other things to do."
—ARobertson, Amazon reviewer

"Once you start, you need to get comfortable because you will stop reading all of a sudden and discover many hours have gone by."
—John Scott, Amazon reviewer

"R. L. King has my purchasing dollars with fun-to-read, suspenseful, character-driven stories…Damn fun reads."
—Amazon reviewer

"I have been hooked on this series from the first book."
—Jim P. Ziller, Amazon reviewer

"Awesome and exciting. Love this series."
—Cynthia Morrison, Amazon reviewer

"Amazing series. The characters are deep and identifiable. The magic is only a small part of what makes these books great. I can't wait for the next one!!"
—Amazon reviewer

"Great series, awesome characters and can't wait to see where the story will go from here."
—Amazon reviewer

"I have read every book in this series and loved them all."
—Soozers, Amazon reviewer

"The writing is extremely good, and the plot and characters engaging. Closest author comparison probably Benedict Jacka and the Alex Verus series."
—MB, Amazon reviewer

## ALSO BY R. L. KING

### The Alastair Stone Chronicles
*Stone and a Hard Place*
*The Forgotten*
*The Threshold*
*The Source*
*Core of Stone*
*Blood and Stone*
*Heart of Stone*
*Flesh and Stone*
*The Infernal Heart*
*The Other Side*
*Path of Stone*
*Necessary Sacrifices*
*Game of Stone*
*Steel and Stone*
*Stone and Claw*
*Shadows and Stone (novella)*
*Turn to Stone (novella)*

### Shadowrun
*Shadowrun: Borrowed Time*
*Shadowrun: Wolf and Buffalo (novella)*
*Shadowrun: Big Dreams (novella)*
*Shadowrun: Veiled Extraction (coming in 2019)*
(published by Catalyst Game Labs)

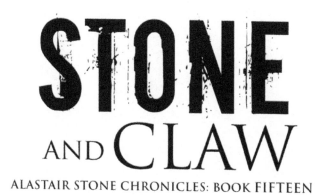

# STONE
## AND CLAW

### ALASTAIR STONE CHRONICLES: BOOK FIFTEEN

# R.L. KING

MAGESPACE
PRESS

*Stone and Claw*
First Edition, September 2018
Magespace Press
*Edited by John Helfers*
*Cover Art by Streetlight Graphics*

ISBN: 978-0999429259

# | PROLOGUE

THE SMELL WAS THE WORST, Viajera decided.

Everything around her, from the hot asphalt of the streets to the swirl of discarded food wrappers to the people passing by as she sat in the taxicab, smelled too strong, too ripe, too—foreign.

She wouldn't have thought it would be such a problem—after all, they had streets and trash and people where she came from, even though she avoided all three whenever she could—but suddenly it threatened to overwhelm her.

This had been a bad idea.

*No,* she told herself firmly. It was the *only* idea. Her sources had been clear, and sure of themselves: this was where it had gone. Whoever had it—whoever had stolen it, or sold it, or hoarded it in some vile collection somewhere—they were here.

And *it* was here. Somewhere.

And she had no idea if it would *remain* here. If it left this area, if it got shipped off to some far-flung location overseas, she might never find it again. Her resources weren't limitless.

No, as distasteful as it was, she'd need to do this.

The taxi stopped at her destination, double-parking next to an old minivan, and she hesitated a moment before paying the driver and getting out. How did people *live* in places like this? San Francisco was supposed to be a beautiful, cosmopolitan city, but she had a hard time believing that from her current surroundings. All along the street she saw neglected buildings, overflowing garbage receptacles, homeless people shuffling along or huddled in doorways, cars stuffed into every available space. As soon as she opened the car door, the smells hit her like a wall.

*It doesn't matter,* she told herself. *Your comfort isn't important. Do what you came here to do.*

The shop was sandwiched between a vacant space and a Moroccan restaurant. The sign over the door read "Antiquities for the Discerning Connoisseur," except some of the letters were missing. She couldn't see inside: the picture window was piled high with haphazard junk, and a shade covered the door.

She consulted the planner in her bag again, where she'd listed several potential locations she'd discovered. This was only the second she'd tried since arriving in the area. The first had been a bust: little more than a junk shop catering to tourists.

She stepped inside. A harsh bell jangled on the door, and the street smells of garbage and gasoline and hot asphalt were replaced by dust, heavy aftershave, and just a hint of wood rot. Her eyes adjusted quickly to the low light, and she immediately picked out the stocky form of a man behind the counter in the back. There were no other customers.

"May I help you, my dear?" the man called.

Viajera continued scanning the shelves as she walked toward him. Of course she didn't expect to see it sitting there among the old dolls and fake skulls and questionable pottery, but stranger things had happened and she couldn't afford to take chances. "I'm looking for something."

"We are all looking for something, I think." His gaze crawled up and down her body, and a slow smile spread over his face. He was shorter than she was, wider, and considerably older, with fussy round glasses, slicked-back dark hair, and more tufts poking from the open front of his lurid Hawaiian shirt. She couldn't identify his accent. Now that she was closer, she had no trouble picking out the alcohol adding to the shop's ambient aromas.

She sighed. She didn't have time for this. She described the object of her search, showing the man a sketch she'd made, and watched him closely for any reaction. If he'd seen it, she'd know.

"May I?" he asked, reaching out for the drawing. He wore rings on every finger except his thumb. When she offered it to him, he touched her hand as he took it, trailing his damp fingers along hers.

She didn't shudder, but it wasn't easy.

"Hmmm…" He studied the drawing a moment. "Well, now—I think this might be your lucky day, pretty lady. I think I *have* seen this."

He was lying. Everything about him, from his scent to his tone to his expression, told her that. "You have?"

"Yes. I think someone brought it in just the other day." His gaze flicked up and settled briefly on her face before traveling hungrily downward. He glanced toward the door, then moved around the counter. "If you'll come with me, I'll try to remember where I put it."

She nodded toward the sketch. "You have this."

"Yes, yes." He moved past her, trying to brush against her as he came around the counter, but she deftly shifted out of his way. "This way. I am so happy I can help you. It isn't often I get such a lovely lady in my shop."

"I don't have a lot of time," she told him. "And I see you're almost ready to close."

"Oh, don't worry, don't worry. I never lose anything in my shop, and I'm pleased to help you. It is my greatest joy—helping my customers find the things they seek. Sometimes even things they don't know they want." He leered again, peering at the shelves as he slipped up the aisle toward the front of the shop.

Viajera tensed, but not with fear. She thought she knew what would happen next. It had happened to her before, more than once. Perhaps one day his type would learn, but she doubted it.

"It's all right," she said. "But I need to be going soon."

"Oh, yes, of course. I understand." He poked at one of the shelves, pulling out an old wineglass, examining it, and then putting it back. "No, no, that's not it. I know I left it near here somewhere. If I could only remember—" He brightened, as if he'd just had an idea. "I know! I have just put some coffee on. It's an exotic blend I get from a friend—most of my customers find it quite...stimulating. Perhaps we could sit and have a cup, and that will help my memory." He rolled his eyes ruefully. "I am not as young as I used to be. Sometimes I need a little help."

"No, that's all right." Viajera was done playing games with this pathetic little man. Every moment she remained here was another moment the object she sought might be even now leaving the area. "Thank you so much for your help. I should be going."

"Oh, please, don't leave yet!" The man moved faster than before, circling around her to reach the door first. He fumbled behind him. "You brighten my shop with your beauty."

Viajera didn't miss the *click* of the lock engaging, but didn't show she'd noticed. "Thank you. That's kind of you to say. But I need to go. Please excuse me."

His expression changed. His kindly smile went sly, and something in his eyes went hard. "Please, not yet. Don't you know it isn't polite to lead someone on and then disappoint him so? Let me find this item for you so you will be happy, and then perhaps we might discuss a…trade?" Once again, his lecherous gaze lingered on her figure.

Now she smelled something else—something more primal—as her senses heightened. He was between her and the door, and there didn't seem to be another exit from the shop.

"Get out of my way," she said. Her voice never rose from its normal pleasant calm.

"I think not," he said in the same tone, but his eyes never left her. "You need a lesson, I think, of why it's not wise to promise what you aren't willing to deliver."

Viajera's heart beat faster, blood pounding through her limbs, energizing them. "I'm only going to tell you once more. Get out of my way."

"Or what, my dear? What will you do?" His words held a challenge.

She took a step forward. When she spoke again her voice was different: lower, deeper, traced with a warning, purring growl. "Or I'll rip your skin from your bones and feast on your flesh."

She saw her glowing golden eyes reflecting in his round glasses, and behind them his own grew wide and terrified as he got a good look at her.

"Uh—uh—" he stammered, scrambling sideways. "You—what—"

As soon as he no longer blocked the door, she calmly flipped the catch to unlock it. "Thank you," she said, once again casual and pleasant, and the glowing reflection in his glasses faded. "I can't say it was a pleasure doing business with you, but at least I can cross one more shop off my list. Have a good evening."

She left him there, stuttering and terrified, and exited the shop. As she did, she smiled as yet another scent joined the existing olfactory cacophony: the strong, sharp smell of fresh fear-urine.

Good. Perhaps he'd think twice before trying that again.

Her amusement faded with each step, though. She still hadn't found what she was looking for, which meant she'd have to implement the most difficult and risky part of her plan. She'd hoped it wouldn't be necessary, but at this point she had no other choice.

She hoped her resources were as good as they claimed, because it looked like she was going to have to test them.

# | CHAPTER ONE

ENDINGS ARE NEVER EASY.

Alastair Stone stood in the upstairs study of his downtown Palo Alto townhouse, gazing out the window at the late-morning light shining into the microscopic backyard. In all the time he'd lived in the house—over four years—he'd never once set foot out there.

The study was empty now, another bare room like all the others. He turned back around, leaning on the wooden sill to regard the lighter spots on the carpet where his desk, his overstuffed sofa, and his ratty leather armchair had stood. He'd already boxed up the books from the shelves with Verity's help, and carefully wrapped and packed the collection of odd items sharing space with them. The prints on the walls were all gone, once again leaving lighter spots behind.

*I probably could have been a better housekeeper,* he mused. *Never did get 'round to hiring someone. Suppose that will need to change.*

The study would be the hardest to leave. It had been the heart of the house for him—even more so than the locked and warded sanctum in the attic. One's magical workspace was a profoundly personal thing, of course, but by necessity all of them essentially had variations on the same theme:

circle on the floor, shelves holding reference books and ritual components, wards to keep the curious from investigating and the errant project from escaping. One's study, on the other hand, was as individual as one's fingerprints—or one's aura. Over the years the place had developed an energy all its own—comforting, steady, conducive as much to research as to the many hours he'd spent slouched in his old chair, plinking aimless melodies on the battered black Stratocaster he should probably think about replacing now that he was in a proper band. Some guitars looked like his because they had character, but he couldn't claim the same excuse: he'd picked it up in a secondhand shop a few years back because he had no idea whether he'd stick with it or not. He supposed he'd earned the right to find a better one. Not a new one, though—new instruments had less character than his old used one did. When he got some time, he'd see about poking around a few high-end shops in London and see if he could find one that spoke to him.

Not literally or anything, of course. That would be too strange even for him.

Chuckling at the thought of a talking guitar—knowing his luck, he'd get one that argued with him about set lists or critiqued his technique—he left the study and drifted toward the door leading to the attic ritual space. It was open, revealing the narrow stairway up. Perhaps inspired by Trevor Harrison and his unexpected mechanical skills, Stone had tackled replacing the heavy metal door himself, after searching around in the garage trying to remember where he'd stashed the original one. His thoughts flitted back to the day when he and Jason had installed the metal door, soon after he'd moved in here. Jason had done most of the work then, but this time Stone had managed the job on his own. It felt strangely satisfying.

The sanctum was the only other part of the house he'd completely packed up, since the place was a furnished rental and most of the furniture remained with it. Verity had helped him with this too, making sure all the magical gear was properly boxed and labeled in ways that wouldn't arouse any suspicion from the movers.

The hardest part had been removing the circle, which he'd painted on the floor. Fortunately, he'd perfected a spell that separated the paint from the wood, so all it took was some effort and a little buffing to eliminate any evidence of mystical goings-on. The wards had been relatively easy to dismantle; they were formidable, but he'd built them himself so unmaking them was a much simpler process than it would have been if they'd been someone else's work.

He stood in the center of the room and turned slowly in place, taking in the empty space. Why was he so sentimental about this place, anyway? He didn't *get* sentimental. It wasn't as if he were leaving his rambling mansion back home in England.

A knock on the door startled him from his thoughts.

"Doc?"

"Yes—up here."

Light footsteps, and Verity Thayer appeared in the doorway. "Everything okay?"

"Fine. Just—reminiscing a bit."

She began pacing the room, pausing to look out the window. Like him, she wore a T-shirt and faded jeans. "Lot of good memories here."

Behind her, Raider stalked with tentative furtiveness, glancing at Stone every few seconds as if confused about why he wasn't being evicted. Normally, the rangy tabby wasn't allowed in the ritual room, so naturally it was a source of constant curiosity. He amused himself sniffing in corners, determined to get in as much exploration as he could before the humans caught on and kicked him out.

"Indeed there are," Stone said, watching the cat fondly.

"Well, you've got the place for a while longer, right? You can always come back here if you need a fix."

"No...no, it's time to go. Are the movers ready?"

"Yeah, they're taking the last few boxes out to the truck."

"Good, good. I suppose we should get going, then."

He still wasn't entirely sure why he'd decided so suddenly to move into the house Adelaide Bonham, a wealthy former client, had bequeathed him. He'd expected it to be a slow process, taking a few things over there every now and then, remaining mostly here at the townhouse for the next few months as he gradually accumulated enough furniture to fill its much larger spaces. The new place, located in a tiny, secluded town called Encantada only a few miles from Stanford, was more than twice as large as the townhouse: three stories, with a detached three-car garage and nearly an acre of land surrounding it.

At this point, the place would be positively cavernous when he moved in. His study would be furnished, but aside from that he'd managed to pick up only the barest necessities: a bed and armoire for the master bedroom, a sofa and coffee table for the sitting room, and a heavy wooden dining set he'd found in an antique shop in Atherton. Aside from that, he'd solicited Verity's suggestions for appliances to replace its previous harvest-gold monstrosities. Following the infusion of a significant amount of money for purchase and expedited installation, he was now the owner of a sleek, ultra-modern kitchen with granite countertops and a massive gas range that would make a gourmand proud. He didn't care, but Verity did, so he gave her his parameters ("nothing fussy—I get enough of that back home") and set her loose with the contractor.

All of this, of course, could have been accomplished on a smaller budget, but ever since his return from Calanar, Trevor Harrison's magic-rich dimension, he'd been plagued with the overwhelming compulsion to make some changes in his life. Perhaps it was because he *hadn't* chosen to remain behind and let Harrison introduce him to areas of study that would catapult his magical knowledge to levels he'd never thought possible. He didn't regret that decision—much—but he did find it made him restless to get out of the ruts he felt he'd fallen into. Perhaps a change of scenery would help with that.

In any case, despite his sudden restlessness, he found over the past few weeks following his return that a big chunk of the low-grade tension he'd been carrying ever since he'd gone black had melted away. He might not have let Harrison teach him the secrets of dimensional travel and teleportation—yet—but he'd been delighted to discover the new magical techniques he'd learned on Calanar translated quite nicely to Earth, thank you very much. Sure, as Harrison had warned him, he didn't have the same level of power he had back there since Calanar was inherently much more magical, but that was fine. He'd expected that. He still had more than he'd had before, and using magic was *easier* now than it had ever been. As long as he didn't overextend himself too much the fatigue he used to get doing white magic had vanished, and likewise he no longer experienced the sensation of slow draining he'd dealt with as a black mage. His only limitation now was the amount of power his body could channel, and as long as he kept himself in reasonable shape, that amount was significant.

And almost best of all, the compulsions to re-create the rush he got when taking power from others as a black mage had all but disappeared. Now, he once again felt comfortable examining auras without the fear he might be tempted to "take a little off the top." That, too, added to his general sense of well-being.

"I should go," he said again, scooping up Raider and taking one final look around the empty space. "I'm not looking forward to unpacking—especially not with the quarter starting soon."

"Take your time," she said. "Moving into a new place should be fun, not stressful. I should get back—got the afternoon shift at the coffee shop today. If you want, I'll come by later and break in your new kitchen with a recipe I've been meaning to try."

"Sounds brilliant. I'll see you then."

After she left, he took a last look around the attic, checking with magical sight to make sure he hadn't left anything behind. Raider struggled in his arms—affectionate and amiable, the cat nonetheless preferred human-feline interactions to be on his terms—but Stone held fast. "Sorry, mate," he said. "We'll be out of here soon, and you'll have a whole new domain to investigate. But let me have a last look 'round, all right?"

He slowly trudged down the stairs, memories flooding in as he did.

A glance in the spare bedroom where he'd kept Raider when he first arrived reminded him of Edwina Mortenson sitting cross-legged on the floor, coaxing the terrified cat into her lap.

Downstairs, the sitting room sofa brought back thoughts of the night Deirdre Lanier had sat there and explained her secret to him. The kitchen recalled all the nights he'd perched at the breakfast bar, chatting with Verity while she puttered away creating all sorts of recipes, glad for the chance to use his more upscale setup instead of the one in her apartment. The hallway called up the night he'd injured Verity with a concussion bolt when he thought she'd attacked Deirdre…

"Enough," he muttered. "Time to move forward, not look back." He shifted Raider to one arm, retrieved the cat carrier from the table by the kitchen door, and headed for the garage.

It was indeed time to move forward.

# | CHAPTER TWO

THE NEXT DAY, Stone was unpacking the stack of boxes piled in his new study when his mobile buzzed. He finished levitating a row of books onto the top shelf—okay, it wasn't strictly necessary to do it that way, but it felt so *good* to be able to again, especially guilt-free—and picked it up from the desk. "Yes, hello?"

"Dr. Stone? Beatrice Martinez."

That was odd. Why was the head of the Cultural Anthropology department calling him at home? The new quarter didn't start for several more days, and he didn't have any meetings scheduled until next week. "Ah, hello, Dr. Martinez. How are you?"

"Very well. Better than I hoped, actually."

Stone put the phone in speaker mode and returned it to the desk so he could continue shelving books. "That sounds encouraging. What's up?"

"I think I might have found you a new colleague—temporarily, at least."

Several books stopped on the way to the shelf, hovering in midair. "Oh?"

She chuckled. "Now, don't get too excited. Nothing's final yet. She'll be joining us as a visiting lecturer, just for this quarter. If things work out, we can discuss where to go from there."

Stone frowned, settling the books into their place and perching on the edge of the desk. "Seems rather—sudden, doesn't it?" Had it already been almost a year since he'd witnessed Edwina Mortenson's death in the Brunderville cave-in?

"It is, and I apologize for that. But with your new status, especially when we thought you might not be back for the Fall, we had to do something. As I'm sure you're aware, Dr. Hubbard has been…quite vocal in his requests to bring someone else on board, so when Dr. Garra expressed interest in the position, we moved fast."

It was a fair point: when he'd had no idea how long his trip to Harrison's dimension would be—or even if he'd return from it at all—he'd told the University he'd planned an extended research trip overseas. Naturally, he couldn't have anticipated the time difference between the dimensions, so when he'd returned after only three days, he'd had to do some fast talking to explain why the "research trip" had to be cancelled due to logistical difficulties. He wondered if bringing someone on without consulting him about it was Martinez's way of getting back at him for putting her in a tough spot. If so, he couldn't exactly blame her. "Er—all right, then. Brilliant. I look forward to meeting her."

"Well, actually, that's why I called. I'd love for you and Dr. Hubbard to get together with her for a chat soon. Are you free for lunch tomorrow?"

"I am—not much going on right now. Just moving into the new place."

"Oh—right. I forgot about that. Are you settling in?"

He glanced around at the half-empty boxes scattered around the floor, including one Raider had claimed for his own. "Getting there. I'll see you tomorrow."

"Faculty Club at noon. I think you're going to like Dr. Garra. She's young, but she's got some good experience."

As Stone hung up and resumed shelving the books, he glanced at Raider. "Lot of things changing these days, aren't they?"

The cat leaped out of the box he'd been sitting in and strolled out of the room, as if to say, *Your problem, Dad. Me, I'm just a cat.*

# | CHAPTER THREE

WHEN STONE ARRIVED at the Stanford Faculty Club shortly before noon the next day, Mackenzie Hubbard loitered in the courtyard outside, finishing a candy bar. Despite the late-summer heat, the older professor wore his usual baggy pants, polo shirt, and rumpled cardigan sweater.

"They're not here yet," he said without greeting. "I checked."

"Ah. Well, at least I'm not late today. That's something."

Hubbard popped the last of the bar into his mouth, crumpled the wrapper, and tossed it in a nearby trash receptacle. Then he looked Stone up and down, his brow furrowing.

"Something wrong?"

"Sorry. You look…different somehow. Can't put my finger on it."

Stone shrugged as if to say *can't help you*. Of course he knew exactly what it was: the grueling physical training Harrison's associates had put him through back on Calanar had added noticeable muscle to his slim frame and trimmed his already-trim waist even more. It wasn't immediately obvious to anyone who didn't know him well—he'd been thin before and he was still thin—but he liked both the look and the increased strength, and had thus made it a point to spend more time at the gym so he didn't lose them. He found it comforting that Hubbard hadn't paid enough attention to him to notice the change.

"Eh, anyway. Sorry to hear your research trip got cancelled, but I can't say I'm sorry you won't be around this quarter. At least it sounds like Martinez might finally have found somebody to help out. About time."

"Well, we're hardly found on every street corner."

"I just hope this one's better than the last few we've interviewed. I'm desperate, but not *that* desperate."

"We'll see, I suppose. How's the latest book going?"

Hubbard brightened. "Still outlining—hoping to start writing soon, especially if we get somebody in to help with the class load. Still waiting to hear back on the last one I sent out a few months back."

Stone made a noncommittal noise and nodded. He'd lost count of how many horror novels Hubbard had written and failed to sell since they'd met many years ago. He supposed he should admire the man's dedication, if nothing else.

"Dr. Stone! Dr. Hubbard!"

Stone, pleased he wouldn't have to hear the plot of Hubbard's latest masterpiece, glanced up to see Beatrice Martinez approaching with another woman.

"I like her already," Hubbard muttered from behind him.

"Down, boy," Stone murmured. "You're a married man."

He couldn't fault Hubbard, though: the woman who followed Martinez was attractive, no doubt about it. Tall and lithe, she stalked along on stiletto heels with the easy grace of a cat. As the two women approached she looked Stone and Hubbard over, her eyes narrowed with cool amusement.

"Ah," Martinez said. "You're already here. Hope you didn't have to wait long." She smiled and indicated the woman. "Gentlemen, this is Dr. Marciella Garra. Dr. Garra, may I present Drs. Alastair Stone and Mackenzie Hubbard."

"It's a pleasure to meet you both," Marciella Garra said. She shook Hubbard's hand first, then lingered a moment longer over Stone's with a strong, firm grip. "Dr. Martinez has told me so much about both of you." She spoke in low tones, with a hint of a Spanish accent.

"The pleasure's ours," Stone said, using the handshake as an opportunity to study her for a moment before they broke off to head inside. She wore a conservative, dark-red business suit with a narrow skirt, a high-collared white blouse, and a simple gold chain around her neck. Her long, shimmering black hair swept back from a high forehead, revealing golden-brown eyes and sculpted cheekbones. A sly, impish smile tugged at her full lips, as if she were fully aware of the effect she had on men.

They followed Martinez back to the same small, private dining room where Stone had met with Larry Duncan and Bryce Riley from *The Other Side* a few months ago. After they'd all settled in and ordered drinks, Martinez addressed Stone and Hubbard. "As I said when I contacted you, I know bringing on Dr. Garra has been quite sudden, but it's only for the one quarter, so we can all see how we work together. As much as I know we're all still mourning the tragic loss of Dr. Mortenson, I know both of you have been eager to bring someone else in to help with the course load." She shifted her gaze briefly to Hubbard as she said this.

"I'm so sorry for your loss," Garra said. "I read some of Dr. Mortenson's work after Dr. Martinez and I began talking, and I wish I'd had the chance to meet her."

"She was a remarkable lady," Martinez agreed. "But we do need to move forward—as you know, the department has become quite popular over the past few years—" this time her quick glance fell on Stone "—and it's not fair to ask the two of you to handle the work on your own. Dr. Garra has only recently become available, so I felt it would be in all of our best interests to invite her to join us. She'll be acting as a visiting lecturer, for the fall quarter at minimum. Afterward, we'll all evaluate our options going forward."

"Brilliant," Stone said. "Dr. Garra, what's your area of expertise? I don't recall seeing your name in any of the journals."

Garra smiled. "I'm not surprised—most of my work has been practical in nature, and my work has appeared only in Spanish-language publications."

"Ah, that explains it, then. I'm afraid I've never learned the language."

Her smile broadened. "It doesn't sound like you grew up in this area."

"What was your first clue?" he asked, chuckling.

"To answer your question, my studies have centered mostly around the occult myths and legends of the Quechua people of northern Peru. The people there have rich and fascinating traditions. If you're interested, I might be able to locate a couple of translations of articles I've written."

"I know I would," Hubbard said. "That's an area I don't think we cover enough in our program here. I'm sure the students will find it fascinating."

Stone raised an eyebrow at him. That was the most interest old Hubbard had shown in anything outside of his novels in years.

"That was my hope as well," Martinez said. "It never hurts to broaden our areas of study."

Stone sat back, sipping his drink as the three of them spent the next several minutes discussing South American occult traditions. He focused his attention on each of them equally, but took the opportunity when no one was specifically watching him to shift to magical sight and study Marciella Garra's aura. It blazed a bright, vibrant green next to Hubbard's more subdued orange and Martinez's steady turquoise.

He realized as he got a better look at her that she wasn't quite as attractive as he'd initially thought—certainly lovelier than most female professors he'd met, but a significant portion of her appeal came from the way she carried herself: confident, graceful, sensual, but with the kind of straightforward focus one didn't see that often. She looked like the kind of person who didn't take anything from anybody, and that was sexy all by itself.

*Stop it,* he told himself sternly as their entrées arrived and he caught himself checking for any signs of illusion or other magical subterfuge. Ever since he'd gotten back from Calanar, he'd had to remind himself that people on Earth didn't generally put up illusions to make themselves look more attractive, like the Talented routinely did.

"So, Dr. Stone," Garra said, turning her easy smile back on him. "As I said, I've heard a lot about you. I've read some of your work—it's impressive."

"Thank you."

"I understand you're quite popular around here."

"Well… that's not really what it's all about, is it? I just hope the students are getting something useful from my courses."

"Dr. Stone is too modest," Martinez said. "He teaches some of our most popular courses, and he's responsible for significant enrollment growth in the Occult Studies program."

"That's wonderful," Garra said. "I hope we'll have the opportunity for some good discussions this quarter."

"Indeed," Stone agreed with a quick glance at Hubbard. If the other professor minded all the attention Stone was getting, he didn't show it.

"All three of us," Garra added.

They spent the rest of the lunch in pleasant conversation, mostly focused on Garra's experiences in Peru and her questions about the University. By the time they finished and rose to leave, Stone could see she'd already won Hubbard over. He couldn't blame the man—even aside from her attractiveness and obvious intelligence, she definitely seemed to have the necessary chops to handle the job. Hubbard wasn't the only one who hoped she might be the candidate who would bring their department back to three again.

On his way back to his car, Stone's mobile buzzed. "Yes?"

"Al? It's Jason."

"Ah, hello, Jason. How are you? How's the private investigator business?"

He hadn't spoken with Jason Thayer since the events at the end of the summer; he'd been meaning to call, but he still wasn't convinced his friend had come to terms with him and Verity seeing each other. He had no idea if Verity had shared anything with him about what had happened on Calanar.

"That's actually what I'm calling about. I passed, Al!"

"Passed?" He had to think about that for a second. "Ah! You passed your private investigator's exam?"

"Yep. Just found out. Now all I have to do is submit the application and I'll be a licensed PI."

Stone couldn't help grinning at the happiness in Jason's voice. "Well done, Jason. Congratulations! Of course I knew you'd do it, but it must be quite a relief to have that behind you."

"Oh, hell yeah."

"You've already told Verity, I presume?"

"Yeah, called her before I called you. I'm—coming up this weekend, if you want to get together and have dinner or something."

If he didn't know Jason as well as he did, he wouldn't have noticed the slight hesitation in his friend's voice. "I'd say that's up to you—and Verity. If you'd rather celebrate with just the two of you—"

"No." This time his tone was firm. "No, I really want you to be there, if you can make it."

"Absolutely. Just let me know when and where. I'll even buy dinner—we should go someplace posh to celebrate that kind of accomplishment."

"Sounds great—Thanks, Al. Gotta go now—got a few more people to call. I'll see you this weekend."

Verity came by later that evening, bearing shopping bags. "You know, we really need to take you to the grocery store one of these days." She patted the sleek new stainless-steel refrigerator before opening it to unload them. "I hear these big cold boxes are great for storing things other than Guinness and leftover take-out."

"Are they?" Stone shot her a look. "And here's me thinking they were just to fill unsightly little alcoves in the kitchen."

"So, did Jason call you?"

"He did. He sounded quite pleased with himself, as well he should."

"Yeah, he's really happy to be done with the apprenticeship thing. I don't think his was nearly as fun as mine," she added with a sly grin.

"Not to hear you tell it any time I tried to teach you theory."

She waved him off. "I think he's just glad to be getting away from Fran. From what he told me, she was a good boss and he learned a lot from her, but they kinda drove each other crazy."

"So he's still planning to come up here?"

She shoved a produce bag and a knife across the counter toward him. "Here, chop up this onion, will you? And yeah, that's what he said today. It's part of why he's coming up this weekend—gonna stay with me for a few days and see about what he needs to set up his own agency. It'll be a while before he can do that, though, so he'll probably look for someplace he can work for a while."

"Will he be moving in with you?" Stone kept his tone casual as he chopped, and used a gentle magical nudge to shove an over-eager Raider off the counter.

"No. Neither of us think that's a good idea—especially not with you paying the rent. Oh—that reminds me: you don't have to do that anymore. I've got it covered now."

"Do you?"

"Yeah. The coffee shop doesn't pay that great, but I've been making good money on the side doing healing for Scuro. As long as that holds out, I think I've got it under control."

"You know I don't mind—"

"I know." She pulled a pot from a cabinet, filled it with water, and put it on to boil. "But I think Jason's right—I shouldn't be letting you pay my rent. Not since I'm not your apprentice anymore. It feels...weird."

"Fair enough, then. But you know if you ever come up short, I'm happy to help."

"I know, and I appreciate it. But I think I'm good. Anyway, Jason says he's got some money saved up from living with Stan, but he'll need that to find an apartment. It's cool, though—he says it will help him get used to the area again before he branches out on his own."

Stone finished with the onion and levitated the chopped-up bits into a nearby bowl. "So he's all right with us—"

"Look at you," she said, grinning. "That's the old Doc back, using magic just because he can. And yeah, he's okay with it. Mostly. I still think he'd rather it hadn't happened, but you know him—he gets over it. Let's not talk about that right now, though. How's the new quarter? Any interesting students?"

"Not…really. There *is* an interesting *professor,* though."

"Oh?" She tossed pasta into the pot, turned up the heat, and dug in the bag for more vegetables. "I thought it was just you and Dr. Hubbard."

"There's a new one. Dr. Garra. They brought her on rather quickly, without consulting Hubbard or me."

"That's weird, isn't it? I thought they had you interviewing all the candidates."

"They did. She's just doing a guest-lecturer thing for the quarter, so we can evaluate her before they make a final decision. Apparently her availability was rather sudden and they didn't want to lose her—especially since they thought I'd be gone a lot longer than I was." He took the carrots she offered and begun cutting them up, staring off into the middle distance as his thoughts drifted to Garra.

"Something wrong?" she asked. "You zoned out there for a minute—that usually means you've got something on your mind."

He pondered. "I'm not sure," he said at last.

"What's that mean?"

"Probably nothing. I just can't shake the feeling that there's something…odd about Dr. Garra."

"Odd? What kind of odd?"

"That's just it—I can't say. There's nothing unusual about her aura, and it's not as if she's done anything strange to make me suspicious."

"What's she like?"

"She's from somewhere in South America—Peru, I think. I'd never heard of her before, but that's probably because all her publications are in Spanish. She's quite young, too."

Verity grinned. "Is she hot?"

"I suppose she is—for a professor, at least."

"*You're* hot—and not just for a professor." Her grin turned wicked. "Maybe that's it—you want to do her and you don't want to admit it."

"No, that's not it," he said quickly.

She checked the pot, then came over and pulled him into a hug. "It's okay if you do, you know," she murmured. "I'd be a hypocrite if I said anything else, considering how much time I've been spending with Kyla lately."

He sighed, returning the hug but then stepping back. "That's not what's happening," he said. "But even if it were—" He shook his head. "Never mind. Let me keep my mind on cutting these up, unless you want a bit of extra protein in your recipe."

She returned to her spot at the counter, focusing on cooking. After a few moments she looked up as if she might say something, but ended up remaining silent.

Jason arrived the following Friday afternoon, and Verity called Stone during his office hour to let him know. "You still want to get together tonight for dinner?"

"I'd like that." He waved farewell to the student who'd just left his office. "I told him I'd treat you two to something posh to celebrate—I think I can still get reservations at Mandala in Palo Alto, if that—"

"You know what? This is gonna sound weird, but Jason says he just wants to go to the Oasis, if that's cool with you."

"The pizza place?"

"Yeah. We used to go there when all three of us were up here, remember?"

"Of course I do. All right, then—if he wants pizza, it's fine with me."

"It's a plan. Seven, okay?"

"Seven it is."

He sat back, twisting his chair around to look out the window. He actually had a view now, which he supposed was good, but he still couldn't help feeling a bit ghoulish about the whole thing. Moving into Edwina Mortenson's old digs had been Beatrice Martinez's suggestion—it was one of those "suggestions" you didn't ignore if you valued your place in the political hierarchy, but Stone had nonetheless put up a token protest before agreeing. The office, larger and more conveniently located than his former tiny space, had an actual full-sized window instead of a small one high up on the wall, but it was going to take quite some time before entering it didn't bring back mental images of Mortenson's framed tarot-card prints and crystal ball, and her ample, gray-haired figure seated imperiously behind the desk.

Ah, well. It was just an office—just a space he didn't even spend much time in, given how often he was either lecturing or walking back and forth to the middle of campus. He'd get used to it in time.

He pulled his battered leather briefcase from his drawer. No point in remaining any longer today—he had no more classes or office hours, and the afternoon meeting had been postponed until Monday. If he left now, he could get a few things done at home before heading out to meet Jason and Verity at the Oasis.

As he was about to leave, his gaze fell on a small stack of books on the corner of his desk, each one with yellow sticky notes poking out in several places. He'd gathered them earlier that day with the intent of lending them to Garra, but had gotten sidetracked by other tasks. He picked them up now— it would only take a couple of minutes to drop them by her office before he left.

Garra's office was his old one at the end of the hallway. He knocked on her door, hoping she hadn't left for the day already. It swung open, revealing an empty space.

That was fine—he'd just drop them off on her desk with a note. He slipped inside, left the books, and glanced around for a notepad and pen. She hadn't had much chance to move in yet, so her bookshelves and walls were still mostly bare.

He didn't see a notepad, but a brightly colored flyer on her desk caught his attention. It showed images of a jeweled dagger, an elaborately-dressed antique doll, and what looked like a stuffed moose head mounted on a wooden shield. The script across the top read *North County Antiques and Oddities.*

That in and of itself wasn't unusual—perhaps Garra liked antiques or knick-knacks and wanted to take the opportunity to check out the local offerings. However, next to the flyer was the San Francisco phone directory, open to a page of display ads from more antique and junk shops. She'd jotted down several phone numbers on a yellow legal pad, and circled three of them. Stone recognized one of the three: Madame Huan's antiquities shop in Palo Alto.

"Dr. Stone?"

Stone spun. Marciella Garra stood in the doorway, eyes narrowed.

"Er—I'm sorry to intrude," he said quickly. He pointed at the stack of books. "I brought by those books I mentioned earlier about local occult history. Thought you might find them interesting reading. Your door was open, so I—"

"Oh—yes, of course. I'm sorry." Her suspicious expression changed to a smile. "Is there anything else you needed?"

"No—no, I don't think so. Have a lovely weekend." Stone exited the office, slipping past as she stepped aside without ever taking her eyes off him.

"You too." As soon as he was out, she went inside and closed the door firmly behind her. As he lingered a moment longer, he heard the lock engage.

# | CHAPTER FOUR

JASON AND VERITY WERE ALREADY at the Oasis when Stone arrived, sitting at their favorite back booth with a pitcher of beer.

"I'm not late, am I?" he asked, glancing at his watch as he slid in across from them.

"No, you're good," Jason said. "We just got here early. Good to see you, Al." His gaze skated over Stone, then locked back in. "Hey, you look great. Have you been working out?"

Stone chuckled. "You don't miss much—useful trait in a detective, I suppose."

"Just never thought I'd see you anywhere near a gym." He flicked a quick look toward Verity, and an even quicker frown passed across his face.

"You needn't worry—it's got nothing to do with your sister. Aside from the fact that she's been cooking for me periodically, which has to be better than a steady diet of takeaway. It's magic related."

"Oh? That reminds me, we should probably do the power thing soon, right?"

"No need anymore."

"What do you mean, no need? I thought we already went through—"

Apparently Verity hadn't shared Stone's latest news with her brother. "We did. And I appreciate everything you've done for me. But it's not necessary anymore. I've found a new approach."

"A new approach?" Jason frowned. "Are you getting power from somebody else?"

"I don't need power from anyone anymore, Jason. That's what I'm trying to tell you. I've worked out how to manage Harrison's magic."

Jason's wide-eyed expression of surprise was almost comical. "You're shittin' me. Really? You can do it now without burning yourself out?"

"I can. My magic's stronger than ever now."

"That's—amazing. How did you do it? V, did you know this?"

"Yeah, I did."

"And you didn't tell me?"

She shrugged. "It wasn't my thing to tell."

"So—" Jason looked as if he couldn't decide whether to be pleased or annoyed. "How did it happen?"

"That's a long story, better saved for another time." Stone raised his glass. "This is your night, Jason. Let's order an enormous pizza with an embarrassing number of toppings, and I want to hear all about your plans."

Jason hesitated, obviously torn. "Okay. But—you're sure? About the magic? You wouldn't lie to me about it, right?"

"I absolutely promise I'm not lying, Jason. My magic is fine. While I'm still technically black on the white-black spectrum, I'm sort of—outside those considerations now. I feel great. So don't you worry about me."

"Okay…" His gaze lingered for several more seconds on Stone, clearly searching for any sign he was withholding the truth, but he finally gave a grudging nod.

The waitress showed up. They ordered a pizza and another pitcher, then Stone leaned back. "So—tell me everything. How was the examination? Did you pass with flying colors?"

"They don't tell you that—either you pass or you don't. But fortunately they don't make you wait long to find out."

"Was Fran unhappy to find out you weren't planning to stay on working for her?"

"Nah, I never made any secret about that. I think she'll miss having her chief flunky and carrier of heavy things, but she'll get over it. She gave me a good reference."

"Brilliant. So you've already left the job down there, then?"

"Not quite yet, but I had a bunch of vacation time saved up, so I figured I'd come up here and see about finding an apartment and a place to work."

"Yes, Verity was saying you'll have to hold off on your own agency for a while."

"I expected that." He poured another glass of beer. "It's okay, though—it'll help me get used to being up here again. I'm looking forward to being back."

"It will be good to have you back," Stone said.

Jason glanced first at Verity, then at Stone. "And because everybody's avoiding bringing up the elephant in the room—I'm okay with you and V. I know that doesn't matter—not like I could stop you—but I've been thinking a lot about it. I guess if my sister's gonna be with a guy, I can't really think of a better one."

"That's…flattering, I suppose," Stone said, amused.

"It's also none of his business," Verity said, but she didn't look annoyed about it. "And he knows it. Otherwise he's gonna have to deal with me being all up in *his* business next time *he* meets somebody."

"I'll have to anyway," Jason said. "When's that ever changed? But I'm just sayin'. And anyway, I won't have time to meet anybody—I really want to open my own place as soon as I can, so I'll be working a lot. Anyway," he added, "how's life up here for you, Al? We haven't talked much lately. Anything new going on at the University?"

"They've got a hot new professor, apparently," Verity said slyly. "*Another* one, I mean."

Jason shot her a *don't push it* look. "Oh, yeah?"

"They've finally brought someone in—at least on a trial basis—to take Dr. Mortenson's position," Stone said. "She's got some good experience, from what I understand. It was all rather sudden, though, and she's a bit of an odd duck."

"How so?"

"Can't quite work it out yet. I keep getting the feeling something's strange about her, but I can't put my finger on why."

"She's not a mage or anything, is she? Does that job attract them?"

"I don't think so. I've examined her aura, and I don't see anything unusual about it. No traces of magic hovering around her, at least, so if she is, she's not practicing regularly."

Jason frowned, his brow furrowing. "I hate to bring this up, but…when you say 'hot,' you're not talking about Deirdre-level hot, right?"

"No." Stone sobered as his thoughts returned to Deirdre Lanier's unearthly, unnatural beauty. He hadn't thought about her in quite some time, and felt suddenly guilty about it. "Nothing like that. Believe me, that was the first thing I thought of. She's quite attractive, yes, but within normal parameters."

"Maybe you should have the Doc introduce you," Verity said. "You two might hit it off."

Stone chuckled. "Give the woman some time to settle in, will you, before I start setting her up with friends." He remembered the flyers he'd seen on her desk earlier that day. "Although you might have a better chance with her if you turned up with an old vase or something."

"Why's that?"

"I popped by her office to drop off some books today. She wasn't there, but she had a lot of flyers for antique shops, junk shops, that sort of thing."

"That's weird," Verity said. "But maybe she just likes that kind of stuff and wants to see if there's anything interesting around here. If she's staying, maybe she needs stuff to furnish her place."

"Probably," Stone agreed. "At any rate, it's none of my business. As long as she does her job, that's all I'm concerned with. The quarter's only just started, but the students seem to like her so far."

The waitress came by with their pizza, and he ordered another pint of Guinness. "So, what have you got planned for the weekend? How long are you staying?"

"Just a few days for now—V and I are gonna go look at apartments, and scope out some potential jobs. Fran gave me some leads, and she said she'd put in a good word for me if she knows the people. She has a lot of contacts up here."

"Good, good. I wish you luck."

They chatted about various topics while devouring the pizza, eventually settling back, comfortably full, to finish off their beers.

"It feels good to be all back together," Verity said. "I miss the days when we used to get involved in all that crazy stuff."

"You miss the Evil?" Jason asked. "Nostalgia's one thing, but that's a little much."

"I don't miss the Evil. But I do miss the—I don't know—the hunt? The thrill? What happened back in July reminded me how good it felt, dealing with that kind of stuff. Don't you think so?"

"I guess so," he said, with less conviction. "But you gotta remember, I don't have the same resources you two do. I gotta solve problems with my brains and my fists."

"Well, at least you'll get the chance to do that," Verity said. "Maybe you'll get some exciting cases up here."

"I hope so. So far it's mostly been following cheating husbands, hunting down insurance fraud, and locating people's birth parents. It's satisfying, sure—couple months ago I found a woman's mother and they had a great reunion—but...yeah, I wouldn't say no to a little more excitement."

"Well, there was Vegas. That was pretty exciting." She sobered. "I wonder how those kids are doing..."

Jason looked thoughtful. "Yeah, me too. I hope they're okay."

"At least they're out of that hellhole and they get a chance to have a normal life. That's better than they'd have had without us." She motioned for Jason to slide out of the booth so she could get out. "Anyway, back in a minute. I gotta hit the ladies'."

When she'd disappeared into the Friday-night crowd, Jason settled back and regarded Stone, who'd remained silent for the last several minutes. "It *is* good to be back."

"Indeed." Stone pondered a moment before continuing. Ever since Verity had told him Jason was returning to the Bay Area with the hope of starting an agency, a thought had been knocking around his mind, but he had no idea how Jason would respond to it. "Jason..."

"Yeah?"

"Have you got a bit of free time tomorrow? I'd like to chat with you about something."

"Uh—sure, yeah. V too, or just me?"

"Just you, for now. This doesn't really concern her—at least not yet."

Jason's eyes narrowed. "You're not gonna—I dunno—ask for her hand in marriage or anything, are you?"

Stone chuckled. "Oh, bloody hell, no. Even if I did intend to ask her to marry me—which I don't, because that isn't what she wants—she'd murder me in my sleep if I did anything so presumptuous."

"So, what then?"

"We'll talk tomorrow. You can come by the house if you like—it's come along quite nicely since you helped me with that floor upstairs. Or we can go have a beer someplace if you prefer."

Jason tilted his head; Stone could almost see the wheels turning as he tried to figure out what this was about. "Yeah, let's have a beer. V has to work for a couple hours tomorrow afternoon, so that'll work out."

Verity returned and slid back in, this time nudging Jason over instead of waiting for him to get out. "Did I miss anything?"

Jason glanced at Stone. "Not sure yet. I guess I'll let you know."

# | CHAPTER FIVE

J ASON MET STONE AT THE FIFTH QUARTER, an upscale sports bar in Palo Alto where they'd gotten together to drink and shoot the breeze several times over the years. He glanced around before he sat down. "Wow, haven't seen this place in a while. Remember we came here after the Evil blew up your old place?"

"Not something I'm ever likely to forget." It had already been nearly four years since the two of them, bloody and rattled from their near-miss escape, had sat in this very booth to discuss their options. Stone hadn't even met Verity yet.

"So what's this about?"

Once again, Stone hesitated. "I've been thinking about something, and I wanted to run it by you to see how you felt about it."

"You look like you're not sure you want to tell me."

"It's not that—it's more that I'm not sure how you'll react."

"Well—just spit it out, I guess." A brief flash of suspicion crossed Jason's face, and Stone was sure he was convinced it had something to do with Verity.

"Right, then." Stone sipped his drink and met Jason's gaze head-on. "I want to invest in your agency."

"*What?*"

"You heard me. You want to open a private investigation agency somewhere in the area, and you need funds to do that. I want to invest."

Jason blinked. His gaze never left Stone, and he looked as if he wasn't sure he'd heard what he thought he'd heard. Finally, he managed: "Why?"

"Why not? I've never been hurting for money, and after Desmond's bequest that's changed significantly for the better. You've certainly done enough for me over the years—why wouldn't I want to help you, and invest in your future at the same time?"

Jason shook his head. "No. Al, no. I can't let you—"

"You're not *letting* me. I want do to it." He leaned forward. "And I seem to recall a friend telling me once that I was quite pigheaded when I refused to accept help when it was offered. Hmm…who could that friend have been?"

When Jason still didn't reply, he spread his hands. "Look: if you're worried I might want to come in and take over, you've nothing to be concerned about. I haven't got the time or the inclination for that. I don't want to be involved in any of the day-to-day decisions. We could set it up so I'm a sort of silent partner. We can even draw up a proper legal agreement if you like." He picked up a bar napkin, pulled a pen from his pocket, and jotted a figure, then slid it across the table. "That should be enough to get you started and keep the lights on for long enough to build a client base. You'll have to do all the work, of course. When I say I don't want to be involved, I mean it."

Jason glanced down at the napkin, then gaped. "Holy shit, Al. This—no. I can't take that much. Hell, that would keep the lights on for a year if I just sat on my ass and played solitaire all day."

"Well, I do hope you're not planning to do that," Stone said dryly. "And don't forget—it's not a gift. It's an investment. I'll be a part-owner in your agency—a silent one, as I said. If you feel strongly about it, you can buy me out over time after you're more successful. Besides, it might be useful to have your services available on occasion."

Again, silence hung in the air as Jason swirled the beer in his glass. "Al—" he said at last. "I don't know. I mean—it's an amazing offer, don't get me wrong. I figured I was gonna have to work for somebody else for at least a few months before I could even get a bare-bones operation going. Either that or go into debt, if I could even get somebody to give me a loan. But—" He sighed. "You gotta understand—I know you understand, because you're the same way. I want to do this on my own. You've already done so much for me, for V—"

"I do get it. I'm sure I'd make the same protests if the situation were reversed. But don't forget—you've done a lot for me, too. If it hadn't been for you, I'd be dead several times over. That *includes* when my house blew up." He leaned back, looking at a point somewhere beyond where Jason sat. "And funny thing—I'm still remembering someone telling me something about how daft it is to be stubborn and refuse to accept help when there's no downside. Took me a while to realize that, but he was right."

He leaned forward, putting his hands on the table. "Listen, Jason—I'm rubbish at asking for help, and so are you. I'd say it's that whole male-pride thing, but your sister's every bit as bad at it as we are. We're really quite a sad lot, when you think about it. Perhaps it's time for all of us to admit that we seem to have a hard time staying away from each other, and let some of that pride go."

Jason swallowed, clearly still torn. "It's so much, though. It'll take me years to pay that back, even if I'm successful."

"Make it less if you like," Stone said. "Fine with me either way. But I'm telling you—remember back when we first met, you asked me if I was 'loaded', and I told you I was more like 'comfortably well off'? Well…after Desmond, I've definitely moved significantly into 'loaded' territory now." He pointed at the napkin with the figure written on it. "I promise you—I won't even miss that. And I can't think of anything better to invest it in than helping a friend I know is going to be a success." He chuckled. "Come on, Jason—go for it. Keep me from buying some ridiculous sports car I have no need for."

Jason had to grin. "You've never struck me as a mid-life crisis kind of guy. But then, V *did* say you're in a band now…By the way, when's your next gig? Maybe I'll come by and check it out."

"Erm." Stone thought, half-amused, half-embarrassed, of The Cardinal Sin's last few gigs and the effect they always seemed to have on Verity. If that happened with Jason around, their fragile détente regarding the subject would almost certainly suffer a setback. "I'll—have to check the schedule. Anyway—what do you say? If you agree to my offer, we can have my solicitor draw up some terms to keep it all nice and legal, and you can get started shopping for office space and night-vision goggles and a tuxedo and whatever else private investigators need to do their job."

"I'm gonna be a PI, not an international spy." He shook his head with a loud sigh, casting another glance down at the napkin. "Can I think about it? I'll give you my answer tomorrow, if that's okay. Believe me, Al, I appreciate it. But I gotta decide if this is something I can deal with." His eyes narrowed. "Hey, you didn't cook this up with V, right? She didn't ask you to—"

Stone held up his hands. "No, no. I promise. She doesn't know anything about it. That's why I wanted to meet with you privately at first. But you know…if you need a consultant, you could do worse than her. She's already proven she can be a big help with missing-person cases."

Jason's gaze lingered on him for several more seconds—it couldn't have been more obvious he was trying to determine to his satisfaction that Stone was telling him the truth about not colluding with Verity. Finally he took another sip of his beer. "That's not a bad idea, if she's willing. Of course, I'd have to figure out how to show my work—can't tell the client we found their missing child using magic—but that's down the road. First I need to decide If I'm going to do it this way at all—and get it off the ground."

He finished the beer and stood. "Thanks, Al. Really. No matter which way I decide, I want you to know I appreciate the offer. And—please don't tell V about it, okay?"

"My lips are sealed. It will remain between us until you decide otherwise."

"Great." He clapped Stone on the shoulder as they both stood to go. "See you later."

# | CHAPTER SIX

STONE HALF-EXPECTED JASON OR VERITY to call later, suggesting the three of them all go out to dinner together. When he looked up from his work and discovered it was already almost seven, he decided they must have made other plans. Perhaps Jason was talking his offer over with Verity after all; Stone didn't expect he'd be too successful at keeping it a secret from her, especially if she checked out his aura.

He closed the book he'd been reading and leaned back in his chair to discover Raider perched on the edge of the desk, watching him with a steady, green-eyed gaze. "Well," he said, holding out his hand to the cat. "Looks like it's just you and me tonight, mate. Fancy a pizza?"

Actually, he wasn't even sure the pizza places delivered in Encantada—he'd never checked, and he didn't recall seeing any in the town's tiny downtown area. Back at the Palo Alto place, he'd occasionally find ads for pizza or Chinese food delivery hanging from his front doorknob, but he supposed they didn't do things that way around here. For one thing, the houses were farther apart and most of them were either set far back from the road, surrounded by walls or fences, or both.

He supposed it was as good a time as any to take a walk into town and check things out. Before he'd officially moved in, his visits had been limited to poking around the house doing his little DIY projects and trying to stay out of the way of the contractors doing the real work. He still had to unpack the boxes in the basement and set up his magical sanctum, not to mention going shopping for some proper furniture so the place didn't look like an upscale warehouse. He had a lot of rooms to fill, but didn't feel in any pressing hurry to finish the project.

Raider was still watching him, still sitting neatly on the desk corner with his striped tail wrapped around him. He'd always been expressive for a cat, but tonight his gaze looked particularly perceptive, almost as if he had something he wanted to say.

Stone reached out and ruffled his fur. "What do you think? Shall I bring you back some pizza? Chinese food? A nice lobster tail with drawn butter? Mouse *à l'Orange*?"

"Meow," said the cat.

"That's not an answer." It amused him how often he carried on one-sided conversations with Raider. Before the cat had come into his life, he'd always thought of such behavior as borderline mental—the province of crazy cat ladies and old men who spent too much time alone. Now, though, after more than a year, he did it without even thinking about it. He supposed he shouldn't worry too much about it unless he did it in front of other people—or unless the cat answered.

"Meow," Raider said again. He padded forward and planted himself on top of Stone's closed book, ducking his head for more petting.

Stone obliged as he gathered up his books with magic and stacked them on the edge of the massive desk. He'd been surprised and pleased at how fast the cat had adjusted to this change in circumstances. After Edwina Mortenson had come by last year to help him deal with the traumatized feline, he'd picked up a couple of books on the subject and learned cats were creatures of routine—they were at their happiest when life moved at a steady and reliable pace, mealtimes occurred consistently, and disruptions were kept at a minimum. Since Stone's life was the very definition of "disrupted," he'd occasionally thought early on that it would be kinder to Raider if he found him another home with someone more regular in their habits.

He kept meaning to do it, but after several months had passed and the tabby seemed to be handling things with aplomb, Stone decided that perhaps his new roommate was an exception to the usual feline stereotype. Of course it had nothing whatsoever to do with the fact that he'd grown attached to the little beast.

Nothing at all.

Ever since he'd stepped out of the carrier into the sparsely furnished living room, Raider had settled in to the new place with the curiosity of a scientist and the demeanor of a monarch surveying his new realm. Stone wasn't sure how much of the place he'd explored—in fact, he worried a bit because he himself hadn't examined the entire house with enough attention to detail to ensure there weren't any small holes or openings Raider could lose himself in—but he'd already located his litter boxes on all three levels, identified several favorite sleeping places, and claimed a perch in front of one of the larger picture windows looking out into the sizable backyard. He seemed pleased at the amount of local wildlife, entertaining himself for hours watching squirrels, birds, roaming cats, and the occasional raccoon. One evening while Stone lounged on the sofa, the cat had leaped into his lap, put his paws on his chest, and looked him in the eye as if to say, "Yes, human—this place will do."

Raider's favorite place, though, without a doubt, was the study. It had been obvious from the moment Stone had done his first walkthrough of the house on the day the solicitor had informed him of Adelaide Bonham's bequest that this room had been designed as a study or library: it had two walls of built-in bookshelves as well as a large window looking over the backyard. As soon as he entered it, Stone felt a sense of peace and contentment, almost as if the room were welcoming him. He still hadn't explained the old book that had dropped off one of the shelves while he was checking it out, but it hadn't recurred so he wrote it off as the house settling or something. Just because the place had a ley line running through it didn't mean there was anything magical going on inside.

At least not before he moved in, anyway.

Raider was still watching him. It was a bit unnerving, honestly—the cat's wide-eyed green stare was pleasant enough, but he usually deployed it on mice, birds, or errant dust bunnies. Now, it was fixed firmly on Stone.

"Something I can do for you?" he asked, ruffling Raider's fur again.

"Meow."

That was the other odd thing: Raider wasn't normally that talkative.

"You'll have to give me more to go on than that, I'm afraid. My feline language skills are regrettably lacking."

Raider tilted his head, held Stone's gaze for a couple more seconds, then leaped from the desk and up onto one of the lower shelves. There, he settled himself on another book.

"Raider, whatever you're up to, you'll have to sort it out on your own. I'm off to get something to eat." He stood, pushed in the chair, and prepared to leave the room.

He stopped when he realized what book the cat was sitting on.

He hadn't unpacked all his boxes yet; several of them, all full of books, still waited for his attention in the room's corner. But Raider wasn't sitting on any of those he *had* unpacked. Instead, he was comfortably positioned atop the same old encyclopedia volume that had startled Stone by sliding off the shelf and dropping to the floor during his walkthrough, seemingly of its own accord. The cat continued to regard Stone with smug interest.

Stone shifted to magical sight. He felt a little embarrassed about doing it, especially when he spotted nothing out of the ordinary. Raider's aura looked as it always did: green and vibrant. Animals' auras were all green. Many humans' were too, of course, but those usually glowed much more brightly unless something was wrong.

"Right, then," he said firmly, shifting back and wondering, not for the first time, if he was drifting toward being one of those sorts who carried photos of his cat around in his wallet. "I'll give you some time to sort out whatever's bothering you. I'll bring you back something from wherever I end up. How's that sound?"

"Meow," said Raider.

"Downtown" was an ambitious term to describe the tiny cluster of buildings comprising Encantada's business district. Spread out along a half-mile of heavily wooded two-lane road, the picturesque village reminded Stone of a smaller version of Woodside or Portola Valley, two more upscale, woodsy little towns not far from Stanford. The difference was that Encantada made it clear, in its genteel way, that it didn't encourage visitors who didn't have reason to be in the town. The main road—the only way in—wasn't well marked. The sign pointing the way tended to get overgrown by vegetation and was rarely maintained, whether by inattention or design, so you either had to intend to go there or take a wrong turn looking for something else. Once you got in, getting out wasn't any easier: at the other end, the road terminated at a large church that dated back almost two centuries, meaning the lost traveler would be forced to turn around and retrace their route to get back out.

To his surprise, though, Stone had discovered something unexpected during his infrequent trips down to pick up something from the tiny hardware store. Encantada's residents, despite their near-pathological passion for privacy, seemed a pleasant lot and not at all the snobbish and elitist bunch he'd been expecting. When he'd first learned of the town, he'd feared he was moving into a nest of the sort of wealthy Americans he despised: the crass, materialistic types who considered others somehow lesser beings because they hadn't had the same advantages in life.

To test this hypothesis, he'd deployed an illusion on one of his early visits, disguising himself as a disheveled young man in torn jeans and an old T-shirt before stopping by a tiny sandwich shop tucked into a secluded alcove. Contrary to his expectation—that he'd either be shown the door or served with cold efficiency while being constantly watched—the shop's proprietor had greeted him warmly and even offered suggestions about some selections he might find to his liking. The worst he could say was that Encantada's residents seemed, as a rule, to treat both newcomers and each other with a kind of quiet reserve. Stone didn't mind that at all. To him, the only thing worse than finding himself in a town full of snobs would be finding himself in one full of busybodies. Snobs, at least, could be entertaining if properly handled.

On this pleasant, late-summer evening, it took Stone less than half an hour at a leisurely walk to traverse the short distance from his home to downtown. On his way, he passed two joggers and one dog-walker, all of whom smiled at him as they passed but didn't stop to chat.

He didn't have a lot of options for food if he wanted to stay in town. The only restaurants he'd discovered were the sandwich shop, an elegant, expensive place that didn't do takeout, a gastropub called "The Enchanted Grotto," and an indie coffee shop that boasted excellent brew but didn't serve food. He supposed he could stop by the tiny gourmet grocery store and pick up something to attempt to cook—though Verity didn't think he'd noticed her subtle efforts to involve him when she prepared meals, he *had* actually managed to pick up a rudimentary skill or two—but that would take too long. If he got back soon, he could get some more work done on his latest magical research project: trying to reverse-engineer the spell they'd used on Calanar to enchant clothing to adjust to its wearer's size. He'd been so busy he hadn't had much time to work on it lately, but he was sure he almost had it. Such a thing could prove quite useful.

Sandwich shop it was, then. He'd pick up something for himself, a small, all-meat version for Raider, and be back home before eight.

The place was popular—a few other customers stood around inside its narrow dining area, obviously waiting for takeout orders. Stone placed his and took a seat at one of the tiny tables, idly watching the others with magical sight: a mother and father with two preteen children, an older woman on her own, and a man in sweatpants and T-shirt who looked like he'd just finished a run. The man got his food and departed, and two more women entered.

As Stone continued to wait, switching off magical sight and instead studying the shop's old-fashioned décor, he noticed one of the children was watching him. The two of them, a boy and a girl, had wandered away from their parents and stood near the opposite wall. The boy, perhaps ten or eleven, ducked his gaze when he realized Stone had spotted him, but then seemed to gather his courage. He whispered something to his sister, then moved closer to Stone.

"Hi," the kid said. He looked nervous, which made sense—children that age had it drilled into them from infancy not to talk to strangers, but yet here he was.

"Hello." Stone glanced toward the boy's parents, who were chatting with the counterman about their order.

"You just moved here, didn't you?"

"Er—yes. Why?"

"I rode my bike past your place and saw you out front talkin' to the truck guy."

Stone had never been comfortable around children. They were unpredictable, difficult to read, and he never knew what they might say or how to respond to it. "Er," he said again, noncommittally.

"That place has been empty a long time. Have you seen the ghost?"

"Ghost?" Well. *This* was interesting, at least.

The boy looked pleased, as if he'd stepped onto firmer ground. His tone took on more eagerness. "Yeah. That place is haunted. Didn't you know? Wow, your real estate guy shoulda told you or something."

Neither the real estate guy nor the solicitor had mentioned anything about the place being haunted—but there *had* been that business with the encyclopedia...

"Is that so? How do you know that?"

"Everybody knows. Some old lady owned it." He leaned forward and lowered his voice. "I heard she died in it and they never found her body."

"Well, that's not true. I knew the lady who owned it. She was a lovely person. Died recently, yes, but not in the house. So if that's who you think the ghost is—"

"Nah." The kid waved him off. "She's not the ghost. S'posed to be some old professor guy."

"Is that right? Where did you hear this?"

"Like I said, *everybody* knows it. He really *did* die in it. Long time ago. They say he just dropped dead while he was readin' a book one night." He looked Stone up and down. "You got any kids?"

"Er—no. Sorry. It's just me."

"Just you? All by yourself in that big ol' house?"

"Aidan! What are you doing?"

The boy's mother had finally noticed her son wasn't where she'd left him. She hurried over, shooting Stone a suspicious look, and gripped the boy's shoulder. "Get back over here—we're leaving in a minute. Don't bother this man."

"Oh, it's no bother," Stone said. He stood and offered his hand and an encouraging grin. "Alastair Stone. I just moved into town recently, and your son has informed me I'm living in a haunted house."

"Oh!" She shook his hand and returned the smile. "It's a pleasure to meet you, then. I'm Tricia Carey. That's my husband Scott, and these two monkeys are Aidan and Hannah."

"Pleasure's mine." Stone could sense her tension dissipating even without looking at her aura—score another one for the charm and the accent.

"I hope Aidan wasn't disturbing you."

"No, not at all. I'm fascinated. Do you know anything about this so-called 'haunting'?"

"He's livin' in that big old place on Wilding Road," Aidan said, excited.

"Really?" She eyed Stone with more interest as her husband came over carrying their bag of sandwiches. "I'd heard someone moved in there—saw a few contractors' trucks when I drove by. Honestly, I was beginning to wonder if anyone would ever live there again. They used to rent it out, but it's been vacant for years. Are you renting?"

"No. I knew Adelaide Bonham, the owner, several years ago. Did some work for her. She passed away recently and left the place to me."

Next to Tricia, Aidan and Hannah's eyes got huge. "The old lady *gave* you that place?" Aidan demanded.

"Wow…" Hannah breathed. She looked to be a year or so younger than her brother.

"Guys, enough," Scott Carey warned. He offered Stone his hand. "It's nice to meet you, Mr.—"

"Stone. It's a pleasure."

"I was tellin' him about the ghost," Aidan said. "Askin' if he's seen it yet."

Tricia sighed, rolling her eyes at her son, then shot an apologetic look at Stone. "I'm sorry. That place is—well, I guess it's sort of a local legend among the kids in town." Once again, she turned sternly to Aidan and Hannah. "Listen, both of you—I know kids sometimes used to go there and look in the windows. No more of that. Do you understand? I don't want you two disturbing Mr. Stone."

Aidan looked disappointed, but nodded. "Yeah. No more." He brightened. "You aren't gonna be havin' a housewarming party or anything, are you?"

"Aidan!"

Stone chuckled. "I'm afraid not, Aidan. I'm not really much of a party sort. But if I see any ghosts, I'll be sure to let you know next time I see you."

"Cool!" Aidan and Hannah allowed their father to herd them off toward the door. "Nice meetin' ya!" the boy called back over his shoulder.

"It is," Tricia said. "I'm sure we'll see you around— everyone eventually gets to know everyone around here. It's a nice, quiet little town. I'm sure you'll be happy here."

Stone picked up his bag and set off toward home, deep in thought. Normally, he would have written Aidan's "ghost story" off as the kind of folklore passed on from child to child regarding anyplace that remained unoccupied for too long.

Especially given the fact that his new house, with its high, steeply-peaked roof and gray stone façade, could easily fit a child's idea of what a "haunted house" might look like.

But there was still the matter of the book falling off the shelf...and now Raider was acting odd. It was well documented, even among mundanes, that animals were often sensitive to things humans couldn't see. Could the cat have noticed something he'd missed, even with magical sight? *Could* the echo of the old professor Aidan mentioned, or even some other echo entirely, still be in the house? Possibly even more than one?

Without consciously realizing he was doing it, Stone picked up his pace to a swift stride and arrived home a few minutes later. "Raider?" he called. "Where are you? I've got something for you."

Raider rarely came when called, but he must have smelled the sandwiches this time. A flurry of footfalls sounded from somewhere upstairs and a moment later the tabby came thundering down, skidding to a stop in front of Stone with his gaze fixed on the bag.

"Ah, I see where I rate." Stone ruffled Raider's fur. "Come on—I want to have a look at you."

He pulled the meat out of Raider's small sandwich, put it on a plate, and set it on the floor next to the dining table. Then he settled back with his own and a Guinness, switching to magical sight as he ate.

Raider, tearing eagerly into the roast beef, looked no different than he had before. His aura glowed the same shade of green as always—the red flashes from the traumatic experience that had brought him to Stone in the first place were long gone and had been for months. Stone was no expert on animals, but from everything he could see, Raider looked like a textbook example of a contented, mellow cat.

He finished the sandwich, tossed the wrapper, and stood in the dining room a moment holding his bottle of Guinness. *Come on,* he admonished himself. *You're not going to believe some fanciful story from a child you met in a sandwich shop, are you?*

But there was the matter of the encyclopedia...and the fact that a ley line ran right through the middle of the house.

Fine. He'd work on the spell later. He could at least take the time to do a quick walkthrough and see if anything turned up.

An hour later, after he'd tramped through the entire house—all three floors, the attic, the basement, and even a quick check around the perimeter outside—and examined each room with magical sight, he dropped into the desk chair in his study with a sigh.

Nothing.

Aside from the ley line itself, the magic items he'd brought with him, and the rudimentary wards he'd put up around the house until he had time to construct better ones, he hadn't seen any sign of magical energy, echoes, or anything else of interest. He paid particular attention to the encyclopedia volume, thinking perhaps the "ghost" might be associated with it in some way, but it appeared as mundane as everything else.

"Well, that was a waste of time," he muttered.

At least it wasn't too late yet. He still had time to get in a decent amount of work on the tailoring spell, and maybe even work on some updates to his next series of lectures. He reached for one of the reference books on the corner of his desk.

Raider sat in the study's doorway, watching him intently.

He frowned. The cat had followed him around during most of his wanderings, but that wasn't anything new. Now, though, he sat in the exact center of the open doorway, tail wrapped around him, unmoving. Only his eyes followed Stone's actions.

"Raider, what's got into you? You're acting quite odd tonight. Is something wrong?"

"Meow."

Wait—he *answered?*

Stone put the book aside and stood. "Did you just answer me?"

"Meow."

Okay, this was strange even by Stone's decidedly liberal standards. "Are you trying to tell me something?"

"Meow." Moving with deliberate calm, Raider padded across the room and leaped onto the desk, all without taking his gaze off Stone.

"Okay..." Feeling foolish, Stone shifted once again to magical sight, this time making an extra effort to sharpen his focus. The magic came easily when he called for it—ever since he'd returned from Calanar, he'd noticed a definite increase in his power level, and his arcane perceptions were no exception.

Still, at first he didn't see anything. Raider's aura was still its usual pale green, just as it always was. Nothing unusual about—

"Hold on…" Stone tensed as he narrowed his focus to Raider's face. Something about his eyes—

There it was. Faint and difficult to see even with the extra power Stone was pumping into the spell, it was nonetheless there: a faint flicker of bright blue around the cat's curious green eyes.

"What the…?" He leaned back, keeping magical sight up so he didn't lose track of the blue glow. "Raider—do you understand what I'm saying? Meow once—no, twice—if you do."

Raider tilted his head, looked him in the eye, and meowed twice.

"Bloody…hell." Stone's heart thudded harder, and an electric flush crept over his body. Speaking with care, he said, "Have you…always understood what I'm saying? One meow for yes, two for no."

"Meow. Meow."

He frowned. "No? So when did you start? Wait, that's not a yes-no question." He thought of the odd way Raider had acted earlier that day—the way he'd seemed so unusually in-tent, and perched on the encyclopedia. "Is it only since you've moved in here?"

"Meow."

Okay, so there *was* something about the house. That was curiously comforting—the thought that his feline companion had been capable of conversation and sentient thought ever since the two had begun sharing space was more than a little disturbing—especially given the number of times Raider had been in his bedroom during overnight visits from Verity and other women. He studied the cat, pondering.

Raider held his gaze for a few more seconds, then leaped off the desk and returned to his spot on top of the encyclopedia volume.

Stone swiveled his chair around. "Is there something about that book you want me to notice?"

"Meow."

It occurred to him then that he'd never actually *examined* the book, nor had he gotten rid of it when he moved in. It seemed logical that he would have done so—who wanted a single volume of an outdated encyclopedia set, after all? Even stranger, when he'd first arrived at the house the shelf had included other volumes of the incomplete set, but he'd gotten rid of those along with other useless items he'd found in other rooms. Why hadn't he trashed this one along with the others?

Curious now, he got up and walked to the shelf. Raider obligingly shifted position, moving farther down while still keeping him in view.

He picked up the book. It was a volume of the *Encyclopedia Britannica,* and looked to be at least fifty years old. Nothing struck him as odd or unusual about its cover; it looked old and well used, weathered and faded from no doubt sitting on a shelf in a vacant house for many years, but otherwise fine. He carried it back to the desk, and Raider followed. The cat seemed unusually interested in what he was doing.

He opened the front cover. No inscription on the flyleaf, which didn't surprise him since it was Volume Fifteen of the set. "Is there some entry in here you want me to see?" he asked Raider. At this point, it didn't even occur to him to feel strange about talking to a cat as if expecting the creature to understand him. His mind had shifted firmly from the mundane to the magical realm now, and in the world of magic, a talking cat didn't even move the meter compared to some of the things he'd seen.

"Meow. Meow."

"No? Hmm...all right, then—we'll do this the hard way." He picked up the heavy volume and began flipping through it.

Puffs of dust rose, and some of the pages stuck together from disuse, but he did his best to flip each one. He had no idea what Raider was trying to tell him—perhaps someone had written something in one of the margins?

The book had a lot of pages, and he almost missed it as he passed the halfway point and re-adjusted his grip on the spine. Something flashed by—something that didn't look like part of the book itself.

"Hello, what's this?" he murmured, returning to the spot he'd passed and flipping pages more slowly.

Stuck between the pages was a yellowed newspaper clipping from the *Stanford Daily*. Dated June 1958, the article included a grainy photo of a smiling, nondescript-looking middle-aged man and the headline, *Benchley joins Chemistry faculty.*

The article itself didn't seem terribly interesting on its own: it merely announced that Professor Thaddeus Benchley, formerly of some university back East Stone had never heard of, had accepted a position in the Chemistry department. He and his family had settled in Palo Alto, and he would begin teaching at the Fall quarter.

Stone looked at the photo, then back at Raider. The boy at the sandwich shop had said the so-called "ghost" was supposed to be "some professor guy" who'd "dropped dead while he was readin' a book one night." Could it be—

"Professor Benchley?"

"Meow." If it was possible for a cat to look pleased, Raider did so.

Stone dropped the clipping and sagged back in his chair. "Bloody hell..." he whispered. He shifted to magical sight again for another look at Raider. The cat's aura remained a steady green, with only the hint of blue around his eyes indicating anything different from usual. Stone saw no sign of agitation—if the echo of a long-dead professor was somehow taking his cat for a joyride, it didn't seem to be causing Raider any discomfort. He knew from past experience that echoes could manipulate inanimate objects—he'd once dealt with one that had taken over the machinery at a meat-packing plant—but he'd never seen one borrow a living being before. Perhaps animals were easier than humans.

He leaned forward again, swiping a hand through his hair. "Er—all right, then. It's—er—a pleasure to meet you, Professor. Is there something I can do for you, or are you just popping in to say hello? Sort of a spiritual Welcome Wagon?"

Raider didn't answer, except to lick his paw.

Perhaps that was too complicated a question for the echo to handle in its present state. Was it constrained by having to use Raider's body—and maybe even his brain?—to communicate? But if Benchley's echo had been hanging about in the house for many years, there was probably a reason for it. Most people didn't produce echoes when they died, and usually if they did, it meant they had some unfinished business they needed to attend to before passing on to whatever awaited them on the other side.

"Do you want me to help you with something?"

"Meow."

Fascinated, Stone picked up the clipping again. "I'll do what I can. Just make sure you don't do anything to harm my cat, all right?"

Raider stalked to the edge of the desk and head-butted him, accompanied by a loud, rumbling purr.

All right, apparently no harm. "What can I—"

On the opposite edge of the desk, his mobile phone chirped. Immediately, Raider leaped off the desk and dashed out of the room.

*Damn.* "Bloody brilliant timing, whoever you are." Stone snatched up the phone.

Jason's familiar number flashed on the screen. He hit the button. "Yes, hello?" He was aware he sounded impatient, but it couldn't be helped.

"Al? This a bad time?"

"Er—no, I suppose not. What is it?"

"Sorry, man. Didn't mean to interrupt anything."

"Don't worry about it. What can I do for you?"

"Can we get together tomorrow? Maybe for lunch? V and I went out to dinner and had a long talk."

That didn't surprise Stone. Jason could no more have kept his offer a secret from Verity than he could have stayed angry with her for her romantic activities. The two of them were too close for anything else. "Sure. You've got an answer for me, then?"

"Yeah. Let's talk tomorrow. I'll let you get back to whatever you were doing."

*Not much chance of that at this point,* he thought with a glance toward the open doorway. "Yes, fine. Tomorrow, then. I'll call you."

After he hung up, Stone went in search of Raider, hoping they might resume their discussion. He found the cat curled up in the middle of his bed. "So, Professor—about whatever you want me to do for you. Can you help me work out what it is?"

Raider barely budged, raising his head only enough to aim a sleepy glance at Stone. A quick check with magical sight confirmed that the faint blue glow around the cat's eyes had departed.

"Some other time, then," Stone muttered.

Raider didn't reply.

# | CHAPTER SEVEN

"SO THEN, WHAT HAVE YOU DECIDED? I assume you and Verity have discussed the situation at length."

Stone sat across from the two of them at a busy little pho house on Castro Street in Mountain View. He was still feeling frustrated—he'd made another attempt to communicate with Professor Benchley earlier that morning, but Raider had remained echo-free. Even so, he'd shut the bewildered tabby out of the bathroom while he took a shower, just to be sure. He wasn't proud of it, but he'd done it nonetheless.

Jason finished slurping up a long stream of noodles before answering. "Yeah. Honestly, I was kind of leaning toward saying no—like I said, it's a fantastic offer and I definitely appreciate it, but I felt like I wanted to make a go of this on my own, you know?"

"But…?"

"But then he talked to me," Verity said with a grin. "And I talked some sense into him."

"Is that so? Given how eager you were for me to stop paying your rent, I'd have thought you would have advised him against it."

"That's different. I'm not your apprentice anymore, so you shouldn't be responsible for my housing. But this is an investment. People get investors all the time when they're starting businesses."

"I'm still not comfortable with it," Jason said. "I still think it'd be better if I got a job somewhere up here, and saved up until I could afford to do it with my own money."

"Let me remind you of something, in case you've forgotten," Stone pointed out, feeling a bit like a fisherman reeling in a prize catch—one he already knew he'd landed. "It's *expensive* to live up here. You might think you'll be able to save money like you did when you were living with Stan, but do you really think it will work that way?"

"That's one of the things V pointed out," Jason said. He glared between the two of them in clearly affected annoyance. "Why the hell do you two live someplace so damned expensive, anyway? This would be a hell of a lot easier if you were somewhere cheaper."

"Well, I don't know about Verity," Stone said dryly, "but I'm offering to invest in your firm—not to relocate. You're a good friend, but not *that* good." He sipped his tea. "So—does that mean you accept my offer?"

"Yeah. I can't think of a good reason not to. But not nearly as much as you said. I can get a really good start—get some office space in San Jose, where it's cheaper than up here, buy a few things I need, and put some away to keep the place going for a few months—on half that. And I do want to do it all nice and legal. I want you to know where your money's going."

"Brilliant," Stone said. "Wouldn't have it any other way. Glad to hear your sister's talked some sense into you."

"Yeah, well, she does that sometimes."

"Kind of my job," Verity said with a grin.

Stone raised his glass. "To new beginnings, and future success, then. I'll call my solicitor tomorrow and we can have some documents drawn up."

Jason lifted his own glass and clinked Stone's. "Thanks, Al," he said, and he looked serious now instead of reluctant. "I'm not kidding—this means a lot to me. I won't let you down."

Stone waved him off. "None of that. You've got a talent for this, and your work ethic exhausts me sometimes. You'll do fine."

"He will," Verity agreed. "And I'm going to help him. I should be able to make some of those missing-persons cases a lot easier to solve."

Ah, so Jason *had* spoken with her about that—or perhaps it had been her own idea. "That should work out well. You two make a good team. I look forward to hearing about your continuing successes."

"That's a good point," Jason said. "As an investor, you'll be part of the company, so I can tell you about the cases."

"Excellent. Actually, as it happens I've got one of my own now."

"You do?" Verity leaned forward with interest.

"Yes—Raider started talking to me last night. That's what you interrupted, Jason, and why I sounded so cross on the phone."

"Wait a second." Jason's eyes narrowed. "Did I hear you right? Did you say your *cat* was *talking* to you?"

"Well, sort of." He quickly told them about what had happened, including the story Aidan at the sandwich shop had related.

Verity listened with increasing delight. "Oh, wow. Can I come by soon? I want to talk to your cat...or professor...or whatever. What do you think he wants you to do?"

"No idea. I'm planning to look him up tomorrow—I'm sure there are records in one of the libraries. But if his echo has hung about this long, he's clearly got some business he needs to sort out before he can move on."

Jason shook his head with an amused, rueful sigh. "Okay. This is out of my league. You two can solve the Mystery of the Talking Cat on your own. Me, I need to get back to more boring things, like finding an office I can afford."

# | CHAPTER EIGHT

T HE NEXT DAY, Stone arrived on campus an hour early
so he could try hunting down information about Professor Thaddeus Benchley. He stopped by his office
first, waving a greeting to Laura, the Cultural Anthropology
department's admin aide. "Morning."

She glanced at the clock with a smile. "You're here early.
I thought you weren't even functional before ten a.m."

"Had some things to do before my class." He held up his
cup. "And I've got some extra-potent coffee this morning."
He started to sweep past her toward his office, then stopped.
"Laura…"

"Yes?"

"Suppose I wanted to find out some information about a
professor who used to teach here. What would be the best
way to do that?"

She put her pen down. "I guess that would depend on
who it is and what kind of information you're looking for."

"Chap named Thaddeus Benchley. He started teaching
here in the late Fifties, in the Chemistry department."

"The Fifties? You mean like last century?"

Stone chuckled. "Unless the Chemistry department has somehow perfected time travel, it would have to be, wouldn't it?"

"What do you want to find out about him? HR would probably have information, but I'm not sure they're allowed to give it out."

"Nothing sensitive like that. Just—who he was, when he died, that sort of thing."

She pondered. "You could try the library—maybe back issues of the *Daily*? Or I could check with the Chemistry department for you if you want."

"No, no, that's fine. I can do it myself. This is sort of a…personal project."

"Now you've got me intrigued," she said.

Laura was known around the department for being a bit of a busybody, but Stone saw no harm in satisfying some of her curiosity. "You know I've finally moved into that house in Encantada—well, I found some papers indicating that he might have lived there at some point—and possibly died there. I was curious to find out more about him."

She shuddered. "Died there? That's creepy."

"That doesn't even rate on the scale of creepy I'm used to dealing with," Stone reminded her.

"So you don't find it unsettling that someone might have died in your house?"

"No. It's not as if he's haunting the place or anything." *Possessing my cat doesn't count as 'haunting,' exactly…*

"I suppose not." She shuddered again, then typed something on her keyboard and glanced at her computer screen. "Anyway—the Chemistry department is probably your best bet. Here's the number of their department office."

"Thanks, Laura."

"Good thing he *isn't* haunting your house—a chemistry professor would probably be a pretty boring ghost, all things considered."

Stone, picturing Raider's earnest, intent stare, didn't reply.

As he approached his office, Mackenzie Hubbard poked his head out of his own, two doors down.

"Thought I heard your voice," the other professor said. "Got a minute?"

"Er—sure. Come on in." This was odd—Hubbard usually hated mornings as much as he did, and certainly wasn't the type to be chatty before noon—or any other time, for that matter. At this rate, Stone would have to postpone his search for information about Thaddeus Benchley until later that day.

He tossed his briefcase on the desk and settled in behind it. "Something I can do for you?"

Hubbard didn't sit. Even more uncharacteristically, the man was smiling. It wasn't much of a smile, true, but given his usual world-weary, laconic demeanor, this qualified as positively ebullient for him. "No," he said. "I just got some news this weekend, and I wanted you to be one of the first to know."

"News?" Stone shifted to magical sight; Hubbard's normally dull orange aura glowed brighter than usual, indicating excitement. What was going on? "What sort of news?"

Hubbard grinned. "Remember I told you I'd sent my latest manuscript out a while back?"

"Yes…" That was nothing new. Hubbard was always sending manuscripts out—Stone could usually tell when he'd gotten his latest rejection slip by his grumpier-than-usual demeanor.

"Well—I heard back from a publisher. They're going to buy it!" He pulled a folded letter from his back pocket and tossed it on the desk. "I got the news on Saturday. They're going to publish it, Stone."

Stone looked at the letter, then back up at Hubbard. "That's—brilliant, Hubbard. Really." He stood and offered his hand. "I'm so pleased for you."

Hubbard pumped his hand with vigor. The man seemed to be practically thrumming with excitement, which was a combination of charming and disturbing. He nodded toward the letter. "I'm getting an advance and everything. Not much—it's just a small press, but they're highly regarded in the literary horror sphere. It was never about the money, anyway."

That was probably a good thing. Stone hadn't read one of Hubbard's manuscripts for years, but the one he *had* read, a purple, densely plotted doorstop about a tentacle creature and its minions attempting to subvert the minds of a small town's population, had served as a pretty good cure for insomnia. Presumably the man had improved since then—either that, or he'd finally found a publisher who shared his affinity for turgid prose and sexual innuendo so deeply buried and symbolic that it wouldn't titillate even the horniest of horror-loving nymphomaniacs.

"I'm very happy for you," he said again. "That's fantastic news. When will it be published?"

"Oh, it'll be a while. Probably not until sometime next year at the earliest. It still needs to go through their editing process, have a cover done, and all that kind of stuff. But that's okay. I'm already working on the next one. And if this one does well, maybe they'll take a look at some of my older work." He picked up the letter and put it back in his pocket. "Anyway—my wife is throwing a little party for me later this week at the house, to celebrate. Nothing fancy, just drinks and that kind of thing with a few friends. Will you come? It's Thursday night. You can bring a date if you want."

Stone had never been certain Hubbard considered him a friend, rather than a mere professional colleague, even though they'd worked together for almost ten years. "Of course I'll come. I'd be delighted."

"Great. Seven on Thursday. I'll send you the address. Thanks, Stone. I'd better go get ready for my class now." He hurried out of the office before Stone could reply, with a spring in his step entirely unlike his usual shuffling trudge.

Stone watched him go, trying to decide if he'd have enough time to look for information on Benchley before he had to leave too. He still couldn't quite believe it—Hubbard had actually sold something to a publisher. It *was* turning into an interesting quarter.

The Chemistry department was located near the medical center, in the northwest part of the campus. It was a pleasant day, sunny but not too hot, so Stone decided to stop by before his class. It took him only a few minutes to get there at a brisk walk, and he easily located the department office.

"I'm looking for information about one of your old faculty members," he told the older woman who greeted him.

Her eyes narrowed. "Old faculty members?"

"Yes—someone who used to teach here. He's been dead for many years, apparently." Stone realized his approach might have been a bit abrupt when her suspicious expression increased, so he deployed the charming smile. "Sorry, sorry. Getting ahead of myself." He flashed his university ID card. "I'm Alastair Stone—Occult Studies department. I've reason to believe he might have lived in my house at some point, and I'm just curious about who he was. His name was Dr. Thaddeus Benchley."

She didn't look as if he'd managed to thoroughly placate her, but nonetheless she pulled her keyboard over and tapped in the information. "Ah. Yes. Dr. Benchley was a member of the Organic Chemistry department faculty from 1958 until 1974."

*Sounds like he had a good run, anyway.* "Do you know why he left? Did he retire?"

She consulted the computer again. "It shows here that he passed away that same year. It doesn't say whether he retired and then died shortly afterward, or passed away while he was still employed. I don't have easy access to that kind of information going that far back. A lot of the older records haven't been transferred to the computer system yet."

"That's fine," he assured her. "That's all I really wanted to know. Thank you very much."

She pointed past him at a hallway. "We have photos of many of our former faculty on the wall there—you might find him among them. I'm not sure, since I've never looked all that closely at them."

"Thank you." Stone glanced at his watch—he'd need to get moving if he wanted to make it to class on time, but he could spare a couple of minutes to scan the photos.

It was a long hallway and there were a lot of framed images hanging along both sides, arranged in chronological order with black-and-white photos from the early part of the twentieth century at the far ends, and more recent ones closer to the lobby. He let his gaze trail along them, checking first the ones from the Fifties. When he found nothing there, he edged along through the Sixties.

He found what he was looking for on the bottom row: the same kindly eyes regarding him from a face that looked a good deal less buttoned-down than the neat, suit-clad man he'd seen in the newspaper clipping. In this faded photo, Dr. Thaddeus Benchley was clad in a dark green sport jacket with wide lapels, an open-collared pale green shirt, and gold, wire-rimmed glasses. His hair, gray now, looked as if he'd forced it into reluctant submission for the photo shoot, and he'd gained a comfortable amount of weight. Overall, the man had the merry look of barely leashed mischief that Stone was all too familiar with in some older professors who no longer cared much what the Establishment thought of them. He suspected his students probably liked him, and that every now and then he'd given demos that probably weren't fully University-approved.

"Hello, Dr. Benchley," he murmured. "Pleased to make your acquaintance. Don't you worry—we'll sort out what you're trying to tell me soon enough."

# | CHAPTER NINE

STONE MADE A QUICK STOP at his office following his class. His intent was to grab a quick lunch and head to the library to look at back issues of the *Daily,* but he changed his mind when he saw Marciella Garra striding past his doorway toward her own office.

Something about the woman still intrigued him. Because he couldn't put his finger on why, she'd occupied a disproportionately large percentage of his thoughts—at least the ones that weren't trying to figure out what was up with his new spectral housemate.

As he vacillated over whether to go talk to her, he thought about what Verity had teasingly said the other night. *Was* he attracted to her? It certainly made sense. She was his type: dark-haired, athletic, sensual, confident, and smart as hell. Could that be all it was—a misplaced physical response, tempered by guilt?

Even though Verity had assured him that not only was she fine with both of them seeing other people but she actively *encouraged* it, Stone wasn't so easy to convince. Not for himself, at least. Perhaps he was more old-school than he thought. He'd never been the jealous type—Verity's relationship with Kyla, which seemed to be growing increasingly closer, didn't disturb him in the slightest. He wasn't sure how he'd feel if she decided to start seeing another man, but he'd cross that bridge if and when he came to it. He doubted it would, though. He knew she'd dated other men in the past; they'd even discussed it one night after a few too many glasses of wine. But unlike her relationships with women, none of the men had made it much past the one-night-stand stage.

None except him, anyway. He supposed he could take that as encouraging.

In any case, he had no intention of pursuing a relationship with Marciella Garra. Even if he weren't seeing Verity, workplace dalliances—especially with someone in one's own department—rarely led to positive outcomes. It had never been a problem before, since Edwina Mortenson had been far too old for him and about as far from his type as it was possible to get while still being female. Hell, he'd met men he was more sexually attracted to than Mortenson, rest her soul.

But now, with Garra, he wasn't so sure.

He couldn't read her signals—which, on further reflection, was probably a big part of what subconsciously bothered him. One of the things that had kept him relatively unscathed in the romantic arena over the years, despite his frequent and enthusiastic participation, was his skill in reading auras. It was a lot easier to disengage from a failing relationship when you could spot the signs before she even realized something was wrong—not to mention having visible auric proof that a potential sexual partner was willing and enthusiastic. It wasn't always easy to offer a cheerful "Good night" and perhaps a chaste kiss when he'd had something more in mind—but a cold shower was a lot safer than pushing things when her aura clearly showed she wasn't on board with the night's potential festivities. It was probably why his track record of remaining on good terms with his ex-girlfriends was as consistent as the relationships' inevitable failures once they discovered the charming Brit in the long black coat came with some pretty strange baggage.

None of that mattered now, though. He wanted to chat with Garra, not ask her out, and if he didn't get on with it soon she'd head out again and he'd have to wait. He got up and strode down the hall.

She was still there, sitting at her desk and jotting something on a notepad. Stone was about to knock softly on the doorframe when she spoke without looking up. "Hello, Dr. Stone. Is there something I can do for you?"

"Er—" he said, startled. He didn't think he'd made any noise on his approach. "Sorry—didn't mean to disturb you."

She put her pen aside and tucked a strand of dark hair behind her ear. "You're not disturbing me. I was just making a few notes about my last class before I went to lunch."

"Ah. Speaking of, would you care to join me? I'm sure you haven't had a chance to sample all the little places around campus. I could show you some of the hidden gems."

Her gaze flicked up and she gave him a cool once-over, almost as if trying to gauge his intentions.

"No ulterior motives," he assured her. "I promise. We haven't had much chance to chat yet, and I thought I could answer any questions you might have about the campus or the area."

She smiled. "All right, then. Thank you, Dr. Stone. I'd like that." She finished her notes, put the pad away in a drawer, and picked up her bag.

"So," he said when they'd left the building, "what do you like? We've got quite a selection of places here on campus, including vegetarian if that's what you prefer."

She chuckled. "No, I'm definitely not a vegetarian. More of a carnivore, really."

"Brilliant—fine with me either way. I've got a bit of a reputation for being willing to try anything once."

She cast a quick, sharp glance his way, then smiled. "Why don't you surprise me, then? Show me one of these 'hidden gems.'"

"Challenge accepted. Do you mind a bit of a walk?"

"I hope not. It seems like *everything* is a bit of a walk from our offices."

"That's true—our department definitely didn't get first choice when they were handing out space."

"It's all right, though. I like a little exercise."

She certainly looked as if she did. Today, she wore a fashionable but professional black skirt suit with a silky golden-yellow blouse, and although Stone wasn't specifically looking at them, he couldn't miss the toned muscles in her tanned calves. Without a doubt she spent some serious time keeping in shape.

He took her to a small eatery frequented mostly by faculty, away from the more bustling places usually packed with undergraduates. They placed their orders and managed to find a table even at the height of the lunch rush.

"So," Stone said, watching her tuck into her beef bourguignon. "How are you settling in? We haven't had much chance to chat since you started. Is Laura taking care of you?"

"Oh, yes, she's wonderful." She looked around. "It's definitely larger here than I'm used to—this is my first teaching position, but the university I attended was much smaller."

"Are the students treating you well? They can be a bit of a handful, but they're a good lot for the most part."

She smiled. "So far everything's been fine."

It seemed as if she'd been on the verge of saying something else. Stone waited, and when she didn't, he said, "But...?"

She looked startled, then chuckled. "Oh, it's nothing, really. Occupational hazard, I'm sure."

"What's that? If something's wrong, I'm sure we can—"

Her gaze focused on him, and something in it changed. "I think it's a problem you might be familiar with as well, actually."

"Oh?"

She hesitated, but when she spoke again she seemed more amused than bothered. "Some of the students are...a little more attentive than I prefer."

"Ah." That didn't surprise him in the slightest—in fact, he'd wondered if she might have trouble with it, and he didn't try to deny that he did sometimes as well. It was one of those things you got used to as a younger professor who was even marginally attractive: students lingering after class, coming by the office for unnecessary meetings, and paying far more attention to lectures than you could attribute to your scintillating speaking style. Stone had weathered more than one crush—mostly from female students, fewer from males—handling them with cheerful deflection until the student eventually got the idea and moved on. With Garra, though, given that young heterosexual males tended on average to be more pushy, he didn't envy her position. "They're not bothering you, are they? If they are—"

"Oh, no." Her smile widened and grew just a little bit predatory. "I can handle them. I've just been told I come on a bit strong, and I don't want to offend anyone when I've only been here a short time."

"If they bother you, don't worry about offending them. They're asking for it. As I said, they're a good lot, but sometimes you have to show them the way things are. If you need me to have a chat with anyone, let me know."

"No, no. I don't need rescuing. Thanks for the offer, though. I appreciate it. I'll be fine." Once again, her gaze changed. "I don't think I'll have much trouble letting people know I'm not looking for a relationship right now."

*Ouch.* Direct hit, right between the eyes. If Stone had harbored any hopes in that direction, they'd just been turned aside with a skillfulness he couldn't help admiring. He suspected this was by no means the first time she'd had to do it.

"Right, then," he said briskly. "Have you had a chance to look around the area at all? There's quite a lot to do, especially if you're willing to range out a bit. Parks, theater, nightclubs, museums—you really must visit the Rosicrucian Museum in San Jose, and don't miss the Winchester Mystery House. It's quite touristy, but still fascinating for anyone in our line of work."

"I've heard that. I'll have to check it out."

Stone focused on eating for a few moments, trying to decide if he wanted to ask the thing that was truly on his mind, or if it might be better to just let it go. As usual, his curiosity won out—if she didn't want to answer, she didn't seem shy about telling him. "So—did you get a chance to take a look at those books I dropped by for you?"

"Just a little. I've been so busy I haven't had a lot of time for side projects. Is it all right if I keep them a while longer?"

"Oh, keep them as long as you like." He paused. "Forgive me for being nosy, but I couldn't help noticing when I was in your office that you seem interested in antiques."

She looked briefly confused, then brightened. "Oh—yes. You saw my list. Nothing to hide there—I've always been interested in old things, especially ones rumored to have some kind of occult significance. I'm sure you understand, given some of the things I've seen on your office shelves."

"Oh, absolutely. I'm a bit of a collector myself."

"Mostly I focus on South American artifacts, but whenever I travel I always make it a point to see if I can find any interesting local pieces. I was making a list of places to check out."

"I can probably add to your list, if you like—more so if you're willing to go a little farther away. Also, I can save you some time. I recognized one of the numbers you had—Huan's Antiquities. Normally I'd recommend it highly. She has some fascinating pieces, especially if she knows you, but her shop's closed indefinitely. She's out of the country."

"Oh, really? That's a shame."

He chuckled. "Madame Huan is one of the most intriguing people I know. She runs the shop because she loves antiques, not because she needs the money. But she also spends more time traveling around looking for new acquisitions than she does actually running the place." He didn't mention that she had two other shops, one in London and one somewhere in China. He had a strong suspicion, though he'd never asked and Madame Huan had never volunteered the information, that she had a dedicated private portal set up between the three shops.

"She sounds like someone I'd love to meet. If she comes back while I'm still here, maybe you could introduce us."

"I'd be delighted." He sipped his pint. "Are you planning to stay past the fall quarter? Or is it too early to make that sort of decision yet?"

"I don't know. I suppose it's not completely up to me, of course—I'm aware I'm being evaluated."

"I wouldn't worry too much about it. The students seem to like you already, and I'm sure Dr. Martinez will be impressed with the new focus you're bringing to the curriculum. We tend to be a bit Eurocentric in our approach here, so some new areas are certain to go over well."

"Well, we'll see," she said. "I do like the students, and it's a beautiful area, but I'm used to something a bit less...populous. I'm not sure how well I'll adjust to living somewhere with this many people."

"Fair enough. There are areas that are less so, but it can get fairly pricey if you want anything close to campus. It's one of the few disadvantages of the area, especially if you haven't lived here for years: the cost of living's a bit frightening. We've lost good candidates in the past to other universities in less expensive areas."

"It is a factor," she admitted. She set her fork down and blotted her lips with her napkin. "Anyway—I should probably get going. I've got a class in half an hour and I need to grab something from my office first. Thank you so much for lunch, Dr. Stone."

"My pleasure. And as I said, feel free to ask if you have any questions about the area."

"I will." She started to rise, then paused. "Oh—before I go—are you going to Dr. Hubbard's party on Thursday night? He invited me, but—" For the first time, she seemed hesitant.

"I am, yes. It's just a little get-together his wife's hosting to celebrate his finally finding a publisher for one of his horror novels. He's been writing them ever since I've known him, and this is the first time he's sold one. It won't be large—I don't think old Hubbard has enough friends to manage a big party."

She brightened, looking relieved. "All right, then, I suppose I'll go."

"Brilliant. I'll see you there."

# | CHAPTER TEN

B ETWEEN CLASSES, MEETINGS, and calling his lawyer about setting up the details of his investment in Jason's agency, Stone didn't make it to the library until later that afternoon. It didn't take him long to find the information he was looking for, though, once he located the back issues of the *Daily*: Dr. Thaddeus Benchley of the Chemistry department had died in the spring of 1974, while still employed by the University. According to the article, he'd been sixty-six years old at the time of his death, which had occurred in his home. A subsequent article a few days later mentioned that his funeral was well attended—he'd apparently been a popular professor—and the following day the paper printed a small puff piece about him, including fond quotes from several of his current and former graduate students. Accompanying the article was a copy of the photo Stone had seen in the Chemistry office, as well as two informal snapshots: one showing him standing behind some elaborate chemical apparatus in his lab with students gathered around, and one of him sitting in a chair with a large cat in his lap.

Stone found Benchley's obituary in the *Mercury News*. It stated that the professor had died of natural causes and would be buried next to his wife, who'd predeceased him by two years, in a small cemetery in Palo Alto. In lieu of flowers, donations were requested to several progressive and anti-war organizations.

*Doesn't sound like anything suspicious,* he thought as he put the microfilm spools away. A lot of people, especially academics, had been active in the anti-war movement in the Seventies. From everything Stone had read, Professor Thaddeus Benchley sounded like the classic older professor: brilliant, a little dotty, beloved of his students. He couldn't be sure, of course, with nothing but a few brief articles and photographs to go on, but at least on the surface Benchley didn't come across as a candidate for any sort of violent or suspicious death.

If that was so, though, why had his echo lingered around the house for all these years, even after others had occupied it? It was possible the place was somewhere Benchley had felt safe and comfortable—that did happen, but not often and usually not in rented houses. Hell, if the man's echo was going to hang about because it had nothing better to do, it made more sense that he'd do it here on campus.

Jason and Verity came to the house that evening for dinner. Verity had called him on his mobile and offered to cook if he picked up a few items on the way home. "I have ulterior motives," she said, her grin coming clearly through in her voice. "I want to talk to your haunted cat."

They were already at the house when he arrived, waiting in Jason's red Mustang. He waved as he passed them and pulled the BMW into the garage. "Sorry I'm late," he told them, pulling the bags from the trunk. "Surprisingly, the commute from here to Stanford normally takes less time than the one in Palo Alto, even though the old place was closer. Got stuck in traffic on the way back from the market, though."

Raider was waiting for them at the door. Verity bent to pet him. "Hey there," she said. "So I hear you're roommates with a ghost now."

The cat's only response was to rub against her legs, purring.

"He doesn't seem very haunted to me," Jason said. He looked around. "You've really fixed this place up since I was here last. A little empty, though. Going for the minimalist look?"

"Going for the 'I haven't had time to pick up much furniture' look." Stone carried the bags to the kitchen and dumped them on the counter. "And as for the haunting—it seems intermittent. Verity, check out his aura. When he was communicating with me, I spotted a faint blue glow around his eyes."

She crouched and peered into Raider's face, then shook her head. "I don't see anything. But you're a lot more sensitive than you were before, so maybe I'm missing it."

Jason flashed her a sharp look. "Sensitive?"

"It's got to do with Harrison's magic," Stone said. "My power levels have taken a healthy jump." He checked Raider himself, but didn't see the blue glow either. "Nothing. I don't think it's a constant thing—the professor only seems to show up when he's got something to tell me."

While Verity got started unloading the bags and pulling out pots and pans, Stone told both of them what he'd found at the library. Raider perched on one of the counters nearby.

"Doesn't sound like much," Jason said. "Sounds like the kid was right—he just keeled over from a heart attack or something. I mean, sixty-six isn't really old, but it's not young either. It happens."

Stone glanced at Raider to see if he had any reaction to Jason's words, but the tabby was intent on licking his paw. "Who knows? As I said, it's intermittent—it might not ever happen again." He set Raider on the floor and refilled his food dish. "By the way, I had a chat with my solicitor today. He's going to draw up some documents based on what we discussed before. If you want to have someone look them over, I can make recommendations."

Jason snorted. "Dude, after everything the three of us have been through together, if I can't trust you by now, something's seriously wrong. Just tell me when to show up and what I need to sign."

"Right, then. He said he'd have things ready later this week. Go ahead and set up a bank account for the business if you haven't already—once everything's all nice and legal, we can do the funds transfer. After that, you're on your own."

"Al, I can't thank you enough for—"

Stone held up a hand. "Enough. Seriously. I'm happy to help, but I'll go bloody spare if I have to listen to you thanking me every fifteen minutes."

"That's not much of a trip," Verity said, grinning.

"And you, apprentice—"

"Not your apprentice anymore, remember?"

"And you, former apprentice—"

Verity laughed and ducked away from his glare. "How's the hot lady professor, by the way? You getting anywhere with her?"

Jason's glare joined Stone's, shifting between his sister and his friend.

"Are you *jealous*, Jase?" Verity asked him, wide-eyed and grinning. "Or—oh my God—are you defending my honor because the Doc might be checking out another woman?"

"No," Jason grumbled.

"You *are*." She patted his shoulder, nodding with wicked amusement. "Don't worry, big bro. The Doc and I are both grownups. We've got this all under control."

"If you two are quite finished," Stone put in, "there isn't any 'this' to have under control. Even if I were interested in such a thing—which I'm not, though I'm not sure why that's any of either of your business—Dr. Garra is focused on her work. I had lunch with her today, and she told me in no uncertain terms that she's not looking for any relationships at present."

"You *asked* her?" Verity demanded, still grinning. "You're usually more subtle than that."

"No, I didn't *ask* her." How did these conversations go off in these kinds of directions, anyway? "She was just telling me some of the male students are a bit more persistent than she's comfortable with. It happens. I've no doubt she can handle it."

Jason seemed relieved, which amused Stone. Before, the two of them had nearly come to blows over Jason's discomfort about him and Verity seeing each other. Now, only two months later, his friend was putting out every indication he was annoyed at the thought of Stone's interest in someone who *wasn't* his sister.

He patted the counter. "Come on up here, Raider," he said. "I need someone to have an intelligent conversation with."

Verity threw a chunk of carrot at him. "Fine. Make your own dinner, then. And I still want to meet your hot lady professor."

# | CHAPTER ELEVEN

I N ALL THE YEARS THEY'D WORKED TOGETHER, Stone had never visited Mackenzie Hubbard's home. This lack of invitation didn't offend him, however; he suspected the older professor wasn't much for entertaining, and pictured Hubbard spending his non-working hours huddled in a cluttered, solitary office, tapping away at his computer while slugging down mugs of coffee delivered by his pleasant, patient wife.

Then again, he'd also always pictured the man living in a classic, upper-middle class tract home somewhere in an established neighborhood in Mountain View or San Jose. Beige, most likely, built in the mid-Sixties, with a two-car garage, a lawn tended by some neighborhood kid, and wooden decorative shutters painted to give the place a dash of color.

Apparently, he was fairly bad at this kind of speculation.

The Hubbards' house was actually in Los Gatos. Not way up in the hills where Adelaide Bonham had lived, but about a mile up a two-lane road near the eastern outskirts of town. The neighborhood consisted of rambling, single-story homes, spaced widely apart and interspersed with mature oak trees. Hubbard's home, a pleasant Eichler near the end of the street bordered at the back by forested land and on one side by a small park, had a woodsy, inviting look. A series of sparkling, fairylike lights illuminating the front walk added to the impression.

Stone arrived half an hour after the start time on the invitation. By then, there were already several cars along the street, so he had to park up near the edge of the woods. He recognized a couple of the cars as belonging to other members of the Cultural Anthropology faculty, but most of them didn't look familiar.

Hubbard's wife Barbara answered the door, smiling when she saw him. "Alastair. I'm so glad you could come. Mac will be happy you're here." She wore a pale blue cocktail dress in her usual conservative, classy style. Unlike her dour husband, she had a vivaciousness that suggested she'd been quite the life of the party in her younger years.

"Wouldn't have missed it." He handed over the bottle of wine he'd brought. "He seemed quite excited when he told me. I'm very happy for him."

"So am I," she said, leaning in with a conspiratorial wink. "You didn't have to listen to him every time he got a rejection slip." The twinkle in her eye took the edge off her words.

"Oh, believe me, I've become quite good at noticing the signs. I'm so pleased he's finally had success."

"Come on—everyone's in the back." She led him down a short hallway and out to an atrium featuring a central fountain with various benches and flowerbeds arrayed around it. Beyond that, an open glass door led to a large living room with a wood floor, beamed ceiling, fireplace, and furniture arranged into a cozy conversation nook. About thirty people lingered in both spaces, chatting and sipping wine. Soft classical music played over unseen speakers.

"Your home is lovely, Barbara," Stone said.

She beamed. "Thank you. It's a little big now that the children have moved out, but I love it, and this area. Mac tells me you've recently moved into a new place."

"Yes, in Encantada. Still getting settled in. I'm rubbish at entertaining, but perhaps you might come by for dinner some evening once I've got actual furniture."

She laughed. "That would be a prerequisite, wouldn't it? We'd love to come whenever you're ready for us. Anyway, please, go enjoy yourself. I've got to refresh the food table."

Stone got a glass of wine and drifted into the atrium, skimming his gaze over the other guests. He didn't recognize most of them, though he did spot familiar faces: Beatrice Martinez and her partner, Laura the admin aide, a couple of the Cultural Anthropology faculty and their spouses, and of course Hubbard, who was holding court on the other side of the living room. He had a small group of people clustered around him, and from the few words Stone could make out, he appeared to be regaling them with the plot of his soon-to-be-celebrated novel.

As Stone came in, Hubbard glanced up, spotted him, and raised his glass. "Stone," he called. "Good to see you. Thanks for coming."

Stone raised his own glass and dipped his head in acknowledgment. He couldn't remember ever seeing grumpy old Hubbard this happy, and he genuinely wished his colleague success, but that didn't mean he was in a hurry to hear about tentacle monsters and mad cultists. He'd congratulate Hubbard later after his entourage had moved on.

A table had been set up on the other side of the room, featuring a large chocolate-frosted sheet cake in front of a vase of black roses, and surrounded by several famous horror novels on bookstands: *Carrie, The Call of Cthulhu, Dracula, The Exorcist, The Haunting of Hill House.* The stand at the far end contained a tome with a plain, black-paper dust jacket, on which someone (presumably Barbara) had hand-lettered *The Creeper at the Gate, by Mackenzie Hubbard* in lurid, fluorescent-green gel pen. Marciella Garra stood near the table, looking over the display and chatting with one of the male professors from the Anthropology department. From her body language, Stone got the impression she'd rather be elsewhere but couldn't extricate herself without making a scene.

"Dr. Garra. You made it," Stone said, approaching the table. Now that he was closer, he could see that the cake read *Congratulations Mac – Future NY Times Bestselling Author!*

She looked relieved to see him. "Dr. Stone, hello. It's good to see you. You know Dr. Darnell, don't you?" She wore a short, slinky black cocktail dress with a gold shimmer that picked up the color in her golden-brown eyes, and a simple gold necklace with a black onyx pendant.

"Yes, of course." Brian Darnell was in his fifties but trying to look younger, dressed in a sweater, sport jacket, and crisp, dark jeans. "Brian, pleasure. I think I saw your wife looking for you." He subtly emphasized the word *wife* and cut his gaze sideways, back toward the atrium.

"Alastair." Darnell looked annoyed, but smiled at Garra. "Perhaps we can talk later."

"Perhaps so," she said noncommittally.

Stone watched him go. "Hope I wasn't interrupting anything."

"Oh, not at all."

On the other side of the room, the group listening to Hubbard describing his novel laughed. Stone hoped he'd just told a joke—he didn't think they'd be impolite enough to laugh at his novel plot at his own party. "Nice place," he said. "I've never been to Hubbard's house before."

"It's beautiful. And his wife is charming."

"She puts up with a lot," he said, chuckling. "When you first meet them you wonder how they've ever stayed together so long, but they're mad about each other. Hubbard just doesn't show it often."

"Oh, it's obvious." She glanced fondly over toward the group. "Some people just belong together, and it's always nice when they find each other."

Barbara approached with a stack of plates and a knife. "If you'll all gather around for a moment," she called, "we'll cut the cake and I wanted to say a few words, and then you can go back to your socializing."

Stone and Garra stepped to the side so she could take their place. "Would you like some help?" Garra asked her. "I could cut while you speak, if you wish."

"Oh, that's so kind of you, Dr. Garra. If you wouldn't mind—"

"I'd be happy to."

Stone watched her out of the corner of his eye while he listened to Barbara Hubbard sharing the story of her husband's book sale with the crowd. She handled the knife with graceful skill, slicing the cake into pieces and transferring each to a plate.

"—and so I'm so happy, and I'm sure Mac is too, to have so many friends on hand to congratulate him on his success."

Everyone applauded. Somebody called "Speech!" and others gently nudged Hubbard, who looked overwhelmed by the whole thing, toward the front.

When he got there, Barbara patted his arm and gave him an encouraging smile. He took in the crowd and offered a more awkward smile of his own. "Thank you, everyone," he said, a slight shake to his voice. "This means a lot to me that you'd all show up to help me celebrate. I know it's not a major book deal—hell, odds are the thing will only sell a few dozen copies, and that's if you all buy one!—but I have to admit I'm pretty proud of it after all these years. So please—enjoy the cake and the wine and have a good time."

The crowd applauded and cheered. Several of them clapped Hubbard on the back or shook his hand before picking up a piece of cake and drifting back to their groups.

Stone remained near the table, though he didn't take a slice. "Well done, Hubbard," he said. "Congratulations."

"Thanks. I'm still thinking I might wake up any minute and find out I dreamed the whole thing."

"If you did, we're all sharing it with you. Enjoy your success. You've earned it."

When Hubbard moved off to chat with another group, Stone noticed Garra had moved a short distance from the table. She had likewise not taken a slice of cake, and seemed inexplicably uncomfortable. "Don't like chocolate?"

"Oh, I do. I'm just not in the mood for it right now. What about you?"

He shrugged. "I've never been much for sweets, I suppose." Under cover of glancing out the back window, where some of the guests had wandered out onto the back deck, he took a quick look at Garra with magical sight.

He expected to see her sudden discomfort reflected in her aura, and wanted to see if he could tell whether he was the cause of it. Surprisingly, he didn't see anything—her steady green remained as untroubled as ever, at odds with her subtle change in expression.

What he *didn't* expect to see was the unmistakable glow of magic around her neck.

He must have looked startled, because Garra's eyes narrowed. "Is something wrong?"

Stone tore his gaze away. "Oh—no. I'm sorry. I was just...admiring your necklace." He realized it sounded lame even as he said it. Still, he forged ahead. "It's quite beautiful—is it an antique?"

Her hand went to it, caressing it between her fingers. "It is. It belonged to my mother." She looked down, then back up at him. "Will you excuse me, Dr. Stone? I—need to touch up my makeup."

"Of course."

He watched her go, shifting back to magical sight now that she was no longer looking at him. From the back, he couldn't see the magical glow—clearly the magic hovered around the onyx pendant, not the entire necklace.

*Interesting.* Could Marciella Garra be a mage? He hadn't seen any indication of it so far, but then, he'd only known her for a brief time. Perhaps she wasn't, but her mother had been. It wasn't at all unusual for the non-magical children of mages to inherit their property, having no idea it was more than it seemed. Stone wanted to get a closer look at the thing—the quick glance he'd gotten hadn't been long enough to discern what kind of magic the pendant contained. Not likely that would happen, though. He couldn't tell if being around him was what had made Garra uncomfortable, but he couldn't very well ask her about it. That would do nothing but make it worse.

*Just back off,* he told himself. *Even if she is a mage, it's none of your business. Leave her alone before you annoy her and she reports you for creeping her out.*

Nonetheless, he lingered for a few more moments near the cake table to see if she returned. When she didn't, he got a new glass of wine and reluctantly allowed himself to be lured out onto the deck to chat with Barbara, Hubbard, and one of the Cultural Anthropology professors.

"It's beautiful out here," he said, looking out over the railing at the forested area beyond. Most of the lights illuminated the deck itself, but a couple shone out over the trees, revealing a thick carpet of old leaves and a meandering creek some distance away. A crisp, woody smell of pine needles hung in the air.

"It really is," Barbara said. "We get all sorts of wildlife around here—sometimes when I come out on the deck in the morning I'll even see deer."

"Usually it's just squirrels and raccoons," Hubbard grumbled, but he didn't sound upset. "They drop nuts and pine cones on the roof at night, which can be annoying when you're trying to get to sleep."

"I think they're cute." Barbara gave her husband a fond smile. "He just doesn't like it that I feed them sometimes."

"Sure. Encourage them. That's a great idea. You won't be happy until the whole house is overrun with vermin." It sounded like an old, playful argument. "Maybe you should invite them in, offer them some—"

Off in the distance, an eerie, inhuman scream sounded.

Stone and the other professor tensed. "What was that?" the woman asked, looking nervous.

Neither Barbara nor Hubbard appeared disturbed. "Mountain lion," Hubbard said, in the same tone he might have said *house cat*. "Don't worry—it's not close. We get them around here occasionally, but they don't come near any of the houses. They hunt out in the forest at night."

Stone took a quick look with magical sight, but saw nothing, corroborating Hubbard's words: the pale auras of the numerous trees would screen out anything but close-up wildlife—even something as large as a mountain lion. "I saw one near Stanford once, when I was out running. It didn't come too close to me, thank goodness, but it was impressive."

"They are," Barbara agreed. "I've only seen a couple of them—or maybe the same one twice. They're really quite shy, and they have as much right to be here as we do."

"I notice you don't feed *them*, though," Hubbard commented.

Stone chuckled and excused himself shortly after that, taking the opportunity when two more guests came out to talk with the hosts. He went back inside, idly looking for Garra, but didn't see her. She couldn't still be in the bathroom, could she? Had she already left? He felt guilty—he hadn't intended to come on too strong, especially since he hadn't been trying to show any sort of romantic interest. She'd made it clear she wasn't interested, and in truth, he wasn't either, but that didn't mean she hadn't construed his attention that way. Especially given the number of advances she probably had to fend off. If he could find her, he should probably offer a brief apology and then get the hell out of her way until she worked through whatever was bothering her.

He couldn't find her, though. A quick check of the living room, the atrium, and the kitchen revealed nothing but other groups of guests drinking, chatting, and examining the books on the table. *Damn,* he thought, his guilt increasing. Had he driven her from the party?

Suddenly, he didn't want to be there anymore. He'd only shown up to support Hubbard; normally he found work-related cocktail parties, full of small talk and people trying to impress each other, to be tiresome, and avoided them whenever he could get away with it. He'd made his appearance, and nobody would fault him for leaving early. If he headed home now, perhaps he could talk with Professor Benchley again, or at least finish working on his tailoring spell.

Fortunately, the party was on a weeknight, so he could make the excuse of early errands he had to run before work the following morning. He said his goodnights to Hubbard and Barbara, thanking them for a lovely evening and congratulating his colleague once again on his book deal, and departed.

With the help of his disregarding spell, he managed to make it out the front door without anyone else stopping him to chat. He stood for a moment on the front porch, looking out over the quiet neighborhood, then headed off down the street toward his car.

As he walked, he shifted to magical sight and scanned the area ahead of him. Perhaps if he was lucky he might catch a glimpse of the mountain lion they'd heard on the deck, though he doubted it would come down this far, especially with so many unfamiliar people and cars around.

He'd almost made it to the BMW, pressing his keyfob to open the door, and was about to switch the sight off when something caught his eye. Whatever it was, it was past the car, just beyond the far edge of the park.

He stopped, narrowing his eyes to focus on it. It glowed green, more brightly than the trees around it, and seemed to be hunched over. An animal? A person? As he continued to watch, he spotted red flashes disrupting the green. That could mean many things, none of them good. Agitation, perhaps, or even injury.

He hit the keyfob again to lock the car and walked slowly past it, entering the park. This time of night it was otherwise deserted, with only a few scattered lights providing illumination. Stone approached carefully and silently, with occasional glances around to make sure nobody else was nearby. This hardly seemed the sort of neighborhood where one was likely to be jumped, but it had happened enough times that he never made assumptions.

As he drew closer, he sharpened his focus. The figure appeared to be huddled behind one of the trash receptacles; if Stone couldn't see its red-speckled green aura, he probably wouldn't have seen it at all. Was it hiding?

"Hello?" he called as he drew closer, then stopped to see if it would respond. If it was an animal, he expected it to either dart off into the forest if it was able, or draw in farther behind the trash can if it was too injured to move. If the latter were the case, he could at least get a look at it and determine if it needed help.

*R. L. KING*

Nothing. The aura continued to glow past the edge of the receptacle. Oddly, some of the red streaks appeared to recede as he watched. What was going on?

More cautiously, he stepped forward. It had to be an animal—an injured person would want help, wouldn't they?

*Unless they were injured doing something they didn't want to be caught at...*

"Is someone there?" he called again, approaching closer.

The aura shifted, and the figure moved, rising to stand behind the trash can.

"Bloody hell..." Stone murmured, shocked.

Now that it was fully upright and illuminated by one of the park's lights, Stone had no trouble identifying the figure.

It was Marciella Garra.

# | CHAPTER TWELVE

STONE HURRIED FORWARD. "Dr. Garra?"

She stepped out from behind the trash can, gripping it with one hand for balance. As she came into the light, Stone's shock increased.

Her hair, pulled back into a neat bun at the party, now hung loose and disheveled. Her dress was torn at the top, revealing a narrow slash on her shoulder. Her arms, too, bled from several small cuts, and she'd lost one of her stylish heels.

"Bloody hell…" Stone said again. "What's happened to you?" Suddenly realizing that whoever or whatever had injured her might still be lurking nearby, he took a quick sweep of the area with magical sight, but spotted nothing.

"I'm fine," she said. Her shoulders rose and fell with her quick breathing, but her eyes were steady. She waved off his approach. "Really—Dr. Stone—I'm fine."

He stopped, confused. "You don't *look* fine. You look like something's attacked you. What happened? Come on—my car's nearby. Let's get you someplace where you can sit down."

She didn't move, but she too scanned the area. "I'm serious. I'm fine. I went out here to get some air before I went to my car. I saw the park and decided to look around, and I tripped and fell. That's all it is."

Stone's magical sight revealed faint red flashes still dancing at the edges of her aura, but they seemed even fainter than before. Whatever had happened to Garra, she appeared concerned but not terrified. "You—fell?" Why would she tell him that? It couldn't have been more obvious she was lying, but why? Was she trying to protect someone?

"Yes—completely clumsy of me, I know. I think it's these new shoes, coupled with the uneven terrain."

He offered his hand. "Come on—whatever's happened to you, you're obviously injured. Why don't we go back to Hubbard's house and—"

"No, Dr. Stone." This time her voice was more firm. She didn't take his hand. "Please. I'm not kidding—I'll be fine. It's just a few scratches and cuts. I'm parked just across the street—I'll head home and take care of it."

"But—"

She gave an encouraging smile and pushed her loose hair back. "But nothing. I mean it. It's kind of you to be concerned, but you needn't be. It was nothing but my own clumsiness—I shouldn't have tried walking in an unfamiliar area in heels."

Stone watched her, frustrated. His instincts urged him not to let this go—clearly she'd lied about what had happened to her, and she wasn't nearly as 'fine' as she was trying to convince him she was—but what could he do? He couldn't force his attentions on her. Even his minimal curiosity before had put her off; what would she do if he insisted on aiding her when she didn't want to be aided?

He studied her again, briefly. The red flashes had settled to where he could barely see them now, her aura glowing its usual bright green. The onyx pendant she wore still shone with magical power—possibly even a bit more than before—but without closer examination he couldn't identify its purpose.

"Are you sure?" he asked reluctantly. "I really do think you should do something about those cuts before you leave. If I'm making you uncomfortable, I could call Barbara, and—"

"Dr. Stone." She gripped his arm. "Stop. Please. This is nothing a bit of antiseptic and an aspirin or two won't straighten out." Pulling back, she met his gaze with a calm, implacable one of her own. "Now—if you'll excuse me, I do want to get home. You have a pleasant evening, and I'll see you at work tomorrow."

Without waiting for a response, she bent and deftly removed her other heel, then strode out of the park with a confidence at odds with her claim that she'd 'tripped.'

Stone remained where he was, watching her until she reached her car, a bright red Honda sedan. She got in, and only a moment later started the engine and drove quickly away.

When her taillights disappeared around a bend at the other end of the street, Stone let his breath out. What the hell had that been about? Why would someone—or something—attack a woman in a quiet residential neighborhood? And more to the point, why would she lie about it?

He turned back to the park, shifting once more to magical sight. Perhaps if he did a bit of looking around, he could pick up some leftover impressions to give him more of an idea of what had occurred here.

One thing he was fairly certain of, at least: Garra wasn't a mage. If she had magical talent, he couldn't imagine her allowing herself to be attacked without putting up a fight, but aside from the necklace, he'd seen no sign of magical energy hovering around her. Perhaps that part of her story, at least, had been true: the necklace had been a gift from her mother and she had no idea of its properties. But if it truly had glowed more brightly now than before—and to be fair, he couldn't be sure it had—that meant it had activated and used its power. Was it protective, perhaps, and saved Garra from further injury?

Curious and wary, he spent the next several minutes pacing the small park, looking for any signs of magical energy. If he could find where the attack had occurred, he might be able to figure out more about its purpose.

He almost didn't find it, because he'd been confining his search to the park itself. As he drew near the rear part of it, though, where a narrow path separated it from the wilder forested land beyond, he moved a few feet into the trees and focused his sight again.

This time, energy lit up the area off to his right. Red and angry, it swirled in the air like crimson smoke.

He narrowed his eyes and studied it more carefully. There had been a fight here, no doubt about it. He couldn't tell how many combatants there had been or their nature, but it hadn't been long ago. A chill ran through him as he pictured Garra walking along the path, then something or someone leaping out and dragging her back into the trees. How had she escaped? He'd been out on the deck with

Hubbard and his wife, not far from this area. In the neighborhood's evening silence, he couldn't have missed a scream or cry for help.

It was darker out here beyond the edge of the park, with only the faint moonlight to illuminate the ground. Stone risked a dim light spell, shifting back to mundane sight. The angry red mist faded, but without it obscuring his vision he spotted two other things: Garra's lost high-heeled sandal lying half-buried in the dead leaves, and a trio of deep slash marks on a nearby tree trunk. *Strange...*

He retrieved the shoe and held onto it, leaning in for a closer look at the marks on the tree. They consisted of three parallel slashes, sinking a quarter-inch into the thick bark. If he didn't know better, he'd have guessed they were made by an animal, not a human—but even the mountain lion he and the others had heard from the deck probably couldn't sink its claws in that deep.

What was going on?

Suddenly, he felt very exposed out here, a chilling sensation crawling up his spine. Had Garra's attacker fled long ago, or was someone even now watching him, observing his every movement from cover and waiting for a chance to attack? He spun, scanning the space behind him with magical sight, but still saw nothing but the trees' pale auras. If anybody was there, they were either a long way off or hiding very well.

*You're being absurd,* he told himself angrily, turning back to the tree. Nonetheless, he summoned a shield around himself. Absurd he may be, but it never hurt to be careful—especially not now, when his heightened power levels made it easier than ever to maintain the protective barrier. Whatever

*R. L. KING*

was out there—*if* anything was out there—it would be in for a nasty surprise if it decided to have a go at him.

He looked around for a few more minutes, but it was difficult to see much without using a much brighter light spell—which would likely attract attention from one of the Hubbards' departing party guests or some other inquisitive neighbor. Cops out here showed up fast when called, and while he could certainly get away from them if he needed to, it wasn't worth the risk.

Not when he had other options at his disposal.

# | CHAPTER THIRTEEN

G ARRA WASN'T IN HER OFFICE when Stone arrived on campus at ten-thirty the following morning. "Morning, Laura," he said, pausing at the admin's desk. "Have you seen Dr. Garra today?"

"She was here an hour or so ago, but she's already left for her class."

"Ah. All right, then—I'll chat with her later. Thank you."

"I enjoyed the party last night, didn't you?"

"Oh—I did, yes."

"I'm so happy for Dr. Hubbard—he's been working for this for so long." Her brows furrowed. "You left early, though, didn't you? I didn't see you go, but I looked for you around nine, and you were already gone."

"Ah…yes. I had a few things I needed to finish last night, so I wasn't able to stay as long as I'd hoped." He thought about asking Laura if she'd noticed anything odd about Garra, but didn't—if he did, he was sure the inquisitive admin would be unable to contain her curiosity about why he wanted to know, and that could lead to nothing good. Especially if it got back to Garra that he was asking. It did strike him as odd, though, that Laura hadn't commented on Garra's scratches. If she'd noticed them, she'd have said something. Perhaps Garra had covered them with a suit jacket.

"Oh, I understand," she said. "I'm glad you could make it." She returned to her work after a quick sideways glance at him.

Stone was convinced, after all the years she'd served as the department's aide, that she considered her job to be as much riding herd over a collection of intelligent but highly eccentric charges as it was answering phones and handling schedules. He wondered sometimes with amusement what she told her friends about him, Hubbard, and the others when she discussed her work.

He had only a single class today, at eleven, leaving his afternoon open for the meeting with his solicitor and Jason to sign the papers formalizing their partnership. Since it was a beautiful day, he decided to get an early start on his walk across campus, and perhaps pause for a cup of coffee on the way. He stopped by a little café halfway between his office and his classroom; he'd started picking up his morning caffeine there since he'd moved to Encantada, as his old favorite place on University Avenue was no longer convenient.

He supposed it shouldn't have been a surprise, or a coincidence, that he spotted Marciella Garra in the café, standing with several others and waiting for her order. The place was on the way to her classes too, after all. What *did* surprise him was that she had the jacket of her usual professional skirt suit off, draped over an arm bared by a sleeveless blouse—and he saw no sign of the cuts from last night. No bandages, either. Her arms, as evenly tanned as the rest of her, were unmarred by any injury.

Almost as if she sensed him there looking at her, Garra turned toward the door. For just a second, an odd expression passed across her face—annoyance, perhaps, or even fear—but then it was gone and replaced by her usual smile. "Dr. Stone, good morning."

"Good morning. You're looking well today." He dropped his volume so only she could hear him, and cast a pointed glance at her arm. "I'm glad to see you're showing no ill effects from last night."

She looked startled, then the smile was back, brighter than ever. "Ah. Yes. I did appreciate your concern. As you can see, though, I was right—it really was nothing. I'm fine."

The barista called her name, and she hurried forward to retrieve her steaming cup of coffee, then returned to Stone. "I should probably wear lower heels—either that, or familiarize myself with where I'm going before I try out a new pair of high ones."

"You'll be pleased to know I found the other one, by the way." He noticed that she was back to wearing her usual gold chain necklace, and no longer wore the one with the magical black onyx pendant.

"The other—?"

"Shoe. I wanted a bit of air myself after you left, so I walked around for a few minutes before I headed home. Found it out in the trees behind the park." He kept both his tone and his gaze light, but held hers firmly. "Odd that I'd find it so far out. Perhaps some animal dragged it out there."

Garra tensed at his words and her own gaze sharpened, just for a moment. Then she chuckled. "Oh—well, possibly. I did see a couple of raccoons when I was walking, and they'll steal anything shiny. I appreciate your retrieving it for me—they weren't cheap."

Stone wished he'd been able to examine her unexpected reaction with magical sight, but staring at her in the middle of a crowded coffee shop didn't seem prudent. "Well, at any rate," he said, "I've brought it with me today, so you can stop by my office whenever you like and pick it up. It's in the black tote bag on my guest chair."

"I'll do that." She nodded toward the barista. "Don't let me keep you—I know you have a class coming up." With a smile and a wave, she swept out of the shop.

For the rest of the way to his class, Stone couldn't get his mind off her. As he strode along sipping his coffee, he kept going over what he'd seen. Even taken individually, the events would be enough to pique his curiosity: a supposed mundane with a magical necklace, someone who could heal injuries overnight—hell, even his general feeling that something about Garra was unusual. Taken together, though, they all began to form an intriguing and tempting puzzle.

*Stop it,* he told himself. He reached the building where the classroom was located, pausing to toss his empty cup before heading in. Even if Marciella Garra *did* present the kind of challenge he regarded in much the same way as cats did catnip, that didn't mean he had any right to pursue it. Garra might have secrets, but so did he. How would he react if she began digging into *his* life? That, and since she didn't know the *reasons* for his curiosity, she'd be justified in assuming he had romantic interest in pursuing her. That could get him in trouble, not to mention simply being an unpleasant thing to do since she clearly wasn't interested.

For now, he'd keep an eye on her—from afar. At least until and unless anything changed.

# | CHAPTER FOURTEEN

"**S**O, IT'S DONE," Jason said. "We should go have a beer or something to celebrate."

They stood outside the downtown Palo Alto office of Stone's local solicitor, where they'd just officially signed the papers formalizing Stone's investment in Jason's agency. "Indeed we should," he said. "Come on—there's a place just down the street."

Jason fell into step next to him. "Too bad V's working, since this kinda concerns her too."

"I'm sure there'll be many more reasons to celebrate in the future." When Jason started to say something, he held up a hand. "No—no more thanks. I meant that. It's done, and now it's time to move forward. Have you had any success finding an apartment, or premises for the agency?"

They entered the bar, a small, high-end place on University Avenue. At this time of the late afternoon, early for the after-work crowd, it was nearly deserted.

"I think I've got a line on both," Jason said, walking to the bar and ordering a microbrew for himself and a Guinness for Stone before Stone could beat him to it. They took seats in a booth at the back. "I put a deposit on an apartment not too far from V's place—about a mile away. It's not huge, but it's got a couple of bedrooms and a carport for the Mustang. And there's some office space for lease in San Jose, down on First Street."

"Excellent."

"Yeah." He took a long pull from his glass, then took a notebook from his back pocket and consulted it. "I honestly didn't expect this to move as fast as it is. So much to do—I need to rent some furniture, get phones, a fax machine, a computer system so I can hook up to the search databases, business cards—hell, I don't even have a name for the agency yet. I was trying to come up with something catchy, but maybe I should just keep it simple and call it Thayer Investigations."

"Why not? It's your venture—why shouldn't it have your name on it? If you like, I'll check with the Graphic Design department at the University and see if anyone wants to make a bit of money designing a logo for you."

"Yeah, that'd be great—and maybe I can get V to help me out with some of this other stuff."

"Good idea. She essentially picked out my entire kitchen—she's good at that sort of thing."

Jason flashed him a sharp look, then sighed and dropped his gaze to his glass.

"Something wrong?"

"Nah."

Stone raised an eyebrow. "Jason, I'd have thought by now you'd have realized trying to lie to me is pointless. Out with it."

For several seconds, Jason didn't answer. He looked as if he were turning something over in his mind. "It's—you and V," he said. "I'm still working through it."

"I thought you said you were all right with—"

"I am," he said quickly. "Mostly, anyway. It's just—"

"Just what?"

"Are you reading my aura?"

"No. Why?"

"Well, don't. It's—I want to have a conversation without you tryin' to second-guess everything you think I'm gonna say."

Stone narrowed his eyes. "I'm not reading your aura, Jason. You should be able to tell if I were, at any rate. So what's the problem?"

He looked at his hands. "This is gonna sound weird, okay?"

"Weird is what I do, remember? Just say it."

"Well—when I first found out, I was mad. You know that."

"I don't think any of us could miss it," Stone said wryly.

"Yeah. Well—can you blame me? I find out my twenty-one-year-old sister's sleeping with her teacher—my best friend—who's nearly twice her age. It was kind of a shock, especially since I didn't see it coming at all."

"*We* didn't see it coming," Stone reminded him. "It sort of…crept up on us."

"Yeah," he said again. "I know it's none of my business what V does, but I can't help my feelings, you know? But—this whole situation is weird, and that makes things…different."

"How so?"

"Like I know mages live longer than mundanes, so the age difference shouldn't be as big a deal." His gaze came up. "I mean, damn, Al, I know you're almost forty, but you sure as hell don't look it. You don't look much older than I do these days."

"That's…flattering. But I still don't see—"

"Okay, so here it is," Jason interrupted, holding his hands up to stop Stone. "I guess I'm more of an old-fashioned guy than I thought I was, in some ways. I mean, not in every way—I got no issue with V being bi and preferring women. To be honest, I'm more comfortable with her being with women. I know that doesn't make a damn bit of sense, but there you go."

"So you have issues with her being with a man."

"Yeah—no. No. She's a grown woman. She can be with whoever she wants, and it's none of my business. And like I said before—if it was any other guy in this situation, I'd think it was creepy. You know, older guy hitting on a young hot woman. You know as well as I do what that usually means."

"I do," Stone said. "But we—"

"But you're not like that. I get it. I'm not saying you are." He snorted a laugh. "Actually, for a guy who sleeps around as much as you do, you're probably the closest thing I know to a real gentleman."

Stone raised an eyebrow. "Er—thank you?"

"You know what I mean."

"I'm not sure I do. And I'm *definitely* not sure I see where this is going."

Jason finished his drink in one long swallow and smacked the glass down on the table with a loud sigh. "Okay, I'll just lay it out straight: I'm having trouble dealing with the fact that you two are sleeping together but you're not…*together.* That's where I'm old-fashioned, I guess."

Ah, so that was it. He should have guessed. "So…" he said, "You'd be fine with it if we had a more…conventional sort of relationship."

"Yeah. And like I said—whether *I'm* fine with it or not doesn't even matter. I'm not saying it does, or that either one of you should do anything different. It's not my business. But you asked me what I thought, so I'm tellin' you."

"Did you tell Verity?"

"No. She's still a little defensive about the whole thing, so I figured it's better if I just don't bring it up."

That was probably true. As close as Jason and Verity were, she still suffered from a bit of leftover 'little sister syndrome,' causing her to push back rather more than she might have otherwise done whenever she perceived Jason trying to direct her life or influence her decisions. He spread his hands. "Jason, I told you before: it's not me. It's never been me. It's her choice, and I respect it. I thought we settled this."

"I thought so too—but then you two started talking about this hot professor in your department, and you—"

"Wait—just wait a moment." Stone raised a hand. "I am *not* seeing Dr. Garra. Even if I wanted to, she's made it clear in no uncertain terms that she's not looking for a relationship. So if Verity is speculating about that, you can set your mind at ease." He narrowed his eyes. "But that doesn't mean I *won't* see anyone, if I should decide to."

Now it was Jason's turn to blink and focus closer on him. "That sounded like *you* being defensive, Al. What's up?"

Stone shook his head. Once again, his habit of associating with overly perceptive people had come back to bite him. "She's made no secret that she's fine with it. She's *encouraged* me to do it, on numerous occasions, in fact. I think she rather hoped I *would* get something going with Dr. Garra."

"Why?"

"Your guess is as good as mine. Perhaps she feels guilty about her feelings for Kyla, and thinks she'd be more comfortable if I were seeing someone else as well. Or perhaps—" He let that trail off and stared into his pint glass.

"Perhaps what?"

"I think perhaps it would help her maintain a sort of...distance. To give her an excuse to avoid the entanglements she doesn't want to encourage."

Jason pondered that. "So you're sayin' that you *don't* want to hook up with anybody else, even if V thinks you should?"

"Yes—but not precisely. I'm not saying I wouldn't be open to it, should it occur. But it seems it's occurring quite a bit less lately, by my own doing."

"What's that mean?"

It suddenly dawned on Stone that this discussion wasn't one he wanted to have—with Jason or anyone else. At least anyone who wasn't Verity. He waved a dismissive hand and forced a chuckle. "Never mind. I'm a bit off my game, to be honest. I shouldn't have even brought it up."

"Al—"

"No. Really. We should be celebrating the birth of Thayer Investigations, not discussing my personal life." He raised his glass. "To a long and successful venture."

Jason held his gaze for a few more seconds. He clearly wanted to say something else, but finally he sighed and raised his own empty glass. "And good friends."

Stone's next words came out before he had a chance to filter them. "Jason…I think I might actually have an inaugural case for you."

"Huh?"

*Don't do this. You're starting down a rabbit hole that can only lead to a bad end.* "It has to do with Dr. Garra."

"What about her?" His eyes narrowed. "This isn't about V anymore, is it?"

"No. I attended a little get-together for Dr. Hubbard at the University last night, and something…odd happened."

"Odd? How so?"

Still feeling as if he'd made a decision he'd later regret, Stone gave Jason an abbreviated version of the events at the party last night. He told him how he'd suspected something unusual about Marciella Garra from the moment he met her, and how the magical necklace, her accident or attack last night, and her lack of any sign of injury this morning had only added to his suspicions. As an afterthought, he even described the series of junk-shop flyers and phone numbers he'd found on her desk.

Jason listened in silence. When Stone finished, he said, "So…what do you want me to do about it? You don't want me to follow her, do you?"

"No. I don't think that would be wise. If there *is* something supernatural going on with her, I wouldn't send you after her without more information. But you can trace information about people, right?"

"Sure. That's a big part of what PIs do."

"Well—what I'd like, if you're willing, is for you to look into her background a bit. I'll give you all the information I have—which isn't much, unfortunately—and we'll see what you come up with."

"Uh—yeah, I can do that. But—"

"But what?"

"Well—if you think she's tied up with the supernatural, why don't you just *ask* her? Don't you guys have ways to scope each other out? Can't you tell from her aura or something?"

"In answer to your first question—I can't just ask her. It's possible even if she *is* connected with my world somehow, she's just doing what I'm doing: trying to keep her head down and do her job without arousing suspicion. I think I'm already making her uncomfortable—in fact, I wonder if she hasn't already suspected that my curiosity is a bit more than professional. If you come back with something troubling, I might have to talk to her, but for now it seems prudent not to."

"What about her aura?"

"I've checked. Aside from the magical necklace she wore at the party, I see no sign of magic around her. That doesn't mean she *isn't* a mage, but it does mean if she is, she's not using it much, and definitely not at all around me."

Jason looked troubled, but finally nodded. "Yeah, okay. I'll do a little poking around and see what I come up with. It'll give me an excuse to get moving. It'll take a few days, though—still gotta get a computer and get it hooked up, get database access, all that kind of thing."

"Not a problem. I'm probably getting worked up over nothing. I think my best bet is to stay away from Dr. Garra, for a while anyway."

# | CHAPTER FIFTEEN

S TAYING AWAY FROM DR. GARRA proved not to be a problem, since she seemed to be actively avoiding him. She wasn't obvious about it—it wasn't as if she changed direction when she passed him on the way to class or back to their office or anything blatant like that—but it almost always worked out that she wasn't in the same place as he was. If he didn't know better—and in truth, he didn't—Stone might have thought she'd studied his schedule to make sure she wasn't in the office at the same time he was. He even stopped seeing her at the coffee shop in the morning.

If that was the way she wanted it, it was fine with him. He had plenty of things to keep him busy, between work, spell research, and slowly fixing up the Encantada house.

The echo that seemed to have possessed Raider didn't re-appear, despite his best efforts to coax it out. He tried calling the cat by Professor Benchley's name, examining him with focused magical sight, paging more carefully through the encyclopedia volume looking for other clues, and even setting up a small circle to try summoning the echo. Nothing worked—in fact, Raider no longer showed any interest in the encyclopedia at all. Stone suspected it hadn't been the tome at all that the echo had been trying to draw attention to, but rather the clipping inside. Once he'd found that, there was no more need for the book.

Even so, he didn't get rid of it. He left it on the shelf with the rest of his library, lying on its back so Raider could sit on it if he so desired.

"I have no idea what you're trying to tell me," he said one night in the middle of the week after Hubbard's party. Raider sat in front of him, watching him with his intent green gaze, but seemed unaffected by his words. He rubbed against Stone and purred, but that was all.

Jason called Stone the following week. "Hey, you want to come by and see the new office? Not much here yet, but I've got enough that I can put up my shingle and start looking for clients. And I got something you might be interested in."

"News about what I asked you to look into?"

"Yeah. Come on down and I'll tell you what I found out."

Jason's new office turned out to be in the middle of an unremarkable office-park building about a mile from the courthouse, sandwiched between a law office and a private security firm. It had a picture window in front that still read "Big Boy Bail Bonds," featuring the image of a muscular, grinning man. The locked door sported the slogan, "*You Ring Us, We Spring You!*" Stone spotted both Jason's red Mustang and Verity's black SUV in the parking lot.

"Decided to switch to a more lucrative business?" he asked wryly as Jason unlocked the door.

"Nah—got your girl from the Graphic Arts department coming over to redo the window tomorrow. We're not officially open yet."

Verity waved from behind a desk in the back, where she'd been tapping something into a computer. "Hi, Doc. What do you think of the place?"

"It's...nicely minimalist," Stone said with care, looking around. The small office was mostly one open space, with a doorway in the back probably leading to a storage room and restroom. So far, the space had two desks, each with a computer and phone; three file cabinets; a printer and fax machine on another table on the other side of the room with two boxes of printer paper stacked next to it, a sturdy-looking cabinet; and a tiny waiting area with a loveseat, chair, and table, all three of which looked like they'd been rented from some office-supply firm. The otherwise bare walls contained only three items: a poster-sized map of the San Jose and Peninsula area, a small, framed document that had to be Jason's private-investigator license, and a whiteboard with "Thayer Investigations" printed on it. A cartoon figure of a grinning Sherlock Holmes holding a large magnifying glass was most likely Verity's work.

"Yeah," Jason said. "Just the bare bones for now, but we'll jazz the place up a little as we go. We've got a water cooler coming in next week, and a little fridge for the back room."

"And some art prints," Verity added. "Need a couple of those to class up the joint." She pointed at Sherlock. "Unless you want more of my originals."

"Yeah, that's okay, V—as an artist, you're a really good mage."

Stone glanced at the second desk. "Has Jason decided to hire you officially, then?"

"Nah. I'm just helping out today because I've got the day off. He offered me a job as his assistant, but I'm not exactly the sit-behind-a-desk-all-day type. I'm gonna consult on missing-persons cases, though."

"Excellent. I'm sure you'll be good at that."

"Yeah, but I still need to find an assistant—somebody to handle the clerical stuff and records and that kind of thing," Jason said. "Right now, though, since we don't have any cases yet, I think I can keep on top of that myself."

"You *do* have a case," Stone reminded him. "Speaking of which, you said you had something for me."

"Yeah, I do." He pulled a file folder from his desk drawer. "You were right, Al. There *is* something up with Dr. Garra."

"Indeed?" Stone perched on the edge of the desk, leaning forward. "What is it?"

"This was a good test for my skills, I'll tell you that—I had to pull in some friends, including Stan Lopez and Fran, to track down this info." He opened the folder, withdrew a sheet with a black-and-white photo on it, and offered it to Stone.

He studied it. The print quality wasn't the highest, but he could see it depicted a woman in her forties with a sharp, piercing stare, heavy brows, and dark hair pulled back from her face in a severe bun. "Who's this?"

"That's Marciella Garra."

"What?" Stone stared at it in shock, then back up at Jason. "What are you talking about?"

Verity drifted over, but said nothing.

"It's true," Jason said. "The reason I had so much trouble with all this was that not only were almost all the resources I needed in Spanish, but this lady does *not* want to be found. She's very reclusive. That photo was taken several years ago."

Stone studied the photo again. He didn't recognize the woman—she didn't even bear a family resemblance to the woman he knew as Garra. "I don't understand, Jason. Explain."

"Okay. Let me start at the beginning." He pulled out a few more printed sheets and spread them on the desk. "I started with those papers you gave me—the ones your professor's supposed to have written."

"She didn't write them?"

"Well, yeah—she did. The *real* Marciella Garra did. She really is an expert on anthropology and folklore, but she hasn't been active for several years."

"So Garra—or whatever her name is—has—what—stolen her identity?" Stone pushed himself off the desk. "But that doesn't make sense, Jason. I've spoken with her about her areas of study. She clearly knows what she's talking about. No one's complained about any of her lectures, and there's no way she could have made it through the interview process without—"

Jason shook his head. "I don't know. I don't have that info yet. So far all I've been able to figure out is who your Garra *isn't.* I can't find a damn thing about who she *is.* But the real Professor Garra lives—or at least *used* to live—somewhere in the sticks in Peru, where she's doing a damn good job of keeping her head down. I couldn't find a current location for her, but there's no way your Garra is the same person. This lady would be in her fifties by now."

Stone paced, pondering. "None of this makes sense. The University wouldn't hire someone without a thorough background check."

"You did say they were kind of in a hurry about this. Maybe they cut a few corners—although all the official stuff I was able to get access to looks pretty convincing."

"What's that mean?"

"Well…" Jason riffled through the papers in his folder. "What it means to me anyway is that somebody did a really good job of faking this information. Way better than your average layman should be able to do."

"So…" Verity said, pointing at the papers, "you're saying you think this fake Garra could be working with somebody else?"

"Maybe—she might have paid somebody to set up this fake identity for her, knowing the chances of somebody tracking back to the real Garra were pretty slim, given how hard she is to find. Or she might have done it herself."

"Which means if she did, she's not 'your average lay-man,'" Stone said. This situation was getting stranger by the moment. "But *why?* Why would she fake being an Occult Studies lecturer? It's not exactly the highest-prestige position at the University. What would she stand to gain by it?"

"I have a thought…" Verity put in. "It's a long shot, but—"

"Let's hear it," Stone said. "I've got bugger-all right now, so I'm open to anything."

"Well," she said, "you did say you caught her with ads and phone numbers for antique shops, including Madame Huan's place, right?"

"Yes…"

"Maybe she's looking for something—something magical. If she knows stuff about Occult Studies—and you said she's keeping up with the job just fine, so she must—maybe she heard about the opening in the department, and decided to use it as a cover while she looks for whatever she's trying to find."

"Yes, but—if she's looking for something in this area, why would she need to pretend to be a professor? Couldn't she just come here and ask? It's not as if poking around junk shops is illegal or anything."

"True...but if she's looking for something that's *really* magical, especially if she isn't a mage herself, having a job like that might give her extra credibility when she goes looking around. Or maybe she doesn't want people to *know* she's looking for something, so she needs a cover for being here long enough to find it. You *did* say she knew her stuff—maybe she borrowed the real Dr. Garra's identity because she has the knowledge, but knew she couldn't get hired at the University without the academic cred."

Stone sighed. "Sounds like a lot of work to me."

"Yeah," Jason added. "I'd almost say she was trying to get close to you—like maybe if she knew you were a mage—except you said she's been avoiding you."

"More than ever, lately. I think I might have spooked her when I found her in the park after whatever happened the other night. For whatever reason, she doesn't want me to know what actually did happen."

"Do you think it has anything to do with the magic necklace she was wearing?" Verity asked. "Maybe somebody tried to steal it from her."

"Possibly..." Stone said, half to himself. He wasn't convinced, though. He'd bet good money she wasn't a mage—the fact that he'd seen no magical traces on her when he found her in the park meant she hadn't used any magic to protect herself. That wasn't definitive proof—she might be the kind of mage whose spells didn't lend themselves to combat situations—but he still doubted it. There was definitely *something* unusual about her, but he didn't think it was that.

"Are you going to turn her in?" Verity asked.

He snapped back to the conversation. "What?"

"You know—to the University. Are you going to tell them she's a fake?"

"I—" Once again, he considered. On the one hand, the fact that she'd faked her credentials to get hired—and done a damned good job of it, because the University *did* do thorough background checks on all its hires—disturbed him. If she truly wasn't what she claimed to be, and especially if she was connected somehow with the supernatural world, she could be putting the students and his colleagues at risk.

But on the other hand, his curiosity wouldn't let this rest. If he shared his knowledge with Beatrice Martinez, Garra—or whoever she really was—would be terminated immediately. She could even be subject to prosecution for identity theft. And even if the University didn't pursue that angle, he was certain she wouldn't stick around long enough for him to get to the bottom of her subterfuge.

"Not yet," he said at last. "I think I'll keep a closer eye on her for a little while, and see if I can turn up anything else."

"You could confront her," Verity pointed out. "You know—tell her what you know. Maybe if she's worried you'll rat her out, she might tell you what's going on."

"It might come to that. But not yet. I'm curious about what she's doing at these antique stores, though. Perhaps it's nothing, but my hunch tells me it's connected with why she's here. Do you two concur?"

"Yeah," Jason said. "I think you're right that she might be looking for something—or some*one*."

"Maybe you can use a little magic to sneak into her office and snoop around in her desk drawers," Verity said. Then she grinned at Jason. "You didn't hear me say that."

"Say what?" Jason pointedly fixed his gaze out the front window. "I didn't hear anything."

It wasn't a bad idea, Stone decided. True, it could get him in a lot of trouble if he got caught—but he didn't intend to get caught. "I'll think about it," he said. "Thanks for the help, Jason—how much do I owe you?"

Jason rolled his eyes and snorted. "You're kidding, right? You bankroll my whole operation, and you think I'm gonna *charge* you for a little poking around? I'm just glad I could help."

# CHAPTER SIXTEEN

EVERY SCRAP OF STONE'S GOOD SENSE told him this was a bad idea. Even with magic, there were too many ways it could go wrong—some of them possibly even putting his career at risk. Tenure didn't protect you if you were caught breaking into a fellow professor's office and rifling through her locked desk. Especially when half the department was sure he was romantically interested in her. That was the kind of thing that got you restraining orders, if not outright sacked.

None of that meant he didn't plan to do it, though. Especially with his recently augmented magical abilities, the risk was minimal. He'd just have to be careful.

Laura stopped by his office that evening before she left at six, giving him a sideways glance. "I didn't think I saw you leave. Is everything okay? You're usually long gone by now."

He looked up from the book in front of him. "Ah—lost track of time, I guess. I'm working on a bit of research and I don't want to take a break until I've finished." He indicated the several other open tomes arrayed around him in a semicircle, and the large cup of coffee he'd picked up on his way back from his last class.

She paused in the doorway. "Well—all right, then. Don't work too hard. Do you need anything before I go?"

"No, thank you, Laura. I'm fine. I'll be leaving soon. Have a good evening."

"You too." She lingered a moment longer, then he heard her footsteps recede down the hallway.

He couldn't blame her for being confused: he almost never stayed this late unless he had a seminar or a specially-arranged office hour, preferring to do most of his research at home where he wasn't likely to be disturbed by unexpected students. In retrospect, it probably would have been better for his cover story if he'd left with her and then sneaked back, but it was too late now.

*You're overthinking this,* he told himself firmly. It wasn't as if the far-flung Department of Occult Studies offices were Fort Knox or the Louvre, and his plan was to steal the Mona Lisa under the noses of a cadre of watchful guards and extensive electronic surveillance. Hell, half the time the professors didn't even lock their offices. Why would they? It wasn't as if a rash of office-supply thefts was a problem.

As he put away his books, an amusing memory struck him, of the time he and the wild-talent cat burglar Zack Beeler had recently broken into the New York City penthouse of the enigmatic and powerful mage Thalassa Nera. Between that job's formidable wards and deadly traps, not to mention being tossed out a seventy-story window, this one hardly seemed cause for undue concern by comparison.

*Perhaps you should have talked to Kolinsky about hiring Zack to do the job.* That wasn't a bad idea, except for one thing: he'd stopped by Kolinsky's shop yesterday after he'd spoken with Jason, intending to see if his black-mage associate might know anything about the woman posing as Marciella Garra. He found the place closed and locked, with a familiar notice behind the wards indicating Kolinsky was away indefinitely. He could always call Zack directly, of course, but he hadn't reached that stage yet. Especially since he hadn't seen Kolinsky since his trip to Calanar, and didn't want even the hint of owing his friend a favor right now.

No, better to handle this on his own, at least for the moment.

He waited a few more minutes to make sure Laura hadn't forgotten anything, then got up and drifted out to the front office. The door there was locked; the admin's desk was clear and her computer switched off. He took a quick check around to make sure no other professors had remained behind, then pulled a pair of latex gloves from his pocket and donned them. He planned to do everything he could using magic, but better safe than sorry. All he'd have to do was get in and out before the cleaning staff arrived to vacuum and empty the trash.

Garra *had* locked her office door, but that proved no deterrent for Stone's magic. He had it open in seconds and slipped inside, leaving it partially ajar so he'd have a chance of hearing anyone who might come in. He didn't expect anyone, but the definition of 'surprise' was pretty much exactly 'things you don't expect.' Once again, caution was prudent.

As one final bit of prudence, he stopped in the doorway and examined the interior of the office with magical sight. Just because he was convinced the imposter wasn't a mage didn't mean he'd risk going in without checking for traps. Odds were low—he didn't even keep any magical protections on his own office—but it only took a moment to check. It didn't surprise him at all when he found nothing.

Because Garra's office used to be his and she hadn't changed any of the furniture, Stone had no trouble navigating it. He ignored the bookshelves and credenza, heading straight for the single lockable drawer in the desk. Using magic, he tried to open it—perhaps luck would be with him and she hadn't locked it.

Nope. The drawer rattled, but didn't open. Stone glanced toward the open door, then up at the tiny, high window. At least nobody would be able to peer in at him through it unless they got someone to give them a boost. Another application of magical power flipped the lock with a tiny *click*.

*Last chance to give up this mad idea.* For a moment, Stone hesitated. This wasn't like stealing the artifact from Thalassa Nera—that had been for a higher purpose, to save a lot of people from potential injury or death. This was breaking into the private space of a professional colleague. Despite what he'd found out about Marciella Garra's falsified identity, as far as he knew she'd done nothing to invite this kind of treatment. She showed up at work every day, did her job (a good job, too, from what he'd heard from his students) and didn't cause any trouble. Whatever reason she had for pretending to be someone she wasn't, that didn't give him the right to do what he was about to do.

He thought again about the way she'd looked when he'd found her huddled behind the bin near Hubbard's place. Something or someone had attacked her—probably something big and nasty, based on the slashes he'd seen on the tree. She may be a model professor at work, but she was up to something. He needed to find out what it was. If it all ended up being a misunderstanding, he'd admit what he'd done later. Right now, he needed to know.

After another quick look at the door, he slid the drawer open, still using magic so he didn't have to touch anything.

He didn't see much inside: an expensive fountain pen, a small quantity of change, a couple sheaves of paper, and a bound calendar planner. When a scan with magical sight revealed nothing of interest, he levitated the papers and the planner out and put them on the desk.

The papers didn't look like what he was looking for. He riffled through them, but found only pages from the university's employee handbook, information about health insurance, and other administrative documents. Feeling guilty, he did memorize her home address—an apartment in Menlo Park—but then he returned the documents to the drawer as he'd found them.

That left only the planner. If he didn't find anything in there either, he'd have to decide whether he wanted to risk staying long enough to examine the other drawers and the credenza. He glanced at his watch: six forty-five. He probably had another half-hour or so before he had to worry about the janitors showing up, but that didn't mean he wanted to cut things that short.

He gestured, opening the planner and flipping through the pages until he reached the early part of September, just before she'd started at the University. Each double-paged spread covered a single week; he flicked his gaze over the first one, but found only notes about meetings with Beatrice Martinez and Laura, others about the locations of her classes, and the names and addresses of several nearby local restaurants. Normal stuff, in other words.

*You've let your imagination get away with you,* Stone told himself in disgust. *Get the hell out of here before someone catches you.*

He didn't, though. Instead, still using magic, he flipped the page to the following week. This one had a bit more interesting data: in addition to the address and time of Hubbard's party and more notes about class schedules, she'd also scrawled the names of several of the antique and junk shops Stone had seen references to on her desk before. Each one had a time next to it, and all of them were crossed out. Had she visited each of them and failed to find whatever she was looking for? The only one that didn't have a time next to it was Huan's Antiquities, but it was also crossed out. Next to it was the notation, *Cerrado.* Closed.

He turned the page again, to the current week. There was another notation for yesterday, also crossed out, and no more until Friday night. On that date, she had written: *10 p.m. – info on item?,* followed by an address in San Jose.

Stone frowned at the entry. Ten o'clock? That was late to meet someone at one of the shops she'd tracked down. If it weren't for the *info on item?* part, he might have simply thought she had a date. He wished he was more familiar with San Jose—he didn't know the area and had no idea where the address was located in the sprawling city.

He pulled a notebook from his pocket and quickly jotted down the address and the rest of the notation, then used magic to flip to the next couple weeks in the planner. Other than entries about work meetings and a hair appointment the following Monday, he found nothing else.

He was debating whether to check the credenza when he heard something.

He stiffened, checking his watch again. Seven p.m. Had the janitor showed up early? Had one of the other department professors returned for some reason?

As he remained still behind Garra's desk and craned his ears for a better indication of what was going on, he caught snatches of conversation. A woman and what sounded like a young girl, both speaking Spanish.

*Damn.* It *was* the janitor. Stone usually didn't stay late enough to see her, but he'd encountered her a few times after evening meetings, going through the offices emptying trash cans and sweeping the hallways. The girl was probably her daughter, and she'd brought her along so they could finish in time to start their early-evening plans.

He was preparing to return the planner to the drawer when he noticed something poking out from inside the back cover. With another fast glance toward the door, he reopened the book.

Inside the cover was a sketch. It depicted what looked like a cup or chalice, with a large gem set into the front of it and two smaller ones flanking it. The sketch was crudely made and thus didn't provide much detail; Stone wondered if Garra herself had drawn it. Could this be the "item" she was searching for?

Outside the office, the young girl giggled, startling Stone. They were closer now.

*Pull yourself together,* he told himself, annoyed. It wasn't as if he didn't have a right to be here. Well, certainly not inside his colleague's locked office, but there was no reason he couldn't be in the building itself. Hell, he had a keycard that opened it, as did all the other professors who worked here. If need be, all he'd have to do was get out of Garra's office and slip back into his own.

He didn't want to do that, though.

He slipped the sketch back inside the planner, then used magic to return it to the drawer. As he closed the drawer and locked it, he considered his next steps. He didn't think there was any way anyone could figure out he'd been in here, but if someone *did,* it would be best if the janitor and her daughter hadn't seen him at all.

Fortunately, Garra's office was all the way at the end of the hall, so unless the janitor started at the back and worked forward, he had a little time. Also fortunately, his augmented magical powers meant he could hold an invisibility spell for longer than he used to be able to. Not *much* longer, true, but it should be long enough for him to get out of the building while the woman was busy in one of the other offices.

He couldn't help a quick, wicked grin: the last time he'd been stuck inside an office he wasn't supposed to be in, he'd had Grace Ruiz with him, and her rumbling stomach had almost given them away. It occurred to him that he hadn't seen her for over a year, and he wondered idly how she was doing. She might be a good resource if he needed any Spanish translations done.

*Focus.* Moving with care, he slipped over to the open doorway, cast the invisibility spell, and peeked out into the hall—

—and nearly came face to face with the chubby, coverall-clad woman, who was pushing a vacuum cleaner. Her daughter, a little girl around six in a My Little Pony T-shirt, skipped along behind her.

*Oh, bloody hell, this is ridiculous.*

The janitor was heading straight for Garra's office, probably to plug in her vacuum. Stone ducked aside until she passed, then combined a levitation spell with the invisibility and floated out into the hall.

As he did, the little girl began singing something, waving her arms around her. One of them smacked Stone's shoulder as he floated by, and her face scrunched into confusion.

"Mama? I just hit something in the air! Are there ghosts here?"

Stone got out of there just as she flailed her arms again, obviously trying to locate the "ghost." Scooting down the hall, he heard the janitor say something sharp in Spanish (he thought part of it was *"el fantasma,"*) but he didn't wait to see how the girl would respond. So far, the spells were holding—he could levitate for a long time, but already the invisibility was beginning to tire him. He'd have to get out fast.

The one thing in his favor was that it wasn't possible to see the exit door from the office hallway. He slipped around the corner, glanced through the small window in the door to make sure nobody else was approaching from the outside, then pushed it open and zipped out.

He didn't drop the invisibility spell until he was around the corner, hidden in a narrow space between the building and a large tree. He let his breath out in a rush, gripping the tree as he waited for his heartbeat to go back to normal. Only then did he allow himself to think about what he'd just done, and how close he'd come to being caught.

He pulled his notebook from his pocket and made a quick copy of the sketch he'd found in Garra's planner, trying to get all the details right while his memory was still fresh.

Then he flipped pages and examined the address he'd scrawled there.

*I hope this ends up being worth it.*

# | CHAPTER SEVENTEEN

BACK AT HOME, Stone found a map of San Jose and found the location of the address from Garra's planner. It was on the east side of the city, in an area comprising mostly light industrial businesses—auto body shops, warehouses, and similar. Not the sort of place it seemed she was likely to go for a date or any other recreational activity. He checked if any junk or antique shops were in the area, but he didn't see any. If only he could do something about trying to identify the chalice from the sketch, but that would be difficult with his two best experts on ancient artifacts—Madame Huan and Stefan Kolinsky—out of communication. Perhaps he could take it back to England and see if Eddie Monkton could come up with anything, but he knew the odds weren't good—the original sketch had been fairly crude, and his own had even less detail. It was an option, but not one he'd need to use yet. Maybe if nothing came of the address, he'd think about it.

His gaze fell on the articles about Thaddeus Benchley, which he'd pushed off to the corner of the desk, and then at Raider, curled up on his old leather sofa. "Well," he told the cat, "have you got anything else to say to me? I could use a break from this Garra business."

What he could use a break from, if he wanted to admit it to himself, was his guilt. He still had no definitive evidence Marciella Garra had done anything other than fake her identity to get a job at the University. That was bad, of course, but it was the kind of bad you handled through administrative channels, not by breaking into someone's office and rifling through her locked desk looking for clues. Maybe he should confront the woman about what he'd found, and see what she had to say. She could have a good explanation for what she'd done, after all.

Perhaps he'd do that—but not until after he'd investigated the address from the planner. He'd thought before about following her, but now he didn't need to. He knew where she'd be. All he had to do was show up there, hide, and see what she was up to. If it turned out to be nothing, he could put the matter out of his mind and move on, living with his guilt for being a nosy git about the whole thing.

And if it turned out to be *something…*

*Enough. You'll find out on Friday.*

Raider hadn't answered his question—Benchley hadn't made even a token appearance since that first night—but the cat had risen from his sleepy ball, stretched, and leaped up onto the desk. He paused, licking his paw in the nonchalant manner of all cats who didn't want you to think they were up to something, then padded over to the small stack of clippings.

"Is there something in there you want to show me?" Stone leaned forward, intrigued, as Raider appeared to be examining the top clipping on the stack.

The cat did not reply.

Stone picked up the clippings. There were three: the original one he'd found in the encyclopedia, the obituary, and the puff piece. After a moment's thought, he cleared the map off his desk and laid the three of them side by side, leaving a foot of space between each. "There you go," he said, indicating them. "If you want to show me anything, the floor—well, the desk—is yours."

Raider remained where he was, appearing for all the world as if he was pondering his next move. Then he stalked over and stood next to the puff piece article.

"Something in here?"

"Meow."

Stone tensed. "Was that a normal meow, or an answer?"

"Meow."

Quickly, he shifted to magical sight, leaning down to get a good look into Raider's eyes.

As he'd half-expected, the faint blue glow was back.

"Dr. Benchley. Good to see you again. Shall we see if we can get a bit farther along with what you're trying to tell me?"

Raider didn't answer. Instead, he stared intently at the puff piece.

Stone leaned in for a better look. The article covered half a page, including the three photos—the head shot, the candid one of him standing at the lab table with his students, and the one with him and the cat. Quickly he read through it again. It gave a brief overview of his career before and after he'd joined the faculty, and seemed to be focused more on light-hearted memories rather than any kind of rigorous examination of his scientific contributions. Several quotes from graduate and undergraduate students painted him as a cheerful man with a kindly, wicked sense of humor. He apparently cared deeply for his students' well-being, and had been a gentle but tireless crusader for anti-war and other progressive causes.

"Well," Stone said. "This certainly seems to indicate you were a pleasant enough chap. It sounds like your students were quite sad to see you go."

"Meow." Raider extended a paw and patted the photo of Benchley with his students.

"Something about that photo you want me to notice?"

"Meow."

"Can you be a bit more specific?"

Apparently, however, Raider couldn't. Stone had never dealt with an echo possessing a living being before—perhaps there were limitations on how much precision they could muster while dealing with an unfamiliar, non-human body and brain. He almost thought he saw a look of frustration pass across the cat's face, but that might just have been wishful thinking.

"Okay…let's have a look." He examined the photo more closely. Aside from Benchley himself, five other students clustered around the lab bench, clearly interested in the professor's demonstration. There were three men and two women; the caption identified them as Roy Hooper, Del Wright, Valerie DeGeorge, Shari Milius, and Colin Frederick.

He studied each face. It was hard to tell because the article was a photocopy of a grainy original, but he'd guess they were graduate students from their apparent ages. "Are you trying to show me something about the students?"

"Meow."

"Anyone in particular?"

Raider looked up at him, blinked a couple of times, shook his head, and licked his paw. Then he walked across the article and head-butted Stone, purring and looking confused.

"Bugger...you've popped out again, haven't you?"

No reply, and when Stone lifted him up and peered into his eyes, the blue glow had vanished.

At least the phone hadn't rung this time. And he did have a bit more to go on: apparently, one or more of the five graduate students might have more information about whatever Professor Benchley wanted him to know. He took out a pad and jotted down all five names. If they were in their early to middle twenties in the mid-Seventies, they'd be in their sixties now. Some of them might even be dead.

Would the Chemistry department have kept track of them after all this time? It sounded like another trip back there would be his next step.

At least it would help keep his mind off Marciella Garra for a while.

# | CHAPTER EIGHTEEN

STONE DIDN'T GET BACK TO HIS OFFICE until after noon the next day. "Dr. Stone?" Laura called as he passed her. "Dr. Garra was looking for you."

"Oh?" That was odd, after how much she'd been avoiding him. "Is she here now?"

"Back in her office."

Interesting. He paused to drop off his briefcase in his own office, then headed down the hall and knocked on her open doorway. "Laura said you wanted to see me."

She looked up from the paper she'd been writing something on. "Oh. Yes. Do you have a moment?"

"Of course." He studied her as he sat; she wore a bold purple blouse and her usual gold-chain necklace, with her shining black hair pulled back into a thick braid that hung down her back.

She finished what she was writing, then met Stone's gaze. "Dr. Stone, were you looking for something in my office?"

Stone barely kept the shock from his face, and from his aura. How could she have known? "What? Why would I be in your office?"

"I don't know. Someone was, and I'm trying to figure out who."

He narrowed his eyes. "How do you know someone was in here? I mean—I popped in to drop off those books, but that was a while ago. Perhaps Laura was—"

"No, I don't think it was Laura. Someone was in here last night. When I opened my desk drawer, I found things moved around. Not much—just enough that I know I didn't leave them that way."

"That's...odd." Stone searched his memory—he'd been so careful to put everything back exactly as he'd found it. Had he gotten something wrong in his haste to get away? "The cleaning people come in at night—perhaps they—"

"It's a locked drawer. I doubt the janitors have keys." She glanced down, then back up again. "It *is* odd. Don't get me wrong—I'm not accusing you of anything. I don't keep anything very valuable in my drawer, and nothing was missing. They didn't even take my nice pen. It's just—creepy, to think somebody was going through my private things. You know?" She met his gaze squarely as she said it.

The sudden feeling hit Stone that she knew *precisely* what he'd done. It was absurd—how could she possibly know?— but there it was. Still, he doubted she could prove it, and he couldn't exactly come right out and admit it.

He submerged his guilt and focused on keeping his expression neutral and mildly indignant at the thought of someone taking advantage of her. "Indeed—I can see why you're concerned. But I assure you, I haven't had any reason to be in your office, let alone in your locked desk. I'm not sure why you'd think I would have been."

For a moment they held each other's gazes, each daring the other to flinch. Finally, hers dropped. "I'm sorry. I guess I overreacted. Since this used to be your office..."

"You thought I might have held on to a copy of the desk key." He could have turned the guilt back around on her if he'd wanted to, feigning offense that she'd think such a thing of him. Instead, he merely shrugged. "I don't know what to tell you, Dr. Garra—I turned in all my keys when I moved to Dr. Mortenson's old office. If you're concerned, we could get Campus Security involved—"

She didn't call his bluff, thank goodness, but instead shook her head and waved him off. "Oh, no, no. It's not worth that. Like I said, I don't keep valuables in there. Or maybe it didn't happen at all, and I just misremembered how I left things. I'm sorry I brought it up. Now that I say it out loud, it sounds a little silly, doesn't it?"

"Of course not," he assured her, standing. "You've got every right to feel secure in your office. If you're that worried about it, at least ask Laura to have someone in to change the lock on your office and your desk. That should give you some peace of mind."

"That's a good idea. Thank you, Dr. Stone. And I *am* sorry for sounding like I was accusing you."

"Think nothing of it. If there's anything I can do to help, let me know."

*Bloody hell! How did she* know?

Stone had intended to spend some time going over student essays in his office, but after the meeting with Garra, he had to get out of there. He crossed the campus with a purposeful stride designed to let any students tempted to stop him for a chat know it was a bad idea. It took him until he almost reached the central quad before his heart slowed to normal.

How could she possibly have known he was in her office? Had she been lurking around and spotted him? Had the janitor seen through his invisibility spell and told her? Had he shown up on some security camera he didn't know about? Had the child's talk of "ghosts" somehow made her mother suspicious?

*She doesn't know. She can't. She's just guessing because she already suspects you of something, and you're the best candidate to still have a key.* Even if she *did* suspect him of looking through her desk drawer, though, there was no way she could have figured out what he was doing in there. She'd said herself that nothing was missing.

Unless he'd somehow put the sketch back in the wrong place…

*Just—don't worry about it,* he told himself. *She can't do anything about it, and after tomorrow night you might have more answers.* Besides, if she threatened to accuse him of the break-in, he could always pull out his hidden ace and reveal he knew she was an imposter. It even provided a reasonable motive for why he might have done the deed, though probably not an excuse for it.

He didn't have another class for more than an hour. He'd already had lunch, so instead he continued north toward the Chemistry building. He hadn't planned to stop by today, but since he couldn't go back to his office yet without facing Garra again, it seemed as good a time as any.

The same woman greeted him as he entered. "Ah, you're back. Did you find out what you needed to know about Dr. Benchley?"

"Sort of. I did find his photo in your collection, and located a couple of articles about him at the library. I was curious, though—I'm sure you keep records about former students, but would you be able to tell me anything about some of them? I thought perhaps I could contact them for information."

She eyed him with suspicion. "This seems like a lot of trouble for tracking down information about a man who used to live in your house."

"What can I say? I'm a bit of a history buff, especially about old houses. I understand if you can't give me information about them, but if I gave you their names, would it be possible for you to let me know if they're still alive, and perhaps pass a message on to them that I'd like to contact them? That way we can leave it up to them whether they want to get back to me."

"Well…" She glanced at her computer screen, then back at him. "Tell me their names and I'll see what I can do when I have some free time. Are you in a hurry?"

"Not really—whenever you can get to it is fine." He flashed the charming smile and pulled the notebook page from his coat pocket. "I do appreciate your help. It's very kind of you."

She smiled back. "It *is* an interesting project, I'll admit." She glanced at the page. "Oh! Well, you'll be happy to know I think I can help you right away, at least with one of the names on your list."

"Oh?"

"Yes." She pointed at the second name, *Del Wright.* "Dr. Wright is on the faculty here. In this department, as it happens."

He stared at her. "Really?" Things didn't often go that well for him. "Are you sure it's the same Del Wright?"

"His photo will be on the wall—I'm not sure when he started here, but it was before my time. Probably sometime back in the Eighties."

"Indeed? Excuse me a moment." He hurried down the hall and scanned the photos again, starting shortly after the one of Thaddeus Benchley and working his way through the more recent ones. It couldn't be the same man—that was too easy. But the age was right…

When he saw the photo, he was sure. It was in the section covering the late Eighties, so that would make Wright only about fifteen years older than he'd been in the *Daily* photo. Even accounting for the graininess in Stone's clipping, the resemblance was too close to be a coincidence. Both had wide foreheads, curly dark hair, and easy, laid-back smiles.

He returned to the admin. "You're brilliant—that's him, all right. Is he in his office right now? I'd love to chat with him."

"He's not—he doesn't spend much time here, since he only teaches a couple of courses a week." She typed something and consulted her screen. "He should be in on Monday. Why don't you give him a call then, or stop by? Maybe he can help you find out what you're looking for.""

"That's great. Thank you so much."

# | CHAPTER NINETEEN

FRIDAY EVENING STONE DROVE DOWN to San Jose, stopping for dinner at A Passage To India on the way.

Marta Bellwood, the proprietor, smiled as he came in. "Alastair. Haven't seen you in a while. How have you been? You look like you're finally getting some sleep, at least."

"I am, yes. How are you?"

She indicated the dining room, full of couples and groups enjoying their meals. "Can't complain. Want to try the tandoori chicken? Nikhil really outdid himself tonight."

"Sold."

When it was ready, she delivered it to his table herself. "Do you mind if I sit with you for a few minutes, or are you meeting someone?"

"Please." He indicated the chair across from him. "Not meeting anyone—I'm on my own tonight."

He'd thought about asking Verity or Jason to accompany him on his scouting mission, but Verity was spending the weekend in San Francisco with Kyla, and had told him last time they'd talked that Jason had a date with a woman who worked at the law office next door to his new agency.

"Dunno if it'll go anywhere," she'd said slyly, "but maybe if he gets some action he'll quit giving us the side-eye."

"What brings you down here?" Marta asked. "Are you heading back home for a bit?"

It was a reasonable question—he'd been using the portal in the restaurant's downstairs storage room quite a lot this past summer to travel back and forth between California and England, helping his friends Eddie Monkton and Arthur Ward convert Caventhorne, the late William Desmond's massive manor house, to a resource center for use by the magical community. He'd also been doing quite a lot of research about his family's dark past following the shocking revelations he'd discovered. He hadn't been back since his trip to Calanar, however.

"No—got some things to do down in San Jose."

She brightened. "Jason and Verity stopped by the other day. I'm so glad he's back in the area again. I think it'll be good for you to have your friends back."

He chuckled. "It's not like we're setting up play dates, Marta. They've got their own things to do. Jason's busy as hell getting his agency started."

"Oh, I know—he told me. But still—I think he's glad to be back too."

Stone lingered over the chicken—it really was delicious—chatting with Marta about innocuous topics for the next hour, as the restaurant's customers gradually trickled out following the dinner rush. Finally, though, he couldn't stall any longer, and stood.

"Please send my compliments to Nikhil. I promise I'll stop by more often. Got to go now, though."

"Take care of yourself, Alastair. And if you're off to do something dangerous, I don't want to hear it. Unless I can talk you out of it, at least."

"Nothing dangerous—I hope. Good night, Marta."

Stone was right about the area containing the location of Garra's meet: it was a run-down section of east San Jose, dominated by warehouses and uninspiring light-industrial buildings. Surprisingly, though, the address he was searching for was not either of these, but an abandoned school.

He'd deliberately headed there nearly an hour before the scheduled time, so he could scope the place out before either Garra or whoever she was meeting with arrived. He parked the BMW on the next block, cast a disregarding spell over it so it would blend in with the surroundings, and activated his disguise amulet to make him look like a twentyish man in a hoodie and jeans. Then he walked back, looking the place over as he approached.

It was hard to see much, as it was quite dark around here. The only illumination came from two street lights and a few perimeter spotlights placed at strategic points around the razor-wire-topped chain link fence surrounding the buildings. From what he could tell it had been a typical California elementary or middle school: most of the buildings single-story, with a few two- or three-story ones scattered around. It had clearly not been occupied for quite some time; even from where he stood outside the fence, Stone could see signs of scrubby weeds poking up through the asphalt of the playground, and graffiti-sprayed plywood covered many of the windows.

He paused, hands in his pockets, and took the place in as best he could from where he stood. Garra was meeting a contact *here?* He couldn't be sure this had anything to do with her search for antiques or artifacts, since the planner entry hadn't provided any clarification, but what else could it be? It hardly seemed likely she was meeting someone here for a romantic encounter.

Frowning, he had another thought: Garra had faked her identity to get the job at the University. That showed her willingness to lie—perhaps she'd lied to him about her reasons for seeking the antique shops, too. If the chalice in the sketch was her target, could she perhaps be planning not to buy it, but to steal it? Her aura hadn't budged when he'd asked her about her interest in the shops, but that might not mean anything. If she had connections to the supernatural world, she might even know how to conceal her reactions— or she might not have any to start with.

But if she wasn't looking for items to add to her collection—either the chalice alone or others, too—what *was* she looking for? Or, alternatively, maybe she *was* looking to add to her collection, but having failed to find what she was seeking by legal means, she'd branched out and now sought to obtain items by less aboveboard methods. Perhaps she didn't plan to steal them herself, but to arrange with someone else to do it for her.

That actually made the most sense of anything so far, given the meet's location. A thief or fence might not operate from a fixed location, or might not want to reveal that location to someone he wasn't familiar with.

He wondered if the attack outside Hubbard's party had anything to do with this. If she'd tried this before, perhaps she'd somehow gotten on the bad side of some shady character, who'd decided to come after her. *That doesn't make sense either, though,* he thought, frustrated. Why would someone follow her all the way out to Los Gatos? Surely there would be better places to jump her if that was their intent.

*You won't know until you check out this meet, so you'd best get going.*

He glanced around with magical sight to make sure nobody was watching, then pulled up a disregarding spell and levitated over the fence. When he touched down on the other side, he dropped to a crouch and looked around again, but nothing moved.

There was one major problem with his plan: he had no idea which of these buildings Garra would be meeting her contact in. When he'd seen the address, he'd expected it to be a warehouse or other single structure, making it easy for him to hide somewhere and observe, but this made things much more difficult. Even though the school wasn't a large example of its kind, it still spread out over two or three sizable blocks. Long, narrow classroom buildings mixed with larger gym, auditorium, and administration buildings, with wide expanses of cracked blacktop and scrubby dirt playgrounds separating them. There were all sorts of places she could go, and if he picked the wrong one it would take him enough time to cross the campus and reach her that he might miss her—especially if the conversation or exchange took place quickly. If she was doing something illegal, he doubted they'd hang about and chat afterward.

He looked around again, pondering. He still had some time—he could take a walk around the area and look for open doors, uncovered windows, or some other indication of a convenient meeting spot. That would take quite a while, though; if either Garra or her contact showed up early, they might spot him wandering around. Even if they mistook him for a homeless squatter or teenage tagger, it still might spook them into relocating.

His gaze fell on the auditorium building. It was some distance away, located in the center of campus. More importantly, though, it included a bell tower rising above a tall, steeply pitched roof. He smiled. *There we go.*

Less than five minutes later he was in the tower, perched where he could look down and observe nearly every other part of the campus.

It was a better vantage point than he could have hoped for. The space inside the top of the tower that had once held the bell—it was long gone now—was only about four feet on a side, with open arches in all four directions. Below his feet, a trap door in the dusty wooden floor no doubt covered a ladder downward, but it was locked. Nobody would sneak up on him from there. It wasn't ideal—since the tower was at one end of the auditorium, he couldn't see what was going on at ground level at the other end—but if he turned around frequently and used magical sight, he should be able to spot anyone approaching from nearly every angle.

He glanced at his watch—a little less than half an hour until the meet time, and he expected both Garra and her contact to show up early. Hell, the contact might already be hiding somewhere inside one of the buildings, waiting for her to show so he could get a look at her as she approached. That couldn't be helped, though—magical sight was a versatile thing, but it didn't let him see through walls.

So now, all he had to do was wait.

It was quiet out here; except for the occasional distant rumble of a car or truck driving by or the occasional far-off howl of a police or ambulance siren, Stone heard no other sound of human habitation. It made sense: most of the businesses out here wouldn't be open this late, and the school had obviously been derelict for a long time. With the possible exception of homeless people seeking shelter or perhaps drug dealers using the place to conduct business, it was unlikely anybody else would go through the trouble of finding a way through the stout chain-link fence.

He pulled his coat closed against the light wind. It was starting to get chillier at night now, in mid-October, but at least it wasn't raining. The moon shone bright in a clear, black sky, providing a bit more illumination now as Stone's vision adjusted to the darkness.

Where *was* she? He glanced at his watch again: nine fifty-five. If she didn't want to be late for her ten o'clock appointment, she'd need to already be on campus somewhere. Had he managed to miss her? Had she come in from the one side he couldn't see from his vantage point?

The longer he crouched there, scanning as far around the area as he could, the more convinced he grew that she had entered the campus behind him. Hell, she could be directly under him now, conducting her business inside the auditorium.

*I'd better check, or I'll be sitting here all night.*

He rose, took one more look around, then cast a disregarding spell on himself. He could use invisibility, but since no one would expect someone to be floating around high overhead, this one should be fine to conceal him for his brief scouting mission. He stepped onto the roof and levitated upward, drifting to the opposite end of the auditorium building. Once there, he activated magical sight and repeated his sweeping scan. If Garra was here, her green aura would glow brightly against the drab, lifeless darkness of the abandoned campus.

Nothing.

He checked the walkways, the playgrounds, even along the edge of the chain-link fence, but spotted no sign of Garra or any other human presence. The only living thing that showed up was the faint green aura of a cat creeping along the perimeter of the gymnasium, probably out hunting for careless mice. He felt a certain frustrated kinship with the cat—apparently neither of them was finding what they were looking for. Perhaps in his haste he'd misread the address, or the time, or—

A loud, screaming snarl ripped through the silence.

# | CHAPTER TWENTY

STARTLED, STONE JERKED IN THE AIR and nearly bobbled the levitation spell. He caught himself an instant before it slipped and sent him plummeting to the ground, then quickly reoriented and scanned the area again.

What the hell had that *been?* It had come from in front of him—probably inside the gym—and whatever it was, it hadn't sounded human. It hadn't even sounded like an animal—unless a tiger or some equally large predator had escaped from a local zoo. He had time for two absurd thoughts: had the sound somehow come from the stalking cat he'd spotted, or had the mountain lion from near Hubbard's house managed to make it all the way to San Jose?—before he dropped lower and flew toward the gym.

It occurred to him that the sound might be a diversion—had someone spotted him and used it to draw him away from the action? But there were a lot easier ways to do that than to mimic the scream of a predatory beast. Whatever was in there, it had to be connected with Garra's meeting.

The scream sounded again, followed by the unmistakable *crack* of a gunshot.

*Bloody hell!* Stone touched ground and immediately dropped both spells, swapping them for a shield. He took off at a run, scanning the building's sides for a way in.

*There!* At the far end, he spotted a closed door. Was it unlocked? Was that the way they'd gotten in? It didn't matter—locks wouldn't stop him. He picked up his pace and reached the door in a few seconds as the roar once again echoed from inside. There must be a window broken or open somewhere, since the walls were far too thick to hear it through. He couldn't see it, though, and didn't have time to search for it.

The door was locked. Stone popped it with a flick of his mind and flung the door open, darting inside and ducking quickly to his left to take in the scene.

The door led directly into the open expanse of the gym's floor—enough moonlight streamed in through windows high above him to tell that—but the cavernous space was otherwise dark. Stone looked around for a flashlight beam or other clue about where the scream might have come from; when he saw none, he switched to magical sight.

He stiffened at what he saw.

Far away, on the other side of the gym, three figures' auras lit up. Two were tall, hulking men, broad-shouldered and powerful. The third, crouched and growling on top of a tall bank of half-destroyed bleachers, looked like—

Was that some kind of *jungle cat?* It was so black it seemed to blend in with the shadowy darkness, but its aura blazed bright green. Right now, it seemed fully focused on the two men ahead of it, and as Stone watched, it leaped from the bleachers, paws out and claws extended, toward one of the men.

The gun went off again. The cat screamed defiance, jerking in the air and landing hard on its side, but then it rolled up and darted away.

What the hell was going on?

Stone shifted his gaze back to the two men. Both were running after the cat, seemingly unafraid of facing it. As they passed through a patch of moonlight, he got a brief look at their faces: feral, focused, as predatory as the cat itself. They moved with athletic, muscular grace, intent on the creature. Startled, Stone noticed their auras: one man's was red, the other gold, but both had thin bands of green at their edges.

The cat had leaped to the top of another bank of bleachers. Its bright green aura shone as strong as ever, but red patches in it indicated that at least one of the men might have hit it with their shots. Before they could draw a bead on it again, it launched itself toward them, yowling its rage.

This time, one of them didn't get out of the way in time. The cat landed on him, taking him down. He was almost as big as it was, and it wasn't a small creature.

Stone expected it to be over quickly, but the man yelled something—it sounded more angry than frightened—and scrabbled until he got a grip on the cat, then wrenched it free of him and flung it away. Once again, the cat landed on its side and rolled quickly to its feet.

Meanwhile, the other man had spotted Stone over by the door. "Help us!" he yelled. "This thing's a maneater! It'll kill us all if we don't stop it!"

The cat roared, moving with frightening speed, and dived at the second man. He barely got out of the way in time, throwing himself to the side. The cat's wide-open, fang-filled jaws snapped shut on air, barely missing his leg.

Stone hesitated, unsure of what he'd burst in on. Did this have anything to do with Garra's meet, or had he somehow stumbled upon something completely unrelated?

The cat twisted with inhuman grace, spinning around and raking its claws across the man before he could scramble back to his feet. He screamed as his shirt ripped, his aura flaring red.

Stone made a decision. None of this situation was making sense, but until he sorted it out, he'd have to take the side of the humans over the enraged jungle cat. He raised his hands and grabbed hold of the beast with a telekinetic hold, sliding it across the ground and slamming it into the side of the bleachers. He didn't want to use magic in front of the men, but if he was careful he could hide the worst of the evidence under cover of darkness.

The cat screamed, its own aura flaring as brightly as the men's. It twisted again, vaulted up, and disappeared under the bleachers as both men fired their guns at it.

Stone ran to the side, keeping low, scanning the area beneath the broken risers for the cat. As dark as it was, it might be able to hide itself in shadows, concealing it from its would-be captors, but it couldn't mask that blazing green aura. Stone quickly picked it up again and headed toward it.

Surprisingly, though, the men seemed to have no trouble tracking the cat as well. They separated, one heading to one end of the bleachers where it hid, and the other to the opposite end, clearly intending to box it in. To get out, it would have to run past one or the other of them—and they both had guns.

This didn't seem to disturb it, however. Its screaming cry echoed into the gym's high rafters and it was on the move again, keeping low. Stone watched through the bleachers' slats as its aura zigzagged from side to side, almost as if it were aware of the gun and trying to present an erratic target. It didn't have enough room to execute a mighty leap this time, so instead it launched itself forward with its powerful hind legs and bull-rushed the man, bowling him over. Two gunshots sounded—one from the stricken man, the other from his partner.

Stone, closer now, flicked a quick magical scan back toward the other end. As he did, something on the floor lit up against the darkness, only a few feet away from him. Staying crouched to avoid getting caught in the two men's gunfire, he darted over and snatched it up.

He recognized it instantly—because he'd seen it before, only a few nights ago.

It was Marciella Garra's black-onyx pendant—the magical one she'd worn to Mackenzie Hubbard's party. Its gold chain was broken, its arcane energy flickering faintly.

*What? How can this—*

*Wait—*

*No. It couldn't be. That's not possible. It's insane!*

As farfetched as it was, though, it was the only thing that made sense.

He spun toward the first man, who was clambering back to his feet as the cat came in for a second pass, and pointed his hand, releasing a thundering, wide-beam concussion bolt.

The bolt slammed into the man with the approximate surface area and speed of a bowling ball flung by a giant, hurtling him back into the bleachers. He tumbled over and over, yelping in pain, and came to rest splayed on his back across several rows of risers. He lay still, stunned.

"What the *fuck*?" the other one yelled, whirling to open fire on Stone.

The bullets *spang*ed off his newly augmented shield. Pink pinpoints flared up where the projectiles hit, but the shield held. *Damn,* but it felt good to have this kind of power at his command!

*Don't get cocky. You still don't know what's going on here.*

The cat, meanwhile, hadn't been idle. Yellow eyes gleaming in the faint light, it streaked on silent paws toward the man who'd just fired on Stone, forcing him to redirect his attention. He managed to squeeze off two shots before the cat took him down, screaming its eerie cry.

"Wait!" Stone yelled, running forward. "Don't do this!" He focused his concentration again, using a telekinetic grip to grab the man and yank him free of the cat's grip, flinging him across the room into the nearest wall. He hit hard and dropped in a heap.

Stone ran toward the cat. "Stop," he yelled. "We can—"

The cat roared, and an instant later something slammed into him from behind. Startled, he let his shield slip for only a second—but that was long enough for the man to get hold of him. Before he could react, he was sailing through the air, far higher and faster than a normal human should have been able to throw him.

*Bloody hell, he's not a normal human.* The thought was all he was able to process before he hit the wall hard and rolled down the bleachers.

*Okay, change of plans.* He rolled up, puffing, and reformed the shield around himself. The hit had hurt, but another side effect of his physical conditioning and extra time at the gym was that he'd been able to twist in the air and land in a more advantageous position. He'd have bruises tomorrow, but nothing was broken or bleeding.

*Yet.* That could change if he didn't deal with these guys soon.

One of them was firing at him again, crouched behind some debris a short distance away. He quickly rolled to the side, putting the edge of the bleachers between them and considered his options.

Meanwhile, the other attacker was focused on the cat. The beast had leaped away, ducked low, growling, stalking its opponent. Stone could see from the rippling muscles under its inky pelt that it was prepared to move if the man took another shot at it.

It didn't appear that was his intent, though. He brought the gun up and feigned a shot, but when the cat jumped to the side, he launched himself forward in the same direction toward it.

*He's going to* wrestle *it?*

The man moved fast—as fast as the cat, which shouldn't have been possible. He came down on top of it before it could jump free, and as the two rolled on the dirty gym floor, Stone caught the flash of metal in the man's hand—a knife!—as he slashed downward.

The cat screamed again, this time as much in pain as rage, raking the man with powerful claws and flinging him aside, but the second attacker was ready for it. He squeezed off two quick shots. The cat managed to avoid one of them, but yowled as the second one hit.

"No!" Stone yelled. This was getting out of hand now, and if he didn't do something soon the cat could be in trouble.

*Okay, no more easy shots.*

It felt good to gather power to him now—better than it ever had before, using either white or black magic. The energy from magic-rich Calanar flowed into him, raw and potent; he pointed a hand at each of the men and shaped it with his will into the weapons he needed.

"Get *out!*" he boomed, releasing the energy in the form of crackling lightning bolts that streaked across the darkened gym, wreathing their pathways with bright blue-white light.

Both men shrieked in pain, limbs stiffening, short-cut hair standing on end, eyes bulging. They staggered backward, dropping their weapons, and collapsed to the floor, twitching. After a moment they lay still.

Stone hurried over toward one of them. Had he killed them? He hadn't specifically been trying to, but he hadn't held back, either. A quick look with magical sight revealed faintly flickering auras—still alive, then, at least for now. They still had the odd green edging, too, but he didn't have time to figure that out now.

"Where are you?" he called, turning to look for the cat.

His vision filled with darkness as a snarling, furry form slammed into him. It knocked him to the floor, its paws pressing down on his shoulders, its mouth wide open to reveal long, pointed fangs. Its yellow-gold eyes glared at him, full of rage. As he lay stunned, trying to get his bearings, it unleashed a deafening roar only inches from his face. Its hot breath washed over him. Its claws gripped at him, not quite piercing his shoulders but clearly capable of it.

"Wait!" Stone croaked, panting. "Dr. Garra—stop!"

# | CHAPTER TWENTY-ONE

FOR A SECOND THAT STRETCHED to an eternity, Stone feared his wild, mad speculation had been wrong, and the cat would sink its teeth into his throat before he could get his shield back up. He stared up into the creature's blazing eyes, panting, and waited.

After a moment, the pressure on his shoulders lessened—but only slightly. The cat pulled its head back, still glaring down at him but closing its mouth. It growled something that almost sounded like words—and then it was changing.

The massive, heavily muscled black jaguar seemed to melt away, backing off, rising to a standing position. And then it was gone, replaced by a familiar—and naked—figure, blood running down her body from several wounds.

Stone, still panting, scrambled to his feet. "Dr. Garra..."

Garra's glare had not receded in the slightest following her transformation. She was still looking at him as if regretting she hadn't torn his throat out, and didn't seem at all self-conscious or embarrassed about her lack of clothing.

"Stone..." she said, and her voice held the same growl as the cat's had. "I should have known..." She didn't seem worried about the wounds, either.

"What—?" Stone began, but then looked down at himself, realizing the illusion generator was still active. He switched it off; the hoodie changed to his normal black T-shirt and long, dark coat. He stared at her. "Bloody hell, you *are.*"

"I should kill you…" she snarled. "I knew it was you—you couldn't fool me with that illusion. It didn't hide your scent—just like I couldn't miss it in my office. I should have known you were a mage."

Stone didn't stop to wonder how she knew about mages. He risked a glance at the two fallen attackers. "Listen—unless you're planning on killing me just now, we should get out of here. I suspect those two are going to wake up any moment. I don't know where they got strength and resilience like that, but I don't fancy seeing it in action again right now, do you?"

"Give me my amulet," she ordered, thrusting a hand toward him. "I saw you pick it up."

Stone pulled the onyx pendant from his pocket. "What is this thing, anyway? Your own version of my illusion generator?" He focused on her face; despite her confident stance and clear lack of concern about her nudity, he nonetheless found her impressive figure distracting and it was throwing him off his game.

She snatched the pendant from his hand, but her angry expression turned to one of dismay as she held up the chain. "No…it's broken…"

Stone shrugged out of his coat and offered it to her. "Here. This should do for now until we can find you some clothes. If you let me take a look at your amulet later, I might be able to sort it out for you."

"You stay away from me," she snapped, but she did grab the coat.

"I'm not your enemy, Dr. Garra—or whoever the hell you are." He backed off, turning pointedly away to give her time to cover up. "I just want to know what's going on. I think you owe me that much for saving your life."

She snorted. "You didn't save my life. I would have handled them just fine on my own if you hadn't come along."

"I'm not so sure. Do you know who they are? Or why they're after you?"

"No," she said after a pause, and now she sounded more troubled than angry. "I don't know who they are. I've never seen them before. They're far stronger and tougher than normal humans." The glare resurfaced. "Perhaps they're mages—like you. Perhaps you're working together."

"Don't be absurd. Why would I be working with *that* lot?" He jerked his head toward the door. "Now—you're injured. Do you want to wait until they wake up and have another go at us, or shall we get the hell away before they do?"

She studied him for several more moments, with the same sort of look he got when examining auras. "All right," she said grudgingly. "Let's go." She'd donned Stone's coat and buttoned it; it hung down nearly to her ankles, effectively covering her. Without waiting for his response, she stalked toward the door.

Stone glanced back toward the two fallen attackers, both of whom were already showing signs of stirring. Then he jogged after her, noting that she didn't move like someone who'd just been shot.

"Will you trust me?" he asked. "It's fairly deserted around here so I don't know if anyone heard those gunshots, but if they did, the police will be here soon. Best if they don't find us when they arrive, yes?"

"What are you going to do?" Suspicion still laced her voice.

"Make it less likely that anyone will notice us. Where did you park?"

She pointed in the same direction as Stone had left the BMW. "A couple of blocks away. I've got some extra clothes in my car."

"All right—let's go, then. Stay close to me."

She didn't ask questions, but merely glared at him and moved closer.

Stone settled a disregarding spell around them and started toward the fence. Garra easily kept up with his long stride despite being barefoot on uneven terrain.

"How did you get past the fence?" he asked when they drew near it. "Did you find a hole somewhere?"

"I jumped over using a trash can. The person I was supposed to meet said he'd leave a gate open on the other side, but I didn't trust him."

"Let's make things a bit easier, then. Hold still."

"What are you—"

He cast a levitation spell on both of them, lifting them up and over. When they'd touched down again, she let her breath out. "I don't know if I should trust *you*, either."

"Well, you've got my coat, and my wallet's in there. So if you take off at this point, I could be in trouble. Suppose we trust each other, at least until we get out of this?"

She grunted an affirmative and set off down the street.

As it turned out, she'd parked less than two blocks away from the BMW, farther up the same street. They passed his car first and he dropped the disregarding spell he'd cast on it.

Garra frowned. "I walked right past this spot. How did I not notice your car here?"

"Magic. Get in—no point walking two blocks in bare feet."

The suspicion rose again, but after a moment she climbed into the front seat. "Why were you following me?" she asked in the darkness as he rolled off.

"That's a bit of a long story. I have questions for you, too—would you be willing to go somewhere with me to talk about it?"

He thought she might decline when she drew a sharp breath, but then she let it out. "I suppose I don't have a choice. I still don't trust you—but I don't think you're involved with those men."

"Well, that's a start, I suppose. I assure you, I'm not. Are you all right? They hurt you. I thought I saw one of them shoot you."

"I'm fine. I…heal quickly."

"Yes, I noticed that the other night."

They reached her red Honda and he pulled in behind it. "You said you've got clothes in your car—I can use an illusion to cover you while you change if you like."

"It doesn't matter to me," she said with a shrug. "People have such issues with nudity. It's ridiculous. But I suppose it will make things easier if no one sees us."

Stone kept watch while she ducked to remove a key she'd left in a magnetic case under her car, then opened her trunk and pulled out a folded set of clothes. "All right—go ahead and change. You won't see anything different, but I promise, the rest of the world—including me—won't see anything but empty street. Tell me when you're finished."

Surprisingly, this time the suspicion didn't return. Either she believed him, or she didn't care if he watched her dress. Either way, he did as he'd told her he would, scanning the area around them with magical sight to make sure the two attackers weren't approaching.

"All right—I'm ready."

He dropped the illusion to reveal her standing behind her car, clad now in jeans, T-shirt, and dark-red leather jacket, holding out his coat. "Thank you," she said.

"Think nothing of it." He put the coat back on and looked around again for anyone approaching. He didn't hear any sirens, which was a good sign. Perhaps the area *had* been too deserted for anyone to hear the gunshots.

She slid behind the wheel of the Honda. "So, what now? Where do you want to go?"

"Just follow me—I think I remember passing a restaurant on the way over here. It's not too far. I think we could both do with a cup of coffee. I'd actually prefer a stiff drink or two, but that's probably not the best idea at present."

# CHAPTER TWENTY-TWO

TEN MINUTES LATER, they were seated in a booth at the back of a dimly-lit Mexican diner, both of them casting occasional glances out the window to verify no one had followed them. Stone regarded Garra over a large cup of steaming coffee. "So—suppose you start."

She flicked her gaze up, a shadow of the old anger flashing across her face. "Why me?"

"Because you're the one who faked her identity to get a job at the University, and—oh, yes—changes into a giant black panther."

"How did you know that?" she asked, eyes widening in surprise. "That I faked my identity, I mean."

"Yes, I figured. The cat bit was rather obvious. What are you, anyway? Some sort of—panther shapeshifter? I've heard of shifters, but I've never met one. I wasn't even sure there were any anymore. They've got to be quite rare, yes?"

"Yes. Jaguar, actually." She looked down at her hands. "Rarer by the year, unfortunately. Most of us don't live among normal humans. Those who do make a point to keep their heads down and remain…discreet. And most don't live in such populous areas." She sipped her coffee. "How did you figure it out?"

"It wasn't difficult, once I found the amulet. I wasn't sure I was right—when I first came upon you and those two men, I thought I'd stumbled into something that had nothing to do with you. That's why I helped them at first."

"What changed your mind?"

"I saw their auras. They were—strange. And I made the connection between you and the amulet. Remember, I asked you about it at Hubbard's party?"

"Yes..."

"That wasn't because I was admiring its design. I saw it was magical, and that raised my curiosity. I don't often see mundanes wearing magic items. That meant either you weren't a mundane, or you had some connection to someone who wasn't."

"Is that why you broke into my office?" Her eyes narrowed. "You *did* do that, right?"

"Guilty," he admitted. "How did you figure it out? I was careful to—ah." He nodded as he put it together. "I *was* careful—but I couldn't disguise my scent."

"Exactly. You were nervous, I could tell. But I don't know what you were looking for. Were you trying to find the amulet?"

"No—I was suspicious when I saw how quickly you healed the injuries from the night of Hubbard's party, and wondered if it had any connection to your antique hunt."

"I see." She glanced out the window, then back at him. "So that's how you knew I had a meeting tonight. And why you followed me."

"Yes. I thought it odd that you'd be meeting someone about antiques that late, and in that part of town. I thought perhaps you might be pursuing something illegal, dangerous, or both. Those men who attacked you—you truly don't know who they were?"

"No...not specifically. But I might know what they wanted."

"Does it have something to do with the chalice you had a sketch of in your planner?"

She glared at him. "You *are* thorough in your snooping, aren't you?" But then she sighed, and nodded. "Yes."

"Did they attack you in the park after Hubbard's party?" Suddenly he remembered something and another puzzle piece fell into place. "That night, when I was out on the deck chatting with Hubbard and his wife, we heard a wildcat scream. They said it was a mountain lion. It was you, wasn't it?"

"Yes. Only one man tried to attack me that night. I think they underestimated my capabilities. I drove him off without too much trouble, but he must have slashed me with a knife or something. You found me before my injuries healed completely."

Stone pondered that as he sipped his coffee. "So, why *are* you here, Dr. Garra? Why did you go to all the trouble to fake your identity and get a job as a university lecturer? I assume you're here looking for that chalice, yes?"

"Yes."

"Let's start at the beginning, then: *how* did you fake your identity? You do know there's a real Dr. Marciella Garra, right?"

She gave him a withering look. "Of course I do. She was an old friend I knew when I was a young girl."

"So she knows who—and what—you are?"

"No—not precisely. I lost touch with her years ago, but she's not teaching any longer. I'm not even sure she's still alive, but if she is, she's very reclusive. I was sure no one would track her down, and her work is obscure enough that with a little help, I was able to fake some of her publications as my own. They didn't check that closely—I think they were fairly anxious to bring me on. And I really *am* a scholar of anthropology. It's just that my schooling wasn't… conventional."

"You learned from the real Garra?"

"No, but I learned a lot of things from her when I was young. Including quite a lot about magic."

"Indeed?" Stone leaned forward. "She's a practitioner, then?"

"She's a witch, yes."

"Ah—did she make that amulet of yours?"

"She did. I've had it for years. You were right—it's an illusion generator, attuned to me specifically. As you noticed, we have a bit of trouble with clothing when we shift. It's one of the reasons you don't see many of us in cities. Even though *we* don't have a problem with nudity, human society tends to frown on people walking down the street stark naked. Most of us, if we come out at all, we do it at night."

"I see. Well—I was serious when I said I can probably fix it for you, if you'll trust me to do it."

Her gaze chilled. "I'm still not sure I do trust you, Dr. Stone. I…have a lot of reasons not to trust your kind."

"My kind?" He remembered the last time he'd heard that, from the Harpies. "Mages? Or men?"

"Mages."

"But you said your friend was—"

"Marciella was a witch, not a mage. She specialized in more subtle arts: healing, enchantment, potions. She didn't seek to rip the world apart with her will."

Stone struggled not to roll his eyes. He was getting very tired of being accused of that. "Look," he said, annoyed, "I'm not trying to rip anything apart—not even those two men who came after you. They do disturb me, though. Their auras were unusual. I wonder if they weren't under some kind of magical influence."

"I wouldn't be surprised, if I'm right about why they were after me."

"Suppose you tell me. What *is* that chalice, and why are you looking for it?"

She didn't answer for a while; instead, she sipped her coffee, gazed out the window, and toyed with her napkin.

"Dr. Garra—I can help you, if you let me. Assuming you're not trying to hurt anyone, you might find advantages in having me on your side. World-ripping aside, I know this area—including the stranger aspects of it—much better than you do."

She glared at him. "How did you find out about the real Dr. Garra, anyway? *I* don't even know where she is, if she's still alive. She dropped off the face of the earth years ago."

"I had a friend—a private investigator—check up on you after Hubbard's party."

Her glare intensified. "You *checked up* on me? So someone else knows?"

"Don't worry—he's a good friend, and very discreet. Aside from him and my former apprentice, who's also discreet, nobody else knows. But if I'm to keep your secret, you need to convince me that the students and faculty aren't at risk."

"Why would they be at risk? Has anyone complained about my teaching?"

"No. I've heard nothing but good reports about you in that regard. But given what happened tonight, I'm concerned about what might happen if someone came after you in a more public place."

She stared into her cup. "I don't think that's going to happen—but I can't be certain. I don't even know how they found out I was here."

"Who did you think you were meeting at that school tonight?"

"I know…I was a fool. I should never have done it. A man contacted me, saying he'd heard I was looking for the chalice. He told me he didn't have it, but he might be able to get it. He said I'd have to meet with him first, though. I thought he might be a thief or a fence—but I'm willing to deal with whoever can help me find it. I don't care about legality at this point."

"Dr. Garra—tell me about this chalice. Is it a magical artifact?"

"Yes. A very old one."

"Where did it come from? Did you hear something about it? That it's around here somewhere?"

Garra's gaze came up, flashing anger. "It was stolen, Dr. Stone. From us."

That wasn't what Stone had been expecting to hear. "Us?"

"My clan."

"So there's a whole group of you?"

"In Peru, yes. In the Amazon rainforest. They mostly stay well hidden and don't interact with human society."

"But you do."

"My upbringing was unusual. After my father was killed, my mother fled our clan and fell in love with a human man. He knew what my mother was, but I spent a lot of my childhood among humans. As I got older, I tried to return to the clan, but you know that old saying about 'you can't go home again'? That happened with me. They tried to accept me, and I tried to fit in, but it didn't work. It had been too long. We're still cordial, but I was away so long that living with them isn't really an option for either of us."

"So what did you do?"

"That's where the real Dr. Garra came in. She met me through the others, and we talked a lot because she wanted to learn more about shifter society. As I said, she's a witch and an anthropologist. We became friends when I was a child."

"And where does the chalice figure in? You said it was stolen from your clan?"

"Yes. They've asked my help in recovering it, and I've managed to trace it to somewhere in this area."

"What is it? What's its purpose?"

Her gaze was steady, and sad. "Life, Dr. Stone."

# | CHAPTER TWENTY-THREE

"LIFE? WHAT DO YOU MEAN?" Stone studied Garra, shifting to magical sight. For the first time, her aura seemed troubled—not as if she was lying, but more a deep sadness that mirrored the look in her eyes.

She considered her words carefully, swirling the remains of the coffee in her cup. She waited as the waitress came by to give her a refill and drop off a basket of chips and salsa. "I mean exactly what I said. If you're a mage, I'm sure you're aware that magical power in the world used to be higher than it is now."

"Yes, of course." It had long been speculated among magical scholars that, as the world grew ever more technologically advanced and belief in the supernatural waned, the ambient arcane energy suffusing the Earth had correspondingly decreased in power. It was one of the reasons ancient magic artifacts were so valuable—because it was difficult or even impossible to duplicate them given the current levels of magic, even in areas where multiple ley lines converged. Stone remembered the frightening potency of the set of game pieces he'd dealt with earlier that summer; no doubt there were many other, equally powerful items out there in private collections, or buried in the ruins of long-dead civilizations.

"I'm sure you're also aware that weaker magic in general also means any creatures that need magic to function have been correspondingly weakened."

"Or have disappeared entirely," Stone said soberly. He'd never seen proof of it, but many scholarly mages believed that a number of the Earth-based magical beings immortalized in folklore—vampires, werewolves, faeries, even dragons—had existed at one point, but couldn't remain viable in modern times due to decreased magical energy. Stone didn't know whether he believed that, but he'd met enough strange things and people in his life to consider it possible. The question remained, though: even if such beings and creatures *had* existed, what had become of them? Had they died out, or had the features that made them special simply waned along with the magic, leaving them nothing more than normal humans and animals? As far as Stone knew, no one had more than theories. "What's that got to do with you, though? Obviously if you and your lot still exist, then there's enough magic to sustain you."

"Yes. But..." Her grip on her cup tightened. "We're dying out, Dr. Stone. And that's where the chalice comes in."

"Dying? How?"

"I don't mean we're literally dying. Our kind lives a long time, and nothing's killing us directly. But...we're not replacing ourselves. Not fast enough. Cubs are rare, and many of them die either before they're born or shortly after."

Stone frowned. "Why? Has something changed in your environment?"

"No one knows. It might just be the lack of magical energy catching up with us. It might be nature trying to tell us we don't have a right to exist anymore. But whatever it is—we don't just want to let it happen. Nobody wants to die, Dr. Stone. And nobody wants to watch their children die."

Stone dropped his gaze. "I'm sorry," he murmured. "That's terrible. Is this only happening with your clan—with jaguars—or…I assume there *are* other types of shifters, aren't there?"

"Of course. There are different clans and groups all over the world. Most of them are isolated and reclusive, but they exist. I don't know if they're having the same issues we are, but right now I hope you understand that I'm mostly concerned with what's happening to my own people."

"Of course. But I still don't see—"

"The chalice is a magical artifact," Garra said. "It's been in the possession of our people for countless generations. On its own it has value as an artifact, of course, but its main purpose—the purpose it was created for—is of use only to us."

Stone made a 'go on' gesture.

"When used by females of our kind, it can produce an elixir that increases our fertility—and allows us to produce healthy, strong cubs despite the lessened magical level."

"I…see. And you say it was stolen?"

"Yes. Three months ago." Her features twisted with hatred. "By *your* kind."

"Mages? But why would they—"

"The clan doesn't know why they stole it. They think they were treasure hunters—the sort who seek out magical artifacts for their own collections, or for wealthy patrons. They must have heard about it somehow, and decided to go after it. We're not even certain if they knew its true purpose, but only that it was highly magical and therefore valuable. Several of my people were killed trying to protect it, but they couldn't do it."

"And you've traced it here."

"Yes. My people may live primarily in their true forms— their animal forms—but they're not without resources. Through a combination of mundane and magical means, they tracked it to this area. But it wouldn't be practical for the other clan members to travel to an unfamiliar area. So they came to me."

"Because you've got experience with the human world," Stone said.

"Yes. And because I understand, as no one but one of our own people can, how important it is to get the chalice back. Already our females are having trouble conceiving, and the only two cubs born since then have both died in their first few days." She fixed blazing eyes on Stone, and her voice shook with emotion. "We *need* our property back, Dr. Stone. It's not a toy or a bauble for some rich mage to study, or display in his collection. It's our *lives*."

Her gaze dropped, and she snatched up a chip and plunged it into the salsa bowl. "So there it is. You know my story now. I don't care if you don't believe me—it's the truth. And I won't let you or anyone else get in my way. If you want to tell the University I'm a fake, go ahead. I'll find another way to get the chalice back."

Stone didn't respond right away. Instead he studied her again, across the table. She looked different from what he'd grown used to, in T-shirt and leather jacket instead of her usual stylish, tailored suit. Her hair, normally pulled back into a bun or braid, hung loose around her shoulders now; it would have given her a vulnerable look, except for the steady, resolute way her gaze met his. This, he could see, was a woman who would do whatever was necessary to accomplish her mission. He found it oddly compelling on several levels.

"I believe you," he said softly. "I won't tell anyone about you, as long as you continue to do your job and you don't put anyone at risk. And I'll help you, if you let me."

The resolute expression changed back to suspicion. "Why would you help me? And what can you do? I've been to every junk and antique shop between here and San Francisco, and found nothing. I haven't found many dealers in magical items, but the ones I've found haven't heard of it either. I can tell when people are lying to me—their scent changes. That's how I knew for sure you'd been in my office. No one has seen it. I'm terrified that the thieves might have brought it here so they could ship it off somewhere—to China, maybe, or Russia. Or else—I've heard rumors of other shifter clans who've heard of it. I didn't think they'd be dishonorable enough to steal it from us. The clans—especially the different animal types—don't usually interact, but if they came to us, we could make the elixir available to them as well. But perhaps one of them has grown as desperate as we have."

"I can help you in a number of ways. I'm much more familiar with the magical community around here—and I guarantee I know of at least one collector of artifacts you haven't met yet."

"You do?" She asked quickly, leaning forward. "Who?"

"I won't say. He's a very private man, and he's not in town right now. But I can talk to him for you—ask about the item. Even if he hasn't seen it, he might have heard of it, or be able to track it."

"How do you know he'll tell you the truth? You should bring me along when you talk to him. I will know."

"I'm not so certain you will, to be honest. He is a...unique individual, and very powerful. There's little that happens around here he doesn't know about. But if you want me to chat with him when he returns, you'll have to trust me."

She closed her eyes and let her breath out. "It seems I don't have a choice, do I?" Her gaze rose again, and Stone could see the rage of the jaguar lurking in her golden-brown eyes, and the hint of a feral snarl around her full lips. "All right. I will trust you, Dr. Stone—for now. But if you betray me, I promise, magic or no magic, I will rip your throat out."

He didn't doubt her for a moment.

# | CHAPTER TWENTY-FOUR

STONE STOPPED BY the Chemistry department office after lunch on Monday afternoon, hoping perhaps his conversation with Del Wright might prove more fruitful than his search for Marciella Garra's stolen chalice.

He'd spent most of the weekend doing research: he sent out a few subtle feelers to some magical-artifact dealers he knew, including a handwritten note delivered through the mail slot at Stefan Kolinsky's shop. The black mage was still away, or at least the shop was still closed and the sign was still behind the wards, but perhaps he checked in every now and then. Stone even popped over to London to consult with Eddie Monkton, who promised to check his reference material for any mentions of the chalice. In all of these inquiries, he didn't bring up the existence of the shifters, but merely framed it as an object he might be interested in acquiring.

It had only been three days, two of them on a weekend, so it didn't completely surprise him that nothing had come back yet, but it *was* odd that none of his sources seemed to know anything at all. It was generally difficult to keep the existence of an item that powerful in the area secret for long, even if it involved nothing more than rumors.

Aside from that, Raider had remained echo-free. He'd tried to talk with the cat a couple times over the weekend, but every time he checked Raider's eyes, the blue glow had been nowhere in evidence. He'd finally given it up; if Thaddeus Benchley had anything else to say to him, he could bloody well make an effort.

"Hello, Dr. Stone," the admin—whose name, he'd found out, was Pamela—greeted. "I wondered if you'd come by today."

"Is Dr. Wright here? I've got a bit of time, so I figured I'd drop by and check."

"He is. He's in his office, and I don't think he has any meetings scheduled for a while. Second floor, number 213."

"Brilliant. Thank you."

Room 213's nameplate read *Dr. Delmar Wright, Organic Chemistry.* Several newspaper clippings, chemistry-related cartoons, and pages from published papers adorned the door, along with two photos of a professor in a lab with students, reminiscent of the one of Thaddeus Benchley in Stone's puff-piece clipping. Stone knocked softly.

"Yes, come in," a cheerful, distracted voice came from inside.

Delmar "Del" Wright didn't have curly dark hair any-more—now what little of it remained was gray—but Stone still had no trouble recognizing him as an older version of the man in the photos. "Dr. Wright? I'm Alastair Stone, from the Occult Studies department."

Wright's eyebrows went up. "Occult Studies? That's interesting—I'm not sure I've ever heard of that one."

"I'm not surprised—most people outside the department haven't."

"You haven't come to put a hex on me or anything, have you?" he asked with a chuckle.

"Not today. Do you have a few minutes?"

"Of course, of course. Sit down." He waved Stone to an empty chair and pushed his work aside. "I could use a break, to be honest. I only teach one day a week these days, so things tend to pile up on me when I'm here. What can I do for you?"

Stone studied the man, taking a quick look at his aura. It was a medium gold, with a few darker patches that could indicate the man wasn't entirely well. It might just be age, though—the older people got, the more their auras tended to pick up flaws. "This is going to sound a bit daft, so please bear with me."

"Daft? I'm intrigued. Let's hear it."

"It's about Dr. Thaddeus Benchley."

Wright looked startled. "Dr. Benchley? That's a name I haven't heard in a long time. What about him?"

"Well—as it happens, I've just moved into a house he used to live in. In Encantada."

"Really?" Wright shifted his papers around again, stacking several books on the corner of his desk and closing a spiral-bound notebook. "How do you know that?"

"I found a newspaper clipping inside a book when I first moved in." He gestured in the vague direction of the downstairs department office. "As I mentioned to Pamela downstairs, I'm a bit of a history buff—I actually inherited the house, so I'm looking into some of its previous residents."

"Well…" Wright's brow furrowed. "I'm not sure how much I can help you, Dr. Stone. What did you want to know?"

"You were one of his graduate students, yes? When I researched him in the library, I found an article that included a photo of him with you and some others." He pulled his copy of the article from his briefcase and slid it across the desk.

Wright examined the photo, then slid it back. "That *was* a long time ago. I'd forgotten about that. I don't even remember what he was showing us in that lab anymore."

"Can you tell me about him? What was he like?"

"He was a fine teacher—quite a mentor to me as well. I worked closely with him during my graduate studies."

"So you got on well?"

"Of course. Dr. Benchley got along well with almost everyone. He had quite the sense of humor. He took his work very seriously, of course, but he wasn't above the odd practical joke. Never at anyone's expense, though—except his own."

Stone nodded. "I understand he was active in the anti-war movement."

"I'm not sure 'active' is the right word," Wright said, considering. "He supported it, definitely, and I remember him taking part in a couple of demonstrations on campus. But he wasn't militant about it." He smiled. "He wasn't the type to be militant about anything, honestly. Just a good, decent guy who loved his job and his students."

That information certainly corroborated what little Stone had gotten from Benchley's echo so far. "You knew him around the time he died, didn't you?"

"Yes. I was very sad to hear about his death. By that time, we'd grown to be friends as well as colleagues."

"From what I understand, he actually died in his home—my home, now."

"Why do you—" Wright looked startled again, but then smiled, nodding. "Ah! I see now. You're from the Occult Studies department, and you're asking about a man who passed away in your home." The smile turned sly. "You're not suggesting Dr. Benchley might be *haunting* your house, are you, Dr. Stone?"

Stone chuckled. "Hardly. Just because I teach about ghosts and witches and things that go bump in the night doesn't mean I believe in them. But I must admit, finding out he'd died there is what piqued my interest in finding out more about him."

"Well…I don't know what else I can tell you, honestly. His death was a shock to all of us. He wasn't a young man, but he was in good health for his age, as far as I knew, at least. Heart attack, if I remember correctly. Such a shame. But I suppose none of us can count on tomorrow, can we? At least I knew he lived his life doing what he loved. Can't ask for much more than that."

"No, I suppose we can't." Stone stood and retrieved the clipping. "Thank you, Dr. Wright—I won't take any more of your time. One more thing before I go: are you still in contact with any of the other people in this photo?" He held it out so the man could get another look.

Wright peered at it. "I'm afraid not. I think Shari Milius got married and changed her name, and Colin Frederick passed away recently. The other two—no idea. We all lost touch years ago. I'm sorry, Dr. Stone."

"Quite all right. Thank you again for your help."

# | CHAPTER TWENTY-FIVE

WHEN STONE RETURNED TO HIS OFFICE, he found an envelope waiting on his desk. Fine and cream-colored, it had nothing written on its exterior. However, the red wax seal holding it shut, embossed with a stylized *K*, told him instantly who'd sent it.

"About time, Stefan," he murmured, opening it as he sat down. Inside was a matching card with only two handwritten lines:

> *I will be in my shop tomorrow afternoon.*
> *Please call at your convenience.*

He wondered what Laura must think when a suit-clad courier showed up to deliver the missive—it certainly hadn't been the first time. There was no point in getting frustrated with Stefan Kolinsky and his odd, old-fashioned ways, though; if the man could tell him what he wanted to know, the relatively minor inconvenience was worth it.

Jason and Verity came by for dinner that evening. This time, he'd insisted on picking up takeout on the way home. "No, no," he'd told Verity when he called she'd offered to cook. "I'm not getting into the habit of taking advantage of you."

"You're not taking advantage of me," she protested. "I *like* to cook. Especially in that amazing kitchen of yours. It's not like *you* ever get any use out of it."

"Oi. I made toast the other day…"

"You're hopeless, Doc," she said, her tone laced with fond amusement. "Fine. If you want to feed us Chinese take-out, go for it. But next time I'm cooking."

"Deal."

"So," he said, when the three of them were settled around the big wooden table in the dining room with several steaming cardboard cartons between them, "how was your weekend with Kyla, Verity?"

"It was great." She opened one of the cartons and transferred the contents to a serving dish. "We mostly stayed around her place, but it was fun. Got to hang with some of the Harpies on Saturday night."

"Oh?" Both Stone and Jason shot her sideways looks.

She mock-glared back at them. "Yeah. We went out and caught a guy who'd been mugging old people in the Haight. Tied him up and left him for the cops. Hezzie and I hung around with disregarding spells up until they showed up and took him away. Felt good to get scum like that off the street."

Stone supposed there was no point in bringing it up again that he was uncomfortable with this new aspect of his former apprentice's life. She was just that—his *former* apprentice—and if she wanted to use her magic to play Batwoman with her girlfriend's gang of female vigilantes, that wasn't any of his business. It didn't mean he had to like it, but it did mean he had to keep his mouth shut about it.

Given what he got up to, anything else would have been hypocritical.

Jason, apparently, hadn't come to the same conclusion, judging from the disarray in his aura. He didn't say anything, though, probably in deference to the fact that they were guests in Stone's home. Stone suspected the two of them would get into it at some later date.

Verity had clearly seen the signs, though, because she quickly changed the subject. "Hezzie's teaching me alchemy."

"Indeed?" Stone glanced up from his plate.

"Yeah. She's really good at it—at least as much as she can be at her power level. She's frustrated because she knows a lot, but doesn't have the power or the money to really make it happen the way she wants to. She figures maybe she can teach me to do it better."

"I'll be interested to hear how that goes," Stone said. "I've always been rubbish at alchemy."

"Not surprised," she said with a grin. "I've seen you try to cook. That's all alchemy is, really—magical cooking. Or chemistry experiments. Or maybe a little of both."

"Well, perhaps you can give me some pointers when you get better at it. I might be a bit more motivated to learn alchemy than I am to learn cooking."

"I hope so. When you mess up a cooking recipe you don't dissolve the bones in your hands."

"Obviously you've never seen me attempt a vindaloo. Ah—that reminds me: speaking of chemistry, I had a chat with one of Dr. Benchley's former graduate students today."

"Yeah?" Jason asked. "How'd you find him?"

"He teaches at the University, as it happens. Didn't find out much useful, though."

Raider, almost as if he suspected he was being talked about, jumped onto the empty chair across from Stone and put his paws on the table.

"Sorry, mate—no Chinese food for you," Stone said.

"You sure that's Raider?" Verity asked.

Stone took a closer look, but the blue glow wasn't there. "Nothing but cat." He used magic to gently nudge the confused Raider off the table. "But yes, apparently Dr. Wright and Dr. Benchley were friends, and Wright remembers when he died. Heart attack, he claims. Understandable—people smoked like chimneys back then, and from the look of him I doubt he got a lot of exercise."

"It's weird," Verity mused, spooning more kung pao chicken onto her plate. "It just doesn't make sense that a happy, content guy who died of natural causes in his office would hang around haunting the place after all these years. Does it?"

"It's not unheard of," Stone said. "But it *is* rare."

She returned to eating for several moments, but he noticed she looked troubled, as if she had something on her mind. A quick glance at her aura confirmed it.

"What is it, Verity? I can tell there's something you're not saying."

She swallowed and sighed. "Well…something just occurred to me, but I didn't want to bring it up. It's probably nothing, and I don't want to upset you."

"Upset me? How?"

"Well…" she said again, idly petting Raider, who'd jumped back up on the table. "I was just thinking about someone else who supposedly died of natural causes, but that turned out not to be the case."

Stone tensed. "Desmond."

"Yeah. I'm sorry—like I said, I don't want to upset you. But if Dr. Benchley's echo is hanging around here and it's unusual for them to do that without a reason, maybe he *has* a reason. Maybe he didn't die of a heart attack."

Stone almost dismissed it as absurd—but *was* it? It made sense, and would give Benchley's echo a reason to remain behind, waiting for someone he could communicate with to show up. He glanced at Raider again, shifting to magical sight, but there was still no sign of the blue glow indicating the professor was driving. "Dr. Benchley—this might be an excellent time for you to join us, if there's anything to what Verity's saying."

Raider licked his paw and attempted to stick his nose in one of the empty cartons.

"Why would anybody want to kill an old professor, though?" Jason asked. "Didn't you say his students liked him?"

"Yes—by all accounts, he was a pleasant chap, very popular. Unless…"

"Unless what?" Verity asked. She picked up Raider and set him back on the floor.

"Well…he was active in the anti-war movement. Dr. Wright said he wasn't militant about it, but perhaps someone took exception to his views."

"Enough to kill him, though?" Jason asked.

Stone shrugged. "Who knows? If I could get him to come back and talk to me, perhaps he can shed some light. But until then, your guess is as good as mine. I haven't got the time to look into it in detail."

"Why not?" Verity asked. "By the way, did you ever sneak into Dr. Garra's office and check out her desk?"

"I...Best if I don't answer that," he said with a sideways glance at Jason. "But I *did* find out quite a lot more about her. We had an illuminating conversation on Friday night. I know why she's here now, and why she faked her identity."

"You do?" Verity looked surprised. "Can you tell us?"

"I can tell you some of it. Not everything, because I promised her I wouldn't." Quickly, he caught them up on the meet at the school, the ambush, and some of the details about the chalice she was seeking. He left out anything about Garra being a shifter, and the chalice's specific purpose.

"Holy crap," Jason said. "I gotta say, Al, if there's any kind of weird supernatural shit going around, you sure do manage to find it. So what now? You're gonna help her track down this chalice?"

"That's the plan. Stefan's back from wherever he was off to, so I'm going to have a chat with him tomorrow. If it's in the area, chances are he's either heard of it or can find out where it's gone."

"Well—let me know if I can help. I don't have any other cases yet, so I've got time."

"I thought you'd be *busy*," Verity said. She waggled her eyebrows at him. "You didn't tell the Doc how your date went on Friday."

"That's because he doesn't *care*, V," Jason said, shaking his head. "Unlike *some* people I know, he minds his own business."

"All right, you two," Stone said, and set Raider on the floor again. "Enough squabbling. You'll upset Dr. Benchley."

"At least maybe that way he'll come back and talk to you," Verity said.

Raider remained silent and stalked out of the room.

# | CHAPTER TWENTY-SIX

STONE APPROACHED STEFAN KOLINSKY'S disreputable little East Palo Alto shop with more trepidation than he had in a long time.

He hadn't seen his old associate since before he'd gone to Calanar; as far as Kolinsky knew, he was likewise still a black mage, dependent on power drawn from other people to fuel his magic.

Would Kolinsky notice a change just by looking at him? Ever since he'd nearly died on Calanar, impaled on a crystal spike and caught in the leading edge of a manastorm in the weird, magically deadly wasteland comprising much of that dimension, he'd noticed his aura had changed: instead of its former purple and gold, it now included a third color, a band of silver around the outside. Oddly, though, he was apparently the only one who could see it. So far, none of his magically talented friends and colleagues—Verity, Eddie, Arthur Ward, even Trevor Harrison—had commented on it, despite his making no attempt to hide it. Harrison, well, his motivations were frequently inexplicable, and it was entirely possible he *had* noticed and not said anything about it. But if any of the others had seen anything unusual, Stone had no doubt they would have mentioned it.

Kolinsky, however, was (with the exception of Harrison and Madame Huan, neither of whom were presently available, and the late William Desmond) the most powerful and knowledgeable mage Stone had ever known. Even though they'd known each other for nearly ten years, exchanging favors and bits of useful information to mutual advantage, Stone still didn't feel as if he understood the man much better than he had when they'd first met. Kolinsky raised being secretive and enigmatic to an art form, and held both his knowledge and his possessions close to him while doing his best to ferret out anything he could about others.

Still, Stone couldn't draw out avoiding Kolinsky forever—not if he wanted to continue his association with the man, and that association was far too valuable to let wither. Even if the black mage asked him about the change, that didn't mean he'd have to answer. Not without some fairly hefty *quid pro quo,* anyway.

He pushed open the door, noting the sign was gone now. He wondered if anyone other than him had even seen it. Kolinsky's "shop" was one in name only; you couldn't even see the door past the illusions and wards if you weren't magically talented, and the black mage didn't even make a pretense at maintaining any sort of regular business hours. Madame Huan, at least, kept her junk shop open to the public when she was in the area—not that anyone could ever *find* anything in it, but at least they had the chance. With Kolinsky, if you didn't know he was there and didn't have reason to visit him, you were out of luck.

Stone descended the familiar stairs, opened the door at their foot, and passed through the deserted front part of the shop without stopping. The door leading to the back was open.

Stefan Kolinsky stood at the display case in the middle of the floor. He had his severe black suit coat off and his sleeves rolled up, revealing the intricately-designed tattoos covering his powerful forearms. As Stone entered, he held up one hand without looking away from the carving laid out in front of him on a black cloth. "One moment, Alastair, if you please."

"Of course." Stone hung back and watched as Kolinsky moved his hand over the carving, which was roughly round, a foot in diameter, and etched with concentric circles of tiny, closely-spaced text that Stone couldn't read. Each place Kolinsky's hand passed over glowed momentarily, then faded again as he moved on. He leaned in for a closer look, using magic to turn the carving over.

Stone shifted to magical sight, curious about the object. As he expected, it lit up with arcane energy, each section of tiny carved letters or sigils glowing with a different color. It was a beautiful piece, obviously brimming with power, but he couldn't determine its purpose without more study.

He was about to switch the sight off and wait for Kolinsky to finish when he got a glimpse of the black mage's aura. He tensed, blinking.

*Well.* That's *interesting...*

Kolinsky didn't appear to be masking or dimming his aura, but that wasn't unusual. The man didn't make any apologies for his power level, and his ego eclipsed Stone's—which wasn't an easy feat. The normal dual hues, red and purple, erupted around Kolinsky's body as brightly as they ever had—

—but now there was a third one.

Stone narrowed his eyes, focusing with more care. He had to be mistaken, right? He'd been so obsessed with wondering whether Kolinsky would notice the new third color in his own aura, perhaps he was projecting his fears onto the man himself.

But no…there it was: another narrow band of purple around the outside. This one wasn't the same color as the shade in Kolinsky's original aura; instead, it had the same intense, almost ultraviolet hue Stone had seen in Trevor Harrison. Like the silver in Stone's aura, it was much thinner than the other two colors, but it had a crackling, kinetic quality Stone had never seen before—not even in Harrison or in his own new silver "addition".

"Alastair?"

Stone jerked his head up, dropping magical sight instantly. Had Kolinsky caught him checking? He knew his friend wouldn't consider it rude—mages examined each other's auras all the time—but would no doubt consider that level of scrutiny to be unusual. "Er—yes. Hello, Stefan. How are you?"

"I am well." Kolinsky regarded him through narrowed eyes for a beat, then turned his attention back to the carving on his display table. Using magic, he wrapped it in the black cloth, placed it in a cabinet on the other side of the room, and engaged the lock on the cabinet. Then he returned to his familiar place behind his antique roll-top desk and indicated for Stone to take a seat. "I have not seen you in some time. I trust you were successful in dealing with the matter we discussed during our last meeting."

"Yes. Thank you again—I couldn't have done that without your help. I doubt you care, but a lot of lives were saved."

"I am pleased to hear that."

Stone didn't think it mattered to him one way or the other, nor did he think Kolinsky cared that he knew it. "I stopped by a couple of times, but you were away. Another artifact-gathering trip?"

"Among other things, yes."

When Stone had first met Kolinsky, the man rarely left the Bay Area, but over the past few years, that had changed. These days, it seemed he was away more often than he was home. Stone wondered what had brought about the change in habits, but didn't ask. With Kolinsky, every question was a trade, every bit of information a transaction. Curiosity aside, some were worth more than others. He nodded toward the locked cabinet. "New acquisition?"

"Indeed. One of my associates made me aware of its discovery recently, so of course I was compelled to investigate." He made a note with a fine fountain pen, then looked back up at Stone. "How may I be of assistance, Alastair? I assume this is not a social call."

*So far, so good.* If Kolinsky had examined his aura and discovered the extra bit, he hadn't said anything about it. It was hard to tell with him, since he'd always been good at hiding his use of magical sight. "Yes, as it happens. I have a question for you."

"Yes?"

"I'm looking for an item, and I know there aren't many magical artifacts that come through this area without attracting your attention."

"Indeed. What sort of item?"

"It's a chalice. Made of bronze, with silver highlights and several semi-precious stones set into it." He pulled a folded page from his pocket and spread it out on the desk. "That's a crude sketch, but it gives the basic idea."

Kolinsky studied the sketch. "What makes you think it would have appeared in this area? And how have you heard of its existence?"

Now the dance began. "I'm not at liberty to say how I've heard of its existence, but I found out from the same source who told me it was in the area."

"I see."

"So—do you know anything about it?"

"I do."

Stone tensed. Knowing Kolinsky, it wasn't at all unexpected that he would know, but things didn't usually go this easily for him. "So—can you tell me where it is?"

"Not at present, no."

"Yes, yes," he said with a sigh. "I know—you want something in return, of course. But I need to know how much you know before I can make an offer. If you've got the thing in your back room, that's not the same as if you've heard rumors of its existence."

"I do not have the item in my possession. But I can provide you information you might find useful for tracking its location."

Well, that was something, at least. More than he'd had before, anyway. "Okay. It's a start. Tell you what—a while back, while going through Desmond's library, I found an old book containing some very interesting summoning techniques. Bit dark for me, but likely right up your alley. For now, the offer is to allow you some time with it. If you can actually help me find the item, you can have it." He'd have to be careful: he'd almost offered his standard arrangement of refreshing Kolinsky's wards, which he could do again—probably better than before—now that he was no longer limited to black-magic techniques. But he wasn't ready to share his newfound status with his associate yet.

Kolinsky considered, then inclined his head. "I accept your offer."

"Brilliant. I'll bring the book back next time I go home—is that acceptable?"

"Of course. I have quite enough to occupy my time at present."

Stone leaned forward in his chair. "All right, then: what can you tell me about it?"

"It was offered to me several weeks ago."

"Offered to you? You mean someone wanted to sell it to you?"

"Yes."

"But you didn't accept?"

"I did not."

"Why not? From what I understand, it's a fairly powerful item. I'd think it would have intrigued you, if nothing else."

"It did intrigue me." Kolinsky made a note on his pad, pulled the sheet free, and stowed it in a folder in one his lower desk drawers. "But contrary to what you might believe, I am not indiscriminate in my acquisitions. This one held no connection to my current areas of interest, and the price the seller was asking was somewhat exorbitant, even by my standards. I am certain I could have persuaded him to take less, but I did not attempt to do so."

"Did you examine the item?"

"Briefly, yes. A more thorough examination would have been the next step, should I have been interested."

Stone pondered. "Can you tell me anything about the person who tried to sell it to you?"

"I can. But I will require a bit more from you for that information." He held up a hand as Stone started to protest. "Not possession of the volume you spoke of—not yet, at any rate."

"What, then?"

Kolinsky consulted another small notebook, then slid it back into its cubby and resumed his steady scrutiny of Stone. "If my cursory examination was accurate, the item was not the sort of thing *you* would find interesting, either. So I am curious about why you seek it."

"What did you discover about it?"

"Only that it was a benevolent artifact related to fertility, and possibly has some connection to shapeshifters."

"You know about shapeshifters?" Stone asked, surprised. He supposed he shouldn't have been. Stefan Kolinsky made it his business to know about most things related to magic—this shouldn't be any different.

"They are not a particular area of focus, but I am aware of their existence."

Stone got up, pacing as he considered. "All I can say is that I'm...acting as an agent for someone else who's looking for the chalice. They've tracked it to the Bay Area, and I agreed to help them look for it."

"So you do not seek it for your personal collection?"

"No." He gave a short laugh. "When have you ever known me to be interested in fertility artifacts? If anything, I'd more likely be after the opposite."

"Circumstances change," Kolinsky said mildly.

"Not that much. Anyway—I've told you all I can. Is it enough for you to give me the information about the seller?"

"It is. In fact, I will even give you one more bit of information, free of charge."

"Yes?"

"The seller did not share his name with me, but I am familiar with him, nonetheless. And I am certain he did not obtain the item from its original location himself."

"What does that mean?" Stone dropped back into the chair.

"I strongly suspect that he stole it from someone else. Most likely when it was en route from one location to another."

"Stole it? Why do you think so?"

"He specializes in such things. I have dealt with him previously."

Stone didn't even bother asking whether that meant Kolinsky routinely dealt in stolen goods. He had no doubt that was true—when the black mage set his mind on something he wanted, little could effectively stand in his way. Why *else* would he have an expert magical cat burglar on his payroll? That didn't mean getting tangled up in it was a wise idea, though. "So—do you know who he *did* obtain it from?"

"No. He did not say, and since I was not interested in acquiring the item, I did not ask."

"Right, then. It sounds like my next step is to track him down and find out what he *did* end up doing with it. You don't know where he is, do you?"

Kolinsky regarded him over steepled fingers and waited.

Stone supposed this cat-and-mouse game of trades and bargaining could get old, but on the other hand, Kolinsky had never given him erroneous or inaccurate information. Wasn't that worth a little inconvenience? "What else do you want? The book?"

"No. I cannot provide you with the chalice, so an opportunity to peruse the volume will be sufficient." His hawklike gaze sharpened. "My price is the answer to a single question."

*Uh oh.* "What...sort of question?"

"Your aura has changed. I would like to know why."

Stone blinked, unable to hide his surprise. "You can see that?"

"Of course. Did you expect to conceal it from me? It did not appear you were making any effort to do so."

"I..." Stone paused, considering his next words. Even telling Kolinsky that so far no one else had spotted the change constituted useful information—information that, according to Kolinsky's own rules, was valuable and therefore not to be given away. Instead, he narrowed his eyes and gave the black mage a tight smile. "I could ask you the same question—and I'll probably get about as far with you as you will with me."

Kolinsky tilted his head. "Oh? I am not sure I understand."

"I'm not the only one whose aura has changed."

"I assure you—my aura has not changed."

Stone almost protested that yes, of course it had, but stopped. Kolinsky had never, at least as far as he was aware, purposely lied to him. If the black mage was telling the truth—if his aura *hadn't* changed—that meant something in

Stone *had*, allowing him to see something he couldn't see before. Could it be that—

"Alastair? You look troubled. Is something wrong?"

"No. No, nothing's wrong." He met Kolinsky's gaze head-on. "I'm sorry, Stefan, but that's not something I'm willing to tell you right now. I'll give you *an* answer—it will be truthful, but probably not the one you want. But you have to give me your word that you won't ask me—or anyone else—anything else about it."

It was an audacious response, and he thought Kolinsky would turn him down. So far, there had never been an instance when the black mage had refused him a bit of information due to his unwillingness to meet the required price. Sometimes he'd altered the deal, but never outright denied him. Stone thought it might be because he enjoyed the bargaining as much as he valued the information. This time, however, it seemed as if this might be not be the case.

At last, though, he inclined his head. "Give me your answer, then. You have my word. I admit I am curious, but it is your choice."

"All right, then." Stone stood again, considering his words with care. "Yes, I'm aware my aura has changed. I don't know exactly why. It happened a few weeks ago, during a ritual, and I'm certain I couldn't duplicate it."

That was stretching the truth, but it wasn't a lie. Technically, the entire trip to Calanar had resulted from a ritual, and while he could certainly re-create the process that took him there, he was equally certain he couldn't duplicate the confluence of the crystal spike, the unpredictable magic of the Wastes, and the savage manastorm that had likely led to the change. Or possibly enhanced it, if Madame Huan's observation three years ago had been related.

Kolinsky's obsidian-chip gaze bored into Stone. Clearly, he wasn't satisfied with Stone's answer. "All right," he conceded. "I will do as I promised, and not ask any further questions about this change. I hope you will understand, however, that this promise does not preclude examinations of my own."

Stone gave him a wry smile. "As if I could stop you. And if you work anything out, I'd appreciate it if you'd share it with me. I'm sure we can come to an understanding. So—about the thief…?"

"Yes. He is based in Oakland. He goes by the name 'Jimmy Tanuki,' though I am certain it is a pseudonym."

"And you don't know his real name."

"I know nothing else about him. It is none of my concern. He knows it would not be a wise decision to attempt to cross me or deceive me."

"When was the last time you saw him? You said you dealt with him before—did he try to sell you anything else after the chalice?"

"A couple of months ago. I have not seen him since then."

"And you don't know if he's sold the chalice to someone else?"

"I suspect he probably has—it is in his best interests not to retain possession of items for too long, in case their original owners might come searching for them."

"But you don't know who."

"No. As I said, it is none of my concern. After I chose to pass on the item myself, I put it out of my mind."

"All right. One more question: what does he look like?"

"Observe." Kolinsky swiveled his chair to face the display table where he'd been examining the disc. After a moment, the air began to shimmer, and a few seconds later it formed into an illusionary figure that hovered a few inches above the table's surface.

Stone got up to examine the figure more closely. It was an impressive illusion, three-dimensional, almost like a hologram from a science-fiction movie, and depicted a short, slender, pale-skinned man in his middle thirties. He wore a stylish black leather jacket, black jeans, and a gray turtleneck sweater. As Stone continued to watch, the man's gaze darted back and forth, as if he expected someone to jump him.

The illusion persisted long enough for Stone to study it in detail, then winked out. "Thank you, Stefan. I'll bring the book back soon—you needn't be in a hurry to return it."

"I look forward to seeing it—and wish you luck in your search."

# | CHAPTER TWENTY-SEVEN

STONE STOPPED BY MARCIELLA GARRA'S OFFICE late the next morning. "I've got some information," he told her. "Have you had lunch yet?"

They returned to the little place he'd first taken her. He could sense her tension on the walk over, and she nearly pounced on him as they sat down with their food. "What did you discover?" she demanded. "You didn't find the chalice, did you?"

"Not yet. But I've got a lead." He told her what Kolinsky had given him, without revealing the source of the information.

Her eyes narrowed. "So this...Jimmy Tanuki person didn't steal it from my people?"

"That's what my source says."

"I tend to believe it. From what I understand, the thieves were powerful—some of them magically talented, others strong warriors like those two men who attacked us at the school."

"I don't think Jimmy is either of those—he seems more the sneaky sort. Both I and my source think it's more likely that the original thieves were doing it on the orders of someone else. Jimmy managed to find out about it and stole the chalice while it was en route here."

She gripped the table, eyes flashing. "We need to find him, then. Do you know where he is?"

"Oakland. But that's not a small city, and my contact didn't know—or wouldn't tell me—anything more specific."

"Take me to this contact," she growled. "I will convince him to reveal it."

"No—trust me, that wouldn't be wise. But it just occurred to me—I might have another way."

"Oh?"

"I can't trace Jimmy—or the chalice—magically, since I've never met or encountered them. But it's possible I can do it the old-fashioned way. Let me look into that and get back to you."

"You'd better not be stalling. If I go looking for this Jimmy and find him, it won't go well for him."

Stone made the call as soon as he got back to his office, and his contact returned it within the hour.

"Hey, Stone. Haven't heard from you in a while. How have you been?"

"Thank you for calling me back, Detective. I have a favor to ask."

"What do you need?" Detective Leo Blum of the San Francisco Police Department dropped his volume so Stone could barely hear him. "Please tell me you don't have something else nasty and magical going on."

"I do—but it's more personal this time. No threat to the public, at least not as far as I can tell."

"Great. Well, that's something, at least. What do you need? I don't have a lot of time, but I'll give you what I can."

"I'm looking for a man who goes by Jimmy Tanuki." He described the figure in the illusion Kolinsky had shown him. "From what my sources tell me, he's based in Oakland."

"Okay...I got some contacts in the Oakland PD. Who is this guy? He one of your kind?"

"Possibly. He's a thief, primarily. He steals magical artifacts and sells them to other mages."

"And you think mundane cops are gonna find him before you do?"

"It's possible he steals more than magical items. I know it's a long shot, Detective, but I don't have any way to trace him myself. If need be, I'll come up there with an associate and we'll see what we can find, but I'm hoping you can save us some of that legwork."

Blum sighed. "Okay. I'll do what I can. Don't get your hopes up, though."

He didn't hear anything else for the next three days. Garra stopped by his office each morning to ask about his progress, clearly growing more suspicious and impatient each time. "I can't wait any longer," she said on Friday, closing his office door and leaning menacingly forward over his desk. "The chalice could be anywhere by now. They could have already shipped it overseas, or—"

Stone's mobile phone buzzed in his pocket. "One moment," he said, holding up a hand to stop her. "I know—I get it. Just let me just take this."

The number, to his surprise, was both familiar and timely. "Detective. We were just talking about you."

Garra leaned farther forward, almost as if trying to hear the other side of the conversation.

Stone waved her to a seat, put the phone down, and cast a warning look at her accompanied by a finger to his lips. "You're on speaker, Detective. Have you got anything for us?"

"Yeah, maybe. Sorry it took so long, but you didn't give me much to go on."

"Did you find Jimmy Tanuki?"

"I think so. You're not gonna like what I found, though."

"Why not?" Stone asked, tensing. Garra, who'd sat down, leaned forward again.

"He's dead. Or at least he is if the guy they found is the one you're lookin' for."

Stone and Garra exchanged glances. "Dead? When? How?"

The line crackled as Blum paused. "That's where things get weird, and why I'm thinkin' this *is* the guy you're lookin' for."

"Tell us!" Garra snapped.

"Who's that?"

Stone shot another glare at her. "A friend. She's involved in this too—best if you don't know too much. What did you find?"

Blum's sigh came through even over the tiny speaker. "He was found a couple months ago, inside his residence in the Oakland Hills. A deliveryman called the police when he got the wrong address to drop off a package, and smelled something odd inside the house."

"And—?"

"Well...the guy wasn't just dead. He'd been ripped to pieces. Literally. I got a copy of the report from my friend in the Oakland PD, and the crime-scene photos weren't pretty. They're calling it some kind of bizarre mob or gang hit, but so far they have no leads."

"Ripped to pieces..." Stone said, with another look at Garra. "You mean...like by an animal?"

"Not unless the animal was some kind of super-strong ape."

"What do you mean?"

"There weren't any slashes or bites, but—you know that line in *Star Wars* about Wookiees ripping people's arms off? Yeah, well, I doubt this guy was killed by a Wookiee, but...you do the math."

"I...see."

"Do you know anything about this, Stone?" Blum's tone took on an edge that hadn't been there before.

"About the murder? No. As I told you—if this was Mr. Tanuki, he stole something that my friend here is trying to get back. They didn't find a bronze chalice inside the residence, did they?"

"That's what you're lookin' for? I don't think so, but this report doesn't include a list of everything in the house. The Oakland guys are tryin' to find next of kin, but so far they haven't turned up anything."

"Do they know the victim's real name?"

"Hang on a sec...Yeah, here it is. The house's owner is listed as Ricardo Estevez, down in L.A., and he says he leased it to a guy named Wayne Poole. They had to identify him with dental records—he'd been in there a while when they found him. Not a neighborly guy, apparently, and the houses up there aren't too close together."

"So you think this Wayne Poole was Jimmy Tanuki."

"It's a good guess. Same basic build and description as the guy you told me about—as much as they could tell, anyway. And it sure as hell sounds to me like something supernatural could have killed him."

Stone tapped a rhythm on his desk, thinking. He had an idea—it was a long shot, but he'd dealt with worse before. "Detective, could you give me the address of this house? Is it currently occupied?"

"Stone...what are you planning?"

"Best if I don't tell you. But unless you can get me access to the place officially..."

"Yeah, that's not happenin'. Nobody's livin' there right now, though. They released the scene a while ago, but Estevez is gonna need to have some serious cleanup work done in there before it's habitable again. What are you thinkin' about doin'?"

"Nothing," Stone said. "I'm not thinking about doing anything. But a violent death like that is bound to leave traces behind—traces someone like me might be able to interpret."

Blum let his breath out. "I don't wanna hear it. Just don't tell me. Far as I know, you don't have a damned thing planned. But off the record—if you get caught, don't call me. I won't be able to help you." He read off the address. Then, in an offhand tone, added, "It'd be a shame if the place had a burglar alarm, you know? I can think of about 7,243 reasons why it might..."

Stone made a note. "Don't worry, Detective. I won't say a thing to anyone. Thank you for your help—it's most appreciated."

"Yeah, no problem. Give me a call next time you're up my way and we can have a beer. Good luck. Oh, and Stone?"

"Yes?"

"If you *do* figure out what's behind this, even if you can't say anything about it officially, I'd appreciate a heads-up. I really want to know we don't have to start worrying about a rash of giant apes dismembering people in their homes."

"That's a promise, Detective. I don't think it will be a problem, though. As I said, I think this one is...smaller in scope." He glanced at Garra, who nodded. "I think it was related directly to this item, and won't be repeated."

"I sure as hell hope you're right."

Stone broke the connection and hadn't even gotten the phone back in his pocket before Garra said, "I want to go with you."

"Yes, I assumed that."

"Tonight."

"Dr. Garra—"

"Tonight," she repeated firmly. "I heard the address too—if you don't go, I'll go myself. I can't wait any longer."

He didn't like it—he would have preferred a bit more time to prepare—but he also knew she wasn't kidding. "Fine. We'll go tonight. I haven't had a chance to fix your amulet yet, though."

"That won't stop me. When can we leave?"

"I've got a meeting this afternoon—I can't get out before six. But best if we go under cover of darkness anyway."

Frustration crossed her face—clearly she wanted to get up and leave immediately—but she sighed. "Fine." Her eyes narrowed. "I'm guessing if you went through my desk and set a private investigator on me, you know where I live."

"Guilty, yes."

"Pick me up there, then. If you don't show up by seven, I'm going without you."

# | CHAPTER TWENTY-EIGHT

TRAFFIC WAS HEAVY heading up toward Oakland on a Friday evening, even by the standards of a typical Bay Area rush hour. Garra sat in the passenger seat, the impatience sluicing off her like waves obvious even without a glance at her aura.

In an effort to get her mind off the gridlock, Stone said, "Tell me more about this chalice. How does it work?"

"I don't know exactly." She glared out the front window as if trying to will the cars in front of them out of the way. "As I said, it's been among my people for many years. When a female wishes to conceive, she seeks out the elders of the clan and they make it available to her."

"Is there some sort of alchemy involved? Where does the elixir come from? The chalice doesn't produce it, does it?" If it did, that would indeed be wondrous: even magic couldn't produce something permanent from nothing.

"No. I don't know if the liquid used matters. From what I understand, water is sufficient. The chalice's magic transforms the liquid into the elixir we need."

"So you've never used it yourself? Forgive me if that's an inappropriate question."

"No, I haven't. I wish to have a cub someday, but I don't know if it will be possible, since I don't participate in the clan enough to find a mate." She gave a tight smile. "Before you ask, yes, it's possible for us to reproduce with humans, but most of us find it distasteful."

"I thought you said your mother married a human man."

"I said *most* of us, not all of us. And I didn't say we don't have sex with humans—just that it's thankfully difficult to conceive children with them." She gave a bitter chuckle. "Most humans find our kind sexually attractive—both the males and the females."

"You're very—er—open about that sort of thing."

"Why wouldn't I be? Sex is a part of life. You humans are far too psychologically unhealthy about things like sex and nudity."

"Yes. Er. I suppose we are." Stone fell silent, focusing on driving. That particular subject was not one he wanted to think too much about tonight.

"What about you, Dr. Stone? Do you have a mate? Children?"

"No. Well—it's a bit complicated."

This time, her chuckle was more amused than bitter. "See what I mean? How can it be complicated? You either do or you don't."

"I don't have any children. At least not that I'm aware of."

"But you have a mate? I didn't see anyone with you at Dr. Hubbard's party…"

Stone shot a sharp glance her way; she was watching him, her eyes glittering in the darkness. "No. Not…*per se.*"

He thought about Verity. He'd considered asking her to come along tonight—though he didn't expect to encounter any opposition, it was always good having more magical punch on his side. Before he had a chance to call her, though, she'd called him to let him know she'd be spending the night in San Francisco again. Scuro, the magical tattoo artist she did freelance healing for, was doing a big job tonight and he wanted her help, so she figured she could spend some more time with Kyla afterward. She'd asked if he minded.

*No, of course not*, he'd answered. What else could he have said?

"I'm sorry," Garra said. "Am I prying?"

"No," he said without looking at her. "Not prying."

She didn't speak for a while, as he picked his way across to the fast lane and increased their speed a little. "If you don't mind my saying so," she said at last, "you seem troubled about something. Is there any way I can help you? I know it might not be the most professional of offers, but I think perhaps after last Friday night we've moved a bit beyond a purely professional association." She looked around, glaring at the cars crawling along near them. "And it might take our minds off this glacial traffic."

He almost shook his head and brushed her off. He barely knew her, after all, and half the time she seemed more inclined to bite his head off than to offer a sympathetic ear. He focused on the soft music playing on the stereo, and spoke before he had a chance to second-guess himself. "I haven't got a mate, but I do have...someone."

"Someone?"

"I told you—it's complicated. She was my apprentice, and over the past few months, things have…changed between us."

"You've become romantically involved?" The words were clinical, but her voice was gentle.

He made a small snort. "I wouldn't call it romantic, exactly."

"Sexual, then."

"Yes," he said, wincing. "Mostly that's how it's worked out."

"There's nothing wrong with that." Still, her tone was gentle. "Not if you both want it. Do you?"

He flashed her a look. "Oh, yes. Definitely. No doubt about that."

"So, then, I don't see—"

"I love her," he said softly. He shook his head, letting his breath out, and gripped the steering wheel tighter. "I shouldn't be discussing this."

"Why not?" A long pause, and then: "May I make a guess about you, Dr. Stone?"

"If you like."

"I'm guessing you don't have many people you discuss such things with."

"You'd be correct. I shouldn't be discussing them with *you*. But—" He trailed off and sighed again. Part of him, the part that observed and usually kept him from such things, couldn't believe he was saying them. Not while sober, any-way. But Garra (*or whoever the hell she is*, he reminded himself) had the unusual and appealing qualities of being both detached and encouraging.

"Does she love *you*?"

"I…think she does. But there are…complicating factors."

Garra waited for him to continue. As impatient as she seemed with the traffic around them, her presence was otherwise calm.

Stone tightened his grip again. What was he doing? This wasn't any of Garra's concern. "She's…considerably younger than I am."

"I don't—"

"She's also bisexual, and prefers women."

"Ah…" She gave an understanding nod. "I think I'm beginning to see."

"I doubt it." His laugh was bitter. "Honestly, I'd be amazed if you were."

"She loves you, but she won't commit fully to you because she doesn't want to give up her relationships with women."

He threw her a quick, surprised glance. "That's…most of it, yes. But that's her right. I would never ask her to change who she is, for me or anyone else. That's where she is this weekend—with a woman up in San Francisco."

Garra settled back in her seat and watched the traffic. "Do you resent her doing that?"

"Seeing this woman? No. It's true," he added hastily. "I know that sounds odd, but it is."

"I believe you. Remember, even in this form I can read scents far better than a human. I can tell when you're lying to me."

A useful skill—sort of like olfactory aura reading. "I want her to be happy, Dr. Garra. Isn't that what love is supposed to be?"

"It is, although it's been my experience that most humans don't treat it that way." She stretched her long legs. "You want her to be happy, but you want more than she's offering."

He thought about it, still wondering why he was doing this. "That's…sort of right. Not quite, though."

She waited.

"I—" The traffic around them had begun to pick up speed, and he nudged the BMW up accordingly. "She's made it clear she has no issues with my pursuing other relationships. As far as I can tell—and I'm better at reading auras than she is at hiding hers—she's not lying. She's genuinely fine with my seeing other people. It's not just because *she's* seeing someone else."

She chuckled. "That sounds like the kind of relationship most human males would consider a gift from the gods, Dr. Stone."

"Yes, well—I'm not most human males."

"No…I can see that. Wait a moment," she added, twisting in her seat to face him. "I think I understand now. She encourages you to pursue other relationships, but you're finding it difficult because you consider it disloyal to her."

Stone swiped a hand through his hair, wishing he'd never allowed her to draw him into this conversation. "Dr. Garra—"

"That's it, isn't it?"

He gave up, gripping the wheel again and increasing the car's speed. "Yes. That's it." He sighed. "I've always had a bit of a reputation in that regard—I've been with a lot of women over the years. They usually don't last long, though. They move on when they get a glimpse of the odd bits in my life. But always one at a time."

She gave a sage nod. "So you feel if you see anyone else now, you're cheating on her—but she won't make the same commitment to you."

"I don't *expect* her to make the same commitment to me. That's what's so buggered up about the whole thing. It's just like you said—most men would consider this the ideal situation. So why can't I get past it?" He made a bitter snort. "Anyway, enough about this. I don't know why I told you any of it in the first place. You're my colleague, not my therapist."

"A bit more than your colleague at this point." She paused. "I haven't thanked you for helping me, Dr. Stone. I genuinely appreciate it. If it hadn't been for you, I wouldn't have gotten this far. I don't think I was prepared for what I was getting myself into."

"Not a problem." It was a relief to get back to familiar, comfortable ground again. "This is intriguing to me as well. I hope I can help you. If we find any traces at Jimmy Tanuki's place, with any luck I can use them to track down the people who have the chalice."

"Or I can. Let's hope that between the two of us we can find something we can use."

Once the rush-hour congestion thinned and Stone could open the BMW up, they made good time to Oakland. Jimmy Tanuki's house was in the Oakland Hills, the eastern part of the city marked by more upscale properties. As Garra navigated, Stone drove up a winding, tree-lined road, slowing to peer at addresses on mailboxes. The homes up here were spaced widely, as were the street lights; he hoped that meant no one would notice their presence and call the police.

"There it is," Garra said, pointing.

The single-story house was small by neighborhood standards, situated at the top of a rise. It was visible from the road but surrounded by trees. The neat yard sported an equally neat NO TRESPASSING sign. Stone drove past it and parked a short distance away. When they got out, Garra retrieved a dark backpack from the rear seat and slung it over one shoulder.

Stone cast a disregarding spell over the car, then another one over himself and Garra. "Let's go."

They left the road and slipped into the trees so they'd be less visible to anyone driving past. "Keep that nose of yours going," Stone said, switching to magical sight. "If you notice anything at all, let me know." At the moment, he didn't spot anything beyond the pale-green auras of the trees and the occasional brighter one of a small animal or bird moving through them.

Garra paused as they reached the edge of the trees near the house. She raised her head and sniffed at the air, looking around. "I don't notice anyone out here—but my senses aren't as strong in this form."

"I don't see anyone either. I don't think we need to worry about it—I doubt anyone's watching the house at this point. Come on—let's get inside. I can keep us invisible long enough to get through the door, which I hope will foil any motion-sensor lights."

"I wouldn't have thought of that…"

"I wouldn't either, until recently. My law-enforcement friends have been rubbing off on me. Speaking of—" He pulled two pairs of latex gloves from his pocket and handed her one. "Put these on, so we don't leave any fingerprints."

He held the invisibility spell as they crossed the yard, noting as he drew closer that the NO TRESPASSING sign he'd spotted from the road also read, BY ORDER OF OAKLAND POLICE DEPARTMENT. As he'd hoped, no floodlights came on—either there weren't any or the spell fooled them. The heavy wooden front door had a sign posted on it, likewise warning would-be intruders that entering the house was a violation of the law.

Stone exchanged glances with Garra, then popped the lock on the door and the two of them slipped inside.

Immediately, a strident electronic beep began to sound.

"Burglar alarm," Stone said. "Quickly—let's find it. Code is seven-two-four-three."

It didn't take long to find the panel, just down the hall. It glowed in the darkness, flashing its red light and emitting its harsh, rhythmic warning. Stone entered the code and pressed the *Disarm* button, and it immediately shut up. "Thank you, Detective," he murmured.

Behind him, Garra let her breath out.

"Are you all right?"

"Something definitely happened in here, and not too long ago."

"What do you smell?"

"Death. Blood. Maybe fear—hard to tell unless I shift."

"Don't do that yet—I don't think it's a good idea to have the police find jaguar prints in here. We should look around. Whatever it is, it's probably not hard to find."

"Let me go first—I can see in the darkness better than you can."

It didn't take long to find the scene of Jimmy Tanuki's murder. After checking the living room, the kitchen, and what looked like an office, Garra stopped in front of a closed door at the end of a wide, tiled hallway. "I think it's in there. That's where the scent is strongest."

"Can you tell if anything's alive in there?"

"Not with all the interference. I don't think so, though."

Stone motioned her to flatten herself against the hallway wall. He did likewise across from her, then used magic to open the door, shield ready in case anything leaped out or took a shot at them.

Nothing did. The door opened on a large room, mostly empty except for a king-size bed on the far wall, two dressers—one low and squat, the other tall and narrow—and an overstuffed chair.

Even with only the light from the moon shining in through a skylight, it was obvious something had gone wrong here. The bed, nothing more than a mattress and box spring now, was splattered with dark stains. More stains covered the carpet around it, and still more spattered the walls. Whatever had happened in here, it had been violent. A faint hint of decomposition hung in the air.

"My friend the private investigator once told me that when these sorts of things happen, the police don't handle the cleanup," Stone said, his voice low as he scanned the room. "Best they do once they've finished their investigation is give the victims the numbers of crime-scene cleanup companies. It's down to them to handle it."

"That's horrible." Garra spoke softly too. "I can't imagine how it must be for a family to have to deal with such a thing in the midst of their grief."

"Works to our advantage this time, though. The owner's down in Los Angeles—he probably hasn't got 'round to arranging anything yet." He began pacing the room. "I'm going to take a look around magically. You do whatever you do—with luck, one of us will get something."

He shifted to magical sight. The first thing that showed up was Garra's bright green aura, lighting up the darkness as she too circled the room. He concentrated a moment to mute it, then focused on the bloodstains, starting with the bed.

The murder had occurred long enough ago that he knew he wouldn't get solid readings—even something this horrific faded eventually. But even two months' time hadn't taken all the edges off the psychic energy, especially with his heightened senses.

He got more impressions than specific information. He narrowed his eyes, frowning. The largest and strongest feeling he got was terror, which was completely expected. Jimmy Tanuki would have been frightened even if this had been a "normal" murder, but most home invasion victims didn't expect to have their limbs torn off.

What Stone didn't expect, though, was how much confusion he was picking up. If he was reading the scene correctly, Jimmy Tanuki hadn't only been afraid of his attackers—he'd had no idea why they were there, or their nature had been so unusual that they'd caught him off guard.

"Are you getting anything, Dr. Garra?" he murmured, without shifting back to normal sight.

"It smells…odd," she said, sounding distracted. "I can't get a better idea unless I shift, though. The blood smell is too strong—it's masking something else."

Stone glanced toward the window, covered by blinds. It was a risk—what if the police came back here and found big-cat prints on the carpet?—but they had to find out as much as they could about what had occurred here. "Do it," he said. "But let me levitate you so you don't leave prints."

She gave him an odd look, but then nodded. "All right." She slipped off her jacket and began unbuttoning her blouse.

"What are you doing?" Stone asked, startled.

"I like this outfit. I don't want to destroy it." She flashed him a wicked smile as she tossed the blouse on the bed. "I thought we'd already discussed this whole nudity-taboo thing."

Stone pointedly stared at the blood-spatter pattern on the far wall as Garra continued shucking clothing. He *didn't* have a problem with nudity—under the right conditions. However, having his partner in crime—his very attractive partner in crime—blithely stripping off in the middle of a gore-strewn murder scene was a bit beyond his usual experience.

"All right, ready."

He turned back. She stood in the middle of the floor, stark naked, her clothes in a neat pile on the bed. "Er…"

She laughed. "You're so funny—I thought you had a reputation as quite a ladies' man. You act like you've never seen a naked woman before. Now, are you going to levitate me so I can do this? It's chilly in here."

"Right. Sorry." Focusing on her face and trying to concentrate on anything but her trim, athletic curves, he raised his hand and visualized the spell pattern. Immediately she rose off the ground.

"Hold on tight," she said, still clearly amused. "I'll get heavier in a moment."

The transformation was fascinating to watch—so much so that he stopped thinking about her human body as he watched it shift and morph, growing larger, more muscular, changing from her normal deep tan to shimmering, furred black. In only a few seconds, a full-grown black jaguar floated a few feet away from him.

Her yellow-gold eyes fixed on him. She made a sound like a rumbling growl, followed by a snuffled chuff that could only be continued amusement. Once she seemed satisfied he wasn't going to drop her, she began looking around the room, sniffing the air.

Tentatively, Stone moved her closer to the bed. When she didn't object, he slowly continued steering her around the entire room, paying particular attention to the bloodstained areas.

After a few minutes, she twisted around toward him and gave a very human-like nod. Then she was morphing again, back to her nude human form. She let her breath out.

"Did you find anything?" Stone demanded. By now, he was so interested in the results of her scan that he barely paid attention to her state of undress.

"It's still hard to get much—the stench of blood and fear is very strong, even now. But I do know one thing for sure."

"What's that?"

She retrieved her clothes and began dressing. "The same people who attacked me at the school in San Jose killed this man."

"That was the same impression I got. The psychic residue is quite muddy—I suspect they probably tortured him to reveal the chalice's location—but their auras were unusual enough that they were hard to miss." He tilted his head at her. "Do you know who they are, or more importantly, *why* their auras were odd?"

"Odd in what way?" Garra pulled on her slacks and zipped them.

"When I saw them at the school, they had a sort of…green overlay."

"And that's unusual?"

"Yes, especially for mundanes. I've never seen anything like it before."

She shook her head, looking contemplative. "I don't know who they were. I think one of them attacked me near Dr. Hubbard's party, but I didn't recognize his scent from before that."

"So you don't think they're the ones who stole the chalice originally?"

"It's possible, but—" She stopped in the act of buttoning her blouse, her body going still and her gaze darting around.

"What is it?"

She held up a hand. "I'm not sure. I thought I noticed a—"

Something crashed through the window, shattering the glass. Before either of them could react, it rolled across the floor and began emitting a cloud of gray, acrid smoke.

# | CHAPTER TWENTY-NINE

"**B**LOODY HELL!" Stone snapped. "Come on!"

Garra was already moving toward the door. Even in her human form, she moved faster than Stone did, and she reached it before him. "Hurry!" she urged, coughing.

Another crash sounded toward the front of the house as another window broke, and then yet another on the other side. More smoke billowed toward them.

Stone crouched, moving as fast as he could, already coughing too. The smoke tasted odd—sweet and cloying. "Fire?"

"I don't smell fire," she said. "Just smoke."

By now, the hallway leading to the front door was a solid wall of smoke. They weren't getting out that way. "Can you shift and break through one of the windows?" Stone called. He flung shut one of the doors where the smoke was coming through, but it didn't help much. He doubled over, coughing harder. Unfortunately, his shield was meant for physical attacks and magic—it wouldn't be as effective at blocking the smoke.

Garra poked her head through another door. "This room's still clear. Come on." She ducked inside and motioned for him to follow.

As soon as he was inside the room, she slammed the door shut. Stone looked around—they stood in a small bedroom, its only furnishings a twin bed and an armoire. He paused a moment, catching his breath.

Garra ran to the window. "I'll shift, and—" She paused. "No!"

"What is it?"

"I can't shift!" She whirled on him in sudden terror. "Alastair, I can't shift!"

"Bugger! It must be something in the smoke! Back up."

She got out of the way. "What are you going to do?"

Stone didn't answer. Instead, he used magic to wrench the armoire free of the wall and lift it. Good—it was made of solid wood, not one of those cheap pressboard things. Struggling not to drop it—the magic came easily, but the smoke had gotten into his lungs and he couldn't stop coughing—he flung it toward the window. It broke through with a satisfying crash. "Come on—let's—"

Another missile sailed through the now-open window and landed on the floor near them, pumping out more gray smoke.

"Damn!" Stone yelled. "Stay close to me so I can shield us."

She hurried over to him. He summoned a shield around them both and levitated them outside. He'd been correct. As soon as they cleared the window, shots *spang*ed off the shield, sending up little pink flares in its nearly invisible wall.

"Can you tell where they are?" he demanded. His eyes streamed from the acrid smoke, making it hard to see anything. He switched to magical sight, but it didn't help. Too much smoke choked the air.

She coughed again. "Let me down. I need to go after them!"

"I thought you said—"

"Let me *down!*" she yelled.

He lowered both of them to the ground, still keeping the shield up. Another round from the unseen shooter hit it from the left side, then one from the right. Two shooters. The same two men they'd fought before? They were strong—were they strong enough to rip a man limb from limb? And more importantly: how did they know Stone and Garra were here? Had they been watching the house?

Garra morphed again, her clothes ripping as the black jaguar shimmered into being. She roared something at Stone and then took off into the forest.

Stone, panting, staggered away from the house. His head felt woozy, his chest tight and throbbing from all the coughing, and he could barely see anything through slitted, watering eyes. At least nobody was shooting at him at the moment. But where had Garra gone?

He moved farther from the house, then levitated up onto the roof for a better view. Fortunately the smoke seemed confined to the house—the attack had probably been designed not to injure them, but to flush them out so the snipers could take them down. *They're still out there,* he reminded himself.

The air was better up here. He was still coughing, but less now. He swiped an impatient hand across his eyes and forced himself to open them more fully, shifting to magical sight. He had to find Garra and help her. Why couldn't she shift inside the house? Had it been the smoke, or had momentary panic overcome her?

At first he didn't see anything, his vision still blurring from the smoke's effects. He swung his gaze left and right, scanning the trees, trying to spot anything against the pale green of their auras. From far off in the distance, he thought he heard a siren. Had someone seen the smoke or heard the gunshots and called the police? They needed to get out of here! But where the hell was Garra?

Something burst through the trees to his right. From the roof, he spotted a low, dark form running with a hitching, jerky gait.

*Bloody hell, she's injured!* Keeping the shield up in case someone was following her, he dropped to the ground as fast as the levitation spell would allow and sprinted toward her.

She was still in cat form, hunched and panting. A wet, bloody streak tore along her right flank, and another, smaller splash stained her left shoulder.

"Dr. Garra!" He crouched next to her, still looking for approaching attackers. "Are they still following you?"

She didn't reply. Her head lay on her massive paws, her sides heaving with her fast, shallow breaths.

"If you can understand me, the authorities are coming. We've got to get out of here! Are they gone?"

Her head tilted up. The golden-brown gaze settled on him, her skin rippled, and then she was human again. She panted harder, wincing, her breath catching. The bloody wound was now on the side of her leg, running up her hip. Teeth gritted, she clutched at Stone. "I'll be—all right—" she got out between breaths. "I...heal fast..."

He hoped so, because there wasn't much he could do for her here. "Are they gone?"

"Took...off...in car..." She indicated the blood on her shoulder. "This isn't...mine. I managed to...slash one of them."

Well, that was something. "Come on—let's get you out of here." He bent to gather her in his arms, all business now, no thought to the fact that she was naked or that she was getting blood on his coat. All he wanted to do was get both of them away from this scene before the police showed up.

She gripped his arm. "Get...clothes...Backpack..."

Even though all he wanted to do was run as fast as he could with her to the car, he knew she was right. If the cops found her ripped clothes or her backpack with spares, it wouldn't end well—either if they traced them to her, or if they ended up on a wild-goose chase looking for an injured woman who didn't exist. "Hang on..." he panted, still coughing a little from the aftereffects of the smoke. He laid her back down and hurried off to collect her shredded outfit and the pack.

By the time he got back less than a minute later, she'd already risen to her feet. She looked unsteady, but much better than she had. "Let's go," she said, her voice still shaky. "I'll get dressed when we're away."

Stone slipped out of his coat, put it over her shoulders, and summoned a disregarding spell around them, but he nonetheless hoped the cops didn't show up until they'd gotten away. The spell relied on making its subjects unobtrusive, helping them blend in to the surroundings so no one would notice them. It worked better if the spell's subject was already unobtrusive, and a man running next to a naked woman in a long black coat didn't qualify under any definition of the word.

This time, they caught a break. Stone glanced over his shoulder when they reached the car, and didn't see the telltale red and blue lights of an approaching police cruiser. "Are you all right?" he asked Garra, who'd paused to lean against the BMW's side.

"I will be." She was still panting, but not as much as before.

He opened the sedan's back door. When she scrambled in, he shoved her backpack in after her. "You'll have more room back there. Stay down—I'll get us out of here."

He didn't speak again until they'd gotten out of Oakland and were heading south down the freeway. He drove the speed limit, staying in the middle lane and doing his best not to draw any attention to them, glancing occasionally in the rearview mirror to make sure Garra was all right in the back seat. He heard her moving around back there as she unzipped the pack and pulled on a T-shirt and yoga pants. "Everything all right?" he asked at last.

"Much better, yes." She did sound better: her voice no longer hitched and she wasn't panting. She tossed his coat over the passenger seat. "Are you all right?"

"Fine." His chest still hurt and his throat was still dry and scratchy from all the coughing, but the woozy-headed sensation had departed as soon as he got some fresh air. "Did you see who did that? You said they drove off?"

"I tried to catch them, but I wasn't moving as quickly as usual—especially after one of them shot me. I got one shot at one of them, but they took off before I could catch up." She sounded annoyed with herself.

"Were they the same ones as before?"

"One of them was. The other was different. Same type, though: large, muscular, very fast."

Stone pondered that. Someone—whoever was trying to prevent them from reclaiming the chalice—was getting hold of some pretty formidable henchmen. Was there some kind of employment agency for supernaturally powerful brutes out there? He'd never seen anything like the men who'd attacked them before. The closest were Lane and Hugo, who'd worked for Elias Richter, but Hugo was dead and these two, while far too strong and fast to be normal humans, hadn't been immune to magic. There was also the matter of the strange green band in their auras. "Well, for now, let's get the hell away from here, and then we can discuss our next steps." He drove for a while more, then remembered something. "You said you couldn't shift inside the house. Was that because those smoke bombs caught you by surprise? Does fright prevent you from shifting?"

"No." Now she sounded sober. "Usually my first response to a threat *is* to shift—I'd rather face it in my jaguar form, if possible. This time, I *couldn't* shift. Something stopped me."

"And that's never happened to you before?"

"No. It was terrifying." In the rearview mirror, she shuddered. "The thought of being stuck in this form is…"

"Hmm. So if you couldn't shift, it had to be the smoke, somehow."

She leaned forward, gripping the back of the passenger seat. "How can that be? How can smoke prevent me from using my abilities?"

Stone shrugged. "Those men have supernatural backing—I'd stake my magic on it. Your chalice uses alchemy. Perhaps the mage who stole it came up with a way to neutralize your powers. He—or she—has got to know you lot will be trying to track the chalice, so it's not out of the question to believe they might have ways of shutting down shifters. That might be how they got it in the first place."

"I didn't think of that..." she mused. "It makes sense. It's still terrifying, though."

"We'll deal with it. Clearly whatever it is, it doesn't stop magic." He glanced in the mirror again. "Are you all sorted back there? Healed up?"

"Yes. The wound was just a graze, but even if it had been a solid hit, I could heal it. We regenerate quickly. The only problem would have been blood loss—that takes longer." Her grip tightened on the seat. "I just wish I could have caught at least one of them!"

"Yes, well, clearly they didn't want to be caught, and they were ready for you. We just need to do some thinking."

They crossed the Dumbarton Bridge and made it back to Palo Alto without incident, though Stone found it harder than he thought to keep to the speed limit. He pulled the car up in front of her apartment building in Menlo Park and waited while she gathered her things.

"Would you like to come up?" she asked as she got out. "We can have a cup of coffee while we discuss what to do next."

He almost said no, but then glanced around, half-expecting that the two men had followed them. She'd clearly proven she could take care of herself as well as he could, but if they knew where she lived, they might be lying in wait. "I think I'll take you up on that, thanks."

Her apartment was on the second floor in a small, up-scale complex. Stone followed her up the stairs, magical sight active, but didn't see any lurking auras. Garra didn't seem concerned, though, and no doubt she'd have caught an intruder's scent. She opened the door, flipped on the light, and tossed her small pack on a chair. "Give me a few minutes," she said. "I'll get that coffee going. Make yourself comfortable."

Stone didn't feel comfortable, still on edge about the at-tack and wondering how the assailants had managed to track them to Oakland. He paced the room, frequently checking the window to make sure no green-tinged auras were approaching them.

Garra's apartment was small, elegant, and she'd clearly rented it furnished. She'd added next to no personal touches to the areas Stone could see, which didn't surprise him—now that he knew why she was here, he likewise knew once she'd found the chalice she'd be returning to Peru. She'd never meant to remain at the University, which was why, despite her excellent job performance and popularity with the stu-dents, she'd never seemed terribly concerned about the results of her probationary period.

His disappointment at the thought of her leaving sur-prised him. Obviously she couldn't stay—she couldn't go on pretending to be someone she wasn't indefinitely. Someone would catch on eventually, especially if they decided to make her an offer for full-time employment after this quarter. And even if she had been who she claimed to be, she didn't have the academic credentials to hold the position. There was no way Stone could think of to make this work, which was irrelevant anyway since all she cared about was getting the chalice back and restoring it to her people.

To his embarrassment, his thoughts returned to the way she'd looked in Jimmy Tanuki's bedroom, standing there naked with no shame or self-consciousness. She was attractive, no doubt about it.

"Here we are," Garra called. "How do you take your coffee?"

"Black, thanks."

She appeared on the other side of the breakfast bar, holding up a bottle of Kraken rum. "I was going to put a little…extra something in mine, to take the edge off the evening. Shall I put some in yours too?"

"That would be brilliant."

She dosed both cups, then brought one to him and took a seat at the other end of the small sofa. "Do you think they'll come after me here?"

Stone glanced at the window again. "To be honest, I'm concerned they might."

"I can handle them if they do."

He didn't answer.

"You don't think I can?" Her eyes narrowed, and a bit of the big cat showed in her expression.

"I do—hell, I saw how well you handled yourself against them before. But those smoke bombs of theirs trouble me. If they can prevent you from shifting—"

"They didn't prevent it for long," she reminded him. "As soon as I got out of the cloud, the effect faded."

He looked into his coffee cup, then took a sip. She'd put quite a generous shot of rum in it, and it felt good going down. He wished he could just have the rum and skip the coffee, but he still had to drive home.

*Damn,* the little voice in his head said. *Too bad she won't ask you to stay.*

*Stop that,* he ordered it, tightening the grip on his cup. To take his mind off her sitting there so close to him, he said, "Perhaps you should stay somewhere else for a few days. Somewhere they don't know about."

"You think they know where I live?"

"I found out. I don't think it's too difficult for someone who has magic."

She gave him a sly, amused smile. "Where do you propose? Your place?"

He jerked his head up, startled. "No. No, of course not. Well—actually yes, but not the way you think."

"What does that mean?"

"I've recently moved into a new place, but I haven't given up the lease on my old one yet. It's a furnished townhouse near downtown Palo Alto. You could stay there. I already took the wards down, but I can put basic protective ones up quickly. You should be safe there."

She didn't answer for a while. "I hate to give them what they want," she said at last. "If I show fear, they'll know it."

"It's not fear. It's prudence. If they find you—if they kill you—you won't be able to find the chalice and bring it back to your people." He leaned forward and met her gaze. "Don't you owe it to them to take all possible precautions?"

She thought about it, looking away. "I suppose you have a point. I'll give it some thought and let you know." She picked up the bottle and added more rum to her coffee, then held it toward him in invitation.

He should have declined, but he didn't. He watched as she poured more into his cup, then lowered it. She was still watching him with that half-amused, half-intense expression, and once again he couldn't help picturing her as she'd stood in Jimmy Tanuki's bedroom.

She tilted her head. "You know…you don't have to leave. You could stay a while." She held up the Kraken bottle and leaned in closer to him. "I don't know about you, but after what happened tonight, I could finish this off, with or without coffee. Want to help?"

He blinked, startled. Had his thoughts caused him to misread her signals? She'd never shown any of that kind of interest in him before. His heartbeat quickened. "I—"

She smiled. "Just a thought…But…you can't deny you want to stay. You can't hide that kind of thing from me."

He drew a deep breath and shifted to magical sight. There was her familiar green aura, blazing as bright as ever—but now it was overlaid with unmistakable red flashes. "Dr. Garra—"

"You know that's not my real name," she said. Her voice was lower, with a hint of the jaguar's rumbling growl.

"I know…"

"I won't tell you my true name—that's only for my clan. But when I left them, I adopted another name: Viajera. It means 'traveler' or 'wanderer'." She chuckled. "Marciella and I both thought it was amusing that her last name, 'Garra,' means 'claw' in our language, given her interest in our people. An appropriate name for one of us, don't you think?"

"Very much so…" he murmured, leaning closer. "But…I shouldn't…"

"Because of your apprentice?"

"Yes. I…" He shifted, drawing back a little again. *Get up and leave now, before you do something you'll regret.*

She took his hand and squeezed it. "You said she didn't mind. That she encouraged it. Did you mean that? Did she? I know you can tell."

And he *could* tell. Verity hadn't learned to hide her aura from him yet, and he knew she truly *didn't* mind. How could she? She was in San Francisco tonight with Kyla. It wasn't as if he were cheating on her.

She leaned closer. "It's up to you, Alastair. But I can see you want me…can you deny it?"

"No…" he whispered. "No…I can't deny it."

"We both nearly died tonight. I don't want to be alone. Do you?"

He didn't. He thought about what would happen if he left: he'd go home to his cavernous, under-furnished house, with only Raider for company—and that was only if Dr. Benchley didn't decide to hijack the cat for another appearance.

"No," he said again. "I don't." He reached out, pulled her into his arms, and kissed her.

She came to him readily, her strong, lithe arms tightening around him, her lips meeting his. She tasted like coffee and rum and something primal.

# | CHAPTER THIRTY

R AIDER WAS WAITING FOR HIM at the door when he arrived home late the following morning. It was absurd, but the cat's wide green eyes seemed accusing. Either that, or Stone was projecting his current state of mind.

"Sorry, sorry," he told Raider. He tossed his overcoat on a nearby chair, then headed to the kitchen to check on the cat's food and water bowls.

After refreshing them, he paused by the sink, gripping the counter and gazing out into the wild backyard. *Really must see to having someone over to take care of that,* he thought idly. *Need to find a housekeeper, too.* This place was far too big to handle on his own, even if he wanted to. He'd only gotten away with it in the townhouse because it had been small and hadn't required much attention to keep it at acceptable levels of tidiness. This place would be overrun with dust in weeks if he didn't do something about it.

*Yes, because you really want to think about* dust, the little voice in his head said. It sounded unusually snarky today.

Thinking about dust was easier than thinking about last night, though.

The trouble was, he couldn't *stop* thinking about last night.

He'd never experienced anything like that before. Garra—*Viajera,* he reminded himself—had responded to him with a level of white-hot passion that hadn't let up through most of the night. He'd never been with a woman who matched—and most likely exceeded—his strength, and when combined with her insatiable hunger and her aggressive technique, he felt like he'd gone two rounds with some kind of amorous superwoman. Two very *pleasurable* rounds, but still. Her feline side came through in the scratches on his back, the way she'd clamped her teeth, gentle but insistent, into his shoulder , the way her cord-strong arms pulled him tight against her. She'd driven him to the kind of performance he'd be afraid to try on another woman, for fear of hurting her. If anything, he was a bit concerned she might hurt *him.* And all the while the red flashes danced around her green aura, mingling with those in his. Neither of them had gotten much sleep.

He pushed off the counter with a loud sigh, pausing to scratch Raider's ears before trudging out of the kitchen toward the stairs. He'd taken a quick shower this morning at Garra's place, but his clothes still smelled like the cloying gray smoke from the house, and that reminded him of what had happened in Oakland. He'd have to come up with some way to track those men before they came after Garra—or him—again. And he'd also need to get to fixing Garra's illusion amulet, so if she had to shift again she could cover herself when she—

As he mounted the stairs, his mind once again spun off images of the exquisitely nude Garra, this time standing behind his car back in San Jose…

His mobile phone buzzed in his pocket.

He snatched it out gratefully, driving back the disloyal thoughts as he glanced at the number. *Gerry Hook,* the screen read.

Why was Hook calling him—

*Oh, bloody hell, I forgot.* "Hello, Gerry."

"Hey, Stone. I didn't wake you up, did I?"

Stone glanced at his watch: after eleven. Even he didn't normally sleep this late. "No…bugger, I know what you're calling about. We've got a thing tonight, don't we?"

"A thing" was a performance by The Cardinal Sin, the band Stone had joined a few months back. Composed of four Stanford professors from various departments, the Sin played classic, hard-rock covers a few times a year at faculty functions and parties, along with occasional private gigs at local bars. Tonight's performance was to be at a place on Castro in Mountain View. A friend of Hook's knew the owner, and they were being paid in food, drink, and a small fee none of them cared about. Stone, who played lead guitar, had known about it for a couple of weeks and even put it on his calendar, but the business with Garra, the chalice, and Raider's ghostly hitchhiker had driven it from his mind.

"We do," Hook said. "Guess it's a good thing I called to remind you. Maybe we need to start scheduling practices more often, yeah?"

"No…no, it's fine. It did slip my mind, but I'll be there, don't you worry."

"Great. It's just two short sets, so we should be done by ten. Show up at eight-thirty so we can set up, okay?"

"Got it. Thanks for calling, Gerry."

He put the phone back in his pocket as he reached the top of the stairs. Well—at least he had something to do tonight, to take his mind off his night with Garra. As he passed the open door to his study, he glanced at the black Stratocaster on its stand next to his desk, where he kept it so he could noodle melodies while trying to work out problems. He reminded himself he'd planned to pick up a better one, but he hadn't been back to England in the meantime.

His thoughts strayed to Verity, and an uncomfortable surge of guilt ran through him. *Stop it,* he told himself, annoyed. He had no reason to feel guilty about what happened. *She* certainly wouldn't want him to feel guilty. She'd probably be glad—possibly even relieved—about what he'd done. As much as he knew she cared for him, and auras didn't lie, he hadn't missed her uneasiness whenever she thought he was taking things too seriously.

Would he tell her? He didn't know yet. He supposed he'd have to play it by ear. He wondered if she'd be at the show tonight. She knew about it, but hell, *he'd* nearly forgotten about it and he was in the band! If she decided to spend the rest of the day up in San Francisco with Kyla, he probably wouldn't see her until at least Monday.

Ah, well. Shower first, a change of clothes, and then he'd spend the remainder of the afternoon sorting out Garra's amulet. He'd need to get back to helping her track down the chalice, but that could wait until tomorrow.

# CHAPTER THIRTY-ONE

STONE GOT TO THE BAR a little after eight. Gerry Hook wasn't there yet, but Radha Unger, the lead singer, was already in the back, halfway through setting up Hook's drum kit. She waved as he approached. "Gerry had to take a call so I'm helping him set up. Want to give me a hand?"

"Sure." He set his pint glass of Guinness down on the edge of the stage and leaped up. "How have you been, Radha? Haven't seen you in a while." He found the bass pedal and crouched to attach it to the drum.

"Not bad. Busy. Prisha is starting her sophomore year, and Ajay just started junior high, so I haven't had much time to rest lately. What about you?"

Stone smiled ruefully as he thought about the events of the last couple of weeks. "Busy too. Bit of an understatement, actually."

"Ah, right—you've moved into that fancy new house, haven't you? Well, at least you've finally got someone else to help you out in your department. How is she working out?"

His thoughts turned to last night. "Fine. The students quite like her."

Gerry Hook came out from the back hallway as more customers began trickling in. "You made it, Stone." He grinned at Radha. "He almost forgot. I had to remind him this morning. He's turning into a real prima donna, this one is."

"Set up your own bloody drums," Stone muttered, amused. He jumped down from the stage, took a drink from his pint, and retrieved the Strat from where he'd left it on the end of the bar. As he removed it from its bag, hooked it up to the bar's amplifier system, and began tuning it, he caught himself glancing over the small crowd. He didn't see Verity anywhere among them. Would she show up? She hadn't missed a performance yet, and every time the two of them had staged a "performance" of their own after the show, either at her place or his.

After last night, it was probably best if she didn't attend this one, though. He'd already decided today, while working on Garra's magical amulet, that he would tell Verity about what had happened. She made no secret of her relationship with Kyla, after all—honesty was definitely the best approach on both sides. And besides, he didn't have a "relationship" with Garra. Nor, he'd realized to some surprise when he'd awakened next to her that morning, did he want one. It had been an enjoyable night for both of them; he didn't regret it, and he didn't think she did either, but last night had been more the product of adrenaline, passion, and shared peril than anything deeper.

He finished his Guinness and went to the bar for another. Jake Cohen, the group's bassist, and Radha waited there, looking over the area.

"You ready?" Cohen asked. "Not a bad crowd tonight. I think word's getting around that we don't suck. So let's not suck, okay?"

"Got it." He nodded toward the Strat. "Note to self: set the 'don't suck' switch."

"Better get right on that," Radha said. "We're up. Let's do this."

Stone took a quick drink from the new pint, then set it on the edge of the stage near the bar and leaped up. He slipped the guitar's strap over his head and took another glance at the crowd. Still no Verity. No Garra, either, but he had no reason to expect she'd be there. She didn't even know about The Cardinal Sin, as far as he was aware. He certainly hadn't told her—and in any case, she had far more important things to do than come watch one of her colleagues play in a bar band. *Forget about them,* he told himself as Hook banged his sticks together to set the starting tempo, and then they were off into their first number.

As always, Stone forgot about everything else as he played. He still felt a little embarrassed when he thought about it, but jamming with the Sin brought him a rush of excitement that not much else—aside from magic and good sex—could match. Who'd have thought, less than a week shy of his fortieth birthday, that he'd be on a stage playing the hard-driving music he loved for an appreciative crowd? That was the kind of thing you did when you were twenty—that he *had* done when he was twenty. Every once in a while, he couldn't help wondering what his father would think of him if he were alive now. *He'd probably approve of the magic,* he thought with a wry grin as the crowd applauded. *But the band? Not so much.*

The songs they played weren't musically rigorous—mostly rock covers from the Sixties through the Nineties—so he let his gaze roam over the crowd as he played. Maybe forty or fifty people, which was good-sized for one of their performances. This one was a public show, not a party for some professor or family member, so most of these people were either here because they wanted to see the band or else they were friends of friends. Stone shifted to magical sight, watching the dancing, rainbow-hued auras blend and crest against each other. Some of the group pressed close to the stage, writhing along with the music, clapping their hands to the beat. A thrill went through him as he played a riff and they responded.

He was about to shift back when he spotted a familiar, emerald-green aura near the back of the room by the door.

Verity was here after all?

He tightened his focus and the aura resolved itself. It *was* Verity. He recognized the figure standing next to her too, its bright blue aura as sharp as her own. Jason. They'd both come out to see him play.

They pushed their way forward as the band finished its first set and the others adjourned to the bar for a quick refresher. "Doc!" Verity called with a big grin. "You guys sounded great as always."

Stone headed to the edge of the stage where he'd left his pint, then jumped down. "I thought you'd forgotten about the show."

"Yeah, right, like I'd forget." She flashed him a significant look, then cut her gaze toward Jason. "Besides, Jase wanted to see you play."

Jason clapped him on the arm. "You sounded awesome, man," he said. "I had no idea you guys were that good."

"We do all right." Stone swiped his damp hair off his forehead and took a long pull from the pint. "It's just a short show tonight—you should come see one of the longer ones."

"Definitely. Wouldn't miss it."

From slightly behind him, Verity rolled her eyes at Stone.

He got the message—there would be no post-show festivities tonight—but that was all right. He'd never tell them, but it felt good to have them here, taking time away from their busy lives to come hear him play.

"Listen," he said, still breathing a bit hard from the exertion. "We should be done a bit after ten—do you two want to have a drink or something after?"

"Yeah, that'd be great," Verity said. Her expression clearly suggested she had other things on her mind, but she was being a good sport about it. She hooked 'devil horns' with one hand and waggled them. "Go get 'em, Doc. Rock on."

Jason raised his beer in salute, and the two of them moved off, back into the crowd.

Stone grabbed one more long drink—the Guinness tasted a little flat, he observed idly, making a mental note to pick up a fresh one after the set—and joined the rest of the band on stage. They'd do four or five more numbers, and then he, Verity, and Jason could go someplace where he could catch them up on the latest developments in the Garra situation. Or most of them, anyway.

They launched into the second set with a vigorous version of *Highway to Hell*. Stone backed up Radha, who belted out the song in her bluesy, throaty voice, her grin matching his. People tended to underestimate her: nobody expected the prim, slender Indian woman to have the growly pipes of a rock star, and Stone knew she enjoyed setting them straight.

It was one of the things he liked most about the band: none of them were what they seemed. Okay, so the other three used it as a welcome escape from the staid life of academia and he was a mage who battled horrific extradimensional threats, but hey, who was keeping score?

He wiped his arm across his brow again. Damn, it was getting warm in here—must be all the extra people packing the small space. It was good they only had a few more songs to do, otherwise he'd need to take a break for a cold drink. He eyed his half-full glass on the edge of the stage; maybe he could grab it between songs. Even flat, it would take the edge off the heat.

A sudden, sharp pain lanced through his midsection, causing him to jerk his hand and miss a chord. Jake Cohen glanced at him in question, but he waved him off. It was probably a muscle pull from last night—sometimes those took a while to show up. Either that, or the turkey sandwich he'd picked up on the way over was disagreeing with him. He focused his attention, getting back into the groove with the rest of the band. Across the crowd, he met Verity's gaze and shrugged.

This song seemed to be going on forever! Sweat ran down from his forehead, getting in his eyes, and more soaked through his black T-shirt. What was going on? Why didn't they turn up the bloody AC in here?

When the pain hit again, it nearly doubled him over. It felt as if someone had plunged a spear into his stomach. He clamped his teeth together as his hand slipped and hit all the strings at once, sending a discordant clamor shrieking from the amps.

What was going on?

Terror sluiced through him as yet another jolt of pain ripped across his body, followed by a sudden, shuddering chill. Heart pounding, he heard an uproar around him as if it were coming from somewhere far away. Somehow he was on his knees, but he didn't remember how he got there. His hands slipped off the guitar, letting it dangle on its strap.

"Somebody get a doctor!" a woman yelled—or at least he thought that was what he'd heard. The words sounded muddy and indistinct: *Sumuddy ge' 'okker!* The music behind him hesitated and stopped, and then hands were clutching at him as he pitched forward off the stage.

*Never did a stage dive before,* he thought, just before Verity's terrified face appeared in front of him.

He didn't quite pass out as the hands lowered him gently down and laid him on his back on the floor. His thoughts raced, making only occasional sense of the stimuli around him: someone yelling *call 911*, the smell of beer, the sea of feet and faces around him, a melting ice cube lying next to him, another searing pain slicing through his gut, his heart hammering hard. He tried to focus, to shift to magical senses, to find a friendly face among the swirl. He tasted blood, bright and coppery in the back of his throat.

"Everybody get back!" a familiar, authoritative voice called, rising above the cacophony. Jason—it had to be. The swirling faces receded.

A cold hand settled over his forehead, and another familiar face swam back into view. "Doc…Alastair…it's okay…It's me…" Verity. "You're gonna be okay." Her eyes were wide with fear, though. "The ambulance is coming…" She leaned in close and dropped her volume. "I'm gonna see what I can do in the meantime."

"V…Verity…" he whispered, then winced and clenched his eyes and jaw as yet another pain hit. He clutched feebly at his abdomen, which now felt like it was on fire. What was going on? His thoughts wouldn't stay on track, but a quick one surfaced before the pain drove it off again: *there's no way a turkey sandwich could have done this.* But what could—

And then, a moment of clarity.

The beer.

He clutched at Verity's arm, his vision blurring so hard he couldn't get a grip on her. "Verity…" he whispered.

"Shh…Doc…let me concentrate…"

His flailing hand touched her arm and he clamped hard, trying to pull her down before she got away again. All around them, Jason was using his cop's booming voice to drive the crowd back, to give them space. "Verity…the beer…the…the glass…"

He could tell she'd been ready to shush him again, but then her slim arm went rigid under his grip. "Oh my God…" she whispered. Then, louder: "Jason!"

And then the pain surged anew, and during the instant before he finally passed out, he was sure an unseen blade had sliced him in half.

# | CHAPTER THIRTY-TWO

THE FIRST THING STONE SAW when he awoke was Verity, seated in a chair next to him. He blinked until his vision cleared, raising a hand to his head. An IV tube snaked from the back of his hand.

Verity started from her light doze, the open book in her lap tumbling to the floor. "Doc?"

He closed his eyes a moment, then opened them. He lay in a hospital bed, clad in a blue-dotted gown and covered with a light blanket. Next to him, several beeping machines went about their business in the background. He settled his gaze on her. "Verity..." His voice barely had any volume behind it.

She clutched his hand with a gentle grip, avoiding the IV. "Oh, God, I'm so glad to see you awake. How do you feel?"

He pondered that, trying to remember how he'd gotten here. All he could recall were swirling faces, a knifing pain in his gut, and chaos. His other hand scrabbled at his midsection as a sudden terror rose: *had* something sliced him in two? But no, his lower half was still where it belonged beneath the blanket, and his stomach didn't hurt anymore. "Tired..." he rasped. He looked around him again; clearly he was in a hospital, but it didn't look like a standard patient room. "How...long?"

Her grasp on his hand tightened. "Two days. It's Monday now, about seven at night."

"Two...*days?*" He thought he'd misheard her. That couldn't be right. "Verity—what—"

"Shh..." She put a cold cloth on his head. "Just be calm. You're going to be okay. Jason's coming in a little while. We've been taking turns sitting with you, and I've been going by your place to feed Raider."

Something in her tone troubled him—something she wasn't saying. He turned his hand over and closed his fingers around her wrist, amazed at how weak his grip was. "Tell me...what happened," he ordered.

She glanced over her shoulder, as if expecting a doctor or nurse to be coming in, then turned back to meet his gaze. "You almost died," she said softly, tears glittering in the corners of her eyes.

"What?" He tensed. "How could—"

"I don't know. We haven't been able to figure it out yet." She leaned in even closer and dropped her voice to a whisper. "Do you remember the beer glass?"

He searched his memory, trying to sort out the discordant images and sensations from the bar. "I remember it...tasted odd. Not bad. Just...flat."

"I'm really glad you said something before you passed out. Jason was able to get it in the chaos. I poured the rest of it in a bottle I had in my bag, and we took the glass and the bottle away." Her expression sobered even more. "Doc—I looked at it with magical sight. There was magic around that beer."

Stone couldn't hold a thought. They darted around inside his brain like pinballs, making it difficult to pin them down. "Magic—in the beer?"

"I haven't had a chance to analyze it yet. I'm gonna take it to Hezzie—she's better at it than I am. But I'm guessing somebody put something alchemical in your Guinness when you weren't watching it."

He struggled to remember—everything after he started feeling strange was a blur, but he did remember leaving his glass on the corner of the stage and not paying much attention to it during the set. Quite a few people had pressed up close, and the lights had been dim; any of them could have slipped something into it. But why would anyone have done that? As far as he knew, nobody wanted him dead. At least not immediately.

Unless…

He gripped her arm again, frustrated at his lack of strength. "Verity…where's my mobile?"

"Uh…in your jeans pocket, I think. They took all your stuff and locked it up for you."

"I need it."

"What's wrong? You can use mine if—" She reached for her bag.

"No…no…I don't have the number memorized." He struggled to sit up.

"Doc, please. Lie down. I'll find somebody and get your phone back, but it's probably not charged up after all this time. Who do you want to call?"

"Dr. Garra."

She blinked. "Why?"

"She might be in danger. Verity—please."

"Okay. Okay." She got up. "But Doc, you gotta stay down. I'm not kidding—you nearly died. If I hadn't gotten to you when I did—" She patted his shoulder. "Hang on. I'll be back."

Stone lay back against the pillows and stared up at the ceiling. Two *days* he'd been out. If he could believe Verity—and she wasn't prone to exaggeration about such things—he'd come closer to dying than he had since…well, since he'd been impaled on a crystal spike on another dimension two months ago. But this time it hadn't been anything so fantastical, but merely some arcane poison someone had slipped into his pint at an overpriced hipster bar in Mountain View.

He looked around, noticing his surroundings for the first time. He wasn't in a normal room: this place had walls on either side and the back, but no windows, and only a closed curtain blocked the front. Beyond it, he could hear the sounds of doctors and nurses moving around, calling to each other. Was he in intensive care? "Bloody hell…" he whispered.

The curtain moved, and a tall nurse clad in blue scrubs slipped in. "Ah, you're awake," he said, smiling. "I'm just here to draw some blood. I'm really glad to see you looking better tonight." He moved next to Stone and began wrapping a rubber cord around his upper arm.

"Wait—wait a moment, please."

"Just let me finish this. The doctor will be in soon. Hold still, and it'll only take a second."

Stone winced as the nurse tightened the cord around his arm and pressed the needle in. "Nurse—please. Can you tell me what's happened to me?"

"You'll need to talk to the doctor," he said. "We called her as soon as you showed signs of waking up." He fluffed the pillow. "Is there anything else you need?"

"Just…information." Even the brief conversation tired him.

"You'll get that soon enough, Dr. Stone, I promise. Now, don't hesitate to press the call button if you need anything." He finished his blood draw and departed with the vial as the curtain parted again to admit Verity.

"They won't let me have your phone, or any of the rest of your stuff," she said, looking annoyed. "You'll have to authorize it before they will."

Stone let his breath out in frustration. If someone had come after him, they'd probably come after Garra too. She could be dead now. But he didn't think he could even get out of bed at the moment, let alone go after her. "All right," he said, shaking his head. "It's too late to call the University—no one will be in the office."

"Why are you so worried about her?" She pulled up her chair and sat next to him.

"It's a long story. I haven't told you everything about her. But I think I know who tried to kill me—in a general sense, at least—and I think they might be after her as well."

"Who?"

"Did you say Jason was coming?"

"Yeah—I called him, and he should be here any minute. Why?"

"I need you two to go to her place." He gave her the address. "See if she's there. If she is, tell her about what happened, and that she's probably in danger. Let her into my old place downtown—she can stay there. You might need to tinker with the wards a bit to let her through—she's not entirely vanilla human." He closed his eyes, then met her gaze. "And be *careful*. If they're watching the place, they're dangerous."

Her expression sharpened. "Who are *they*?"

"Magically enhanced men. Very strong, very fast. Though I didn't spot any of them in the crowd that night, so there might be others involved. Please, Verity—go check on her. Get her settled, then come back here."

"Okay, Doc. Okay. We'll do it. But you have to promise me you'll stay here."

"I don't think I'll be going anywhere just yet."

"Okay. We'll be back as soon as we can."

As she got up to leave, Stone reached out to her again. "Verity—"

"Yes?"

"Thank you. It sounds like you saved my life. Again."

She flashed a faint, tired smile. "Not the ending I was hoping for that night, but hey—I do what I can."

She'd only been gone for a few minutes when the curtain opened once more and another woman came in. This one wore a white lab coat and a stethoscope around her neck. "Hello, Dr. Stone. I'm glad to see you awake. I'm Dr. Zhang."

"Pleasure. So...how am I? The nurse wouldn't tell me anything."

Dr. Zhang didn't sit, but instead stood at the foot of the bed. "I'd like to ask you some questions, if I may."

"I'll answer yours if you'll answer mine."

"Fair enough. Your friends say that you became ill while at a bar in Mountain View."

"Right. Some of my colleagues and I have a band—we were performing there."

"Do you remember anything about what happened? How did you feel?"

"You mean when things started to go bad? Hot, weak—mostly my stomach hurt like someone had jammed a knife in there."

Her expression changed, and her tone took on a careful edge. "Dr. Stone—do you know anyone who wishes you harm?"

*How long have you got?* he thought wryly. "Er—no, I don't think so."

"And…there's no reason why you might wish to…harm yourself?"

"What?" He struggled up to a sitting position, glaring at her. "Dr. Zhang, that's absurd. Harm *myself?* What are you trying to get at?"

She sighed and glanced at his chart. "We don't have any explanation for what happened, Dr. Stone—or rather, for *how* it could have happened. We found significant evidence that you ingested something highly caustic." She shook her head. "Frankly, everyone I've consulted with is amazed it didn't kill you instantly. But I'm also baffled at how you could have swallowed it at all."

"Why do you say that?"

"This substance—it would have had a highly distinctive and unpleasant flavor and odor. Enough that it would have been immediately noticeable when you tried to drink it. Were you perhaps suffering from a cold, or other difficulty smelling or tasting?"

"No. Nothing like that. Believe me, Doctor—I didn't notice anything except that my pint tasted a little flat. It certainly didn't taste of—what—industrial drain cleaner or something?"

"We're still trying to figure out exactly what it was—it's nothing we've ever seen before. I've sent a sample out to be analyzed, but it hasn't come back yet. We were hoping you might be able to help us."

"Sorry. As I said, I didn't notice anything out of the ordinary." He pushed himself up a bit more in the bed, once again grateful Verity had been there. If she hadn't, it sounded like whatever he swallowed would have killed him in minutes. "So—how am I now?"

He didn't miss the troubled look passing across her face as she consulted the chart again. Finally, she looked up with a sigh. "Lucky, Dr. Stone. That's all I can say with certainty at the moment."

"Lucky? You mean that I survived?"

"That, too. But it's more than that. You shouldn't even be awake, let alone having a conversation with me. But yet, here you are. How do you feel?"

He shrugged. "Tired, mostly."

"Any pain?"

"No—I figured you had me dosed up on the good drugs, though."

"We do. But even at the dosage you're currently on, you should be experiencing some discomfort."

"No discomfort, aside from my standard dislike of hospitals in general."

She regarded him a moment in silence, then shook her head. "We've got you scheduled for another scan soon to check on how things are progressing. But there's one other thing that's confused everyone."

"What's that?"

"As I said, all the evidence suggests you drank something extremely caustic—but yet we found no damage to your mouth, throat, or esophagus. Which should be impossible."

He narrowed his eyes. "So I somehow managed to drink something that nasty, but it didn't take effect until after I swallowed it?"

"Strange as it may sound, that's what the tests show. If I didn't know better, I'd say the only way it could have happened that way is if the substance was injected directly into your stomach."

*Or else it was combined with some alchemical concoction to mask it on the way down,* he thought. That must have been what the magic had been for—that, and to obscure the taste and odor of whatever they'd poisoned him with. Whoever had done this wanted to make good and sure their nasty little mixture killed him. Once again, he thanked whatever gods who looked after him that Verity and her healing magic had been there.

He ran a hand through his tangled hair. "I don't know what to tell you, Doctor. I definitely don't feel *good* at present—I'm not ready to leap up and run any marathons or anything—but I certainly don't feel like half my gut's been dissolved with acid, either."

She made a note on the chart. "All right, Dr. Stone. Get some rest. I'll talk to you again tomorrow, after the scan results come back. And…when you're feeling up to it, the police would like to come by and ask you a few questions."

Brilliant. The last thing he wanted was to get the police involved, especially since there was no way they could help. "Later, please. I *am* getting tired."

This time, it wasn't even a lie.

# CHAPTER THIRTY-THREE

VERITY DIDN'T SHOW UP until late the following morning, and this time she had Jason with her. By that point, Stone had been moved out of the ICU and into a private room.

"Hey, Al," Jason called as they came in. "How are you feeling?"

Stone didn't miss both his and Verity's worried expressions. "Still like I got hit by a truck. But better than last night." He tilted the bed up to a seated position. "Did you find Dr. Garra? Is she settled in?"

Verity shook her head, frowning. "She wasn't home when we got there. I even used magic to sneak inside and look around, but I didn't find any sign of foul play. No blood, no traces of magic. Everything looked fine."

"Bugger. That's not good."

"It's not?" Jason asked. "Maybe she was just out for the night. You said she was hot—maybe she had a date."

"I doubt it. She's too focused on her mission to be out carrying on with someone." Stone thought once again about their night together, but that had been different. He pushed himself up more. "Bloody hell, I've got to get out of here. She could be anywhere. I've got to find her."

Verity looked alarmed. "Doc, you can't go yet. You nearly—"

"Yes, yes, I know. I nearly died. But I *didn't* die—thanks to you. I'm not at my best yet, but I'll be all right. They did some kind of scan on me last night, and they're utterly stumped, since they didn't find any sign of damage."

"Wait." Her eyes narrowed. "You say they found *nothing?*"

"That's what the doctor said when she came in this morning. I could see from her aura that they're all completely baffled about what's going on. I suggested that perhaps the initial examination might have been in error, but I don't think they're buying it. Now they're all looking at me like I'm some sort of medical anomaly."

Verity glanced at Jason, then back at Stone. "Doc—I don't get it either."

"What do you mean?"

"I healed you, yeah—at the scene before the ambulance showed up, and then again a couple times when I was sitting with you. But I couldn't fix all of it. You were messed up big-time. I don't think the doctors' tests were mistaken." She scooted her chair forward. "I haven't had a chance to show that sample to Hezzie yet, but I looked at it again last night. There's definitely something alchemical in there."

"I'm not surprised. Last night, the doctor told me I swallowed something that was essentially industrial-strength drain cleaner. I didn't notice it, and it didn't hurt going down. I'm thinking the alchemy was to cover up whatever it was until it got where it needed to go."

"Fuck, Al," Jason said, fists clenching. "Somebody really wants you dead. Don't you think it's time to fill us in on the rest of what's going on? What's this got to do with Dr. Garra?"

"Wait," Verity interrupted, holding up a hand. "That's important too, yeah, but I still want to know how he's doing this well. It doesn't make sense. I'm good, but I'm not *that* good."

Stone shrugged. "No idea. Maybe you *are* that good. You've been growing steadily as a healer for a long time now." He waved her off. "At any rate, I haven't got time to worry about it. I'm just going to thank both you and the doctors for whatever you did, but I need to find Dr. Garra. You don't happen to have my mobile charger, do you?"

Verity dug in her bag and handed it over. "We stopped by your place this morning to feed Raider and drop your car off."

Stone had already convinced one of the nurses to return his phone. He glanced at the door, then used magic to plug in the charger and hit the button for Garra's number.

It rang three times and went to voicemail.

"Damn," he muttered. "She's not answering."

"People don't answer their phones all the time, Al," Jason reminded him. "She might be busy."

"She's probably gone off looking for them on her own. If—" When Stone broke the connection, he spotted his own voicemail icon with a tiny *4* next to it. All the numbers were different; he recognized Gerry Hook's and two from different people in the department office. The remaining one was Garra. He selected that one and listened.

"*Alastair? It's me—Viajera. Please call me back as soon as you can. I think I found a lead on the chalice and I want to investigate it as soon as possible.*"

The message's timestamp was Sunday afternoon.

"Damn!" He clenched his fist around the phone. "She *has* gone off somewhere. Hold on—" This time he hit the button for the department office. When Laura answered, he said, "Laura? Stone."

"Dr. Stone?" She sounded dumbfounded. "My God. We heard you were in the hospital!"

He glanced at the small collection of get-well cards on the table next to his bed. "I still am, at the moment. But listen, Laura—I need to ask you something."

She still clearly hadn't gotten past the shock of hearing his voice. "How—are you?" she asked, careful and breathless. "They said it was serious…that you—you—"

"—almost died. Yes. But it wasn't as serious as they thought initially. Not feeling great, but I'll be fine. But I need to talk to Dr. Garra. Is she in today?"

Laura paused. "Dr. Garra?"

He cast a look of frustration at Jason and Verity, who were watching him closely. "Yes, Laura. Dr. Garra. Is she there?"

"No, Dr. Stone. She wasn't in the office yesterday. She didn't call in, and I couldn't reach her all day. We're assuming she had some kind of emergency she had to attend to."

*Damn.* Stone glanced at his watch, which he'd also convinced the nurse to return. Nine-thirty a.m. He tightened his grip on the phone. "And she hasn't been in yet today?"

"Well, she doesn't usually come in this early. Do you…think something's wrong?"

"Not sure yet. Thank you, Laura. I don't know when I'll be back—figure I'll be out until the end of the week. I'll let you know if that changes."

"I—All right. I'll let the others know. Are they letting you have visitors yet?"

He glanced at Jason and Verity again. "Er—let's hold off on that, shall we? I might be out of here soon. Thanks, Laura. Talk to you later." He hung up before she could reply and flung the phone down on the bed. "Bugger!"

"What's going on?" Jason asked.

"Garra's disappeared. She left me a message that she was on to something Sunday afternoon, and she wasn't at work yesterday, with no call to the office."

"Don't you think you should tell us what's going on?" Verity asked. "Everything, I mean."

"Yes. Definitely. But first I need to get the hell out of here."

"Are you sure that's—" Jason began.

"I don't *care*." Stone located the call button and pressed it. "They can't keep me here against my will. And their own tests show I'm fine. I've got to get started looking for her. Can you two wait for me out front? I suspect this little scene won't be pretty, so you don't need to watch it. I'll call you when I'm ready."

Verity put a hand on his. "Doc—please. This is a bad idea. You don't even know she's in trouble."

"She's got to be in trouble, or she would have called me again." He looked past her to see one of the nurses coming in. "Now, off you go. I'll call you shortly."

She and Jason exchanged resigned glances. She squeezed his hand, and then they left the room.

❖

They were in the waiting room when an orderly rolled him out in a wheelchair nearly two hours later, a nurse trailing behind them. Both of his friends jumped up, and he didn't miss the concern on their faces.

"Are you sure you don't want to reconsider, Dr. Stone?" the nurse asked, eyeing him sternly as he got up. "Dr. Zhang strongly advises against leaving yet. She wants to order some more tests, and you need to—"

"What I need is to get home," Stone said firmly. "Thank you for everything, Nurse. I've already spoken with Dr. Zhang, and I'm absolutely grateful for everything you've all done. Brilliant care, all around. But I'm feeling much better now."

That wasn't entirely true. His stomach didn't hurt anymore, but he'd been forced to use an illusion to hide the fact that he was swaying like a drunk. He wasn't sure if it was the drugs they'd given him or some leftover fatigue from the poison, but whatever it was, it wouldn't kill him.

The nurse sighed. "All right, then. We can't keep you here against your will. But please follow your discharge instructions, and call your physician if you—"

"—if anything goes wrong. I promise I'll do that. Thank you so much. Cheers."

After the nurse and the orderly left, both looking over their shoulders as if expecting him to keel over right there in the waiting room, he turned his attention back to Jason and Verity. "Did you bring the car 'round?"

"Yeah. Right out front."

Verity was eyeing him suspiciously. "You aren't fooling me with that illusion, Doc. Are you gonna be okay?"

"I will, yes. Stop at some drive-through place on the way home, will you? I'm starving. I need some real food."

They walked outside, the two of them on either side ready to grab him if he fell. Verity's black SUV waited in the loading zone. "Shouldn't you go easy on that?" Jason asked as he opened the rear door and Verity hurried around to get behind the wheel. "You *did* just swallow magical Drano three days ago."

Stone fell gratefully into the seat and leaned back, dropping the illusion and tossing aside the stack of papers he'd had to sign before they'd let him out. "Stop worrying about me, you two. Verity's healing job did the trick. I'm a bit of a zombie from the drugs at present, but that will pass."

"Fine," Jason muttered. As Verity drove off, he turned in his seat. "So, spill it. What's going on with Dr. Garra, and why are you so worried somebody's done something to her?"

Stone, eyes closed and slumped against the side window, told them the whole story of what had happened with Garra, omitting only the events after their return on Friday night. He finished at the same time they rolled through the front gate of the Encantada place.

"Holy shit," Jason said. "So Garra's some kind of shapeshifting jaguar from the Amazon jungle?"

"I didn't think shapeshifters were real," Verity added. "I thought they were just in books, like fairies and dragons."

"I didn't believe it either until I saw her." Stone allowed them to flank him as they all walked toward the house. Stubbornness and willpower aside, even with the rest he'd had on their ride over his legs felt like jelly. "They're very reclusive, apparently, which is why I don't know of anyone who's ever met any."

"So you guys don't know where this chalice is now?" Jason asked.

Raider accosted them as they entered the house, winding himself around Stone's legs until Jason picked him up. All four adjourned to the living room. "Lie down," Verity insisted, dropping the bags they'd picked up from In-n-Out Burger on the table. "I'll get you something to drink."

Stone obeyed without arguing, kicking his boots off and propping himself against the pillows at one end of the sofa. "No, we've no idea where the chalice is. Obviously these magically enhanced men killed Jimmy Tanuki and took it, but we hadn't had the chance to investigate further before everything went pear-shaped." He pulled a burger from the bag, but didn't unwrap it yet. Raider sniffed it hopefully.

Verity returned with three glasses of ice water on a tray. "So what are you going to do next?"

Stone had already tried calling Garra again on their way over; once more, he'd gotten voicemail. This time he'd left a message, asking her to call him the instant she got it. "I suppose I'll have to do a ritual."

"How can you do that?" Jason asked. "You don't have anything of hers, do you?"

"He can use the amulet," Verity said. "Right, Doc? You said it was attuned to her, so it should be easy."

"Yes. I hate to risk destroying it, but I can build her a new one." He sighed, looking down at the still-wrapped burger. "But I'm concerned that she's dead. Those men were trying to kill both of us. They got the drop on me, and the only reason they didn't succeed is because Verity was there to heal up the damage before it got too bad. If they managed to find her too...I can't see it ending well." He unwrapped the burger and took an experimental bite, half expecting his stomach to erupt in pain again when he swallowed. When it didn't, he realized how hungry he'd been and tore into the rest.

"You're gonna need to rest a while before you can do any rituals," Jason said. "Even *I* can see that. So how about I go back to the office and see if there's anything I can do in the meantime."

"Like what?" Stone finished the burger, except for a small piece of the patty he offered the insistent Raider, and chased it with several swallows of water. To his relief, there were still no signs of pain.

"I can check local hospitals and police reports to see if anything's turned up."

"You mean any bodies—or mysterious big cat sightings."

"Yeah. I'll...check morgues, too. I don't have a lot of contacts up here yet, but—"

Stone used magic to pull a notebook and pen to him from the table. He wrote down a number and offered it to Jason. "That's Detective Blum's number. Don't call him unless you need him, but if you need to cut through any red tape, he might be able to help. I've already consulted him about some of this. He doesn't know about Dr. Garra being a shifter, though, so keep that bit under your hat."

"Got it." He finished his own burger and stood. "I'll get on that right away." He glared at Stone. "Stay put for a while, okay? And call me if you end up doing this ritual and finding anything. If you go looking for her, you'll need all the backup you can get."

"I promise—I won't go anywhere on my own."

Jason looked surprised, as if he hadn't expected to hear that. "Yeah, okay. I'll call if I find anything."

After he left, Verity dropped down on the other end of the sofa with sigh.

"You look tired," Stone said. "You should get some rest."

"I'm okay. *You're* the one who should be resting."

He shifted to magical sight. Her aura—green like Garra's, but a darker, deeper shade—included a few dimmer spots. "How much sleep have you had since Saturday night?"

"Enough. I caught a few catnaps at the hospital."

"You should sleep now. Much as I hate to acknowledge it, I don't dare try the ritual right now. I've only got one shot at it with the amulet, and I don't want to take the chance of botching it."

"I really ought to take that beer sample up to Hezzie so we can analyze it. It might help us figure out who's behind this."

"There's time for that." More softly, he added, "If Dr. Garra's already dead, taking a bit more time to find who killed her won't matter. And if she's not, I doubt anything will happen in the next couple of hours."

"I guess not," she said reluctantly.

"Verity…" He shifted position so he was mostly seated on his end of the sofa. "It's all right. I'll be fine."

She slid over until she sat against him, her head on his shoulder. "You didn't see you that night, Doc. Everybody was scared to death. You seemed fine, then you just—fell off the stage. You were so pale…"

He put his arm around her. "And you were there to set things right. You can't know how grateful I am to you for that."

"I was scared shitless. You were so messed up inside—I didn't know whether I'd be able to do it before they took you away."

"But you *did* do it." He pulled her closer. "Verity, I am so proud of you. Not just for this—for everything. When I started training you, I had no idea what kind of amazing mage you'd turn out to be."

She buried her face in his shoulder. "I almost didn't come to the show. Kyla wanted me to stay up in San Francisco Saturday night, and go to a party with her. I told her I couldn't miss your show—but she almost convinced me to stay."

"It's all right…" he murmured.

"It's *not* all right. If I hadn't been there, you'd have—"

"Shh…Come on. You can't keep dwelling on that. That's *my* trick, remember? Tearing myself up about what might have been?"

She gave a wan chuckle. "Yeah…I guess so."

He thought about Garra, and a stab of guilt went through him. "Verity…"

"Yeah?"

"I've…got to tell you something."

She pulled her face out of his shoulder. "What is it?"

"I—" He couldn't meet her gaze.

"Are you okay? Do you need something?"

"No. No. Sorry…this is a bit difficult for me, but I can't keep things from you."

Her brow furrowed, and she tilted her head. "Okay…" Her gaze shifted. "Your aura's kind of a mess right now. Are you sure you're not—"

He wanted to get up and pace—the compulsion was so strong it was nearly physical—but he didn't think his legs would handle it right now. "It's not that." He took a deep breath. "Verity—remember what I told you about Friday night? When Dr. Garra and I went to Oakland?"

"Yeah. Of course. You got ambushed by those guys, but they got away. But—"

"I didn't tell you everything." He drew back from her as much as he could, forcing himself to look at her. *No ducking this. You don't get that right.* "I—After they left, I took her home. She invited me in for a cup of coffee. We were both still quite stressed from what happened."

Her eyes narrowed. "Doc…are you trying to tell me you and Dr. Garra slept together Friday night?"

Of course she caught on that fast. He dropped his gaze—he couldn't help it. "Yes," he whispered. "We did."

He waited, afraid to look up, not sure what to expect. Would she get up to leave? Would she be staring at him with anger, or disappointment, or betrayal?

She took his hand. "Look at me," she murmured.

He did, reluctantly, and blinked.

She was smiling.

It wasn't a big grin, but it was there, wistful and amused. Her eyes glittered. "You were afraid to tell me that, weren't you?"

"I—"

"Why?" When he didn't answer, she said, "Because you were afraid of how I'd take it?"

"Well—yes." He covered her hand with his other one. "I shouldn't have—"

"Why not?"

"What?"

"Why not? Why shouldn't you?" She pulled him forward, toward her.

At first he resisted, but when she tugged harder he allowed her to pull him into her arms.

She propped her chin on his shoulder. "Doc—did you think I was kidding before? Did you think I was just telling you I was okay with it because I was supposed to? Because…when you think about it, that's…kinda more insulting."

He flicked his gaze up. "No. No, of course not. I could see you were serious." He chuckled. "You still can't hide your aura from me. The old dog's still got a few tricks you haven't mastered yet."

"Well, then, what? Why were you afraid to tell me?"

He levitated his glass of water over and took a long drink. "I wasn't afraid to tell you. I was…angry with myself."

"Why? You mean for sleeping with Dr. Garra? Why would you be angry about that?" She leaned back and studied him. "Wait. I get it."

"Do you? I'm not entirely sure *I* do."

"You're mad at yourself because you're okay with *me* seeing other people—well, women, anyway—but you still don't think *you* should."

He shook his head, amused in spite of himself. "When did you get so perceptive?"

"It's not tough, Doc. You're not as mysterious as you think you are, sometimes. Not to me, anyway." She pulled him back into a hug. "Can I tell you something?"

"Of course."

"Will you listen to me? Will you *believe* me?"

He stroked her back, his hand shaking a little. "Yes. I promise—I'll believe you."

She remained silent for a while, holding him close. "I love you, Alastair. You know that, right?"

"I...do."

"You can see it in my aura, right?"

He nodded.

"And I know you love me. I can see it in yours, every time we're together. You're better at concealing it than I am, but that's not something you can hide completely."

Once again, he nodded, not trusting himself to speak.

"Then that's all that matters. That's all I care about. I don't care if you sleep with other women. I don't even care if you *love* them. Love's not finite, Doc. Even if you did love somebody else—hell, I know you *do* love somebody else—it's not the same. It'll be different for them than it is for me."

He blinked. "You...know I love someone else? Verity, Dr. Garra was just—"

"Not Dr. Garra," she said gently.

"Then—"

"I saw how you looked at Imogen when we were in England. I know you're always going to love her, even though you know nothing will come of it anymore." When he started to say something, she held up her hand. "But that's not my point. All I'm trying to say is, it doesn't matter what you do with other people...or what *I* do. It won't affect what's between us. Does that make sense?"

"Honestly...I'm not sure. But I believe you. It's—just a bit harder for me to get my mind around it."

She tightened her grip and kissed him. "You do what you want, Doc," she said, her voice gentle. "I just want you to know—and really *believe*—that I'm okay with whatever you decide. We'll still have what we have, either way, for as long as we both want it. And if you want to hook up with Dr. Garra after we find her, you have my blessing."

He chuckled. He had no idea why she always seemed to make him feel good even when saying things he had trouble accepting, but she did. "I don't deserve you, you know."

"Probably not," she said cheerfully. "But you're stuck with me, so you might as well deal." She got up. "Now lie down and try to sleep for a while. You're gonna need your strength for that ritual. I can—"

The phone rang.

Stone raised his hand and brought the handset to him. "Probably someone from work, checking up on me." He hit the button. "Yes, hello?"

"Stone."

He stiffened, a cold thrill of dread shooting through him. The voice was male, low, and sounded as if the speaker was trying to disguise it. He glanced at Verity, who was looking at him with concern. "Who is this?"

"Stay away from the chalice. You should be dead, but we won't fail next time."

"Where's Dr. Garra? What have you done with her?" He tightened his grip on the handset until it shook.

"Last warning, Stone. Mind your own business."

The line went dead.

# | CHAPTER THIRTY-FOUR

"**B**LOODY HELL." Stone threw the handset on the sofa and leaped up. A quick rush of lightheadedness hit him, but passed quickly.

Verity jumped up too. "What is it?" she demanded. "Who was that?"

"I've got to get started on that ritual. No more time to wait." He started toward the stairs.

She hurried to catch up and grabbed his arm. "Who was it?"

"One of the people who tried to kill me. He said to leave the whole Garra thing alone, or they wouldn't cock it up next time." He gripped the railing and started up the stairs.

"Did they say anything about her? Do they have her? Did they kill her?"

"He didn't say."

"How can you do the ritual, though? You're wiped out. Do you want me to—"

"I'm all right. Feeling better, surprisingly. I just need to grab some things from the study before I start." He reached the top, avoiding Raider, who'd streaked up behind them, and pushed open the door.

The first thing he saw, as the cat darted inside past him, was his old Strat on its stand. "Oh, bugger."

Verity winced. "Yeah...I forgot to tell you in all the chaos. Sorry..."

The guitar had definitely seen better days. Two of its tuning pegs had broken off, the whammy bar was bent, and it had a big chunk out of the glossy black paint at the bottom. Stone regarded it for a moment. "Ah, well," he said. "I'd been meaning to pick up another one—perhaps this is the universe's way of telling me to get on with it. It'll have to wait, though." He hurried to the desk and began pulling open drawers.

Verity waited in the doorway, but Raider couldn't sit still. He leaped up on the desk, watched Stone for a few seconds, then jumped down and crossed to the other side of the room, where he put his paws up and scratched at the wall.

Stone, focused on what he was doing, flicked an impatient glance at the cat. "What are you on about, Raider? I haven't got time to feed you right now. You've got a full dish downstairs."

"Meow," the cat said, and continued scratching at the same spot.

"Doc," Verity said suddenly, "do you think he's trying to tell us something?" Without waiting for an answer, she approached Raider and examined the area he was scratching.

"See anything?" Stone asked, still digging through a desk drawer.

"Not that I can tell." She prodded at the wall, feeling around. "I don't see anything with magical sight, and it's all smooth so if there's a concealed passage or something, it's pretty well hidden."

Raider raised up to his full height, stretching his front paws as high up the wall as he could. "Meow."

"Got it," Stone said, grabbing Garra's amulet from the drawer and slamming it shut. "Let's go. I want to get started on this. Sorry, Raider—or Dr. Benchley—but you'll have to wait."

Stone hadn't had time to prepare his new attic ritual area since he'd moved in, since he planned to enlist Jason's help with installing a new slate floor where he could inlay a permanent version. He paced the room, pulling materials off shelves and arranging them on a nearby table. "Help me with this, will you?" he asked Verity. "I'm not sure how much bending and crawling around I'm up to right now."

"You direct, I'll draw," she said, and grabbed a large piece of chalk.

She didn't need help with the basic circle—she could do those almost as well as he could now—so he continued pacing, examining some of the other objects on the shelves lining two walls. He'd have to get around to arranging them soon, but until they figured out what had happened to Garra it wasn't high on his priority list.

To avoid dark ruminations on how close he'd come to never seeing his new home again, he turned his thoughts back to Garra and the chalice. For the last few days, something had been scratching at him, as insistent as Raider had been at his wall upstairs, but he couldn't quite pin down what it was. Barely realizing he was doing it, he began to mutter to himself. "Why would they be so protective of this thing?"

"What's that, Doc?" Verity asked. She was crouched on the wooden floor, sketching out the circle's structure with green chalk.

"Nothing—just thinking aloud. Wondering why whoever has the chalice is so protective of it that they'd try to kill me, and possibly kill Dr. Garra, to keep us away from it."

"Well...it *is* a pretty powerful magical item, right? That would make it valuable."

"True. But it's also fairly single-purpose, if Dr. Garra can be believed. It's valuable for its artifact status, and there are definitely mages out there who collect such things, but their methods of protecting them tend to be a bit less...proactive."

"What do you mean?"

"Remember Thalassa Nera? Her place was full of death-traps, but you actually had to get inside before they went off. She didn't send people out to murder anyone who might be after her property."

"She didn't *know* you were after it, though," Verity pointed out. "Maybe she would have if she did."

"You have a point there. But this just seems like overly extreme behavior for a collector. Most collectors of that caliber are quite wealthy. They own multiple warded properties, and with the portals it would be laughably easy for them to simply make the chalice disappear to somewhere it would take even another powerful mage a long time and a lot of effort to locate. That's assuming they didn't keep it moving for a while to elude detection. Even Kolinsky wouldn't have an easy time tracking an artifact if its owner was actively trying to conceal it."

"So what are you getting at?" Verity used magic to pull a blue hunk of chalk to her from the table and continued with her sketch.

"I'm wondering if whoever has it *isn't* a mere collector."

She glanced up, pausing in mid-line. "You mean you think they're *using* it? But how could that be? I thought you said it was for helping shifters reproduce. You didn't see any shifters, did you? Those guys with the weird auras, maybe?"

"No—the men who came after us did have odd auras, but I never saw any of them shift. And Dr. Garra doesn't have the same kind of aura." He continued pacing, pausing to examine Verity's work so far. "I wonder if shifters might not be involved, though."

"Some other clan trying to use it for themselves?"

"Possibly. If that were true, they might not have the same resources as a wealthy collector, but they're bloody good at tracking. It's possible they decided killing any pursuers might be easier than trying to run from them."

"What about the alchemist, though? You know they've got one—trust me, that stuff you drank had to be highly magical, if they managed to disguise that kind of corrosive substance well enough that you'd drink it. I'm guessing even the poison itself was magical."

"Possibly the chalice is purpose-built for the jaguar clan, and they need an alchemist to make alterations to the elixir before it will work for a different species. I don't know."

Verity sketched for a while before she answered. When she did, she sounded dubious. "I dunno, Doc. That still leaves a lot of loose ends. We don't even know who all the players are. Did the people who have the chalice now steal it from Dr. Garra's clan in the first place? Or did somebody else steal it and these guys killed Jimmy Tanuki and took it from him? And who are the guys who came after you and Dr. Garra? You said they were stronger and faster than normal people. Are they mages too? Are they like those guys we fought up in Woodside last year? The magic-immune ones?"

Stone leaned against the wall and shoved his hands in his pockets. "All good questions, and I don't have answers to most of them. All I'm certain of is that the men who attacked us weren't like Lane and Hugo. And I'm reasonably sure they weren't mages. Or shifters, because of the auras."

"But they've got to have magic associated with them, if they're that strong and fast."

"Yes, that's a reasonable assumption."

"Maybe that's why the alchemist wanted the chalice," she said, standing up and stretching as she surveyed her work. "Maybe they've figured out a way to use it as a starting point to make other things—like an elixir to enhance people."

"Hmm…" Stone considered. "That's not a half bad idea. The only problem is, if the chalice is an artifact-level magic item, it would be extremely difficult to alter its purpose without breaking it. I'm not saying it's not possible, but it would be a big risk. And if it's true, it means we're dealing with some impressive power levels."

"How impressive?"

"To alter the basic purpose of an artifact-class magic item? I'd say Madame Huan's or Kolinsky's level, at minimum. Of course, it's also possible that the chalice isn't actually as potent as Dr. Garra implied, which would make it easier." He waved her off. "It's all just speculation, though, at the moment. Let's finish the circle so I can see if I can find Dr. Garra. Depending on what the ritual discovers, we can make our plans from there. But first let me call Laura and see if she ever turned up. It would be a bit embarrassing to expend all this effort tracking her to her lecture hall at the University."

No such luck, however. A quick call to the department office revealed that Garra still hadn't shown up, nor had she called to reveal her whereabouts.

"I'm getting worried, Dr. Stone," Laura said. "She's missed two classes today already. Should we call the police?"

"Might be worth having them do a welfare check on her," Stone said, already knowing they'd find nothing. "Let me know if she turns up, will you?"

"That's it," he told Verity after he hung up. "I hope this ritual works."

With Stone taking over and Verity assisting, they finished the circle in a few minutes. Stone gathered the materials he'd need, including the amulet, and stepped into the center.

"You sure you're okay to do this?" Verity asked. She'd been watching him like she expected him to pass out ever since they'd arrived in the attic.

"I'm fine." Surprisingly, he *did* feel fine. Even the lightheadedness from before had passed. Perhaps it was the adrenaline from his concern about Garra, or perhaps it was a testament to Verity's growing healing abilities, but either way he wasn't arguing. "Just keep an eye on me in case anything goes wrong."

He sat cross-legged in the circle's center, twisting to light each of the candles around its perimeter with magic. After taking a few centering breaths to calm his jangling nerves, he dropped into his meditative state, switched on magical sight, and fed power into the circle. The familiar shafts of arcane light shimmered into being, satisfyingly strong and steady, joining the points into a pulsing pattern. Yes, he was definitely getting to like this new power level.

"Here goes…" he murmured, reaching out with his magical senses to focus on the amulet on the floor in front of him. Even though it was broken, its illusion effect no longer functional, it had still been designed and built specifically for Garra. That kind of bond was the best kind for a tracking ritual, even with a mundane object. When added to the sexual connection they'd shared, he was confident he could find her.

If she was alive, of course. If they'd killed her, the strongest ritual in the world wouldn't have a chance of locating her.

The spell locked on to the amulet, and after a few moments a white, searching tendril extended upward and disappeared up through the basement's ceiling. Stone closed his eyes and focused his concentration. This would be the crucial part—if Garra was dead, the tendril would collapse on itself in the next few seconds. If she wasn't, it would continue its search, trying to meet up with the corresponding auric essence in its target.

He clenched his fists, heart pounding as he waited to see which it would be. "Come on, Viajera…" he murmured. "Where are you…?"

The tendril didn't collapse. Instead, it continued ranging out, poking this way and that like a curious snake, trying to get a fix. *She's not dead. She's out there somewhere…*

But where? The tendril seemed to be having trouble committing to a direction. That could mean one of two things: she *was* alive, but behind wards or some other kind of magical protection, or she was outside the spell's relatively short range. Possibly both.

"You're not getting away from me," he growled, feeding more power into the spell. With his new connection to Calanar, the power came strong and steady to his call. He'd have to be a bit careful, since after his recent ordeal his body wasn't back to its full strength yet, but even now he had more to draw than he had before. "Come on…let's see you…"

The little tendril seemed to settle on a direction. It searched around for a few more seconds, then darted off to the north. A thrill shot up Stone's spine: she was alive. It wouldn't be that decisive if she was dead. *Focus—don't let it get away from you.*

It was trying to. The tendril writhed and shifted as if it were uncomfortable. It continued its northward progress, but already Stone could sense it beginning to lose potency. "No, damn you…" He fed more power in, trying to keep the thing together by sheer willpower alone. "Show me where she is!"

The tendril strained, already nearing the end of its ability to remain coherent. "Come on…" Stone urged, sensing it was getting close. "Just a bit further…"

The tendril shuddered and dissolved into a shimmer of light, drifting off into astral space as the connection broke. But in the instant before it disappeared, Stone sensed something else that made him stiffen.

Something had reached out to *him.*

For less than a second, before the tendril could no longer hold its connection to the circle, something from the other end had made contact with it.

"Bloody hell…" he whispered, dropping the power keeping the circle running and slumping backward.

"Are you okay?" Verity's worried voice called.

He swallowed and sat back up. In front of him, Garra's onyx pendant lay in a broken heap, the stone cracked and the gold setting melted around it. "That was close."

"Did you find her?" She hurried into the circle and grabbed his arm to help him up.

He let her pull him to his feet. Already his heartbeat was returning to normal—it hadn't been fatigue that caused it this time, but fear. "I think she's alive. Fairly certain of it. She's somewhere north of here." He grabbed the map he'd laid out near the circle and consulted it. "Very close to the edge of the spell's range."

"How far is that? I know yours is wider than mine—probably even more now."

He continued studying the map. "Yes, but I think they might have her behind wards, which decreases its power significantly. There," he added, pointing with his pen at a spot north of San Francisco. "Somewhere up there. Not sure how far, though."

"That's a lot of territory," she said dubiously.

"Yes, but we have a direction now. We can go up there and do the ritual again."

"Can you? The amulet's slagged."

He let his breath out. "Yes. I might be able to do it without a tether object now, though. Especially since—"

"Since you slept with her," she said matter-of-factly. "Yeah, that'll help." She glanced at the ruined circle. "What was the 'bloody hell' for, though? You looked scared there at the end."

"Yes. We need to hurry. Just as I got to the end of the spell's effective range, I felt something…touching me. Trying to track the spell back to its source."

"Shit. Did they do it? Do they know where we are?"

"No. It collapsed before they got a chance. But it means they know someone is looking for them, and I suspect they're bright enough to figure out who. Come on."

She followed him toward the stairs. "Doc?"

"Yes?"

"You said 'fairly certain'. What's that mean? I thought the tracking spell knew for sure whether someone was alive or not."

"Normally it does. But we're dealing with some powerful individuals here. It could be a trap. We'll need to be careful. Let me call your brother and we'll go from there." He pulled out his phone as he reached the bottom of the stairs and hit the button for Jason's office.

Jason answered on the first ring. "Thayer Investigations."

"Jason. Did you find anything?"

"Hey, Al. No, not really. No suspicious deaths around the area. Still got some checks out to the hospitals, to see if anybody matching Garra's description turned up."

"Don't focus on this area. Can you do a quick check to see if anything's shown up in the area north of San Francisco? Up in the Sonoma area?"

"I'll see what I can do. What am I looking for?"

"I don't even know. I found something with the ritual, but it's inconclusive."

"What are you gonna do?"

"Drive up there and try the ritual again."

"I want to come along. Come pick me up—I'll see what I can find before that."

Stone didn't want to take the time to drive to San Jose, but Jason's help would be valuable. "All right—we're coming now. But we can't wait long, so be ready."

# | CHAPTER THIRTY-FIVE

THEY FOUND JASON AT HIS DESK, focused on his computer screen. "Did you find anything?" Stone demanded as soon as he shoved open the door, Verity trailing behind him.

"Maybe. I dunno if it's related, but it's in the area and it seemed weird, so I noted it. I was just checking for anything else."

"What is it?" Stone hurried over.

"A woman's body found up in Sonoma a couple days ago."

Stone froze. "Do they know who she is?"

"No. They haven't been able to identify her, and there aren't any missing persons reports or next of kin turning up. Her face was mangled, and her hands were messed up so they couldn't get fingerprints. They'll need to use dental records."

"Sounds like they were *trying* to make sure nobody could identify her," Verity said.

"How long has she been there?" Stone forced himself to remain calm. Odds were good this wasn't even related to Garra's case, but that didn't help.

"That's the thing—a guy called it in. He said he was out hiking Saturday night and saw somebody dump something.

By the time he got close they were gone. It's a pretty remote area, though."

Stone and Verity both leaned in, trying to peer over Jason's shoulder. "Do they have a description?"

"Yeah. Not a good one, though—looks like she was pretty messed up."

"Could it be Garra? Late twenties, tall, black hair?"

Jason sighed. "Yeah. That fits."

Stone clenched his fists. "Damn."

"Wait," Verity said. "How can she be dead? You found her with the ritual. You said even though you couldn't find exactly where she was, you were pretty sure she was alive."

"*Pretty* sure," he repeated. "Normally I'd say certain, but considering the power levels we're clearly dealing with here, it's possible they could have set a trap for me." He stepped back. "Come on—we need to get up there. Jason, can you use your private-investigator credentials to convince them to let us take a look at the body? I won't know for sure until I see her in person."

"Probably. Especially if I tell them I'm working on a case with a missing woman."

"That's not even a lie. Let's go—I've already got my magical paraphernalia in the car."

"Wait," Verity said suddenly.

"What?"

"Can we drive up through San Francisco on the way? I really want to drop that poisoned beer sample off with Hezzie so she can examine it. I wanted to help her, but she can do it without me. It might give us some useful information about who's behind this."

Stone didn't want to waste a moment, but Verity had a point. "Fine. But we can't stay."

"I'll give her a call so she's expecting us. Let's go."

By the time Stone found a parking space two blocks from Hezzie's apartment building an hour later, he could barely contain his impatience. "Let's make this quick," he told Verity, glancing at his watch. It was after five, and already dark.

Hezzie, a member of the Harpies, the all-female vigilante gang Stone and Verity had encountered a few months back while tracking an ancient, malevolent set of game pieces, lived in a rundown apartment building in the Mission District.

"She can afford a nicer place," Verity commented when Jason looked around the area with distaste, "but she has more room here, and fewer nosy neighbors. Everybody minds their own business."

The witch's place was at the end of a long hallway with only three other doors along it. The faint strains of a rap song filtered out through one of them, and a baby's cry from the opposite one. The air smelled like strongly-spiced Mexican food locked in an olfactory battle with a squadron of smelly gym socks.

Stone switched to magical sight as Verity knocked, and immediately spotted the ward protecting the door. It was a simple but effective working, designed to subtly discourage anyone who might be tempted to break in.

Before he could study it in more detail, the door opened to reveal Hezzie. "Hey, V. Wondering when you'd get here. C'mon in." A pale, plain-faced woman in her middle twenties with short hair and big, dark eyes, she wore torn, faded jeans and a heather-gray T-shirt featuring a cartoon witch and *Resting Witch Face*. Her glance flicked to Stone and then to Jason, her smile fleeing.

"Hey," Verity said. "You remember Dr. Stone. And this is my brother Jason. Jason, this is Hezzie."

"Good to see you again," Stone said. "Unfortunately we can't stay long."

Inside, Hezzie's apartment looked a lot nicer than might be expected from its exterior. The shades were drawn, but the soft glow of a stand lamp with a red shade illuminated a cozy sitting area with overstuffed sofa and chair, old-fashioned wooden coffee table, and a small TV atop another table covered in black velvet. Two cats, one gray and one calico, crouched on top of the sofa watching the visitors with wary, suspicious gazes. Stone got a brief impression of several pagan-themed prints on the walls, and the kitchen was just visible through an open doorway on the far side. Unlike the feuding aromas in the hallway, the apartment smelled of spices, a hint of something more pungent but not unpleasant, and tomato sauce.

Hezzie eyed Stone. "You look good for a guy who drank Drano three days ago."

"It's all thanks to Verity and her stellar healing abilities."

Verity pulled the little bottle with the sample from her bag. "Can you take a look at this, Hez, and let me know what you find? I know it's magic, but I've only got this little bit and I don't trust my alchemy skills enough yet. I don't want to screw up the analysis."

"You wouldn't." Hezzie's fond smile returned as she once again focused on Verity. "I can already tell you've got a real knack for it."

"Well, I hope that's true." She handed over the vial. "I already gave you the details. Do you know how long it'll take to analyze it? It's not something we can wait for, is it?"

Hezzie flicked her gaze at Stone. "Not something *he* can wait for, judging by how impatient he looks. I can see you guys are trying to get out of here. I'll take a look at it tonight and give you a call with what I find out."

"Any chance you'll be able to trace it to its maker?" Stone asked. "That would be the most useful at this point."

"Probably not. Not if they're any good, anyway. But I should be able to tell you what's in it, and that might give you a clue. Alchemists are like chefs—they all have their own touches, and their own individual recipes. I've never heard of a poison like you describe, so maybe I can get something. We'll see."

Stone shifted to magical sight again. Hezzie's aura, a deep purple, showed signs of tension, but even without that extra clue he could tell she was uncomfortable. "Well," he said briskly, "we'd best be going, then. Thank you, Hezzie. I appreciate whatever you can find out."

"Yeah, sure, no problem."

Verity gave her a quick hug. "I'll see you soon. Still on for next week's session?"

"You got it." She glanced at Stone and Jason again, and it couldn't have been clearer that she wanted them out.

Jason waited until they'd left and were heading back toward the car before he spoke. "What's her problem?"

"She's not crazy about guys," Verity said.

"It sure looked like she wasn't crazy about havin' Al and me in her place. I kept expecting her to shove us out the door."

"Yeah, it's nothing personal. I'm not gonna say much about it because it's not my place, but she had some bad stuff happen to her when she was younger. She'll do a good job on the sample, though, so don't worry."

Stone picked up the pace. "Come on—it's more than an hour once we get out of San Francisco, and I want to get there before it's too late to talk to the authorities about the body."

They got on the road again, picking their way through the typically heavy San Francisco traffic toward the Golden Gate Bridge. "What do you suppose Raider was trying to tell us?" Verity asked suddenly from the back seat, gazing out the window at the Bay as they crept across the bridge.

"Huh?" Jason asked.

"He was scratching at a particular spot on Doc's study wall today, but we were in a hurry so we didn't get much chance to check it out."

"You think he was possessed again?"

"Probably," Stone said. "It was quite odd—he kept stretching up like he was trying to reach something, but there wasn't anything there. Verity checked—no seams, hidden compartments, or magic."

"We were in a hurry to get the ritual going, though, so we didn't look too closely," Verity said.

"Weird," Jason said. "I wonder what Dr. Benchley is tryin' to tell you."

"I still think somebody killed him." Verity shifted in her seat and leaned forward. "Why else would he stick around all this time?"

Stone was silent, visualizing the area of the room Raider had focused on. He hadn't been in the study for that long so he didn't know it as well as the Palo Alto place, but Raider's interest had definitely been on part of the wall where no bookshelves covered it. Was there perhaps something hidden behind the wall—something he'd need to break through to get to? Given the craftsmanship that had gone into the woodwork in the house, he wasn't fond of destroying or even defacing it on a vague hunch. It wasn't that bad to have the echo of a long-dead professor occasionally taking his cat for a joyride, was it? Raider didn't seem to mind, and even if Benchley *had* been murdered, it wasn't as if Stone could prove anything. Hell, the murderer was probably dead too. In any case, he'd have to deal with it later. Right now, if they could ever get out of this gods-forsaken traffic, he had more important things to concern himself with.

Still, his mind kept going over the way Raider had stretched, almost as if Benchley were straining to reach something too high for the cat's body to touch.

"Maybe somebody poisoned him," Jason said. "You know, like they did to you. You don't need alchemy for that."

"The authorities would have caught it, though," Stone said, but the nagging thoughts wouldn't stop. Jason's words only set off another flurry of them. "Wait," he said suddenly.

"What?" Jason and Verity asked at the same time.

"I think there might be a vent high up on the study wall—you know, for the air conditioning."

Verity leaned forward further, gripping Jason's seat. "Oh, wow. That might be it! Maybe Benchley's trying to point out something in there."

"What, though?" Jason asked. "You think something in a vent could have killed the guy and nobody detected it? The report said he died of natural causes."

"Chemistry!" Stone said.

"Huh?"

But Verity got it too. "Yeah! Dr. Benchley was a chemistry professor!"

It only took Jason a couple of seconds to catch on. "Holy shit, you could be right. There've got to be chemical compounds that could mimic a heart attack, and nobody'd think to look too closely because he was an old, chubby guy who smoked too much."

"We need to look in that vent," Verity said.

"First things first," Stone said. They reached the other side of the bridge, and traffic began to thin. "As curious I am about what's going on with Dr. Benchley, Dr. Garra takes priority."

# | CHAPTER THIRTY-SIX

THE HIKER HAD FOUND the woman's body a short distance outside a small town called La Rosita, about five miles from Guerneville. Jason called ahead and talked to the police as they drove.

"They're not crazy about draggin' the ME out after hours to let us see the body," he said when he finished. "They wanted me to come back tomorrow, but I convinced them. We're meeting him at the police department, then he'll take us to his office. That's where they're keeping her for now, hoping somebody will come forward and identify her."

Stone remained tense as they drove into town and located the police station, a small, single-story building surrounded by trees. It was unlikely the body would be Garra—he was fairly sure, with the power he'd put into the ritual, that they couldn't have faked the result he got. But if he was wrong—if it *was* Garra who'd been dumped in some rural area—then his options became severely limited. If he couldn't track her, he had no idea where to begin looking for her killers. *And the chalice,* he reminded himself. If Garra had died searching for it, the least he could do was make an effort to find it and get it back to her clan.

*First things first, though. Let's make sure she's not dead before we do anything else.*

The La Rosita police station reminded Stone a bit of the one from Ojai, down in southern California. They probably didn't get much crime around here normally, so it wasn't necessary to have a significant police presence. A uniformed cop leaving the building eyed the three of them with curiosity as he passed, but said nothing.

Jason introduced himself to the sergeant on duty, a stocky, blonde woman whose name badge read *COREY*, and showed her his investigators' license. "This is my sister Verity, and our friend, Dr. Alastair Stone."

The sergeant's eyes narrowed. "When you called, you didn't say anything about three of you. Are they part of your investigation too?"

"Verity's assisting me on the case. Dr. Stone is a friend of the woman we're looking for. I'm hoping he can identify whether this is her."

For a moment, it looked as if she'd turn down their request. Then she sighed and tossed her pen on her desk. "We don't get cases like this very often, Mr. Thayer. In fact, it's been years since there's been a murder here, let alone a Jane Doe." She glanced up, past them. "Ah, here's he is. Evening, Carlo. Sorry to drag you out for this. Mr. Thayer, this is Dr. Carlo Menendez, our medical examiner."

Carlo Menendez was about fifty, barely taller than Verity, with light brown skin, a receding salt-and-pepper hairline, and a burly frame. He wore a plaid shirt, jeans, and athletic shoes. "You're the ones who wanted to see the body?" he asked, looking the three of them over.

"Yes, sir," Jason said. "Thanks for letting us have a look—we're up from the San Jose area."

"It's okay. Wasn't doing anything important anyway. I can't stay long, though. If you need anything more extensive, you'll have to come back tomorrow."

"We shouldn't need much of your time, Dr. Menendez," Stone said.

"Good, good. Come on—you'll have to come to my office. It's just up the street. It's good you called when you did, since we won't be able to keep her for long. If nobody identifies the body in the next day or so, we'll probably have to send her to Santa Rosa." He shook his head ruefully. "I feel terrible for the poor girl—someone's got to be missing her somewhere."

As they got back in the car and followed his battered tan station wagon, Verity's phone rang. She pulled it out.

"Hey, Hezzie. What's up?" She listened a few moments, then sighed. "Yeah. Thanks. I owe you one."

"What did she find out?" Stone asked without taking his attention from Menendez's car.

"That stuff you drank was definitely alchemical. And definitely nasty."

"Well…yes. We knew that already."

"No, you don't get it."

Stone glanced at the rearview mirror. Verity's expression was grim. "What don't I get?"

"It was some heavy-duty stuff—something it would take a powerful alchemist to create, mostly because of how hard it would be to conceal otherwise. I shouldn't have had time to heal you."

"But you did. I think you underestimate yourself, Verity."

"Maybe." She let her breath out, and didn't sound convinced. "But anyway, she also said the components for it were really rare, and only found in parts of the South American rainforest."

"That's...interesting," Stone mused.

Jason pointed. "He's pulling off."

Stone had been about to say something else, but instead he quickly turned the wheel and made a sharp right to follow Menendez into a small parking lot.

The medical examiner pulled into a space. "This is it. We don't even have a hospital here," he said when he got out. "Closest one is in Guerneville, about five miles away." He looked the three of them over as he unlocked the front door. "By the way, what did you say your connection was to this woman?"

"We're investigating a missing-persons case," Jason said. "Her description sounded enough like the one we're looking for that we figured we should check."

"You came all the way up here from San Jose for that? If you'd called, I could have emailed you photos." He flipped on a light and led them down a hall past an empty reception desk.

"No, we wanted to see her in person. It's...complicated."

Menendez flicked a sharp gaze toward Jason. "Well, in any case, I'm not going to say I hope she's who you're looking for, but it will make my job a lot easier if you can provide an ID."

He unlocked a door at the end of the hall, switching on another light.

Stone looked around the small, neat room. A stainless-steel examination table with a drain at one end dominated the center, flanked by a series of cabinets on one wall beneath a counter and sink on the near side, and two steel doors he recognized as body lockers on the far one. The upper door was open, the lower closed.

"All right, let's do this," Menendez said. "I can't let you take any of your own photos, you understand."

"We don't need photos," Stone said.

"Good." He opened the locker and pulled out the stainless-steel platform. A body, shrouded in a white sheet, lay on top of it. With a quick glance to make sure his visitors were ready, he folded the sheet down to reveal the body's face and shoulders. The roughly stitched top ends of the Y-incision from the autopsy peeked above the cover.

Stone let his breath out.

"That's not her," he said, surprised at the sudden intensity of the relief flooding his body.

"You sure?" Jason asked.

It was a fair question. The body had clearly been damaged to make identification more difficult—and if the hiker who'd called in the discovery had seen someone dumping her, that meant it hadn't been done by time or animals. The woman had black hair and light brown skin; her face and shoulders indicated she was slim and athletic, like Garra. The superficial resemblance was strong enough to allow some doubt.

But Stone had no doubt. "I'm sure. That's not her." He shifted to magical sight, knowing he wouldn't get much time to examine the body.

Menendez sighed. "Well, I'm certainly glad for your sake that this wasn't your friend. I sure hope someone turns up to identify her soon, though. Such a shame, the way she died."

"How *did* she die, Doctor?" Jason asked casually.

"Well, that's the odd part." Menendez covered the body and rolled it back into the drawer. "Everything that was done to obscure her identity was done post-mortem. The COD was actually complications from pregnancy."

"Pregnancy?" Verity looked surprised.

"Shocked me too. I can't tell if the baby died with her, but it's possible it didn't, and now it's out there somewhere without a mother. The police are looking. Don't say anything about that to anyone, please—they haven't released it yet."

"Weird that they'd do this to her," Jason said. "Mess her up, I mean."

"Maybe not." Verity watched as Menendez closed the locker door. "Maybe they don't want anybody to know who she is because they wanted to take the baby for themselves. That happens."

"Well, in any case, I'm glad it's not your friend," Menendez said, clearly wanting to get out of there now. "Sorry you came all the way up here, but it's got to be a relief."

"Absolutely," Stone said, still distracted. "Thank you, Doctor."

He didn't say anything else until they were back in the car. "Jason," he said, "do you have a specific location where that body was found?"

"Uh—yeah, pretty close. Hold on." He retrieved his messenger bag from the back seat and found his notes. "Not too far from here—a few miles? This is the nearest town. Why? We're not interested in her, are we, if she's not Dr. Garra?"

"We may be."

"Why?" Verity asked.

"Because I'm fairly sure she was a shifter."

# | CHAPTER THIRTY-SEVEN

"**Y**OU THINK THE DEAD WOMAN was a shifter?" Verity demanded. "Why?"

They'd stopped at a diner up the street from Menendez's office so they could grab a quick meal and compare notes. Stone glanced out the window as he sipped his strong, black coffee. "The body didn't have an aura, obviously, but I saw traces of magic around her. They were faint—I probably wouldn't have noticed them if I hadn't seen Garra's aura before."

"So they don't—I dunno—change back to their animal form after they die?" Jason asked. "Which is their true form, anyway? Human or animal?"

"I don't know enough about them to know the answer to that," Stone admitted. "From what Garra's implied, the animal form is their preferred one. But perhaps if they die, they remain in whatever form they've assumed at the time. In any case, the fact that she was pregnant disturbs me."

"Why? Are you worried there's a baby shifter running around out there somewhere?"

"No, that's not it. Remember what the purpose of the chalice is?"

"To help shifters be more fertile..." Verity said. Her eyes widened. "You think somebody's *breeding* them?"

"It's possible." Stone set his cup down.

"But why?" Jason asked.

"Hard to say. There are some powerful and unscrupulous mages out there, though—perhaps there's a black market in shifter cubs. I'd imagine they would bring a significant sum from the right buyer."

"But why dump the mother, though?" Verity asked. "Even if she died unexpectedly—assuming they didn't kill her—wouldn't they be afraid she'd be traced back to them?"

"Good question. Remember, someone spotted them in the act of dumping the body, which they probably didn't expect. I'm guessing they probably assumed she wouldn't be found for quite some time, since it was a remote area."

"Don't mages have easier ways to get rid of bodies, though?" Jason asked.

"Not necessarily, when they're dead. You can't ash a dead body. Perhaps they wanted to get rid of the evidence fast, and weren't worried about having it traced back to them." Stone finished his coffee. "Finish up—I need to set up the ritual again. If Garra's alive, she's certainly in danger."

"Doc..." Verity said suddenly, her expression turning horrified.

"Yes?"

"Jason, you said this woman was found Saturday night, right?"

"Yeah, so?"

"And Dr. Garra disappeared sometime after Sunday afternoon?"

A chill that was almost painful shot through Stone as he caught her line of reasoning. "Oh, bloody hell…"

Jason wasn't far behind. "Shit…" he breathed. "Are you thinkin' they might have grabbed her to replace the woman who died?"

"It fits, doesn't it?" Verity asked.

"It does," Stone said in a monotone. "That could explain why they've been trying to kill her before—to keep her from finding them—but why now she might still be alive." He stood quickly. "Come on—we've got to find a place to do that ritual."

One of the main problems with doing magical rituals in unfamiliar areas was finding a location with enough space do them. The town of La Rosita was too small to include a motel, and between the chill and the light wind, performing it outside wasn't a viable option. Finally, as Stone's impatience grew, they found someone at the local market who recommended a series of cabins on the outskirts of town. Twenty minutes and a healthy "service fee" to the proprietor later, they parked in front of the largest of those cabins.

"Well, this is a dump," Verity commented, looking around the wooden structure in distaste. The place looked like its décor hadn't been updated in at least thirty years, and though it appeared clean, the furnishings were shabby and obviously well used.

"I don't care if it's a *literal* dump," Stone said, already beginning to unload ritual materials from his black leather duffel bag. "As long as it's got enough room to do what we need." He gestured, lifting a sofa off the floor, flipping it on its end, and leaning it against the far wall. "Let's get the space cleared out so I can see what I've got to work with."

Verity and Jason got started, the former with magic and the latter with muscle power, and in less than ten minutes they had all the furniture pushed back against one wall, stacked on top of each other to provide maximum floor space.

"Aren't you worried about them catching on if you try finding her again?" Verity asked, watching as Stone sketched a circle on the cleared floor. "If they noticed you before, they might be ready for you this time."

"It's a chance I'll have to take. I'll build a couple of precautions into the ritual to conceal my presence, but we don't have any other options."

He wished they did, because he'd already thought about Verity's question and it did concern him. With his greater power level he could *probably* conceal himself, but since he didn't know how strong his opposition was, he couldn't be sure. If they caught him again, would they send someone after him, either in the astral or physical world? That, he could deal with if necessary. But if they decided to cut their losses and kill Garra to prevent him from finding her, he'd never forgive himself.

If only there were some other way he could track them. Now he wished he'd had the presence of mind to grab something from one of the men he'd knocked out back at the school ambush. There was no guarantee they were here, of course, but if he found one of them nearby, he could make a reasonable assumption he was wherever Garra was being held. Whoever had set up those wards probably didn't waste time protecting henchmen. If he had a bit of their clothing, or better yet some blood, he could—

*Hang on...*

He leaped up from his crouch. "Yes!"

Jason and Verity both jumped, startled. "What?"

"Is something wrong?" Verity hurried to the edge of the circle.

"No. Something might be *right*." He glanced around the room until he spotted his black overcoat, which somebody had tossed over the upended sofa. He used magic to pull it to him, then turned it inside out.

"What are you doing?" Verity asked.

He didn't answer, focused on tightening his magical sight. At first he didn't see anything, and feared it had been too long. But then, as he scanned the upper part of the inner liner, he spotted it: a faint glow of magical energy near the left shoulder. "There!"

"What?" Jason demanded.

"Jason, do you have a pocket knife?"

"Yeah, but—"

"Let's have it."

"Al—" Jason dug it from his pocket and handed it over. "You want to tell us what the hell you're doing?"

Stone spoke as he unfolded the knife and carefully began excising the section of liner from the coat. "On Friday night, when those men attacked us in Oakland, Dr. Garra shifted to her jaguar form and chased them. One of them shot her, but she also got her claws on him before he managed to escape. Some of his blood sprayed her shoulder."

"So? Why is it on your coat?"

"When she shifts back, she's naked. I let her use my coat to cover up until she could get to her spare clothes." He finished cutting out the bloody section, set it aside, then focused on the lower part. The magical traces there were stronger, because there was more blood. He cut that section out too. "This is Garra's blood. If I do the ritual twice and it leads to the same place both times, I think we'll have our answer."

"What if it doesn't?" Verity asked.

"We'll deal with that if it happens." He tossed the coat aside and carefully levitated the sample with Garra's blood outside the circle. "You two keep a watch—I don't want anyone bursting in on us while I do this."

Nobody burst in on them. Even with the extra care Stone took to make sure he got a good result, the first ritual only took fifteen minutes. "Give me the map," he ordered without moving from the circle's center. When Verity levitated it over, he unfolded it, circled a spot with his pen, and sent it back. "Here's where he is. Take a look, will you?"

Jason and Verity spread it out on a nearby table and examined it under a light. "This is about ten miles north of here," Jason said. "Looks like some kind of animal preserve or something, way up in the sticks."

"That makes sense." Stone, still remaining where he was, used magic to replace the candles and crystals around the outside of the circle. "If they're doing something with shifters, they wouldn't want anyone blundering in on them. See if you can find any reference to it while I finish this. And be ready to go. If I find Garra in the same place, we'll need to move fast."

The second ritual took a few minutes longer than the first one, because Stone built in an extra concealment component he hoped would keep anyone from noticing him this time. He didn't know if it would work, but if he could manage to get a look without being spotted, they'd have a better chance of sneaking in. He lost all track of what was going on around him as he concentrated on following the narrow, twisting tendril to its source, taking care at each stage to keep the concealment spell strong.

This time when he made contact he was not only sure he'd found Garra, but that she was alive. He leaped up as all around him the candles *whooshed* out and the crystals cracked. "Got her!"

"Where?" Verity demanded. "Is she in the same place?"

Stone summoned the map and examined it for only a second before stabbing a finger down near the place he'd circled before. "She's there. Jason, did you find anything out about the area?"

"Yeah. I made a couple calls while you were out. It's private land—used to be an animal sanctuary, but it's been closed to the public for years. The guy I talked to thinks some kind of scientific foundation is using it now. He also said he's pretty sure they're paying off the local cops to leave it alone, so nobody really knows what's going on up there."

"That sounds like just the sort of place we're looking for, then." Stone gestured, gathering the circle components into a small whirlwind and depositing them in a nearby trash can.

"Did they notice you?" Verity asked. She picked up the can, pulled a heavy trash bag from Stone's duffel bag, and dumped the spent components into it.

"I don't think so, but I wouldn't count on it. We need to hurry."

The road they were looking for wasn't on the map. They took two wrong turns, wasting nearly fifteen minutes, before Verity spotted the unmarked turnoff, badly paved and barely a lane and a half wide, between two clumps of overgrown trees.

"They really don't want anybody finding this place," Jason muttered as Stone carefully turned onto the narrow road.

"Would you, if you were breeding shapeshifters so you could sell their kids into slavery?" Verity leaned forward, peering between the two front seats to keep an eye on the terrain ahead.

"I just hope we can *get* up there," Stone said. The BMW bounced over the uneven, rutted surface; every few feet a reaching tree branch scraped the side. He wanted to go faster—who knew what they were doing with Garra while her rescuers poked along a torn-up, potholed road, barely faster than they could walk?—but he forced himself to maintain a slow, even speed. It would take them even longer to get to her if they broke an axle on some unseen hazard.

They'd barely made it half a mile when Verity's soft, strained voice spoke from the back seat. "Doc?"

"Yes?" Stone didn't take his eyes off the road ahead as he shifted between normal and magical sight.

"Somebody's behind us."

Stone jerked his gaze up to the rearview mirror as red and blue lights switched on and a siren blipped.

*R. L. KING*

# | CHAPTER THIRTY-EIGHT

"**D**AMN. POLICE. What the hell do *they* want?"

"No way we can outrun them," Jason said, sounding tense.

"Let's see what they want. Be ready, though. Verity, use your disregarding spell."

"Right."

Stone pulled over as much as he could and brought the car to a stop. The police car stopped behind them, blocking the road. After a moment, two figures emerged. It was hard to see them since they hadn't shut off the headlights or the whirling red-and-blues. One approached, while the other remained a few steps back. The close one motioned for Stone to roll down his window.

"What's the problem, Officer?"

The cop wore a tan uniform and cap, but wasn't Highway Patrol. He looked to be in his middle thirties, with a blunt, fleshy face and a hint of a paunch lapping over his leather belt. Typical small-town policeman, from the look of him.

"What are you doing up here, sir?" he asked. His gaze took in Stone, then looked past him into the car where it settled on Jason. He didn't appear to notice Verity.

"We got lost. Took a wrong turn. I was looking for a place to turn around."

"License and registration, please."

Stone pulled out his wallet and leaned across to retrieve the registration from the glove compartment. "I don't like this," he muttered to Jason. "Be ready."

"Already am," Jason muttered back.

Stone handed the documents out to the cop, weaving a quick illusion so he wouldn't see the correct information. "What's the problem? This isn't a private road, is it?"

"No, sir. But we've had some problems with drug operations up in the hills here. So when we spot a car like this heading up there—" He paused to study Stone's documents, shining his flashlight over them. "Please step out of the car."

"Why?"

The flashlight swiveled up, the beam hitting Stone in the face. "Step out of the car, sir," the cop repeated, more forcefully this time.

Stone blinked, flinching away from the light. "What do you want? I haven't done anything wrong." He pushed open the door—in truth, he *wanted* to be away from the car, which would give him more room to maneuver—and got out, keeping his hands in sight.

The beam lowered, leaving him momentarily blinded—at least with normal sight. When he switched to magical sight, however, he immediately noticed the odd green edging around both cops' auras, and tensed. Though these weren't the same men who'd attacked him and Garra back at the school, their auras had the same unusual quality.

When the other cop moved, heading back toward his car, Stone made a fast decision. With a quick flick of his power, he grabbed hold of the man's foot and yanked it out from under him. The cop flailed and went down, yelping.

Unfortunately, the first must have picked up on his tension, because he acted nearly simultaneously. Moving faster than an out-of-shape small-town cop should be able to, he backed up and whipped out his pistol, leveling it at Stone. "Down on the ground!" he barked.

Before Stone could react, the guy's gun flew out of his hand and sailed into the forest. *Good job, Verity.* He took hold with a telekinetic grip and shoved the man away. Neither of the cops appeared to be wearing mics—Stone couldn't let them get back to their car and their radio.

The cop recovered fast, though—too fast. With a roar, he leaped forward and grabbed Stone, slamming him into the side of the car.

Stone got his shield up in time to blunt most of the damage. "Don't let them get to their car!" he yelled, hearing both passenger-side doors open as Jason and Verity emerged from the BMW.

The second cop, shorter and broader than his partner, made a run for the cruiser, but skidded to a stop as the open door slammed shut.

"Don't try it," Verity warned.

Stone leaped to his feet and drove the first cop into a nearby tree with a concussion spell. It was so *easy* now!

The power didn't make him any faster, though, and these two small-town cops were every bit as fast and tough as the men at Jimmy Tanuki's place. The guy rolled up and launched himself back at Stone, his angry roar almost feral.

Stone barely got out of the way in time, throwing himself sideways along the BMW's flank. He expected to hear a crash as the cop slammed into the car, but the man surprised him again, springing suddenly upward to land on the opposite side. Spinning, he yelled, "Jason! Watch out!"

The cop came down next to Jason, bulling him off toward the trees, but despite his supernatural strength and speed, he clearly hadn't reckoned with Jason's fighting skill. Jason dropped and flung the man over his shoulder into another tree, where he rolled up almost immediately.

Before he could go after Jason again, though, he lifted off the ground and, arms flailing, smashed into another tree before dropping back down, stunned.

The second cop, meanwhile, had disappeared around the back of the cruiser. Stone swept his gaze around, looking for the man's aura, but didn't see it. Where had he gone? Whatever they were using didn't turn them invisible, did it? If he could—

A dark figure dropped silently down from a branch above, driving Stone to the ground. His grasping hands went for Stone's throat, his eyes blazing with wild rage.

Somewhere in the distance, Stone heard a shriek from the other cop, but he had other things to worry about at the moment. He gathered power to rip the man's hands from him and throw him free.

Suddenly, though, the cop's grip slipped on its own. His eyes lost their animalistic glare and went wide and fearful, and something gurgled in the back of his throat. Jerking and clutching his chest, he toppled backward.

*What—?*

"Look out!" Verity yelled.

Stone spun around, still crouched.

328 |                                          *R. L. KING*

The first cop had gotten away from Jason. He leaped to the top of the BMW and came down toward Stone.

No more time to play around. Stone summoned more power, lifted the man in mid-leap, and flung him with all his considerable strength into the thick trunk of a tree just off the road. He thought he heard something crack, but whether it was the tree or the man, he wasn't sure and didn't care. The cop slid to the ground, then staggered up and took off into the forest. In seconds, he was gone.

Jason and Verity darted around the BMW as Stone crouched back down to examine the remaining cop. "What the hell—?" he muttered.

What he was seeing didn't make any sense. The guy writhed on the ground, his breath coming in hitching gasps, his hands clawing at his chest. The harsh illumination from the cruiser's headlights showed a pale, ashen face bathed in sweat.

"What's wrong with him?" Stone demanded. He hadn't hit the man that hard. He'd barely hit him at *all*.

Verity dropped to her knees next to him, her expression growing fuzzy as she picked up his wrist to check his pulse, then shifted to magical sight. "I think he's having a heart attack."

Stone glanced in the direction the other cop had headed, also switching to magical sight. No sign of the man's aura appeared among the faint green ones of the trees. "We've got to go before he brings more of them."

"We can't just leave this guy here to die," Verity said. "Give me just a few minutes. I can help him."

Stone didn't like it—these cops were obviously in league with whoever had stolen the chalice, if their green-tinged auras were any indication—but he knew from experience Verity wouldn't be swayed. "All right. A few minutes. Just get him stabilized, and we'll leave him in his car and go on. Jason and I will keep watch."

As Jason hurried over to the cruiser to retrieve the shotgun inside, Stone continued scanning in all directions, including a few glances upward to make sure no one was stalking them from high branches. As his gaze skated over the sweating cop, he stopped. "Bloody hell…"

"What?" Verity asked, distracted. She sat near the man's side, moving her hands over his chest.

"The green tinges around the edge of his aura are fading."

"Is that important?" Jason asked. He held the shotgun and stood near the BMW's back end, sweeping the barrel around.

"I don't know yet. But probably." He continued to keep watch, his impatience growing as Verity ministered to the fallen man. Even so, he couldn't help feeling pride as he watched her work. He hadn't been the one to teach his former apprentice her impressive healing skills—that had been all Edna Soren from Ojai—but nonetheless he loved seeing her excel.

The next few minutes passed in silent tension, broken only by the stricken cop's heavy breathing. As more time passed and no one else approached, Stone grew more concerned that a whole squad of enhanced small-town policemen would burst through the trees and attack them, probably accompanied by the even more dangerous men who'd attacked them back in Oakland. But as Verity finished her work and rocked back on her heels with a tired sigh, the forest remained quiet and undisturbed.

"Did it work?" Jason asked, still scanning the trees and the road. "Is he gonna be okay?"

"Yeah," she breathed. "It was minor, and I caught it quick. He's—"

The cop's eyes flew open. His body jerked and fear settled over his face as he stared up at Stone and the others. For a moment, Stone thought he'd try to scrabble away, but instead he let his breath out and slumped back. For the first time, Stone took note of his name badge, which identified him as *FOLEY*.

"Holy shit..." Foley whispered. "What—what happened?"

"Stay put," Jason ordered. "You're gonna be okay, but if you try to attack us again, that might not stay true." He'd already relieved the cop of his pistol, which was currently in the back seat of the BMW, but he held the shotgun in a ready position pointed near, but not at, the cop.

Stone looked at Foley with magical sight, but he didn't need to—as he'd suspected, his aura's green edge had vanished, leaving behind a pale orange glow. "Where's your friend gone?"

"What?" Foley swiped a hand over his forehead, then put it to his chest. "My chest—couldn't breathe—did I have a *heart attack?*"

"A mild one," Verity said. "You're okay now. Answer the Doc's question."

"I'm—*okay?* But—how?"

"Don't play stupid with us," Stone snapped. "You're certainly familiar with the concept of magic, given whatever was done to enhance you. Where did your friend go? He took off into the forest and left you here."

Foley's eyes widened. "Keeler...he...*left*?"

"Would he have gone for help?" Jason demanded. "Is he coming back with more like you?"

The cop sat slowly up. He was still shaking, but looked much better than he had before. When he noticed the car, his posture slumped again. "It's a couple miles back to town. If he's coming back it'll take a little time."

"We need to get going, then," Jason said. "Hang on—I'll disable their car so they can't follow us." He glared at Foley. "If you come after us—"

"Wait," Stone interrupted, focusing on Foley. "Officer Foley—I'd say you owe my friend here your life. You know that, right?"

Foley's gaze shifted between Stone and Verity, and then he let his breath out and nodded. "I don't know how—not exactly—but...yeah." He blinked a couple of times. "Wait...did you say...*magic*?"

Stone ignored that. "Right, then. You owe us something in return."

He swallowed, clearly expecting the worst. "What?"

"I want to know how—and *why*—you were so strong and fast. It's worn off now, I can see, but it was there before." He crouched lower, fixing the man with his cold gaze. "I'd strongly advise you not to lie. My friend might have saved you from a heart attack, but she won't save you from what will happen if you don't tell me the truth."

For several seconds, Foley didn't reply. He licked his lips, swallowed again, and ran his hand across his forehead, almost as if he couldn't quite believe what had happened. Finally, he let his breath out. "Yeah. Okay. I'll tell you."

He struggled to his feet. Stone and Verity stood back, not helping but not getting in his way, while Jason kept the shotgun trained near him and continued to watch their surroundings.

"Do you work for the people at the abandoned animal preserve up this road?" Stone asked when he'd made it to his feet. He shifted to magical sight so he could watch Foley's aura as he answered.

"What? No." His aura flickered.

Stone sharpened his glare and took a step closer. "Officer Foley, believe me, I have *no* patience right now. None whatsoever. Would you like to amend that answer? Last chance."

Foley returned the glare, but then his shoulders slumped. "Yeah. Well…sort of. We don't *work* for them, but we leave 'em alone. And we stop anybody we don't recognize who tries to go there."

"Why?" Stone asked. "What are they doing up there?"

"I don't know." When Stone's glare sharpened, he raised his hands. "No—it's true. I don't know and I don't wanna know. None of us do. Safer that way. All I know is it's got something to do with some kind of secret scientific experiments."

"So what's buffing you up?" Jason asked.

"And why?" Stone added. "I saw your town on the map. It's got a few hundred people and a dog. Why do you need that kind of enhancement to deal with drunks and petty theft?"

Foley glanced around, almost as if hoping somebody would show up to extricate him from his situation. Then he sighed. "It's not drunks and petty theft. It's pretty remote up here, and there are a couple of decent-sized drug operations out in the sticks. We've been trying to root them out for years, but they're smart and well-armed."

"So?" Jason paced in front of him, making no effort to hide the shotgun. "Are you sayin' those guys at the preserve are manufacturing drugs?"

"No. They haven't been here long—about a year." He chuckled mirthlessly. "I guess you could say they made us an offer we couldn't refuse."

"And what's that?" Stone asked. "Don't stall, Officer Foley. It won't go well for you if you do."

"I'm not stalling. I don't have any idea how you did it, but I know you guys saved my life. And I know why you had to." His hand moved to his belt.

Instantly, Jason swung the shotgun around and pointed it at him. "Hands where we can see 'em."

"I'm just trying to show you something. No weapons. You took my gun."

"Go ahead," Stone said. "But slowly."

Foley unclipped what looked like a small, metal water bottle from the left side of his belt. "This."

"What's that?" Verity asked.

"The offer we couldn't refuse."

"Wait a moment…" Stone muttered. "Let me see that."

Foley handed it over readily. "I don't want anything to do with that stuff anymore. I thought it might be doing some-thing to me, but I couldn't be sure until tonight."

The bottle was almost full. Stone popped the cap and poured a small sample of its contents into his open hand. The liquid was brown and oily, with a musky, molasses-like odor.

It also shimmered with magical energy.

"Bloody hell…"

"What is it?" Jason demanded.

Stone flicked his gaze to Foley. "This is what you're taking to enhance your speed and strength, isn't it?"

"Yeah." Foley looked miserable. "It also helps us heal a lot faster, and makes it so we can see better in the dark."

"So…the people at the preserve supply your department with this elixir, and in return, you—"

"We leave them alone, let 'em do their thing, and keep other people away from them." At Stone's glare, he raised his hands in capitulation. "I'm not lying to you, man. I have no *idea* what they're doing up there. None of us do. They're quiet, they keep to themselves, and they don't cause any trouble."

"And the elixir they provide supplies you the capability to root out the drug operations in the mountains."

Foley nodded. "*They're* the dangerous ones. The drug guys. Getting them off the street makes everybody around here safer. Some of 'em have even moved on because they know we can deal with 'em better now."

He gestured toward the bottle. "But that stuff—I knew it was too good to be true. I don't know what they put in it—some kind of special herbs, they said—but I've been feeling for a while like it was messing with me. You know—sweating, fast heartbeat, weakness when it wears off…"

Stone pondered. He wanted to ask more questions—perhaps even comment on the irony of using performance-enhancing alchemical elixirs to help chase down drug producers—but they didn't have time to waste. He was sure whoever was up at the animal preserve already knew they were coming, even if Keeler hadn't alerted them. If they had Garra, they could have already killed her, or they could even now be taking her away via some hidden escape route.

He handed the bottle to Jason. "Hold on to this, will you? Verity can analyze it later." Then he turned back to Foley. "I'd love to stay and chat with you, Officer Foley, but time is short. We've got to go. We think they've kidnapped a friend of mine, and we need to find her before they kill her."

Foley's eyes widened. "Kidnapping? Why would they do that?"

"You tell me. But first I've got to decide what to do with you. If we leave you here, you'll run for help as soon as we're gone, even if we disable your car and your radio."

"No, I won't." He seemed to consider his next words; he looked fearful, but when he spoke again his tone held resolve. "Let me help you."

"Help us?" Jason asked. "How can you do that?"

"Look," he said. "I don't know how you did it, but I feel mostly okay now. That's—if I really *did* have a heart attack, even a mild one, that's amazing. I'm never taking that stuff again. But I've lived in this area all my life, and I know the layout of that place. Used to go up there with my family when I was a kid, before the people who owned it went bankrupt and it was abandoned."

Stone couldn't deny it was a useful offer. Having some-one familiar with the area's geography would be helpful, even if he didn't know what the current occupants were up to. But could they trust him?

Foley seemed to pick up on Stone's hesitation. "Please. Let me pay you back. If I'd been one some other call when this happened, I'd probably be dead now. Listen—I've got a wife and a little girl, and if it wasn't for you I'd never see either of them again. That's worth something to me." He glanced over his shoulder. "We should go before Keeler gets back to town and brings help."

Stone shifted to magical sight and examined the cop's aura. It looked stressed and agitated, but that was to be expected given his scare. It also, however, looked sincere. "All right," he said at last. "You can come with us. But we're not giving you back your gun."

"Yeah...okay." He didn't look pleased about it, but he nodded at the BMW. "Let's go."

# CHAPTER THIRTY-NINE

"WHY ARE YOU STOPPING?" Foley asked. "It's still another quarter mile to the gate."

"They already know we're coming," Stone said. "No point in making it more obvious than necessary." He pulled the BMW as far off the road as he could and shut off the engine. "Everybody out. We walk from here. Can you manage, Mr. Foley?"

"Yeah, I think so, as long as you don't plan to run. I'd feel a lot better if you gave me back my gun, though. I'm not going to shoot you—I promise."

Verity, now riding shotgun so Jason could keep an eye on the cop from the back, twisted in her seat. "I believe him, Doc."

Stone waited until they'd all gotten out of the car, then checked Foley's aura as well. The cop looked resigned and nervous, but he didn't sense any duplicity. "All right. Jason, give him his gun back. But Mr. Foley—if you even attempt to use it on any of us, I promise you'll regret it."

"Don't worry—I saw what you guys can do, and I'm not an idiot. I just don't want to be defenseless." He peered around as if expecting something to jump them. "I think if I live through this, I'm gonna look for another job somewhere safer. Like Chicago."

"Fine," Jason said, not sounding happy about it. "But I'm keeping the shotgun."

Stone concentrated on putting a disregarding spell on the car. It wouldn't help if anyone specifically came out here looking for them, but he'd found a wide enough turnout that anyone going by might miss it. "Let's go," he said. "Keep your voices down, and watch for any signs of movement. Especially you, Verity. They're probably watching us, or will be soon."

"What *are* these guys?" Foley muttered. "It sounds like we're not just dealing with some harmless scientist types making fancy energy drinks."

"I doubt that's all they're doing," Stone said. "Now be quiet and keep your eyes open."

The quarter-mile walk to the edge of the complex took longer than Stone hoped. He didn't want to walk on the road and present a perfect target if anyone was watching, but pushing their way through the heavy underbrush without light slowed their progress significantly. By the time they spotted the glow of perimeter lights up ahead, everyone's auras radiated stress.

"Stop here," Stone muttered, looking around in search of auras hiding among the green glows of the trees.

Verity was looking too. "I don't see anything."

"I don't either, but give me a moment to get a look from up high."

"You gonna climb a tree?" Foley asked. He gripped his pistol tightly like a lifeline, and nervous sweat stood out on his wide forehead.

"Not exactly." Stone stepped behind a thick trunk. He concentrated for a moment and faded from view, then levitated upward. He ignored the cop's soft yelp of confusion.

One free of the trees, he shifted to magical sight and took another look around. He still couldn't see much in the darkness; there appeared to be a chain-link fence topped with razor wire surrounding the perimeter, but past a twenty-foot-wide cleared space past it, more trees obscured the remainder of the area. They'd have to get inside to see the rest.

He narrowed his eyes. At intervals of around ten feet apart he noticed tiny pinpoints of magical energy, corresponding to the metal poles holding the razor wire suspended above the fence proper. He couldn't tell without looking more closely, but he was fairly sure he knew what they were: magical detection devices, designed to alert those inside if anyone breached the fence.

*Good thing we're not planning to breach it, then.* But it would still be safer to disable them if he could before taking the group over.

He was about to drop back down when he spotted a faint blue glow in one of the trees just beyond the cleared area. Thankful that his newly augmented powers allowed him to remain invisible longer without tiring, he dropped lower and focused on the glow. It resolved itself into a figure crouched on one of the upper branches, holding what appeared to be binoculars to its face. A long object, probably a rifle, hung on a strap around its neck. On closer inspection, the blue glow showed the faint green edges indicating the watcher was probably enhanced with the same concoction that had nearly killed Foley.

*Ah, they* do *know someone's coming—or at least they've got a guard set. Good to know.*

He was too far away to hit the man reliably with a spell from here, so he lowered himself back to the ground and landed a few feet behind Foley before his invisibility spell faded.

"Did you see anything?"

Foley jumped. "Where did you come from? Where did you go?"

"Didn't see anything moving." Verity scanned the area in front of her. "Just trees."

Stone ignored Foley. "There's a fence a short distance ahead, with razor wire. Beyond that is an open area, and I spotted someone hiding in the trees on the other side. I think he's got a gun, and I'm fairly sure he's dosed up on the same concoction as Mr. Foley and his partner."

"We need to take him out." Jason raised the shotgun. "Can you guys do that?"

"Not without getting a lot closer."

"Razor wire?" Foley peered into the darkness. "That's new."

"We've got to get going," Stone said. "I don't think he saw me, but I'm sure they know we're coming."

"How are we gonna do that?" Jason demanded. "Sounds like they've got a killing zone set up."

"Verity and I will take care of that. Stay here until we get back."

Jason didn't look happy about it, but he glared at Foley. "Fine. I'll keep an eye on our friend here."

Verity followed Stone without question. As they reached the edge of the tree line, she studied the fence. "This seems like an awful lot of trouble for one guy."

"Normally I'd agree with you. But we can't risk this one getting away and warning the others. I've got an idea." He briefly explained it to her.

She grinned. "Sneaky. Didn't I see that in *Jurassic Park*?"

"That might have been where I got it. Let's go."

Stone waited as Verity faded into invisibility and disappeared into the trees. He gave her a two-minute head start, then used his own invisibility spell and floated over the razor wire fence, keeping a close eye on the figure in the tree. The man didn't appear to have noticed either of them yet—at least it appeared the elixir's enhancement abilities didn't extend to detecting auras or seeing through invisibility. That was something, at least.

As Stone floated across the open zone, the crouched figure seemed to be still scanning the area out past the fence. Had he spotted something there, or was he expecting something? It didn't matter either way, as long as it kept his attention focused.

*Just a little further…*

Suddenly, the man stiffened. He rose from his crouch, sniffing the air around him, and pulled the rifle into position. He swung the barrel around in Stone's general direction, tense and wary.

*Damn. I forgot about the scent.*

Hoping Verity was where she was supposed to be, Stone backed off, putting another thick tree between himself and the man. He used magic to pick up a large pine cone from the ground and flung it off to the side into another tree.

The man's aura flared alarm. He jerked the rifle barrel around in the same direction as the pine cone had hit, but didn't fire yet.

Stone ducked behind the tree so his aura wouldn't be visible. *Come on...*

For a moment, it appeared the man would leap free of the branch and to investigate the disturbance. But before he could do that, he stiffened, swayed, and toppled off the branch, crashing to the ground below.

Stone dropped down and hurried over to find Verity standing near the unconscious figure. He flashed her a quick grin. "Clever girl."

She rolled her eyes at him, but returned the grin, bending to retrieve the man's rifle. "Let's hurry. I don't think he'll be out for long. Unless you want to kill him, we'd better be out of here before he wakes up."

Stone didn't see any other lurking gunmen. He took the rifle from Verity and the two of them levitated back over the fence to where Jason and Foley waited with growing impatience.

"Did you get him?" Jason demanded.

Stone held up the rifle. "Let's move. We don't have long."

Foley was eyeing all three of them with stunned terror. "What the hell *are* you people?"

"Best if you don't ask too many questions, Mr. Foley," Stone told him as they crept free of the trees toward the fence. "You'll sleep better that way."

"If I get out of here alive," Foley muttered.

"Stay close, and we'll keep you safe," Verity told him. "Just don't run off on your own."

"Give me a moment," Stone said. "Let me take out the nearest sensors before we go, just to be safe."

"What sensors?" Foley's eyes narrowed. "I don't see anything."

"You wouldn't, would you?" Stone said, distracted. "Quiet, please." He focused his power on the tiny magical glows around two of the metal poles, and snuffed them out. If anyone was monitoring them, they'd know something was up—but then again, they already knew something was up. At least this way they wouldn't know exactly *what.* "There. Let's go."

They crept forward until they reached the edge of the chain-link fence. "You might want to close your eyes just about now," Stone said. "And please keep quiet, no matter what happens. I don't want to alert anyone else to our presence."

"What the hell—?" Foley was beginning to look as if he wished he had taken off into the forest along with his partner. "What's gonna happen?"

"Trust him," Jason said, patting the cop's arm.

Stone didn't wait to see whether Foley followed instructions. "Verity, you get Jason. I'll take care of Mr. Foley."

Together, they cast their levitation spells. The four of them lifted up past the razor wire and settled neatly on the other side.

Foley stumbled as he touched the ground, and would have fallen if Jason hadn't caught his arm. Apparently he *had* taken Stone's advice, because he now gaped at the fence, clearly confused about how they'd ended up on the other side. To his credit, he said nothing but merely took a deep, shuddering breath and waited for further instructions.

"Come on," Jason said under his breath. "I don't like being out in the open like this. Makes us too easy a target."

Together, the four of them hurried across the twenty-foot open zone. Stone scanned constantly ahead of them with magical sight, and it looked like Verity was doing the same thing.

Nothing attacked them. Either the man Verity had knocked out with her stun spell hadn't awakened yet, or he'd run off to look for more help. Either way, the four of them stopped just past the tree line to catch their breath.

"Now what?" Verity asked. "You don't know exactly where they've got her, do you?"

"No." Stone turned to Foley. "Mr. Foley. You said you were familiar with this place from your childhood. What can you tell us?"

Foley was looking around as if he expected to be jumped from all sides. "I don't remember a lot," he said. "It was a long time ago. It looks like we're on the west side now. There are several enclosure things for animals—some of them are sunken, so we need to be careful not to stumble into them in the dark if the fences are down."

"What about buildings?" Stone asked. "Are there still any? If they've got our friend, they're probably holding her in one of them—not to mention whatever else they're up to."

"Uh—there's a visitors' center thing. Should be pretty close. Some barns...I think there's a vet's office somewhere up ahead."

"There's got to be some kind of administration building too," Jason said. "Probably off somewhere away from the public areas. Unless the admin stuff is in the visitors' center."

"Not much to go on," Stone said grimly. "Can't be helped, though. I'd go up and take a look, but I don't fancy getting shot down if they have a way to spot me. Let's just keep on, and keep our eyes open. I doubt they'll sit idle and let us explore."

Picking their way through the darkened forest proved to be an eerie and uncomfortable endeavor. Constantly on the watch for threats, Stone and Verity both kept their magical sight up. Stone tried to look everywhere at once—ahead, above them into the high branches, behind them to make sure no one was sneaking up on them—while still watching where he walked to make sure he didn't stumble into some overgrown pit. He saw no sign of the downed fences Foley had mentioned; either they were gone, or so choked by growth that they were no longer visible.

"This is creepy," Verity whispered as some small animal skittered by on an overhead branch. She sounded as tense as Stone felt.

"Yeah," Jason muttered. He had the shotgun pointed ahead, sweeping the barrel around and jumping at every faint sound. "Reminds me of that movie *Predator*—remember, V?"

"Great," she said sourly. "Now you've got me thinking about invisible space aliens who want to skin us and hang us from trees. Thanks, big bro."

"Hush," Stone said. "You're not far from wrong—except I think they're more interested in pulling our arms off than skinning us. Stay quiet. Is it much further, Foley?"

Foley had a death-grip on his pistol. "I don't think so. I think the visitor's center's up ahead soon, if it's still there."

It felt like at least another hour before they reached the edge of a clearing and spotted the shadowy husk of a building up ahead, but a quick glance at his watch told Stone it had in reality been only a few minutes. He held up a hand to stop the others and sharpened his magical sight. The structure stood black and dead against the glowing green of the trees and underbrush, showing ragged, uneven edges. "Is that it?" he asked Foley.

"I think so. Can't see too well, but I think that's where it was."

"Looks pretty trashed," Verity said. "They wouldn't be keeping her in there, would they?"

"Let's take a quick check," Stone said. "Unlikely, but safer to be sure. Verity, put a disregarding spell on Jason. I'll get Foley."

"Right."

Stone had no idea if the spell would conceal them from the enhanced attackers, but it didn't require much energy and it might give them the edge they needed. He moved forward, scanning the space ahead of him, and heard his companions doing likewise.

"This is it," Foley whispered as they got closer. "This is where people used to buy tickets, and they ran some presentations on the animals they had here. Looks like not much of it's left, though."

Stone stepped over a pile of debris and approached the building. Foley was right: up closer, it appeared that most of two side wings had been knocked down, leaving only the center section. Even that hadn't survived unscathed, with most of its roof, its windows, and big sections of its walls missing. All around, tall weeds and other growth were clearly in the process of reclaiming it.

"See anything?" Jason asked. He'd turned back the way they'd come and was swiveling the shotgun barrel around.

Everything was dark, relieved by nothing but the faint green glows of the vegetation and the brighter ones of their own auras. Stone spotted a large hole in the nearby wall and stepped through, risking a quick, faint light spell. As the others came through behind him, he got dim impressions of broken furniture, including a waist-high counter; molding, tattered carpets; and the torn and faded remains of what had once been brightly colored posters strewn around the floor. "If they're here, they're hiding well," he said. "I think we should—"

"Look out!" Jason shouted from behind him, followed by the echoing *boom* of his shotgun.

The front of the counter splintered, but not before a dark figure leaped free of it and dived at the group with frightening speed.

# | CHAPTER FORTY

J ASON'S WARNING GAVE STONE the time he needed to get his shield up. The shadowy figure slammed into it and rolled aside just as Verity yelped.

"More behind us!" she cried, raising her own shield.

Stone spun, spotting two more of the attackers—one came in through the same hole in the wall they'd used, and the other had apparently been crouched near a broken section in the roof. All of them moved as fast as Garra had, and none of them had visible auras.

That wasn't good—it would make them much harder to keep track of.

Jason's shotgun boomed again, and next to it Foley's pistol, their loud barks echoing in the silence. A shower of debris came down from the ceiling, pattering over their heads. One of the figures leaped at Jason, who dived sideways and barely avoided the attack.

"Stay close!" Stone yelled, his ears ringing from the guns' reports. They'd have to take this lot down—or drive them away—fast, since there was no way they could fight them on their own terms. The attackers knew the area and their enhancements made them faster, stronger, and more agile than his own group. They might have an advantage if they could keep the fight in here, though. If they got outside, these men knew the terrain better and could use it to their advantage.

Time to let loose, then, and take this new power out for a real test drive.

As one of the men leaped toward them and Verity used a concussion beam to blow him into the far wall, Stone focused on the counter. It was large and looked substantial—at least substantial enough to survive the years' worth of decay that had claimed most of the rest of the building. He reached out with his power and gripped it with a telekinetic hold, then ripped it free of the floor with a wrenching screech. He held it there for just a moment, then sighted in on two of the men and flung it at them.

They were fast—faster than he'd thought. One of them managed to leap free before the thing crashed into the wall, but the other one wasn't so fortunate. The full weight of the massive projectile, which had to be at least two hundred pounds, slammed first into him and then into the wall, crushing him. He screamed in pain as the counter's momentum broke through the weakened wall, tumbling both him and the counter out into the clearing. Without the wall to support it, part of the roof came free and cascaded down on top of him.

"Holy *shit!*" one of the other men yelled.

"You want more?" Stone snapped. He didn't think they'd stay intimidated for long, but every little bit helped.

The others, meanwhile, weren't idle. Jason and Foley both opened fire on the one who'd yelled, and Verity followed up by whipping some of the debris into a whirlwind and settling it over him.

Stone took his eyes off the one he'd dropped in the hope of spotting the third one, but couldn't find him. When he turned back to the first one, expecting him to be diving toward him again, he instead saw nothing but the ruined counter splayed on the ground just outside the blasted wall. The man had disappeared.

Two more gunshots sounded. "He's getting away!" Jason yelled, and indeed the second attacker had burst free of the whirlwind and was staggering into the forest, his jerking gait indicating that at least one of the rounds had found him.

"Should we go after them?" Verity asked, puffing as she scanned the area around her.

"No." Stone fought to control the jangling rush of adrenaline still surging through him. "Let's keep going. We'll probably encounter them again, but we haven't got time to waste chasing them."

Jason pulled rounds from his pocket and quickly reloaded the shotgun, eyeing Stone and the broken counter with a new respect. "I agree. Let's keep going and find her fast. Maybe we can get her out of here before they can regroup."

"How long does it take them to heal damage?" Verity asked, then turned to Foley. "Do you know?"

Foley was obviously trying not to look overwhelmed. "I—I'm not sure," he said. "With us it took about an hour— we never had to test it against serious injuries, though, and I think these guys have a better version than we did."

"I'm sure it's faster than that," Stone said. "Let's assume it is, anyway. Perhaps we'll be pleasantly surprised. Let's go."

They exited the blasted building with care, all of them looking in every direction as they tried to spot potential ambushes. "Anybody hurt?" Verity asked.

Nobody spoke up.

"I think we surprised them," Jason said. "I don't think they were expecting that level of opposition. Have they seen you in action before, Al?"

"Yes, but not much."

"They might be tough, but you two aren't anything to fuck with—not even accounting for the guns. They'll be more dangerous next time."

"No doubt," Stone said. That thought had already occurred to him. They had no idea how many of the men were here—they'd only seen three, but he was sure there were more. No doubt when they regrouped, they'd send everything they had.

They soon left the visitors' center behind. After a few more minutes' hyper-vigilant trek through the tangled overgrowth, they passed another building to their left. This one was only a fraction of the visitors' center's size, and the vegetation had nearly reclaimed it.

"That's the vet's office, I think," Foley said, coming up next to Stone. "If my memory's right, there should be one more building up ahead."

"Do you know what it is?"

"No—it wasn't open to the public. I think it was some kind of lab, or maybe where they kept the animals quarantined when they arrive. Not sure."

"We'll check it out," Stone said. "Sounds like a good place to keep a prisoner."

But as they continued forward, nothing but more trees and underbrush appeared in front of them. They walked for five minutes, then ten, with no sign of either any structures or their attackers. A bit further ahead, they spotted what looked like it had once been a clearing, but now tall trees dotted its center.

Foley stopped. "Wait a second…" he said, looking confused.

"What?"

He pointed toward the clearing. "That's it. There's supposed to be a building there."

"All I see is a cleared-out space with some trees in it," Jason said. "Maybe they tore it down since you were here last."

"Yeah…maybe so. I guess it's possible the remains could be overgrown by now. But it's weird that the trees have gotten so tall. It hasn't been *that* long since I was out here."

"Are you sure you don't have the location wrong?"

"I'm sure." He pointed again. "See past it, where that steep hillside's rising? That's the boundary of the park. It couldn't be any farther ahead." He shook his head. "I've gotta be wrong, though. No way the trees could be that far along. Let's head east a little and see if we can find it."

Stone didn't move. "Hmm…" He continued examining the area, shifting to magical sight.

"You think it's an illusion?" Verity asked. "I can't see anything—I've been trying."

"If it is, it's a bloody good one. But there *is* a ley line not far from here, which would help sustain it. Give me a moment."

He moved away from the rest of the group and levitated up into the branches of a nearby tree. Once there, he crouched and focused, directing his attention to the middle of the clearing.

One thing he'd noticed since returning from Calanar with his new power source: he still had access to significant power without doing more than tapping the dimension's energy, but if he wanted extra punch, he had to work a little harder for it. It wasn't an inconvenience—it wasn't as if it hurt or tired him any more than normal—but it did represent an extra conscious step he had to take, and required a bit more concentration than normal. He did that now, narrowing his eyes and trying to envision a building where clearly none existed.

That was the problem with illusions—seeing through them wasn't just about magic. It was about the ability to believe—to *truly* believe—something contrary to what your every sense was telling you. Stone had met plenty of mages, including some with significant power levels, who'd never truly gotten the hang of it because they lacked imagination. The trick was similar to what he'd had to learn when he first mastered magical sight: you had to look *past* what seemed to be there, while keeping your mind open to the possibilities of what truly *was* there. He'd had a hell of a time getting it through to Verity, just as William Desmond had had trouble getting it through to him when he was a teenager.

Now, though, as he let his mind drift and focus at the same time, something began to shimmer into view. Carefully, he forced himself not to look directly at it—doing that would make it disappear again. Instead, he continued to drift until several seconds later the scene shifted to reveal a glowing, hemispherical ward protecting a single-story building.

"Nice…" he murmured. Combining the illusion with the ward meant that neither of them had to be particularly strong—the two reinforced each other, and with the addition of the ley line, produced a neat disguise to keep any curious searchers away. That was probably the ward his tracking spell had partially pierced, warning its caster of a potential intruder. And if that was true, this might be where they were holding Garra.

"Did you find anything?" Verity's voice came from below him.

"I did." He didn't shift away from what he'd spotted, fearing if he did it would fade again. It would be easier to get it back the next time, but the faster he could get it down, the faster they could get to whatever was inside.

With care, he levitated back down. "Keep watch—all of you. I'm going to take that ward down, and I expect someone will object when I do."

"Got it." Her footsteps rustled as she headed off, back to where Jason and Foley waited.

Stone crouched low and headed to the edge of the ward. He summoned a nearly-invisible barrier around him just in case, then shifted fully to magical sight. Now that he knew where the ward was, he could focus specifically on it while ignoring the illusion.

It wasn't an impressive ward—certainly nowhere near as complex as the one on his home, or even the ones Verity could produce on her own. Likely, whoever had produced it didn't specialize in such things, and counted on the illusion's concealment to keep it from having to stand up to any real stress.

Stone had two options: he could either punch through it using main force, or pick it apart to open a way for him and his friends to pass through. The former method would be faster but would certainly get them noticed immediately; the latter approach would take longer but likely give them a bit of a head start on getting inside the building. Both had their advantages and disadvantages, but he'd need to—

"Doc! *Watch out!*"

Verity's shouted warning came less than a second before something large and heavy dropped from above him, slamming into his shield.

# | CHAPTER FORTY-ONE

W HATEVER HAD DROPPED on Stone clearly hadn't expected him to be protected, which certainly saved his life. He leaped up from his crouch in time to see a muscular male figure glance off the shield, roll away, then leap up and take off toward where Verity and the others waited.

"Look out!" he called, already acting. Without dropping the shield—seriously, how had he functioned before he had ready access to this new power?—he flung twin beams of magical energy at the fleeing figure, expecting it to light up and drop.

It didn't. Moving with agility that would have done an Olympic gymnast proud, the man twisted, leaped to the side, then rolled up and resumed his charge toward the others.

Stone had taken only a few steps in their direction when another figure dropped in front of him, legs and arms spread wide. This one glared at him, but didn't attack.

*They're trying to separate us.*

The figure rose to its full height, looming. The man was taller than Stone and significantly wider—not bodybuilder-muscular this time, but big and substantial like a bear. His eyes burned with feral rage. Stone couldn't tell if he was one of the same men who'd attacked them at the visitors' center, but this could easily have been the man who'd torn Jimmy Tanuki limb from limb.

"I don't have time for this," Stone snapped, taking a step back. Beyond the bearish man, he heard the shouts of his friends, followed by the *crack* of Foley's pistol and the *boom* of Jason's shotgun.

"Should've stayed away," the man growled. "Or died like you were supposed to."

"Sorry to disappoint you." Stone feinted to one side, as if trying to slip past his attacker. When the man leaped in that direction, Stone lashed out with a telekinetic grip and took hold of him around the middle, lifting him high and flinging him off into the forest, away from Jason, Verity, and Foley.

"You all right over there?" he called, spotting the telltale sudden glow in the trees, indicating that Verity was using magic.

"Hurry up!" Jason yelled back, followed by the sound of something slamming into something hard.

Stone whirled back toward the ward. Now that he'd lost his focus on it, the illusion had reasserted itself—once again, the area looked like a clearing dotted with mature trees. It didn't matter, though: now that he knew the ward and the illusion were intertwined, he didn't need to see what he was doing. Not for what he intended. *Brute-force method it is, then.* He gathered more energy, reinforcing the shield around him as he did.

Off to his left, the trees rustled. His bearish opponent was already coming back. That wasn't surprising, given how fast and resilient the elixir made anyone who took it.

*Just have to focus for a couple more seconds…*

He loosed the blast just as the hulking figure slammed into him from the side, knocking him off his feet and sending him tumbling. The shield held, though, and as he rolled, he spotted the wide, smoking hole he'd blown into the ward. He jumped back to his feet and caught the man in mid-air as he leaped, tossing him away again. Beyond him, the edges of the blast sizzled and peeled away, revealing a squat, single-story building surrounded by perimeter lights.

"Come on!" Stone yelled, sprinting off toward where he'd left his friends.

The shotgun went off again, followed by a yelp of pain. Jason and Verity pelted toward Stone, with Foley following more slowly in their wake.

"Did you get him?" Verity panted.

"Not permanently. You?"

"I plugged him in the gut with the shotgun," Jason said. "He took off into the forest."

"That will give us some time, then," Stone said. "Come on. We've got to move." He darted a glance over toward where he'd tossed his own opponent, but the guy didn't re-appear. "They might have gone for more help. They're tough, but they're smart enough not to hang about when they're beaten."

By now, the glowing edges of the ward had receded further, making a hole big enough to drive a vehicle through. "Mind the edges and stay close," Stone directed, going through first and ducking to one side, shield at full strength again and covering himself and Jason. On the other side, Verity shielded Foley. Her barrier was more visible than Stone's, and Foley gaped at it, wide-eyed.

A bullet *spang*ed off Stone's shield.

"From the roof!" Jason yelled, pointing.

Stone followed his line of sight, spotting another shadowy figure crouched on the corner of the building. He raised his hand and made a sharp jerking motion, and the figure toppled off the building with a screech and another wild shot.

"Go!" Verity yelled.

They rounded the corner to the building's rear side. Stone paused for a quick glance: The outside of the building looked weathered, its paint peeling from long disuse, its windows covered with thick sheets of plywood. The door, halfway along it, however, was new and substantial, made of steel with a modern keypad lock.

"Can you get through that?" Verity asked. Like Jason and Foley, she scanned the area behind and to both sides of them constantly, with occasional glances upward in case anyone else tried to ambush them from the roof.

Stone studied it for only a moment. "No need." Instead, he focused on the thick plywood sheet covering a nearby window, ripping it free and flinging it to the side with next to no effort.

"Shit, Al, you *have* leveled up," Jason said. He spun back to cover the area behind them, but so far no one else was approaching.

"I'll go in first," Stone said. "Foley next, then Verity and Jason. Hurry."

With his shield up, he scrambled through the opening. The space beyond was a conference room, with a large, oval table in the center surrounded by chairs. Unlike what they'd found in the visitors' center, this place and its furnishings looked modern and well cared for. The door was closed.

The others quickly joined him. "Any idea where they might have Dr. Garra?" Verity asked, looking around.

"No. We'll have to search. I don't think this building is too big. Stay close. I'm going to try something. They like illusions so much, we'll give them—"

The door flew open, so hard it slammed into the wall. A fusillade of gunshots filled the air, smacking into Stone's and Verity's shields with bright pinpoints. As all of them dived for cover behind the table, a small object sailed inside and landed with a *thunk* on the conference table.

"Grenade!" Jason yelled.

But it wasn't a grenade—at least not the explosive kind. Instead, as soon as it rolled to a stop it began pumping out inky black smoke, filling the room.

"Fire!" Foley's coughing voice held panic.

"No!" Stone had seen this before—it was probably the same stuff they'd used back in Oakland. The anti-shifting properties wouldn't affect their group, but the stuff blocked magical sight, too, and that couldn't be allowed. "Verity! Whirlwind! Blow it out the opening!"

"On it!"

A second later, the air in the conference room began to move, picking up speed as it whipped around. The smoke whirled and slowly dissipated as the winds blew it toward the window.

Stone, meanwhile, ran forward, staying crouched so he wouldn't make a good target. As the smoke faded from the doorway, he saw Jason had done the same thing on the other side, holding his shotgun ready and pointed toward it.

"We need to go," Jason said. "They'll be waiting for us."

"Wait. Let me try something. Stay here."

He'd considered and discarded an invisibility spell—the building was small enough he could probably keep it up long enough to investigate a good portion of it, but if they were facing more of the enhanced men, they could probably locate him by scent. Instead, he summoned an illusion of the hallway beyond the door, making it appear nothing had changed as he stepped out. Even if they *could* catch his scent, it wouldn't matter—unless you could see through them, good illusions worked on all the senses. The men's brains would simply filter out any information not consistent with what the illusion presented as reality.

Stone took in the scene. He stood in a long hallway that appeared to run the entire length of the building. Fluorescent panels in the ceiling illuminated beige carpeting. To his right, one door at the end of the hall read *Break*. Another, on the same wall as they were, had a glass panel and said *Lab 1*. Across the hall, a third bore the universal symbol for a unisex restroom, and a fourth said *Storage*.

The hall in the other direction was longer, and split off into hallways on either side. Stone couldn't read the signs on the doors from where he stood, but he didn't miss the two figures concealed around the two side hallways' corners. Both had their gazes locked on the conference room door, and both held guns.

"Two men I can see, both with guns," Stone said. The illusion meant he didn't have to worry about the men hearing him unless they had electronic listening devices. "Verity, come out. Keep your shield up. We'll take them out together."

"Ready," she said from behind him. "I got left."

"One…two…three."

Both men yelped as their guns ripped free of their grips and sailed down the hallway toward Stone and Verity. One, wearing a lab coat, disappeared around his corner. The other, larger and beefier, roared and flung himself toward the fallen guns.

"Now!" Stone called, dropping the illusion.

Jason erupted out of the conference room and snatched up one of the guns as Stone and Verity both took hold of the charging man and slammed him into first the wall, then the floor.

He hit hard with a loud *oof,* but almost instantly he was back up and coming at them again.

A *boom* sounded from behind Stone and the man blew back, clutching his gut as blood welled up. He staggered, catching himself against the wall, then backpedaled and disappeared around the same corner the other man had. Spatters of blood trailed behind him.

"Come on!" Stone snapped, moving forward behind the shield. His ears rang with Jason's shotgun blast. "Jason, Foley—watch behind us."

They continued down the hallway, pausing to check both side halls as they passed them. One was a dead end; the other, where the two men had fled, had the heavy metal door Stone had opted not to open. It was open now. Were they gone? Probably not—just regrouping, or perhaps seeking more help.

Past the cross halls were the entrance to a small lobby on the right, a closed door at the end, and another closed, reinforced door on the left. The sign on it read *Lab 2 – DANGER - Authorized Personnel Only.*

"I think this is it," Stone said, pointing at it. "Be ready. If I'm right, they'll be making their stand in here."

The others crowded up, all of them keeping constant watch on the other potential attack points. Stone felt too exposed here, with too many ways for more attackers to come after them from all sides. They'd have to do this fast.

"Can you open it?" Verity asked.

Stone tried to pull it open, figuring it might be possible it wasn't locked. No such luck—the hefty handle didn't even budge. It had another keypad lock above it like the outside door, with a digital panel flashing *NO ENTRY*. "Not sure. Hold off anyone approaching and I'll try."

This wasn't the usual type of door he could open easily by flipping the lock with magic. Instead, it would prove a good test of his enhanced power, since he didn't have time to finesse it.

"Doc—more coming!" Verity sounded tense, but not scared. "My shield's up, but hurry."

It was hard for Stone not to turn around, but he didn't. He had no idea what was on the other side of the door—was Garra even in there, or had they spirited her away to some other location? There might be a whole cadre of enhanced or armed attackers waiting behind that door to attack them.

Gunfire sounded behind them, and a male voice roared. Jason's shotgun boomed, followed by Foley's pistol.

"Doc! Hurry!"

No more time to wait. Stone focused his power and opened his connection to the Calanarian energy. He took a tight mental grip on the door handle, blocked out all the sound behind him, and wrenched.

Power surged through him, setting his nerves on edge. The handle caught, then ripped free of the door and clattered to the floor.

*Yes!*

Stone couldn't pause to celebrate his success, though. He flung the door open, focusing on keeping the shield solid, and surged through.

He barely got a second's look around before more bullets slammed into his shield. "Hurry!" he shouted, moving in farther to give room for the others to come in behind him. The room was dark, the air heavy with a musky odor. "Close the door and hold it shut!"

As far as he could see with magical sight, there weren't any other enhanced thugs in here. He took a fast glance around, and immediately spotted the twin auras of two figures crouched behind a large, solid lab table in the center of the room. Both had guns and both were firing, but Stone couldn't miss the red flares of fear around them. These weren't combatants.

One shrieked and dropped, probably felled by a spell from Verity. Stone grabbed hold of the other one and tossed him into the back wall; he slid down and crumpled, stunned.

"Find a light," Jason called. "I'll hold the door."

A flashlight flared and Foley appeared. He looked terrified, but seemed to be holding it together reasonably well given what he'd just witnessed. He looked around near the door, then flipped a light switch. More overhead fluorescents blazed to life, revealing more of the lab.

"Bloody hell…" Stone breathed.

Lining two of the lab's far walls were a series of five enclosures, each around seven feet square. Heavy, clear plastic walls with separated them from each other and the rest of the room, and a light, drifting smoke filled each.

"Oh, my God…" Verity whispered.

Each of the enclosures included a sluggish, clearly sedated creature: two wolves, a cougar, a small bear, and—

"Dr. Garra!"

# | CHAPTER FORTY-TWO

S HE WAS BARELY ON HER FEET, her movements jerky and uncoordinated inside the cage. Stone ran over to her. "Watch those two—and keep that door shut," he ordered the others, and didn't wait to see if they complied.

"Viajera! Can you hear me?" He pressed his hands against the cage and shouted, unsure if his voice would carry through the heavy plastic.

She raised her head. Her eyes were dull and listless, her muscular shoulders slumped, but something lit up in her aura when she spotted him—a combination of fear and hope.

"Stand back—I'll get you out of there."

Apparently his voice did make it through, because she backpedaled until she was crouched against the far wall. She kept looking past him, her yellow-gold eyes wide and searching as if expecting someone to burst in.

The locks on the enclosures weren't as substantial as the one on the main door had been, and it took Stone only a couple of seconds to pop Garra's. He threw the door open, then sent a whirlwind of air through the space to clear out the drifting smoke.

In one powerful leap, she was free. She crouched, eyeing the others warily, and growled a warning as Foley swung his gun around.

"Holy shit, man, why did you let that thing out?" the cop demanded. The pistol shook in his hand, but the barrel remained leveled at Garra.

"Don't shoot!" Stone barked, using magic to sweep Foley's aim off track. "She's a friend."

"*That's* a friend? What the hell—?"

The smoke in the cage, apparently, had been the same stuff they had used on Garra back in Oakland. Now that she was free of it, she closed her eyes and her form morphed and surged into her familiar nude human body, crouched on all fours and breathing hard.

"What…in the *fuck*…?" Foley demanded.

Stone ignored him. He slipped out of his coat and threw it over her shoulders, helping her to her feet. "Viajera! Are you all right? Did they hurt you?"

She was still panting, coughing from the smoke, but already her eyes were clearer. "Alastair—oh, gods, how did you—"

"Never mind that. Did they hurt you?"

"No—not yet." Her gaze swept the room, as if expecting someone to attack them. "I thought you were dead. They said they'd killed you!"

"Not dead. But we've got to get out of here." He grabbed her arm and tried to pull her toward the door.

"Wait!"

"What?"

Stone checked the others, impatient. Verity was keeping an eye on the two unconscious scientists; Foley had taken their guns and was now helping Jason hold the door closed, his still-wary attention fixed on Garra.

Garra indicated the other cages. "We can't leave them here. We have to let them out. And there's a cub here somewhere—"

"Al…" Jason called. "I don't think anybody's coming. I don't hear anything outside."

Stone studied the other enclosures, taking a closer look. The two wolves and the bear crouched, as unsteady and out of it as Garra had been. The cougar lay on a gurney, and as Stone focused on him, he spotted a tube snaking free of his body. Blood ran through the tube and gathered in a clear receptacle on the floor. "What…are they doing?"

Garra had shoved her arms into Stone's coat and buttoned it. "Taking blood," she said grimly. "That's why they want us. They're stealing our blood to use in their alchemical mixtures. They sell them all over the world."

"What?" Stone demanded. "Who is? Who's the alchemist? Is he here?"

"I don't know. I think so. I haven't seen him. The others only refer to him as 'the Doctor.'" She still looked tired, and clutched the edge of the lab bench. "I keep thinking I smell something familiar, but I can't place it. But Alastair, we've got to get them all out of here."

"They were—draining your *blood*?"

"Not mine. They had a different purpose for me." Her tone was bitter. "But these others—shifters regenerate quickly, so they can drain us nearly to empty, then give us a few days to recover and do it all over again." With even more bitterness, she added, "The ultimate renewable resource."

Stone barely believed what he was hearing. "Why—why not you, then?" He paused, physically staggering as the answer hit him. "Wait—the other shifter—the one they killed—she was pregnant."

Garra bowed her head. "The others told me about it, and I heard *them* talking." She jerked her head sharply in the direction of the two scientists. "She escaped. Nearly got away, apparently, but then something went wrong and she died giving birth. They couldn't save her. They brought her cub back here, but…"

"But they needed another female."

"Female jaguar," she said dully. "Now that they have the chalice, they can breed more of us. So instead of trying to kill me, they grabbed me instead. They told me they'd killed you…that no one would come for me…"

Stone was only half-hearing her words. "So…that's why they wanted the chalice. They didn't want to sell it, or help some other group of shifters reproduce…"

"No. Shifters are hard to capture." She indicated the sluggish group around them. "These must have taken them a while. But if they can breed us…"

Stone warred between rage and sickness. "Bloody hell…"

"Yes. If they can breed us, they can get more blood, and increase their production. Possibly even start up another lab somewhere else." She grabbed his arm. "Come on—we've got to let the rest of them out. We can't leave them here."

"You're gonna…let *all* of them out?" Foley's eyes were huge now, as his gaze shifted between the door and the other caged shifters. "Those wild animals? They'll kill us!"

Clearly, he barely rated Garra's attention. She continued addressing Stone. "Alastair...please. I won't leave them behind to die."

"Right," he said grimly. "Verity—see if you can find the cub. Jason, you secure those scientists. Foley, watch the door. Viajera and I will get the rest out."

Verity and Jason moved instantly to their tasks. Foley paused a moment, swallowed, then turned away and took cover behind the lab bench near the downed scientists. "Just keep them away from me..." he muttered.

Stone ignored him, already popping the lock on the next cage, which contained the bear. Garra threw it open, and Stone used another whirlwind to clear out the smoke. "Jason," he called. "When you get those two secured, see if you can find where to shut off the gas they're piping into these cages."

"On it."

The bear growled and tried to leap out of the cage, but he stumbled and did an undignified face-plant just past the exit. Garra hurried over to him and put a hand on his back, talking to him softly.

Stone glanced at the door again; so far, nobody seemed to be trying to break in on them. That wasn't good—judging by how fast the enhanced men had recovered before, they must be mostly back to fighting form by now. What *else* could they be doing? With visions of explosives or fire dominating his mind, he picked up his pace and opened the next two cages, containing the pair of wolves.

They must have gotten a smaller dose of the gas than the bear, because as soon as the doors were open, they erupted free of their confinement and ran to each other, nuzzling together. They stood shoulder to shoulder and bared their teeth at Stone and the others, but didn't attack.

Foley, behind the lab table with the gun still aimed at the door, sidled further away from the increasingly large collection of wild animals gathering in the middle of the lab.

"Found him!" Verity called from the far end of the lab, from where she'd disappeared through another door a few moments ago. She emerged now, carrying a woozy, spotted jaguar cub the size of a small dog in her arms. It hung in her grip, its head and paws sagging.

Nearly instantly, Garra was across the room. "Give him to me!" she demanded, plucking the cub from Verity's arms. She held him protectively, murmuring softly to him. He responded with tired little grumbles.

"He was in another one of those cages," Verity told her. "I think he'll be okay when he gets some air."

"Al, we can't stay here," Jason said. "You know they're gonna be back."

"Listen to him," Foley said. "We're sitting ducks in here."

"Not necessarily." Stone opened the last cage and blew out the smoke. The cougar on the table didn't move; his eyes were open, but he looked lethargic and disinterested in his surroundings. "Damn…Verity, help me."

"What do you need?"

"See what you can do for him—if he can walk, it will be easier to get him out of here. I'm going to have a chat with the scientists."

Garra slipped past with the cub, heading for the cougar, and Stone left the two of them to it. Outside, he discovered Jason had zip-tied the two scientists and propped them against the wall. One was still unconscious, but the other watched the proceedings with a combination of fear and defiance.

Stone crouched next to the latter one. "You're going to answer my questions," he said. "And you're going to do it quickly."

"Or what?" The scientist was in his thirties, with short brown hair and a pale, chubby face.

Rage rose, and Stone fought to control it. "Or I'll kill you. It will be neither slow nor pleasant. You've already seen what we can do—I would *not* push me right now, if I were you." He indicated Garra and the other shifters. "And even if I don't kill you myself, I'm sure my friends there will appreciate a bit of payback." To punctuate his words, he raised his hand and summoned a nimbus of dancing blue flame around it.

The man's eyes got huge, the flames reflecting in his enlarged pupils. "Fine," he grunted, trying to shrink away from Stone. "The money's not worth dying over."

"Smart man." Stone snatched another glance over his shoulder. "How many enhanced people are here at the complex? Don't lie—I'll know, and you'll suffer for it." He shifted to magical sight.

"Th-three."

The man's expression didn't change, but his aura erupted into red spikes. Auras weren't necessarily lie detectors, but this guy must have been truly rubbish at poker.

Stone clenched his fist, resisting the temptation to do a *Star Wars*-style Force choke on the guy, and instead took telekinetic hold of his hair and yanked his head backward until it nearly touched the wall. "Bad choice. I told you not to lie. I'll give you one more chance. *How many?*"

"Al?" Jason called.

Stone glanced over. His friend crouched next to the pair of wolves, who were eyeing him nervously but not making any threatening moves. The bear shifter had already switched to human form—a wide, bearded man with tanned skin and copious body hair—and wrapped a spare lab coat around his waist. Garra, who'd left the cougar's cage, was conferring with him in low voices. "A moment, Jason."

He turned his attention back to the terrified scientist. "You're stalling. Tell me how many *now,* or I'll crush your skull." He wouldn't do that, of course, but he *could,* and that came through in his words.

"Okay, okay!" Sweat burst on the man's forehead. "Five. Really. There are five!" This time, his aura showed general fear, but no deception.

"Only five?"

"They don't need many. Nobody ever comes up here." He nodded toward Foley.

"That's what *he's* for—and the rest of the cops in that little hick town, if they were doing their jobs. Plus, with the elixir the guys here are plenty good enough to deal with normal threats."

"All right. Five. Where's the alchemist?"

The man looked even more scared. "I—"

"I know. He'll kill you if you tell me. But *I'll* kill you if you don't."

"No, you won't," Garra said, moving in next to them. "Because *I* will." She bared her teeth, and even in her human guise the bestial snarl was unmistakable. "I will rip his pathetic, useless body limb from limb and use his flesh to feed this cub." She crouched, getting in the scientist's face. "So you'd better talk, because this baby is hungry and you're about to become his dinner."

Garra's words affected the man as even Stone's magical intimidation hadn't. A spreading stain darkened the crotch of his pants, and the sharp ammonia tang of urine filled the air. "Okay! Okay! She's in the admin building! It's east of here, across the creek!"

"She?" Stone exchanged surprised glances with Garra. "What's her name?"

"I don't *know!* They just call her 'the Doctor.' I've never even seen her! You have to believe me!" His voice hitched in a sob and once again he tried to push himself back into the wall.

Stone watched his aura, seeing more fear as the man's terrified attention careened between Garra and the cub in her arms, but he didn't appear to be lying. "What do you think?" he asked her.

"He's telling the truth." She sounded certain—her sensitive nose even in human form was no doubt a better gauge than Stone's aura-reading ability, even with the urine's interference.

"Okay." He focused on the man again. "Why isn't anyone attacking us now? Why aren't they coming after us when they have the advantage?"

This time, it wasn't the scientist who answered, but the bear shifter. "They're protecting their own miserable hides," he growled. His voice was a deep bass, low and rumbling, with a faint accent Stone couldn't identify.

"What do you mean?" Jason asked.

The man's brow furrowed in a scowl. "They've never dealt with anything like you before. You're not what they expected. They're probably pulling back to defend their boss—unless they've all run for it."

"We've got to go," Stone said. He addressed the shifters—the bear and the two wolves. "Can you lot travel? Are you recovered?"

"Yeah, we can make it," the bear-man said. He pointed at the cougar, who still lay nearly unmoving on the table with Verity working over him. "I don't know about him, though."

"Verity?" Stone called. "How is he?"

"He'll live," she said. "He's already getting stronger." She shook her head. "But they nearly drained him of blood—I can't do anything about that."

Jason pointed at the clear plastic receptacle on the floor; it was more than half full of bright red blood. "Can't you—I dunno—put that back into him? Give him a transfusion?"

"It's possible….if we had an hour or so, maybe. I'm not sure I could do it, though."

"I can do it," another male voice said.

Stone turned back to the group. One of the wolves had shifted to human form, revealing a slender middle-aged man with salt-and-pepper hair and a short-cropped beard. He stood, unselfconsciously naked, studying the cougar's semi-conscious body. The other wolf looked tense, crowding tight against his leg.

"You can?" Stone asked, surprised.

"I have some medical training, and I know they've got the facilities here to do it. He'll recover fast once we get his blood back where it belongs, and we can get out." He patted the other wolf's head. "I'll be safe, love. I promise."

The second wolf howled softly and remained stuck to his side.

Stone looked around. "Right, then. We should get out of here. We need to get that cub and the rest of you lot out of here—you're in no shape to fight. After you're safe, we can—"

"No."

Garra, still holding the squirming cub in a gentle but secure grip, stepped forward. Her eyes were hard, her jaw set in grim determination.

"No?"

"I'm going after that alchemist. That's where the chalice is. We can't leave it here. She may already have taken off with it."

"You can't go alone," Stone said. "It's too dangerous." He jerked a thumb at the bound scientist. "You heard him— there are at least five of those men out there, not to mention whatever the alchemist has prepared."

"And what about the cub?" Verity added. "You can't take him into a fight—they'll kill him."

"We'll take care of him."

The voice came from an unexpected place. Stone spun to find Foley facing him. He still looked fearful, but the gun was no longer pointed at any of the shifters. "Foley?"

The cop indicated the others. "That wolf isn't gonna leave without the other one—that's obvious. If they stay behind and take care of the cougar, the bear and I—" he paused and addressed the bear shifter. "What's your name, man? I can't keep calling you 'the bear'."

"Tony." The bearded man looked surprised.

"—Tony and I can take the little guy away from here and get him help."

Stone narrowed his eyes. "I thought you were terrified of these 'wild animals.'"

"I was. I am. But—" He made a sweeping gesture around the lab with the hand not holding the gun. "—this is fucking *barbaric*. The fact that I drank something made of blood they *stole* from intelligent creatures makes me want to puke." He nodded toward Tony and the male wolf shifter. "And they're obviously human. Some kind of human, anyway. I don't have a fucking idea what's going on here, but that doesn't matter—I want to help make this right."

He took a long, deep breath and addressed Tony. "So...can I go with you? I got a car down the road, if these guys will give me the keys back."

Tony glanced uncertainly between Foley, Garra with the cub, and the others. "I want to go along—to help deal with this evil woman. But...yeah. I'll go with you."

Stone turned to Garra. "Is that acceptable, Viajera? Jason, Verity, and I will come with you to find the alchemist, but you have to let the little one go with them."

She looked down at the restless cub, stroking his head, and then her expression hardened. "Yes. Let's go."

Jason tossed Foley's car keys to him. "Be careful, man."

"Yeah." His voice shook, but his resolve was obvious.

Garra gently handed the cub over to Tony, who settled him into the crook of a large, hairy arm. He gripped her shoulder with the other hand. "Don't let her get away," he growled. "Do what needs to be done—for all of us."

"Oh, don't you worry," she said, and the snarling jaguar came through in her blazing eyes and bared teeth. "She will pay for what she did to us." She gave the cub a final pat. "Be well, little one. You'll be back among your people soon."

Stone turned back to the male wolf. "You'll be all right here?"

"We'll be fine." He glared at the seated scientist. "You'll tell us what we need to know, right?"

Next to him, the female wolf growled, showing long, pointed white fangs.

"Yeah…" the guy muttered. "If you don't kill me."

"That remains to be seen." To Stone, he said, "We'll be fine. Go. Find her. And…thank you. All of you."

Garra slipped Stone's coat off and gave it back to him. "Keep up," she warned. The air shimmered, and then the lithe black cat sped off through the door.

# | CHAPTER FORTY-THREE

S TONE WAS HALF CONVINCED Garra would be nowhere to be found when he, Jason, and Verity exited the building. Instead, they found her crouched in the shadows nearby, her tense posture radiating impatience. As soon as she spotted them, she took off at an easy lope into the trees to the east. There was no sound of small animals or birds, but from up ahead came the low babble of a creek. The only light came from the faint moon above and the building's perimeter lights behind them. Ahead was darkness.

"Stay close," Stone muttered. "She can see in the dark, but we can't. Verity, keep magical sight up and say something if you spot any auras."

"Already doing that. I don't see anything but the trees."

"What if she's already taken off?" Jason asked as they picked their way forward with care. Closer to the water, the ground here was more overgrown and choked with fallen branches and rocks; they couldn't move fast in the darkness without risking tripping or worse.

Stone looked around, scanning the trees' upper branches for any sign of lurking auras. "If she does, Viajera will track her. She can't have gotten far yet—I don't think there are any other roads up here."

"Even if there are and she's got a vehicle, she can't move very fast," Verity added.

"Yeah, but—" Jason began, but stopped when Stone held up a hand. "What?"

"I heard something."

All of them fell silent, looking around and craning their ears for any sound. "All I hear is the creek," Verity whispered.

Stone remained quiet, sharpening his magical sight. He *had* heard something—a faint rustling above them—but it might only have been a squirrel or bird.

*It might not, though.*

He kept his shield up and moved forward, noting Verity had hers up as well around herself and Jason. He wanted to look everywhere at once—if the scientist had been telling the truth, there were at least five of those enhanced men out here somewhere, not to mention the alchemist herself—but that wasn't practical. They had to keep moving. Every minute they wasted gave her more time to escape with the chalice.

He couldn't even see Garra's aura up ahead—either she'd increased her pace or she was using the trees' auras to hide her presence. Either way, as they pressed further into the trees Stone's tension increased. He was no woodsman, and if the alchemists' associates had set up a trap for them, they could be walking right into it.

Jason stopped, swinging the shotgun's barrel around, then up.

"Do you see something?" Stone demanded, forcing his voice to a whisper.

"Thought I heard something running through the trees up above us."

Once again they all stopped to listen, and once again only silence and the creek's babble—louder now as they approached it—greeted them.

"Maybe she's got them all pulled back around the building she's hiding in," Verity whispered. "They're—"

"*Up high!*" Jason yelled. He flung himself into her and took them both down just as a dark shape dropped from above and landed in their midst.

The man was as big as the bearish one Stone had seen before—and this time he was armed. In each hand, he held a long, machete-like knife, slashing one toward Jason and the other toward Stone.

Jason barely got out of the way in time, throwing himself sideways into the trees and rolling up.

Stone's shield easily deflected the slash. He backpedaled, noticing another figure dropping down next to Jason, likewise armed with a knife. From behind him, a loud, snarling roar announced Viajera's return to the fight.

She landed on silent paws next to Stone's attacker and clamped her jaws around his left wrist. There was a wet *crunch* and a shriek of pain, then a spray of hot, red blood spattered Stone's shield. The man fell, then righted himself with effort and half-staggered, half-crawled toward the tree line.

Two more men dropped from the trees; Stone sensed them more than saw them as they spread themselves out, trying to separate the four of them. They'd clearly learned from their previous encounters with him and his friends: staying close together was a bad idea, leaving them more vulnerable to magical attacks. They'd use their strengths here: stealth, speed, and supernatural toughness.

But now they had Viajera to contend with, and she was every bit as fast, strong, and tough as they were—perhaps more so, in her jaguar form. Stone had to hope it would be enough to turn the tide. Every minute they wasted was another minute the alchemist could use to escape with the chalice. They didn't have time to let this fight draw out.

Jason's shotgun roared again, not as loud now since they weren't inside a building, but still deafening. This time it was answered by another sort of roar.

Stone spun, flinging his own attacker off in a screeching parabola back toward the forest, trying to see what was happening with Jason. What he spotted chilled him: Jason had either missed with his shot or hit the man somewhere nonvital, because the thug surged forward and slashed at Jason with his machete. Jason yelped as the blade raked across his abdomen, opening a bright bloody furrow that lit up on Stone's magical sight, and then fell.

"Jason!" he yelled, but Verity was already acting. Her aura alight with rage and fear, she raised her hands and picked the man up, twisting and spinning him in the air before turning him upside-down and slamming him back down to the ground head-first. The resulting *thunk* carried even over the babbling rush of the creek.

Stone hurried toward her, intent on reaching Jason, but in his focus on his friend, he didn't see the man behind him. Something slammed into his shield from the back, carrying him forward. Startled, he let the shield waver for a second before re-establishing it, but it was enough for his opponent's charge to drive him into a tree. He dropped, stunned, the shield fading, and braced for another attack.

It didn't come. Instead, Viajera's roar rose again. Claws out, she slashed at the man, forcing him to divert his attention to her. Another one joined him, wrapping his meaty, muscular arms around the jaguar's neck. Clearly they considered her and Stone the worst threats.

Stone dragged himself up, keeping his back to the tree. He glanced around, looking for the others. Garra appeared to be holding her own her two opponents; she snarled and swiped her claws across the nearest one's abdomen, leaving bloody wounds in their wake, then whirled to bull the other into a nearby tree, breaking his hold around her neck. Verity's shield deflected another's dive, and she used a telekinetic grab to toss him into the creek with a loud splash.

That left only Jason. They'd need to finish this quickly, so they could take care of his injuries. Was he even conscious any longer? Stone scanned the area with magical sight, trying to pick up a trace of his friend's blue aura, his fear growing when he couldn't find it. *Oh, gods, no, is he—*

But no—there he was, lying prone against a thick tree. His aura flickered weakly, flaring red around his midsection where the man had slashed him. He appeared to be struggling to a seated position, fumbling at something on his belt.

Stone didn't realize what he was doing until he'd already pulled the object free and held it to his mouth.

"Jason, *no!*" he yelled, rushing toward him.

He was too late. Jason threw his head back and downed the contents of the elixir bottle he'd taken from Foley, then flung the bottle aside.

Stone lost sight of him for a moment as something slammed into his shield. He spun to see two of the men converging on him, muscular arms wide and beastly snarls on their faces. They knocked him over but the shield held; by the time he'd gathered energy and flung both of them free, Jason had leaped to his feet. Now, the familiar green glow tinged the edges of his strengthening blue aura, and the red at his abdomen was already fading.

"Jason!" Stone called.

His friend ignored him. Growling, he dropped the shotgun and threw himself at the man who was already heading back toward Verity. Jason was fast and athletic under normal circumstances, but now he moved with the same blurred grace as the others, nearly too fast to follow. With a yell, he landed on the man's back, his arm snaking around his neck.

"Jason!" Verity yelled. "Don't kill him!"

Stone didn't have time for elaborate analysis, or to worry about what was going on with Jason. They had to finish this fight—it was a diversion, and if they let it go on much longer, the alchemist would either escape or prepare something even deadlier for them.

Enough fooling around. He had the power—it was time to see what he could do with it.

Garra roared again, her bestial rage echoing through the clearing. As Stone watched she lunged, clamping her jaws on her opponent's throat and tearing it out. The spray of blood slicked her sleek, black fur. The man didn't even have time to scream before he dropped, beyond even the elixir's regenerative ability to save him now.

*Two down,* Stone thought with no regret. *Three more to go.*

Jason and Verity, working together now, seemed to have their opponent well in hand, so he focused on the other two. He'd tossed them in two different directions when they'd attacked him, mostly trying to get them away from him so he could check on Jason. Now, they were nowhere to be seen. Damn whatever was hiding their auras from him! Had they taken off, falling back to protect their boss, or were they even now lurking in the trees above, preparing to—

"Doc, look out!" Verity called, still struggling with the man trying to breach her shield as Jason grappled at him from behind.

Stone barely had time to react before another muscular figure bowled him over and slammed him into a tree. His shield held long enough to blunt the impact this time, but the jolt disrupted his concentration.

The shield faltered for only a second, but it was enough. The man grabbed hold of him, pulling him in, hands tightening as they tried to crush his shoulders. "I'll kill you," he snarled, his hot, sour breath hitting Stone in the face.

Stone didn't hold back. If he did, he had no doubt the man would do to him what they'd done to Jimmy Tanuki back in Oakland. Forcing himself to ignore the pain, he bared his teeth and called energy to him, feeling it jangling through his body until he felt he couldn't hold anymore. He reached out and put his palms flat against the man's muscular chest, then released the power.

The man's hands dropped away as he screamed, his entire body lighting up with crackling energy. His arms and legs stiffened, shuddering. His teeth clamped down on his own tongue so hard blood flew from his mouth. His eyes rolled back in his head and he toppled backward, still twitching as if he'd been electrocuted.

"Try it," Stone muttered, then took off at a run toward Jason and Verity's last position.

He found them as Garra came in from the opposite side, fast and silent. She ignored the two of them and leaped past, disappearing once more into the trees.

Verity yelped, backpedaling as her opponent tore at her shield, ignoring Jason. Her back hit a tree and she struggled to gather her power.

Stone was about to help—Verity was an accomplished mage in many areas, but she'd never been as strong in combat magic as he was, even before Calanar—but before he could act, Jason screamed something into the night and reached up to grip a branch as thick as a child's arm. As Stone watched in fascinated horror, he wrenched the branch free of the tree, wound up, and let Verity's attacker have the full force of a baseball-style swing to the side of his head. The resulting sound was like a ripe watermelon being dropped from a third-story window.

The man didn't even scream. The strength of Jason's blow took him off his feet and carried him several feet away, where he spun and dropped.

Verity, panting, darted her gaze from the man to Jason. "Holy…crap…" she whispered breathlessly. "How did you *do* that?"

"He took Mr. Foley's elixir," Stone said, leveling his own accusing gaze on Jason.

"Don't, Al," Jason growled. His face looked subtly different, his eyes blazing, his jaw set. "I did what I had to do, and I don't regret it. Let's get this bitch."

Garra swept into the clearing, still in jaguar form. Blood slicked her shoulders and her flanks, and it was hard to tell whether it was hers or her opponents'—but the stuff staining her fangs held no similar doubt. She nudged Stone with her head and then took off again. Her meaning was clear: *we have to go.*

"You—*took* that stuff?" Verity asked, gaping at her brother in horror now.

"Not now, V," he growled. "Let's go before it wears off." His shirt was still soaked with the blood from his wound, but he moved as if it were no longer a concern.

Verity shot a worried look at Stone as her brother took off after Garra, moving faster and with more confidence than he had before. It couldn't have been more obvious that she was thinking about what had happened to Foley.

Stone gripped her shoulder. "He's right," he said. "It was the only way. We'll sort out the consequences later."

Her glare was fleeting, and quickly turned to reluctant resolve. "Yeah. Let's finish this."

Up ahead, the rush of the creek grew louder. They broke free of the tree line to find Garra and Jason waiting for them, surveying the area on the other side. There still weren't any lights, but neither of them seemed to have an issue with that.

"I don't see anybody over there," Jason said as they drew up next to him. He held up his hands and stared at them as if he didn't believe they were his. "This is...amazing. I can see in the dark, like a cat. Nothing hurts. Check it out." He pulled up the bottom of his T-shirt, where the knife slash had been. Nothing was there now except some leftover drying blood.

"You shouldn't have done it," Verity said. "You don't know what all's in that stuff. It could kill you, like it almost did Foley."

"Didn't have a choice. And I'm fine. I feel...great. *Better* than great. Like I could take on the world." He caught her expression and took her hand. "Don't worry, V—I'm not addicted to the stuff or anything. But it sure as hell feels good to be able to contribute something to the team when we're fighting supernatural stuff. That shotgun barely slowed those guys down."

She focused hard on him for a few more seconds, then finally looked away. "Yeah. I get it. We'll talk about it later. Come on."

Garra was clearly impatient again, growling and nudging Stone toward the creek. It was about ten feet wide and didn't appear deep, which was good because none of them could see a bridge across it.

"Must be further down," Jason said, peering south, where the meandering creek disappeared into some trees.

"We could try to find it—" Verity began.

Garra, having none of it, growled and plunged into the water, her powerful muscles carrying her across in a few seconds. She mounted the bank, shook off the water in a gesture reminiscent of a family dog shaking off a bath, then growled at them again.

Jason pondered a moment, then took a few steps back and set off at a run, clearing the ten feet in a single, powerful leap. Stone and Verity used levitation spells to carry them across. They all paused to check for anyone lying in wait for them, then moved on into the forest.

Stone could sense Garra's tension as she moved silently ahead of them; without magical sight, he wouldn't have been able to see her at all, but her green aura flashed with increasing anger and agitation as they continued forward.

"Stay sharp," he muttered to Verity. "If they had the other building warded and concealed under an illusion, this one will likely be too. Especially if this is where she does her work."

Up ahead, Garra growled and stopped.

Stone hurried up next to her, peering up ahead. He saw nothing but more dark, shadowy trees, even when he switched to magical sight.

He crouched next to her. "Do you see something?"

She made a low, chuffing growl and indicated the area in front of them with paw gesture. Then she raised her head and sniffed the air, a rumble forming deep in her chest.

"She's spotted something," Stone muttered to Jason and Verity, who'd come up next to them.

"I smell something," Jason said. "Not sure what it is, but it doesn't belong here. Kinda like chemicals and blood."

Garra growled agreement.

"Right, then," Stone said. He neither scented nor saw anything, but he trusted Garra's more sensitive nose—and now Jason's, too. "That means she's got an illusion up, and we don't have time to waste being gentle. Give me a moment, and make sure nobody jumps me."

He crept forward and levitated into the branches of a nearby tree where he could get a good view of the scene ahead. This would be more difficult—unlike the research building, he didn't have Foley's description of exactly where it was supposed to be—but now he had a better idea of the kinds of illusions the alchemist was using. He hoped it would be enough to offset the problem, since they didn't have long to locate her hiding place.

With every moment he scanned, his tension grew. The thugs must have recovered by now; he was sure they hadn't killed all of them—perhaps not any of them—and they'd proven they could track their prey with ease through the darkness and thick forest. So where were they?

For that matter, where was the alchemist? A chill ran through him along with a thought: what if the thugs' purpose truly hadn't been to kill them, but merely to delay them long enough for the alchemist to escape? If that was true, she could already be long gone, and them with her, leaving him and his friends to search the area in vain.

The chill deepened as he remembered the shifters they'd released from the admin building: the two wolves and stricken cougar back at the lab, and the bear and jaguar cub fleeing with Foley back toward the cop's car. The bear could probably hold his own against the alchemist's henchmen, but the cub and Foley would be helpless.

Was all of this nothing more than a diversion?

Grimly, he tightened his focus, taking deep breaths to calm himself. He'd never see through the illusion if he forced it. If the alchemist had already fled with the chalice, they wouldn't catch her, but at least they could shut down the lab before they left so she'd have to regroup before she started again. And between his power and Garra's tracking abilities, they'd find her again, eventually.

"Doc?" Verity's soft voice came from below him.

"Yes?"

"Do you see anything?"

It was difficult to concentrate on her words and keep up his search. "Just a moment," he said, distracted. "I've just got to—"

There it was.

A faint shimmer, barely visible, up ahead and to the left. "Shh…" he cautioned, fearful if he took his gaze away from it, he'd lose it again. He focused harder, while simultaneously forcing himself to look past what he thought he saw. As he did so, the shimmer resolved itself, revealing the hazy form of another building behind it. "Got it."

"Can you get through it?"

"She already knows we're here. No time for subtlety now."

He took several deep breaths, pulling in power. If he had time he could take the illusion down with more care, perhaps so the caster wouldn't even know he was breaching it. But he couldn't shake the visions of her sneaking out the back door. If she was smart—and he was sure she was—she'd get out of she could, and live to re-establish her vile little empire somewhere else.

He gathered the power, feeling it raging and swirling within him, picked a point on the illusion, and released it, channeling all his anger and disgust at what this horrible woman had done to his friend, to other sentient beings, for her own gain.

The power contacted the illusion with a great psychic ripping sound. Without magical sight, he knew it looked like he was tearing a hole in reality, like something out of a science fiction show. Behind it, another scene appeared: instead of trees, it was the pale wall of another building. With more brute force than care, he took hold of the two sides of the breach and pulled them to the side.

The illusion resisted—this one was stronger than the one on the lab—but it couldn't stand against the power Stone was pouring into it. At last it gave way, staggering him backward as it ripped free and disappeared.

Jason caught him, gripping his arms with strong hands, and set him back upright. "Holy shit."

Next to him, Viajera growled agreement.

This building was smaller than the lab, light-colored, its windows covered with metal plates instead of plywood. Perimeter lights shone all around it, illuminating a reinforced metal front door that clearly hadn't been original equipment.

Viajera nudged Stone forward, her growl growing impatient.

This was it.

As they moved forward, quickly but with care, they saw no sign of any of the enhanced henchmen. Stone didn't know if they'd fled or if they were inside, but either way it didn't matter. Their objective was clear.

"In the front, or through one of the windows?" Jason asked. He stood on the balls of his feet, tense and ready, his hands clenching and unclenching. It couldn't have been clearer that he wanted to use his newfound strength to rip something apart.

Stone scanned the building's roof line again, checking for ambushers. Even though the elixir hid the men's auras, he wasn't too concerned—it didn't hide their scent, and Viajera would have picked them up if they were there. "Let's go in the front door. But with care—they could be waiting for us inside."

Jason loped off with Viajera right behind him.

Verity glanced at Stone, her brow furrowed. "I don't like this," she said. "He's…different."

"He's young and strong, and this is only one time," Stone reminded her. "Let him enjoy himself."

She didn't look convinced, but hurried after him.

By the time they reached the building, Jason had stationed himself next to the door, eyeing the hefty handle. "Ready?"

"Just a moment," Stone said. "Let me put up an illusion that we're not here. Stay to the side, though, in case they're waiting to open fire."

Viajera's reluctance to wait showed in her every muscle, but she edged to the right side of the doorway and crouched, ready to pounce. Verity joined her there.

Stone took a moment to conjure an illusion he hoped would convince any waiting attackers that the space outside the door was empty. It was one of the things that came easier to him now, after Calanar—he'd always been good at illusions, but the extra power meant he could concentrate more on content and less on maintaining the spell. "All right," he said after a few moments. "Go."

Jason took eager hold of the handle, set his grip, and wrenched.

The metal screeched in protest as his knuckles knotted around it, and for a moment, Stone thought even his friend's enhanced strength wouldn't be enough. Then, with a final howl of protest, it gave way with a metallic *clank* and the handle clattered to the ground. Jason, grinning, stepped back and to the side with a flourish. "All yours, Al."

"You're enjoying this entirely too much," Stone said. If it hadn't been for the seriousness of their situation, it would have amused him.

"Damn right I am."

Taking a few steps back and raising his shield, Stone gestured and flung the door open.

Beyond lay an empty, dark hallway.

"Do you see anything?" Verity asked, holding back from craning her neck around for her own look.

"Not a thing. No sign of her flunkies. There's not even anywhere for them to hide."

"Illusion?" Jason asked. "I don't smell anything."

"Doesn't look like it," Stone said, and Viajera chuffed agreement.

Verity did peer around now. "Wait—I see light up ahead on the left. Under a door."

Stone had been looking for an ambush, so he hadn't spotted the thin line of dim light near the floor.

Viajera moved forward, gently shoving Verity out of the way. She raised her head, sniffing the air, then made a low growl and plunged into the hall at a run.

"So much for being careful," Stone muttered, and hurried after her. The others followed.

The interior door didn't look like original equipment either. This one was double, made of the same substantial metal as the exterior one. Someone had carefully painted odd-looking symbols on both sides. "Wards?" Verity asked.

Stone had already shifted to magical sight. "Yes. Nasty ones, too."

"Can you get through them?"

He glanced at Viajera, who was radiating impatience. "I'd better be able to, or she's going to rip them down by main force. Hold on. Jason, once I get them down, we won't have a lot of time. As soon as I say the word, get that door open."

"Got it."

"Verity—just…be ready for anything."

"You got it, Doc," she said dryly.

Stone took several deep breaths, focusing on the structure of the ward. It was of a type he'd never seen before, but not particularly complex. Whoever the alchemist was, he didn't think wards were her specialty, and these were probably only intended to keep out mundane intruders. He'd never have been able to do this with wards like Thalassa Nera's, even at his new power level.

That was one advantage they had going for them—although she no doubt knew about their arrival, he didn't think she was prepared for this kind of magical opposition. At least he hoped not. They were entering her lair now, and if he was wrong, they could be in trouble.

*Of course, she's probably long gone with the chalice by now, and all this is good for nothing but slowing us down.* He shoved the thought away. They'd deal with what they found.

"All right…" he murmured as he took hold of two sections of the ward. "Get ready, Jason. On three. One…two…three."

He drew the two sections aside, opening a hole in the ward. It resisted, crackling against his senses, fighting to resume its regular shape, but he held it. "Now," he rasped. "Go!"

Jason stepped forward eagerly and grabbed the left-side handle. Muscles knotting, teeth gritted, he repeated his performance with the front door. "This one's…harder…"

"Hurry up. I can't hold this much longer." The buzzing was growing stronger—it didn't quite hurt yet, but Stone was certain that wouldn't be true for long. Wards, by their very nature, wanted to keep the shape they were built to form, and it didn't go well for anything interfering with that desire.

Jason growled, bearing down on the handle with more force. "Move, damn you!" he snapped.

Behind him, Viajera growled with more impatience.

"Maybe I—" Verity began.

The door made a shrieking, metal-on-metal sound. Jason's roar of frustration became one of triumph as the handle broke free and the heavy door swung open.

The jaguar surged past him into the room.

"Viajera, wait—" Stone hurried after her. "We don't know—"

He stopped, taking in the scene in the room.

"Well, then," he said softly.

# CHAPTER FORTY-FOUR

I T WAS AN IMPRESSIVE CIRCLE, but it didn't look like any magical construct Stone had ever seen.

The closest it came was the monstrosity Elias Richter had set up during his attempt to perform the vile ritual that had killed Deirdre Lanier and nearly killed Tabitha Wells. The circle itself was at least fifteen feet across, drawn with precision in glowing green runes and sigils on the cleared floor of what looked like it had once been a large conference room. That much looked familiar, but everything else spoke to a style of magic Stone had very little experience with.

At many points along the circle's perimeter, lit candles alternated with wooden stands supporting various tubing, glass containers, and upright cylinders, all of them bubbling and brimming with liquids that blazed with power. Some of the tubes connected the vessels, while others snaked into the center of the circle, converging on a black iron cauldron three feet in diameter. More glowing runes in green, blue, and red were etched all around the cauldron's surface, and beneath it a fire roared, sending thick smoke up toward the room's high ceiling, where something unseen dissipated it. Along two of the walls, shelves and benches were lined with bottles and vials of various sizes and colors, along with other receptacles, jars, bags, and books. The room had an acrid, earthy smell mixed with musk and chemicals.

"What the hell...?" Jason breathed from behind Stone in the doorway.

"That's an alchemy setup," Verity said in the same soft tone. "Hezzie has a much smaller one in her apartment. I've never seen one anywhere near that big."

"But where's the alchemist?" Jason asked, looking around. "I can't smell anything alive in here—that smoke's covering everything."

Next to Stone, Viajera growled and took another step into the room. Her yellow-gold gaze was intent on the center of the circle.

"I wouldn't," said a voice.

Stone snapped his attention to the cauldron, but even with magical sight he couldn't see anyone there past the smoke. "Show yourself," he called.

He didn't expect it to work, so he blinked when a figure shimmered into being on the far side of the cauldron, watching them with amusement. It was hard to get a good look at her through all the smoke; all he could pick out was that she was short, very thin, and wore some kind of dark-colored robe or gown.

"I didn't expect you to make it this far," she said. "I should applaud you for that, I suppose. But now, you'll be leaving." Her voice was low and harsh, with a thick Spanish accent.

"I think not," Stone said. He stepped in next to Viajera, whose gaze had not wavered from the woman. She still emitted a low, dangerous growl from deep in her chest.

"Not another step," the woman warned. "Not unless you want your prize destroyed forever." She waved a hand, and the air above the cauldron shifted to reveal an object hovering above it.

Viajera let out an agitated whine.

Stone gripped her shoulder, stiffening. Even only having seen the crude sketch she had made, he knew instantly what the object was.

It was the chalice.

# | CHAPTER FORTY-FIVE

THE WOMAN SMILED, her dark eyes glittering with malice. "Ah, you recognize it. That will make things easier." She indicated the cauldron. "The solution in here is highly caustic, with a component built in to neutralize magic. I frankly doubt it will be potent enough to completely destroy the chalice, but I guarantee it will affect its magical properties sufficiently that it will no longer function for its intended purpose." Her gaze shifted to the jaguar. "I wouldn't risk it, Viajera. Your clan would destroy you if they found out you were the cause of its loss." She raised a thin hand. "In fact, please shift back to your human form. Let's take no chances."

When Viajera hesitated, the woman gestured, and the golden chalice dropped a few inches toward the cauldron. Smoke swirled around it, obscuring its contours.

"I won't ask again," she said.

With a growl of resignation, Viajera stepped back, her muscular, furred form transforming to her human guise. She barely appeared to notice when Stone dropped his coat over her shoulders, her cold gaze still fixed on the woman. "So," she said, her voice shaking with anger. "This is what you have become."

Stone exchanged confused glances with Verity and Jason. "You…know this woman?" he asked.

"Oh, yes." Now bitterness joined the anger. She directed her attention back to the woman. "Why would you do this? We were friends. My mother trusted you. My *clan* trusted you. What would make you betray them like this?"

The woman laughed, her contempt visible on her face. "Oh, Viajera, you always were naïve, even after you left the clan with your mother and went to live among the humans."

Stone, watching the two of them, almost asked who she was, and how Viajera knew her. But then he didn't have to, as the answer struck him. "Bloody hell…" he whispered. "Dr. Garra."

Viajera didn't turn in response, but she did speak without looking at him. "Yes. Alastair, meet the real Dr. Marciella Garra. A woman I thought was my friend."

Stone stared at the woman. Magical sight couldn't pierce the smoke sufficiently to see her aura, but as he watched the tendrils dance and waft above the cauldron, he could now see the strong resemblance between the alchemist and the photo Jason had shown him back at his office. She was older now, and almost skeletally thin in her dark robe, but the steady, beady black eyes were the same.

"Why?" Viajera demanded. "You owe us that, at least. Why did you do it? Why would you steal something so sacred to our people, and…*pervert* it like this?" She gestured around the room, nearly spitting her words at the end.

"It's simple, really." Garra remained behind the cauldron as she spoke, focusing on Viajera and the others. "Wealth. Power. Your clan never appreciated my abilities. Oh, certainly they took advantage of them when it suited them, but as much as I wanted—begged for, in fact—access into their inner circles so I could learn everything about their ways, they always shut me out. I wasn't one of you, you see. As much as I did for you, it ultimately didn't matter, because I could never *be* one of you. So I left, to do my own research, my own study."

Viajera's face twisted with disgust. She gestured at the circle. "So you did...*this?* You kidnapped my people, and those from other clans? Held them prisoner? Stole their *blood?*"

Stone, next to her, saw her trembling, but didn't move to touch her. Even in her human form, the look of the jaguar hung over her. He had no idea what she'd do if he startled her.

"There's quite a market for my concoctions," Garra said. Her voice held no hint of regret or contrition. "It seems a large number of individuals—both legal and not, it turns out—have discovered they can benefit from them. Who wouldn't want increased strength and speed? Who wouldn't want to see in the dark, or heal injuries in minutes?" She shrugged. "Your people should have accepted me, Viajera, and none of this would have happened. I loved you—all of you. But you turned your back on me."

"You're disgusting," Jason said.

"I'm not." Garra glanced down into the cauldron, then back at the others. "I'm realistic. I've got markets all over the world. Naturally, since my production batches are small and I had to maintain utmost discretion for my own safety, I haven't been able to move nearly as much product as I'd have liked, but even so, my operation has already made me a wealthy woman." Her gaze settled on Viajera. "It's too bad

Anna Maria escaped, and even more tragic that she died giving birth to her cub. I'd made some alterations to the elixir the chalice produces, which was supposed to increase her fertility even more. Apparently I didn't have it quite right yet."

"So you captured me instead." Viajera couldn't keep the horror out of her voice. "You…were planning to experiment on me. To use me. And not just for my blood. You were going to *breed* me, and use my children for your madness!"

Garra gave a harsh laugh. "Don't sound so sanctimonious, child. Don't forget that *you* used *me,* too—or was there some other reason you claimed my identity so you could pretend to be qualified for your job at the University?"

"Hardly the same thing," Stone said, narrowing his eyes. "Let's think—a bit of well-meaning identity theft versus kidnapping sentient beings and stealing their blood to line your own pockets?"

"Ah, yes. Dr. Stone. You've been quite a hindrance to my plans. In fact, I'd guess that Viajera here wouldn't have gotten near me if it hadn't been for your help."

"That's me—ever helpful." He might have been able to infuse more contempt into his voice if he'd tried harder, but she wasn't worth the extra effort.

"Tell me," she said, making a gesture that caused the liquid in the cauldron to pop and bubble beneath the floating chalice. "Just to satisfy my own curiosity: how are you still alive? You should have died nearly instantly, in agony, from the mixture you drank."

"Sorry to disappoint you. It seems my friend is a bit more competent as a healer than you are as an alchemist."

Garra shook her head. "No healing magic should have been able to do more than provide temporary respite." She waved him off. "No matter. None of it matters anymore. All that matters is that I am leaving with the chalice."

"You're going to kill us, then, are you?" Stone asked. "Good luck with that—it's proven more difficult than you planned in the past."

"No. I'm not going to kill you. You're going to leave here—all of you."

"Like hell we will," Jason growled.

"Ah, I see *you* have benefited from my concoction too," Garra said, eyeing him approvingly. "It suits you. You like being effective around your magical friends, don't you, boy? I'm sure we could come to some sort of arrangement, if—"

"Fuck off, lady."

She shrugged. "Fine, suit yourself. But as I was saying— you will all leave here, get in your car, and go back to where you came from. My men are recovered from their injuries now. They're stationed around the area, concealed where you'll never detect them. If you leave as directed, you won't see them and they won't touch you. If you don't…" She gestured, and the chalice dipped and bobbed above the cauldron. "…then I will drop this in, and send my men after you. You'll probably beat them—you did before, so I have no doubt you could do it again. But you'll never catch me before I escape."

"And set up your operation somewhere else," Verity said. Her voice shook with anger.

"Of course. Somewhere no one will ever find me. With the money I've made already, not to mention the lure of the elixir itself and the abilities it can provide, I'll have no shortage of help to ensure no one can touch me." She snorted. "You can go back to your people, Viajera, and tell them about what happened—if you dare. If you want to risk their wrath when they discover you were the cause of the chalice's destruction."

"But if you destroy the chalice," Jason said, "you'll be screwing yourself over too."

"She won't," Stone said grimly. "It will put an end to her breeding operation, but that's only ancillary to her plans."

"Exactly," Garra said with approval. "I won't deny that having it made things easier—breeding my stock instead of abducting it is safer and more efficient—but it's not as if I haven't done it before."

"You're a monster," Verity said.

"You're a fool," Garra said. "Now—what will it be, Viajera? Will you leave peacefully, or will I destroy your little bauble here?" The chalice dipped lower, until it hovered only a few inches above the cauldron.

"I'll kill you…" Viajera said, her voice a low rumble in her throat, more the jaguar than the woman. "I'll rip your throat out and decorate the walls with your blood. If not here, then somewhere else. I'll never stop looking for you."

"I'm sure you won't, old friend."

"We can't just let her *go*," Jason said, fists clenched in frustration. "Not after all this."

"We must," Viajera said. She sounded resigned, beaten. "The chalice is too important to my people. I can't be the cause of its destruction."

Stone stood next to her. He'd been silent, but his mind hadn't been idle. There had to be some way out of this. Jason was right: they couldn't simply let Garra escape. If she were allowed to set up shop somewhere else—somewhere a lot less accessible than northern California—she would kidnap or breed more shifters, collect more blood, and produce more of her vile concoction. He thought about what had happened to Jimmy Tanuki, murdered by having his limbs ripped from his body, and about what that might mean in the future if more people had access to elixirs that would make them nearly unstoppable by normal means. She could build a private army to protect her.

But how could they do it? Her own power held the chalice above the cauldron. If they took her out, it would drop in before they could grab it. He might be able to wrench it free, but he couldn't be certain, since he didn't know how powerful her hold was. Viajera was fast, but was she fast enough?

They might be able to do something if they could communicate, but that was out of the question. Garra would never allow it. They were in her lair now—how many protections and hidden traps had she built here to ensure her safety? They dared not risk anything direct.

But what about something *indirect*?

Stone gripped Viajera's shoulder. "You're right," he said, with the same level of defeated resignation. He glared at Garra. "You've won. This time, anyway. But you must know it's not just Viajera who won't stop looking for you."

"Oh, I'm aware of that." Garra sounded amused now.

That, more than anything else, told Stone what he needed to know: that there was no way she was going to let them leave here alive. She had something waiting for them out there—that was doubtless why her men hadn't attacked.

He tightened his grip on Viajera's shoulder and squeezed twice, hoping she'd catch on that he was up to something, and be ready for it. "Come on," he said to the others. "We've no choice. We've got to respect Viajera's wishes."

"But—" Verity protested.

"No, Verity. Come on."

They didn't want to—he could see it. He could sense Verity's desire to try something magical, and Jason's to lunge at Garra with his newfound strength and speed, to hope that the alchemist couldn't stop all of them at once before they plucked the chalice from harm's way. He didn't miss the way they were both looking at him—confused and angry at the thought that he'd give up so easily—but he didn't meet their gazes. They had only one chance at this, and everything depended on Viajera.

He waved them ahead of him, back toward the door. After a moment they went, both of them trudging with slow, reluctant steps. He knew what they were thinking: after all they'd gone through to get here, they were just going to let her win?

Viajera didn't go ahead of him, though. She remained a step or two behind, her angry breathing loud and steady.

Jason and Verity reached the door and stepped through. Stone paused, turning back. Garra watched them from the other side of the cauldron, her beady black eyes still and cold.

Then, suddenly, she yelped as the chalice shot upward and flew to the side, rocketing clear of the circle and slamming into the far wall. Behind Stone, Verity and Jason yelled too.

Several things happened after that, most so fast Stone could barely follow them. The most important was Viajera in front of him, slipping free of his coat as she lunged forward with frightening speed, her body morphing as she moved. By the time she reached the center of the circle she was in full jaguar form, her powerful hind legs propelling her up and over the cauldron toward Garra, who'd staggered backward in shock.

Jason, moving faster than Stone but not as fast as Viajera, dived for the chalice where it had landed near the wall on the far side of the room.

Verity grabbed the cauldron with a telekinetic grip and yanked it hard, overturning it. Bubbling liquid poured out, hissing and sending up more clouds of noxious smoke as it ate through parts of the floor, obscuring the circle.

Stone dropped the illusion he'd been weaving, noting Jason's shout of surprise as the chalice he'd been chasing— the illusionary version—vanished. He snatched up the real one, which Viajera—the only one of them he'd allowed to see it—had knocked free of danger with her leap, and pulled it to him.

"I've got it!" he yelled. "Go!"

She didn't need to hear it: she was already going. Garra, as soon as she'd realized she'd been tricked, had dived toward the shelves on the far side of the room, plucking two bottles from the wall. One, she pulled the stopper from and downed. The other, she flung toward the lunging jaguar, sending up billows of black smoke that obscured her from their vision.

"No!" Stone cried, still clutching the chalice as Viajera shimmered and morphed back into her human form, coughing.

"Yeah, not happening!" Verity yelled, gesturing as Jason headed for the smoke. A whipping whirlwind arose from the floor, dissipating the black smoke toward the room's edges.

Jason disappeared through the door, running hard, but as soon as the smoke cleared Viajera was a jaguar again, streaking past him through the open doorway and into the hall.

"Viajera!" Stone yelled, running after her with Verity in his wake.

"We can't let her get away!" Verity panted. Up ahead, another open door indicated Garra had escaped into the night.

Stone shifted to magical sight as he exited the building, scanning the trees. He saw nothing—no signs of auras or running figures. Even Jason had disappeared into the forest. He clenched his fists in frustration and tightened his focus as Verity skidded to a stop behind him. They were *not* going to let Garra get away! Not after everything they'd done, everything *she'd* done—

From the forest to the south came a screaming roar—the triumphant cry of a hunting cat.

Stone glanced at Verity, then both of them took off at a run toward the sound.

Without conscious thought, Stone cast two spells: a globe of light around his raised hand, and levitation to lift himself off the ground. Freed of the fear of tripping over a protruding branch or rock, he flew forward, the light spell illuminating the thick growth ahead of him.

When he burst into a clearing a few yards ahead, he smelled the blood before anything else.

He dropped the levitation spell, shocked, and barely noticed stumbling to the ground. "Bloody hell..." he breathed as he caught himself.

Verity came up next to him, and Jason burst into the clearing from the other side. They too stopped, gaping.

Viajera, in her jaguar form, stood over the fallen form of Marciella Garra. The alchemist's throat had been torn out, her bright red blood pulsing and flowing into the carpet of leaves and pine needles beneath her. Viajera's front legs were spread wide, straddling Garra, her muzzle and long, pointed fangs stained with more blood. As the others entered the clearing she roared again, fixing each of them with wild, rage-filled glare. Her message couldn't have been clearer: *do not get between me and my prey.*

Beneath her, Garra's body twitched, a faint gurgle coming from her destroyed trachea, and then she lay still.

Stone held up a hand, gesturing for Jason and Verity to stay back, then took a tentative step forward. "Viajera," he said gently. "Stop. It's over. It's done."

She made a sound that was half-growl, half-roar, lowering her head and shoulders into a warning stance.

Stone raised the chalice, which he'd carefully tucked in the crook of his other arm. "Viajera. It's over. I've got the chalice. You've got what you came for. Please—step away from her."

The yellow-gold gaze shifted between Stone's face and the chalice in his hand, then back. She growled again, but softer this time, and stared down at Garra's body. The alchemist had bled out by now, her wide, sightless eyes nearly popping out of her head. Silence hung in the air, broken only by the three humans' heavy breathing and the growling chuffs of the jaguar.

Finally, she lifted a deliberate paw and stepped away from Garra, turning fully toward Stone. For a second he thought she might leap at him, but instead she made a humanlike sound of resignation and shifted back. Her hair hung disheveled and leaf-strewn around her face, her entire lower jaw was drenched in blood, and her eyes still held the half-feral rage that had driven her to what she'd done. Even though she was once again naked, there was nothing sexy or sensual about her now. She looked every bit as bestial as she had in her jaguar form.

"It's done," she said. "Give it to me."

Stone approached her slowly, making no sudden moves that might set her off again, and offered her the chalice.

She took it with gentle hands, cradling it as she had the cub. Tears meandered down, cutting tracks along her gore-strewn cheeks. "So much death…" she murmured. "So much horror…and all for—" She gestured back toward Garra's body. "Greed. Envy. Hatred."

"It's all right…" Stone whispered.

Verity approached then, holding up Stone's coat, which she'd apparently retrieved on her way over.

Viajera took it, expressionless now. She refused to give up the chalice, awkwardly donning the coat without setting it down.

Off to the north side of the clearing, they all heard a rustle.

Jason stiffened, preparing to launch himself in that direction, but Viajera raised her hand.

"Let him go," she said dully. "He is nothing now."

She might be right—she probably was. Whichever of Garra's henchmen he was, he'd soon revert to normal human strength and power when the potion wore off, and he no doubt knew it. But that still left another matter to attend to.

"Excuse me," Stone said, and took off before anyone could question him.

412 |                                    R. L. KING

By the time Verity followed him back at Garra's lab less than five minutes later, it was unrecognizable. The parts of the circle the cauldron's mixture hadn't obliterated were gone, the components twisted and destroyed, and every one of the bottles shattered into tiny pieces. Stone had let his power loose, giving vent to every bit of rage he'd been unable to express against Marciella Garra for the atrocities she'd committed or commissioned, and the results were frightening to behold.

"Doc...?" she asked, looking around at his handiwork. "Everything okay?"

"Not really," he said. "But it will be."

She stood next to him, making no move to touch him. "Are *you* okay?"

He wondered if she regarded him the same way he had Garra: as a dangerous force best treated with caution. Maybe that was what he was. He offered a faint smile. "I'm fine."

She mirrored the smile, tentatively. "That was a nice trick with the illusion. You had me fooled into thinking you'd tossed it away."

He gripped her shoulder. "You're rubbing off on me, apprentice. Teaching me sometimes the subtle solution is the best one."

She nodded toward destroyed lab. "And sometimes it's best to just wreck the joint."

"Surprisingly cathartic, I'll say that much. Where are the others?"

"Here," came Viajera's voice. She drew up behind Stone, studying the carnage in the ritual room without comment. She'd buttoned Stone's coat, and still cradled the golden chalice in the crook of her arm like a child.

"And Garra?"

"She's still there." Her eyes narrowed, her expression growing cold. "We could bury her, but why? She doesn't deserve it after what she's done. The authorities will find her soon. They'll think an animal got her."

*Which wouldn't be far from the truth, would it?* Stone thought, but didn't say it. He looked past her to Jason, who seemed oddly subdued. It was obvious the potion he'd taken was wearing off; some of his preternatural grace and augmented musculature had subsided. Stone wasn't sure if it was disappointment he saw in his friend's eyes at the fact that he'd destroyed all the contents of the lab, but he wouldn't have been surprised if it was.

"Come on," he said. "We should get out of here before the authorities arrive, in case Officer Foley's partner went for help."

"Yes," Viajera agreed. "And I've got a child to find. He no longer has a mother, but at least I can let him know he's safe now."

# | CHAPTER FORTY-SIX

"**Y**OU'RE LEAVING TOMORROW, THEN," Stone said.

"Yes. It's for the best, I think."

He and Viajera sat across from each other at a shadowy table at the back of a small Brazilian steakhouse in Los Altos. Anyone who saw them there might think they were on a date—an attractive, well-dressed couple getting to know each other over a carnivorous feast. Even though it wasn't true—romance was the farthest thing from either of their minds—Stone couldn't miss a new calm in Viajera's demeanor. She still maintained the feline grace and watchfulness, but the return of the chalice had drained away a low-level tension he hadn't even realized wasn't a regular aspect of her character.

"I wish you could stay a while longer."

"So do I—but I need to get this back to my people. They'll be waiting for me." She indicated the large, black leather handbag at her feet; even now, she wouldn't allow the chalice to be more than an arm's reach away from her. "I think we may try again."

"Try—you mean you think you might try rejoining the clan?"

She nodded, picking at the blood-rare slice of sirloin on her plate. "The clan leaders were beyond grateful to me for retrieving the chalice. They were shocked when they found out it was Garra who took it. They haven't seen her for years, but she'd always been one of the only humans allowed any kind of access to the clan's inner workings."

"But not enough for her, apparently."

"No."

As the waiter, clad in the wide pants and loose-fitting shirt of the *gaucho,* stopped by to offer them bacon-wrapped filets from his long skewer, Stone's mind returned to the events of the last two days.

They hadn't had any problems getting away from the abandoned complex. He'd expected Garra's men to give them trouble, but aside from a couple of carefully laid magical traps that he'd disarmed easily, nothing or no one had made any effort to stop them. Perhaps once they'd seen their meal ticket lying on the ground with her throat torn out, they'd decided to make themselves scarce rather than risk angering those who'd done it. Stone didn't care—they were murderers, yes, but now they were nothing more than normal human murderers. He'd given Leo Blum a couple of tips that might aid in their apprehension, but aside from that he considered the matter no more of his concern.

That hadn't extended to Garra's operation, though. After destroying the alchemy lab, he'd made a point to take out the research building as well. By the time they arrived back there, the cougar and the two wolves were gone, so Stone once again let loose. Verity, Viajera, and Jason had helped some, but mostly he'd allowed himself to revel once more in exploring his new power and what it could do. When they left the area, the lab had been reduced to rubble, and anything that might identify what Garra had been doing with the animals lay in ruin. Authorities might still figure out that someone was keeping creatures there illegally, but that was all.

Officer Foley had called them as they drove back toward Palo Alto. The bear shifter, Tony, had taken the cub and gone into hiding, but had left contact information for Viajera to reach him. He hadn't heard from the wolves or the cougar, but said Tony had assured him if they'd escaped the lab, they'd be safe.

"Don't worry," he said when Stone had asked him if he planned to reveal any of what he'd seen. "Nobody'd believe me anyway, and I don't want to cause trouble for Tony. He's a good guy. You don't have to worry about me not keeping my mouth shut."

Stone returned his attention to Viajera. "I'm sorry about what happened at the University. I tried to put in a good word for you, but apparently even my increased status in the department isn't enough to offset falsifying your credentials."

She shrugged. "It's probably for the best. I wouldn't have stayed anyway—now that I've got what I came for, I want to get back to my own people. This way, at least, I have an excuse."

"True. And perhaps the department will vet any future candidates a bit more carefully." He gave a rueful smile. "I'm beginning to wonder if we'll *ever* find someone else."

"You will. I'm sure of it. You just have to wait for the right one to come along."

Stone took a sip of wine, his smile growing amused. "I wonder how Verity is doing with Diego. I don't know if she's ever done any child-minding before, but I'll wager she's definitely never done any like this."

"Well…given that when we left, he was cuddled up on your sofa with her, Jason, and Raider watching a nature program, I think they'll be fine."

"It's a good thing shifter cubs require less specialized care than regular ones." He sighed. "I'm sorry he won't ever get to know his mother because of Garra."

"So am I. But he will be well taken care of by the clan, and he'll never want for anything. So you needn't worry about him."

Stone chuckled. "I think the only thing you should be worried about is whether Verity will let him go."

"She can come visit him," she said, laughing. Her expression sobered. "So can you, you know," she said softly. "Visit him, and…visit me as well."

"I might take you up on that, after things have calmed down. I've never been to South America. And now that Verity's gotten into alchemy, she might want to contact the magical community down there. I understand the rainforests are treasure-houses of alchemical ingredients."

"No doubt. Ah, that reminds me." She pulled her purse to her and withdrew a small cloth bag. "Please give this to her."

"What is it?"

"Go ahead and look."

He opened the bag and withdrew a brown bottle stoppered with a wax-coated cork. It was about the size of a small soda bottle, and bore no label or markings. Curious, he held it up to the light and caught a faint tinge of red. "Blood?"

"Mine."

He frowned. "Why would you—"

"She has a strong interest in alchemy, so I thought she might use it for some experimentation. Shifter blood is useful in many applications, I understand. I trust her to use it wisely." Her eyes twinkled. "And tell her that's all she's getting, at least for now."

As Stone bent to tuck the bag into his briefcase, she added softly, "You two suit each other, you know."

"Hmm?"

"You and Verity. I noticed it from the moment I saw the two of you together. The way she looks at you, the way you look at her...and scents don't lie." She smiled. "If you've got any concern whether she's telling the truth about you seeing other people—don't worry about it. I didn't pick up even a hint of jealousy when she saw the two of us together. She's a good one, Alastair. Trust me. I know these things."

"I know it too." He sipped his wine again. "But it's not up to me, is it? Not entirely, anyway."

"True. But that's the best way." She took another bite of the bloody sirloin and made a satisfied face. "Mmm. You do know how to entertain a lady."

"I'm fairly good at entertaining cats, too. In this case, all I had to do was combine the two. Trust me—leave room for dessert. I hear the catnip *flan* is to die for."

As they left the restaurant and walked out to Stone's car in the late-October chill, Viajera took Stone's hand to stop him. "Alastair..."

He stopped in the act of pulling his key from his pocket, catching her change in tone. Where it had been light before, now it took on a lower, huskier edge. "Yes?"

She pulled him into a hug, her strong arms wrapping around him, and kissed him. It was a sensual kiss—her soft, full lips tasted of meat and wine—but not a sexual one. She held it for a few seconds, then pulled back and met his gaze. Her clear, golden-brown eyes were difficult to read. "Thank you. For everything. I…never would have succeeded without you. I wanted you to know…before I go…how much that means to me."

He embraced her, pulling her into the soft wool of his overcoat. "It was an honor and a privilege, Viajera. I'm glad I got a chance to know you."

"Even if it did almost get you killed?" Now her tone was back to its former lightness, and her eyes sparkled.

"Even that." Briefly, he caught himself wondering what might have been if he'd met her a few years ago, but then shook off the thought. It didn't matter. He knew her now, and that was all he needed. Despite her invitation, he wondered if he'd ever see her again.

He broke the embrace and opened the car door for her. "We'd best go now, though, before little Diego destroys my house…or starts giving my cat ideas."

# | CHAPTER FORTY-SEVEN

S TONE WASN'T SET TO RETURN TO WORK officially until the following Monday, but nonetheless he headed to campus late Friday afternoon. He had an appointment he didn't want to miss.

He didn't stop by the Occult Studies department; he knew he'd have to field a plethora of questions from Laura, Hubbard, Beatrice Martinez, and various students when he returned, but today he didn't want to deal with any of that. He had other things on his mind—things that had very little to do with his work.

Pamela, the Chemistry Department admin aide, smiled at him as he entered. "Ah, Dr. Stone. Good to see you again. Dr. Wright is waiting for you."

"Thank you. I appreciate his agreeing to meet with me."

"You're in luck that he had another meeting this afternoon. He normally doesn't come in on Fridays."

He'd made the appointment yesterday, using a bit of charm to convince Pamela he had something important he wanted to talk with Dr. Wright about. She'd added him to the old professor's schedule following his two o'clock meeting. "He won't be able to stay long, though," she told him.

"Not a problem—I don't think this will take more than a few minutes."

Delmar Wright didn't stand when Stone entered and closed the door behind him, but regarded his visitor from behind several stacks of notebooks and folders on his cluttered desk. "Hello, Dr. Stone. I didn't expect to see you again so soon."

"To be honest, I didn't expect to be back so soon."

"Please—sit down. You can move that stack of folders off the chair."

"That's quite all right. I won't be staying long."

"What can I do for you?" Wright's gaze followed him as he paced back and forth in front of the desk. "As I believe Pamela mentioned, I'm only in the office for a short time today, but—"

"I'd like to talk about Dr. Benchley."

He blinked. "Dr. Benchley? I know you were looking for information about him, but I told you everything I knew last time you were here. I don't think there's anything else I can—"

"Died of a heart attack, I understand," Stone continued as if he hadn't spoken, still pacing. Back and forth, back and forth, as he did when lecturing his students.

"Er—yes. That was what they discovered, if I recall correctly. Quite a shame."

"Indeed." He paused, examining the books and papers on Wright's desk. "You know, I found out something the other day. Something I didn't know. Had a friend look into it for me."

"Oh…?" Wright studied him in confusion. "Dr. Stone, I'm not sure I—"

Once again, Stone spoke as if the other professor had not. "Yes, it's really quite fascinating. Did you know there's a chemical reaction that can produce an odorless, colorless gas? One that, when someone with a weak heart is exposed to it, could cause that person's heart to beat erratically enough that it could induce cardiac arrest?"

Wright paled, and tiny beads of sweat broke out on his wide forehead. "I'm sure I don't know what you—"

"You're a professor of organic chemistry, Dr. Wright. Surely you know of methods one might use." He began pacing again, keeping his tone speculative rather than accusatory. "For example, apparently some compounds derived from the digitalis plant are quite deadly if misused. Normally such poisons have to be ingested for maximum effectiveness, but if...say...a brilliant young chemist were to get his hands on some, he might have the talent to create a highly concentrated dose along with little apparatus that would render it into a gaseous suspension. Probably harmless in that concentration for someone who didn't already have heart issues, but in Dr. Benchley's case..."

"What are you *talking* about?" Wright sputtered. "Dr. Stone, this is preposterous! Are you accusing me of—"

His tone was angry, but his aura flared with bright red streaks of fear.

"I'm not accusing you of anything, Dr. Wright. I'm merely passing along some fascinating information I discovered. I thought you, as a chemist, might appreciate it." He paused, then resumed his pacing. "A couple of days ago, I checked the air-conditioning register in the study at my house. The same study, as it happens, where Dr. Benchley passed away all those years ago. Do you know what I found?"

"I—haven't any idea. How could I?" His gaze shifted toward the door, then toward the phone.

Stone shrugged. "No reason, I suppose. But I *did* find something intriguing there." He pulled a palm-sized apparatus from his pocket and set it on the edge of the desk.

Wright's fear flared even higher, and the sweat beads on his forehead grew more pronounced. He pulled at his collar. "What…is that?"

"Ingenious, really. Unless anyone discovered it fairly soon after the event occurred, they might think it a bit unusual to find such a thing in an air-conditioning duct, but not completely unlikely. And why would they look? Dr. Benchley was known to have heart issues, and it's doubtful medical science at the time could have detected anything in his body." He shrugged. "Nowadays things are different, of course, but back then…it could have been the perfect crime."

Wright's gaze, clearly terrified now, skated once again back to the door, but even if Stone hadn't been standing between him and it, there was still the matter of the desk. He clutched at the edge of it, shaking, and then burst out, "I didn't mean to do it! You've got to believe me!"

Stone paused. "Mean to do what, Dr. Wright?"

"I never meant to kill him!" Still clutching the desk, Wright slumped forward, tears forming in his eyes. "Oh, God, you've got to believe me."

"So you did leave this in the vent?" Stone indicated the item on the desk.

"Yes…yes…" Wright's voice shook, and his face had gone dead pale. "I only meant to make him sick—that's all. I thought the compound's gaseous form would be so diffuse it couldn't do more than give him a mild heart attack at worst. I never meant to *kill* him!" He lowered his head into his hands, his shoulders shaking with his sobs, but then his gaze came up and fixed on Stone. "How...how could you possibly have *known*?"

"Why did you do it?" Stone asked, ignoring his question. He did sit now, moving the stack of file folders off the chair and relocating them to the far end of the desk. "Why did you want to make him ill?"

Wright took one final glance toward the door and then gave up. "I was...angry with him."

"Why?"

"He was my advisor. My friend." His hands clenched and unclenched spasmodically on the desktop. "We worked together on all sorts of projects—him and me and the others in that photo you showed me. But...I didn't have a lot of money, and I...well, I had a gambling problem in those days. I got into some financial trouble. I needed a lot of money in a hurry, or I'd have to leave the university." He looked down at his hands and made a strangled little sound in the back of his throat.

Stone waited.

"So..." he said after a few moments of silence, "I used my skills. I started making and selling drugs. I wasn't going to do it a lot—just enough to pay off my gambling debts."

"But then you discovered you liked having the extra funds."

Wright nodded miserably. "Yes. Everything was fine for a while, but then... Dr. Benchley found out about it. He caught me in the lab late one night mixing up a batch. He was sick over it. I was his favorite student, his protégé. But...he was also an honorable man, and he told me he had no choice but to report me. He told me if I promised to stop he wouldn't tell the police, but he had to report it to the university."

He buried his head in his hands again. "I would have lost everything. Everything I worked for. We argued about it, but he wouldn't budge, even when I did promise to stop doing it. So…I worked out the plan to make him sick. He'd already been talking about retiring soon—I thought this might hasten things along."

"You thought if you could do that, he'd have more important things on his mind than reporting your drug activities."

"Yes. I created the compound and put it in the vent while he was in the bathroom. I—I planned to stay and talk to him until the effects hit him, then call an ambulance and be the big hero. I figured he'd be so grateful to me for saving him that he'd never be cruel enough to report me and ruin my future."

"But it didn't go as planned."

"No." Fresh tears appeared in his eyes, and his lined brow furrowed. "It happened so fast. One minute he was talking to me, and the next, he'd gasped, slumped over and…died. I panicked. We were alone in the house and nobody knew I was there, so I just ran. I figured I could pick up the thing from the vent later, but was afraid I'd get caught."

He met Stone's gaze with red-rimmed eyes. "I've been carrying this guilt for decades, Dr. Stone. Eventually I figured nobody would come after me about it, but that didn't mean I didn't keep feeling guilty."

He swallowed hard and put his hands flat on the desk. "You have to tell me—how did you *know*? Even if you found that thing, how did you ever figure out what happened?"

"You wouldn't believe me if I told you."

"Tell me…please. I have to know."

Stone met his gaze. "My cat told me."

Wright blinked. "What—?"

He shrugged. "Perhaps I believe in ghosts a bit more than I admitted. Sometimes people with unfinished business hang about until it's sorted."

As Wright continued watching him in shocked disbelief, he thought back to the day after they'd returned from the compound. He'd examined the vent just as he'd said, and found the apparatus there. A brief back-and-forth with the eager Raider, who was once again harboring Benchley's echo, had confirmed the events. Stone had brought out the photo again, and Raider had pawed at Wright's image. The basic details hadn't been hard to work out from there.

"You're saying…" Wright's voice shook. "Dr. Benchley's *ghost* really is haunting your house?"

"Who knows? Perhaps I just put two and two together, and I didn't really know as much as I implied. You filled in the rest, just as I'd hoped you would."

Wright slumped back in his seat. "So…what now? Are you going to call the police? Turn me in? I know I deserve it…I've gotten away with it for this long, which is far more than I had any right to."

"No."

"No?" He looked surprised, his head snapping up. "You…*aren't* going to turn me in?"

"No, Dr. Wright. I'm not."

"But…why not? Isn't that why you're here?"

Stone shook his head. "No. I'm here to set things to order. To provide a bit of closure to someone who's had this hanging over his head as long as you have. But he doesn't want to see you in prison. Not after all this time."

"He...doesn't?" Wright was now looking at Stone as if he thought him insane.

"No. I believe you when you say you didn't mean to kill him...and he trusts me to be a good judge of that. But I think it's time for you to retire, don't you?"

Wright stared at his hands and nodded, letting out a long sigh. "Yes. Yes, I think it is."

"Quietly. Without fanfare or parties or accolades. Just...fade away."

Again he nodded. "Yes. That's...the best way. You're right."

Moving slowly, like a man even older than he truly was, he stood and offered Stone his hand across the desk. "This isn't what I would have wanted, Dr. Stone. I wouldn't have chosen it. But in the long run...I'm glad you came to see me today. I don't know if I believe you about Dr. Benchley telling you anything, but...I think I needed this closure as much as he did."

Stone gave the man's damp, trembling hand a brief, firm shake. "See that you do something worthwhile with the time you have left, Dr. Wright. I think Dr. Benchley would approve of that."

# | CHAPTER FORTY-EIGHT

**V**ERITY CALLED THE FOLLOWING DAY, inviting Stone out to dinner with her and Jason that evening. "Our treat," she said. "I just think after everything we've been through, we should get together and do something fun."

Given that he'd planned to spend the rest of the day doing as little as possible, he readily agreed.

"Great," she said. "We'll meet you at Antonelli's at eight."

The first thing he noticed, when he arrived and the hostess showed him to the back table where they waited for him, was their twin expressions of innocent anticipation. He paused, tilting his head. "You two are up to something."

Verity grinned. "Sit down, Doc. You really don't know, do you?"

"Know...what?" He edged closer, lowering into a seat across from them without taking his gaze off them.

"Well," she mused, eyes twinkling as she glanced at Jason. "He *has* been fairly busy the past few days. I guess it makes sense he might forget. It happens when you get old, you know?"

And then he realized what she was talking about.

He started to rise, raising his hands and shaking his head. "No. No. Verity, I don't—"

"Sit down, Al," Jason said. "Don't worry—nobody's gonna come over and sing or anything. But you didn't expect us to forget your birthday, did you?"

"Your *fortieth* birthday, even," Verity added. She looked him up and down with a critical eye. "Though I only have your word on that. You sure as hell don't look anything close to that old."

Stone sighed. He *had* forgotten, odd as that might seem to most normal people. He simply didn't consider the occasion to be worth celebration. *Brilliant, I've made it another year around the sun. Hardly cause for any excitement.* Before he'd met Jason and Verity, the day usually passed with barely a moment of notice, except for the obligatory package from Aubrey. This year it had fallen earlier in the week, when they'd all been in the middle of the Garra affair, and he hadn't even thought about it. Either Aubrey hadn't sent anything this year or it had been held up in the mail.

"Honestly," he said, exasperated. "You didn't need to—"

"Yeah. We kinda did." Verity reached across the table and took his hand. Her tone wasn't amused now, but soft and serious. "It might not be a big deal for you, but you never forget ours. And…after everything that's happened over the last year, it's a wonder you're still here at all. So you're stuck with us."

"Just roll with it, Al," Jason said. "We'll buy you dinner, we'll sit around drinking and bullshitting like we always do, and that'll be it. No party hats, no waiters singing off-key, no strippers. Hell, we didn't even get you a cake. We get it."

Stone studied the two of them, and sighed. "Right, then. So I'll just pretend this is another of our regular nights out."

"Well, we *did* get you a gift," Verity said. "Sort of. But that's for later, after dinner."

They settled in and ordered drinks. "So," Jason said, "Garra—I mean Viajera—is gone?"

"Yes. I heard from her yesterday—she's safely in Peru, and she's reconnected with her clan down there. She says it won't be the smoothest sailing since she's been away for so long, but she's become sort of a clan hero for returning the chalice. And she's decided to adopt Diego."

Verity's eyes lit up. "That's fantastic. I figured she might. I wish they were closer, so I could visit."

"We need to get this woman a pet," Jason told Stone.

"Well, she's welcome to borrow Raider whenever she likes. He prefers her to me anyway." He glanced at her. "How's the experimentation coming on the blood?"

"Slowly. I was up visiting Hezzie yesterday and we're trying to figure out what we can do with it, but we have to be careful since we only have the one bottle."

Stone didn't miss the odd way Jason looked at her, and then away. "We haven't talked much about you and Foley's elixir," he said with care.

"What's to talk about?" Jason's response came too quickly, with a hint of defensiveness. "I did what I had to do."

"Yes…" Stone said in the same careful tone. "I understand that. But there's more to it than that, isn't there?"

"What do you mean?"

Now Verity was watching him too. "You want more, don't you?" she asked with sudden revelation.

It seemed he might deny it, but instead he gripped the table. "Does that surprise you? I mean—no, of course I don't want something that came from stealing blood from shifters. But—I can't deny it felt good to be able to keep up with you guys for a change. And I feel like shit about it, but part of me wishes you hadn't destroyed the stuff in that building, Al." He paused, and seemed to be going through an interior struggle. "V…is there any chance you could…"

"Could what? Make you more of that stuff?"

"Well…yeah. Something like it, anyway. Is there some other way to do it, without having to use the blood?"

She looked at Stone, then at Jason, and Stone didn't miss the sympathy in her eyes. She clearly understood where her brother was coming from. "Jason…I don't know. We can analyze the stuff left over in the bottle you drank, and maybe figure out another way to do it. Maybe. But…you saw what happened to Officer Foley. Even if we *could* make something like that, do you really want to risk it? Do you want to be dependent on it?"

He shrugged. "Not dependent, no. But V—you didn't feel it. After that stuff healed me up, I felt like I could do *anything*. Stronger, faster, tougher—I don't know what you guys feel like when you do magic, and I never will. But if I had something like that, it would make a lot of things a lot easier, you know?"

She studied him with a troubled expression for several seconds. "I'll talk to Hezzie. We'll see what we can come up with." She lightened her tone. "Hell, it might make a good practical exercise for me, trying to make something like that. But no promises, okay? No guarantees."

"Yeah. No guarantees. I get it."

"Now come on," she said. Her tone was still light, but her aura wasn't. "It's Doc's birthday dinner. We're supposed to be celebrating. Let's eat and get a little drunk and stop talking about serious stuff, okay?"

They managed it for the rest of dinner. Verity talked about her visits to San Francisco to hang out with Kyla and the rest of the Harpies, and Jason about a potential case he was meeting with a client about next week. Stone had already given them a quick overview of the end of the Benchley situation, but he answered a few more of their questions about specifics. By the time they finished eating and lingered over after-dinner beers, he felt more relaxed than he had in weeks. Maybe things would finally settle down for a while, and he could focus on mundane pleasures like getting back to work and setting up the rest of his house.

Finally, Jason excused himself to head to the restroom, and Verity leaned back in her seat, stretching like a cat. "So," she said, "this wasn't so bad, was it?"

"No," he admitted. "As birthday celebrations go, this one was about as painless as I could have hoped for. Thank you both."

"Well, it's not over yet." She gave him a sly smile. "Maybe I could come back to your place after? You know—without Jason."

"I'm glad you clarified that."

"Yeah, well…"

"And yes…I'd like that very much. The best sort of birthday present I can imagine, actually."

She glanced up and past him. "Don't say that yet."

Stone followed her gaze. Jason was coming back in, carrying a large, flat box wrapped in metallic blue paper. He must have gone out to his car to get it. Several other diners watched him with curiosity as he passed by.

Stone sighed. "I thought we weren't doing this—"

"Don't worry," Verity said. "I think you'll like this. And like I said, it's not *exactly* a present."

Jason resumed his seat. Verity cleared the dishes to the side of the table, and he laid the package in front of Stone. "Happy birthday, Al."

Stone studied the box. It was about four feet long, two feet wide, and six inches deep. "What's this?"

"If only there was a way to find out," Verity drawled, rolling her eyes. "Go on—open it."

With both of his friends watching him with unwavering attention, Stone tore the paper off, revealing an unlabeled cardboard box. He glanced at them again, then grabbed a knife from the table, slit the tape holding it closed, and lifted the top free.

Inside was a guitar—a Stratocaster, like his previous one. Painted a deep wine red with a black pickguard, it clearly wasn't new: the scuffs on its body and the worn spot on the top where the paint had been rubbed off attested to that. But it had just as clearly been restored—it had new strings and at least one of the pickups had been replaced, and it shone with fresh polish.

Stone stared at in shock. "What—"

"You needed another one," Verity said. "Since your old one got wrecked when you took that oh-so-graceful stage dive." She grinned. "But we didn't want to just get you a new one. That's boring. And that's why it's not exactly a gift. Do you recognize it?"

He leaned in, examining it more closely. It *did* look familiar. Carefully, he lifted it free of the box and turned it over. The back included several stickers, most of them frayed and partially coming off. One large, black one near the bottom bore a crude logo and the words *Fever Dream* written in a scrawling, punk-rock script.

He went still in his chair. "Bloody hell…" he whispered.

"Like it?"

"I—" Still holding the Strat, he turned it to view the stickers in better light. "How—how did you find this? How did you know—"

"How did we find out you used to be in a band in college?" Verity's grin nearly split her face. "Aubrey told me. I went over there a couple days ago and talked to him. I wanted to get you a guitar to replace your old one, and I figured he might be able to give me some pointers on where to look. I thought maybe I could find you something cool like Aleister Crowley's old guitar—except I don't think he ever *played* guitar, so that was out. But when I told Aubrey what I was looking for, he got all excited and told me to wait while he hunted around in the attic. After an hour or so he came back with that."

Stone gaped at her, speechless. "This—was in my *attic*?" He turned it over again, taking in its familiar contours.

"Must have been buried fairly deep—he was pretty dusty when he showed up with it. So…you were in a band called Fever Dream? You never tell us the cool stuff, Doc."

"It was…a long time ago. At University. It only lasted a few months." He laid the Strat on the table and wiped a smudge from it with his napkin. "We broke up after the lead singer and the bassist had a falling-out, and at that point I decided I'd better focus on my studies. I had no idea..." He glanced up at them again. Jason was grinning too. "This is—" He knew his voice was shaking a little, but just this once he didn't care. "Thank you."

"Hey, it's hard to find a gift for the guy who has everything," Verity said. "So we just gave you something you already owned."

"Cheaper that way, anyway." Jason said with a grin of his own.

"The ultimate regifting."

Stone put the Strat back in the box. "It's brilliant," he said. "Absolutely brilliant."

"Maybe you can play something for me later," Verity said slyly.

"Get a room, you two," Jason grumbled, but it was clearly affected. "Or at least wait till I leave."

Stone regarded both of them, a deep sense of contentment settling over him. It wouldn't last, he knew—it never did—but for now, he'd take it. He thought about what might happen later that evening, and reminded himself he'd have to shut Raider out of the bedroom for the duration.

He hadn't seen the blue glow in the cat's eyes since he'd returned home last night to share the story of his final visit to Wright's office...but there was no point in taking chances.

Alastair Stone will return in

Book 16 of the Alastair Stone Chronicles

Coming in Winter 2018

If you enjoyed this book, please consider leaving a review at Amazon, Goodreads, or your favorite book retailer. Reviews mean a lot to independent authors, and help us stay visible so we can keep bringing you more stories. Thanks!

If you'd like to get more information about upcoming Stone Chronicles books, contests, and other goodies, you can join the Inner Circle mailing list at **alastairstonechronicles.com**. You'll get two free e-novellas, *Turn to Stone* and *Shadows and Stone!*

## ABOUT THE AUTHOR

R. L. King is an award-winning author and game freelancer for Catalyst Game Labs, publisher of the popular roleplaying game *Shadowrun*. She has contributed fiction and game material to numerous sourcebooks, as well as one full-length adventure, "On the Run," included as part of the 2012 Origins-Award-winning "Runners' Toolkit." Her first novel in the *Shadowrun* universe, *Borrowed Time*, was published in Spring 2015, and her second will be published in 2019.

When not doing her best to make life difficult for her characters, King enjoys hanging out with her very understanding spouse and her small herd of cats, watching way too much *Doctor Who*, and attending conventions when she can. She is an Active member of the Horror Writers' Association and the Science Fiction and Fantasy Writers of America, and a member of the International Association of Media Tie-In Writers. You can find her at *rlkingwriting.com* and *magespacepress.com*, on Facebook at www.facebook.com/AlastairStoneChronicles, and on Twitter at *@Dragonwriter11*.

Made in the USA
Monee, IL
08 August 2023

40696059R00256